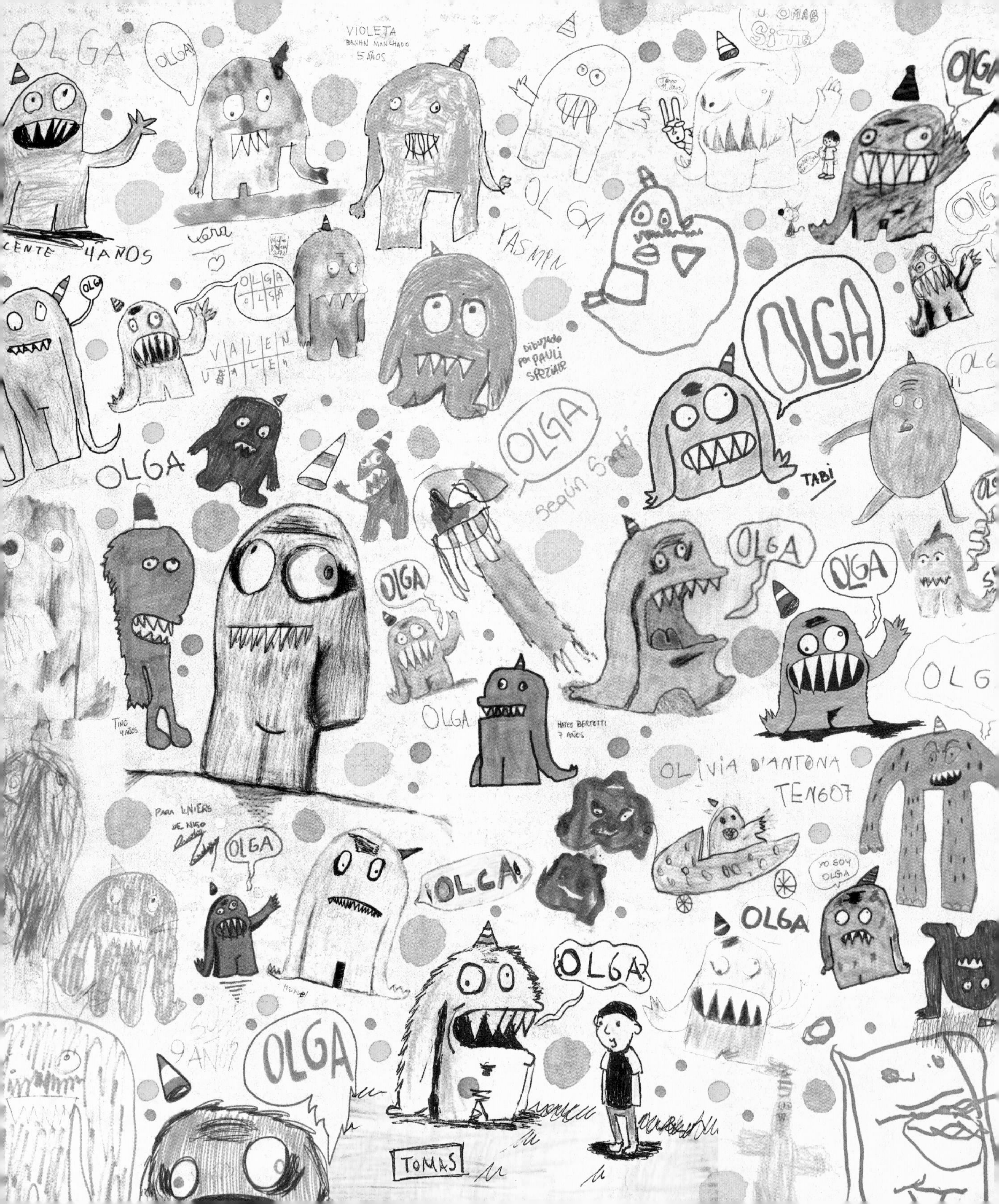
OLGA
OLGA!
VIOLETA
BAYÓN MANCHADO
5 AÑOS
CENTE 4 AÑOS
Vera
YASMIN
OLGA
VALEN
OLGA
Dibujado por PAULI SPEZIALE
OLGA
según Santi
OLGA
TABI
OLGA
OLGA
OLGA
OLGA
TINO 4 AÑOS
OLGA
MATEO BERTOTTI 7 AÑOS
OLIVIA D'ANTONA
TENGO 7
PARA LINIERS DE NICO
OLGA
¡OLGA!
YO SOY OLGA
OLGA
OLGA?
OLGA
9 AÑOS
TOMAS

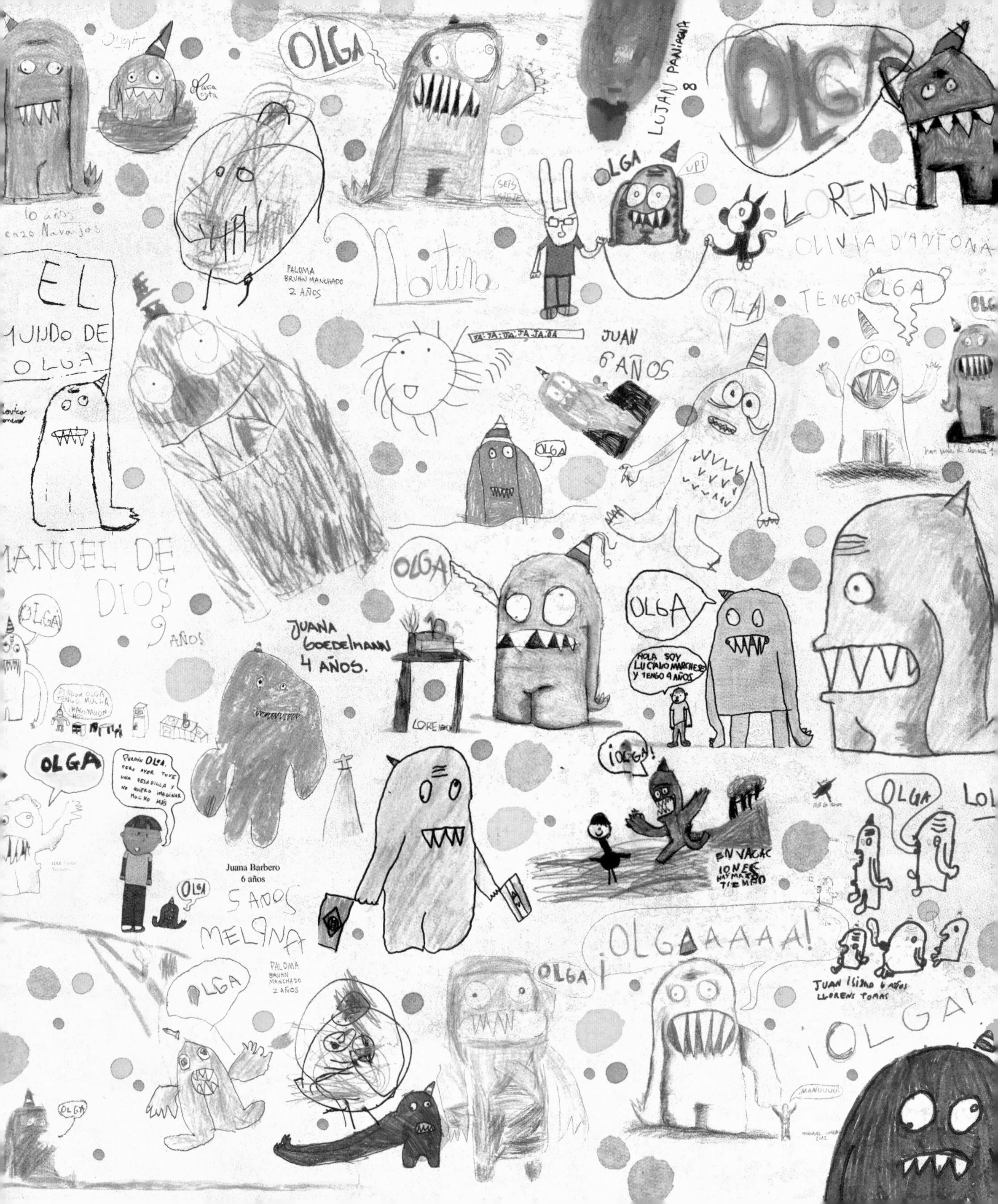
OLGA
10 años
enzo Navajos
EL
MUNDO DE
OLGA
MANUEL DE
DIOS
9 AÑOS
PALOMA
BRUÑAN MANCHADO
2 AÑOS
Martina
UPI
SEIS
SIETE
LUJAN PANIAGUA
8
LORENZO
OLIVIA D'ANTONA
TENGO 7
JUAN
6 AÑOS
JUANA
GOEDELMANN
4 AÑOS.
HOLA SOY
LUCIANO MARCHESE
Y TENGO 9 AÑOS
PERDÓN OLGA,
PERO AYER TUVE
UNA PESADILLA Y
NO QUIERO IMAGINAR
MUCHO MÁS
Juana Barbero
6 años
5 AÑOS
MELINA
¡OLGA!
EN VACACIONES
HAY MÁS
TIEMPO
¡OLGAAAAA!
JUAN ISIDRO 6 AÑOS
LLORENS TORRES
¡OLGA!
MANUUUU

For more exquisite, wonderful, zany moments with Henrietta, Fellini, Mandelbaum, the Sensitive Robot, the Mysterious Man in Black, Oliverio, and others, please look for *Macanudo #1*, *Macanudo #2*, and *Macanudo #3*, also published by Enchanted Lion.

First English-language edition published in 2018 by Enchanted Lion Books
67 West Street, Studio 317A, Brooklyn, NY 11222
English-language translation Copyright © 2018 by Mara Faye Lethem
English-language edition Copyright © 2018 by Enchanted Lion Books
Layout and design for the English-language edition by Marc Drumwright and Sarah Klinger

Originally published in Spanish as *Macanudo #4* by Ediciones de la Flor S.R.L.
Copyright © 2006 by Ediciones de la Flor S.R.L, Buenos Aires, Argentina
All rights reserved under International and Pan-American Copyright Conventions
A CIP record is on file with the Library of Congress
ISBN 978-1-59270-248-0

Printed in China by RR Donnelley Asia Printing Solutions Ltd.

First Printing

MACANUDO

OLGA RULES

BY LINIERS

TRANSLATED BY MARA FAYE LETHEM

ENCHANTED LION BOOKS

NEW YORK

"Knature is kwite kweer."
George Herriman

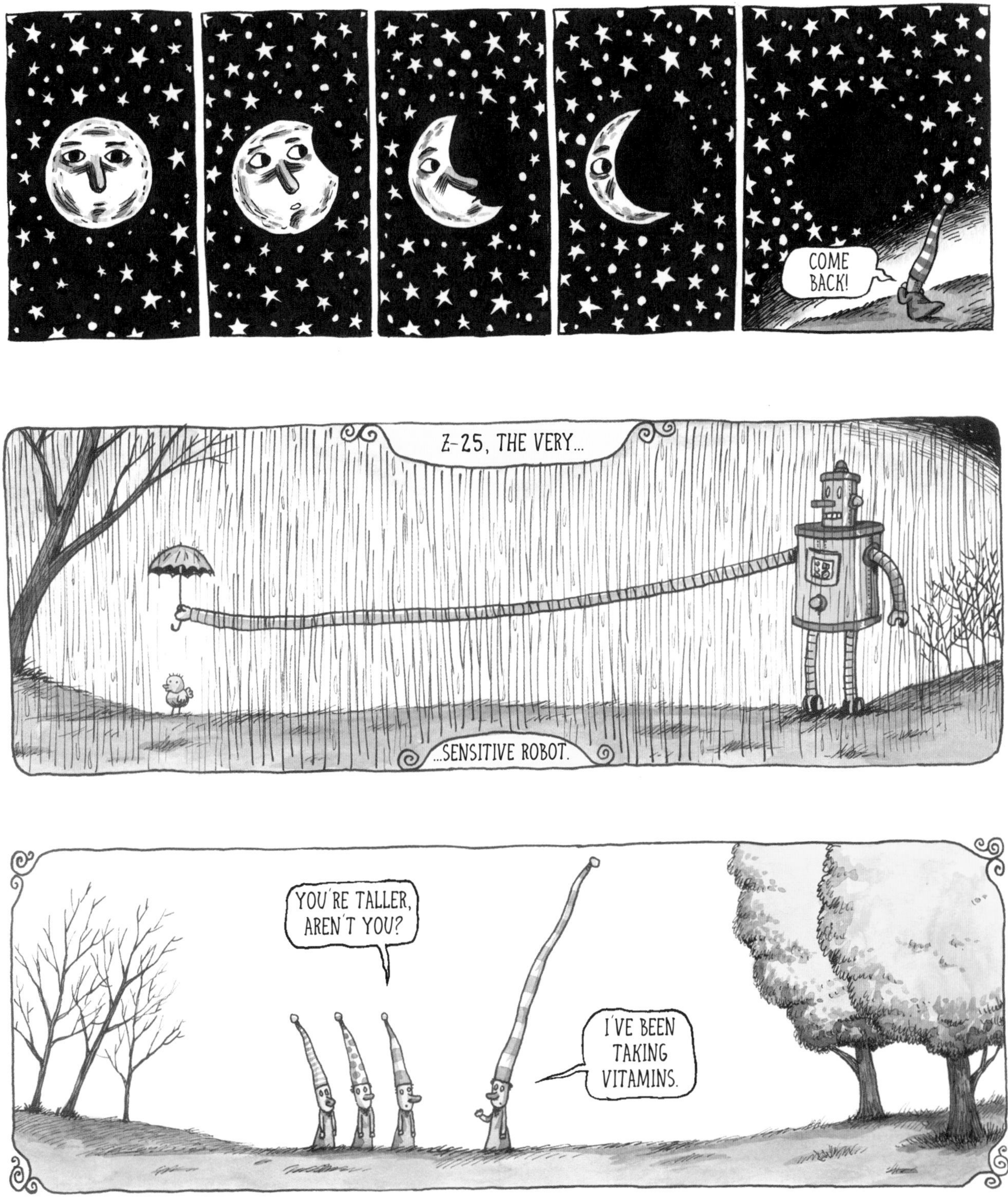
COME BACK!
Z-25, THE VERY...
...SENSITIVE ROBOT.
YOU'RE TALLER, AREN'T YOU?
I'VE BEEN TAKING VITAMINS.

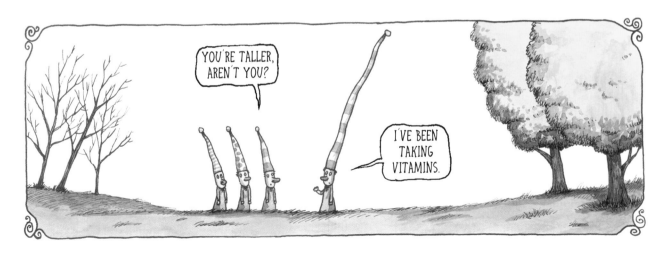

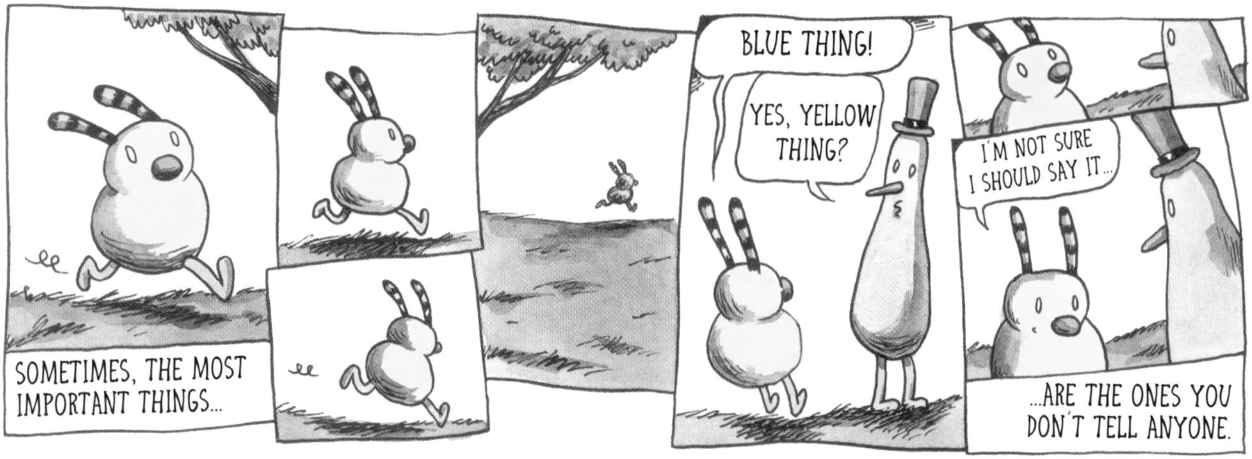
SOMETIMES, THE MOST IMPORTANT THINGS...
BLUE THING!
YES, YELLOW THING?
I'M NOT SURE I SHOULD SAY IT...
...ARE THE ONES YOU DON'T TELL ANYONE.

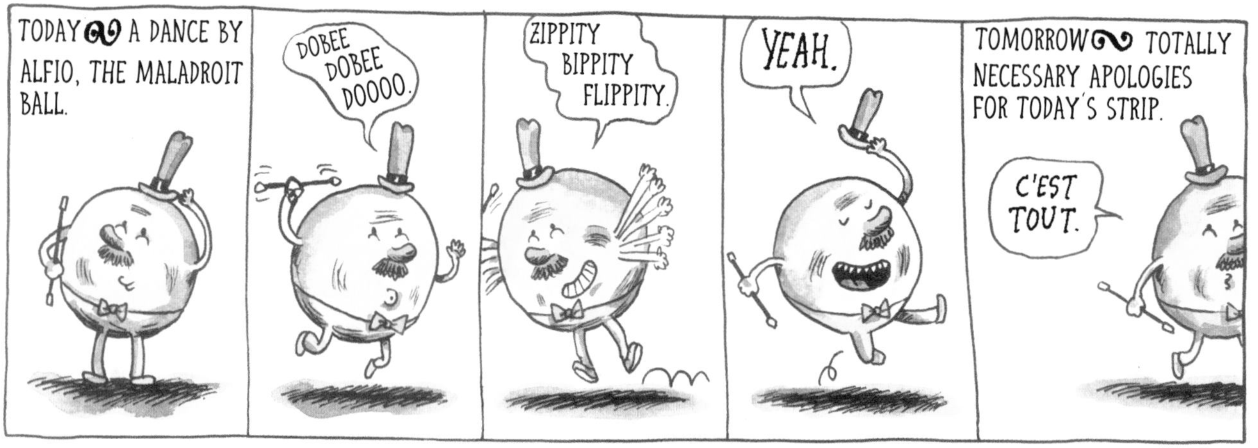
TODAY A DANCE BY ALFIO, THE MALADROIT BALL.
DOBEE DOBEE DOOOO.
ZIPPITY BIPPITY FLIPPITY.
YEAH.
TOMORROW TOTALLY NECESSARY APOLOGIES FOR TODAY'S STRIP.
C'EST TOUT.

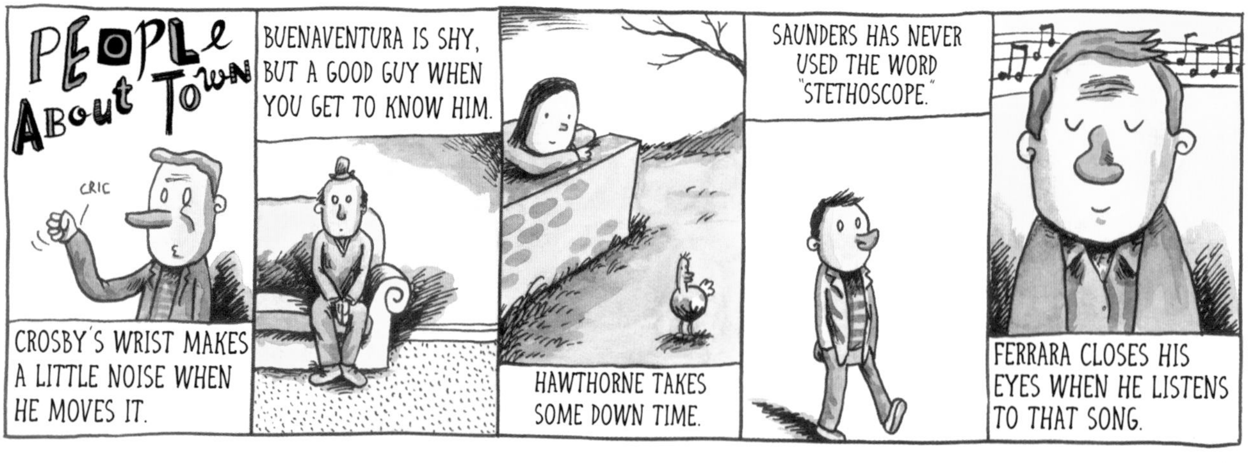
PEOPLE About Town
CRIC
CROSBY'S WRIST MAKES A LITTLE NOISE WHEN HE MOVES IT.
BUENAVENTURA IS SHY, BUT A GOOD GUY WHEN YOU GET TO KNOW HIM.
HAWTHORNE TAKES SOME DOWN TIME.
SAUNDERS HAS NEVER USED THE WORD "STETHOSCOPE."
FERRARA CLOSES HIS EYES WHEN HE LISTENS TO THAT SONG.

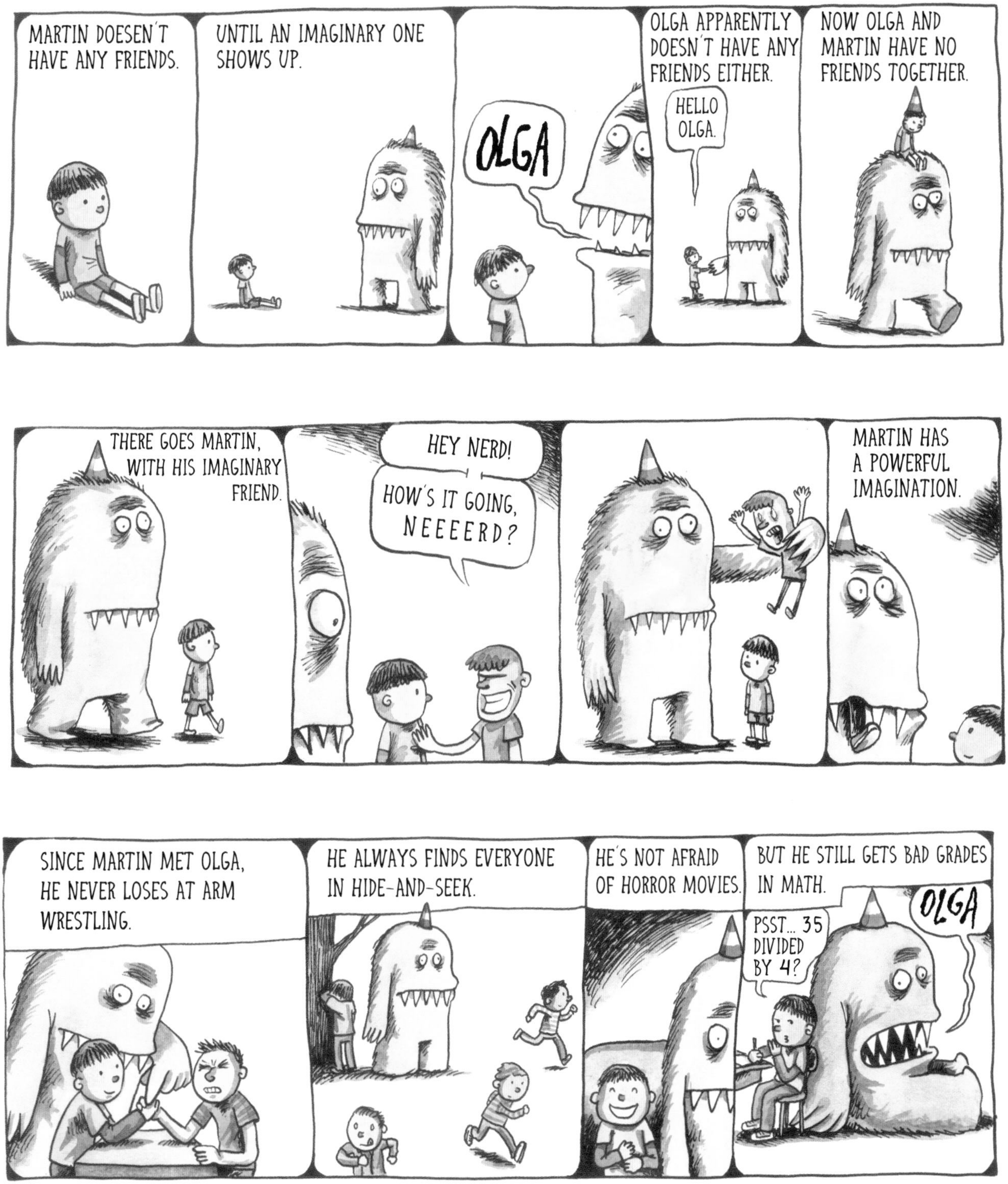
MARTIN DOESEN'T HAVE ANY FRIENDS.
UNTIL AN IMAGINARY ONE SHOWS UP.
OLGA
OLGA APPARENTLY DOESN'T HAVE ANY FRIENDS EITHER.
HELLO OLGA.
NOW OLGA AND MARTIN HAVE NO FRIENDS TOGETHER.
THERE GOES MARTIN, WITH HIS IMAGINARY FRIEND.
HEY NERD!
HOW'S IT GOING, NEEEERD?
MARTIN HAS A POWERFUL IMAGINATION.
SINCE MARTIN MET OLGA, HE NEVER LOSES AT ARM WRESTLING.
HE ALWAYS FINDS EVERYONE IN HIDE-AND-SEEK.
HE'S NOT AFRAID OF HORROR MOVIES.
BUT HE STILL GETS BAD GRADES IN MATH.
PSST... 35 DIVIDED BY 4?
OLGA

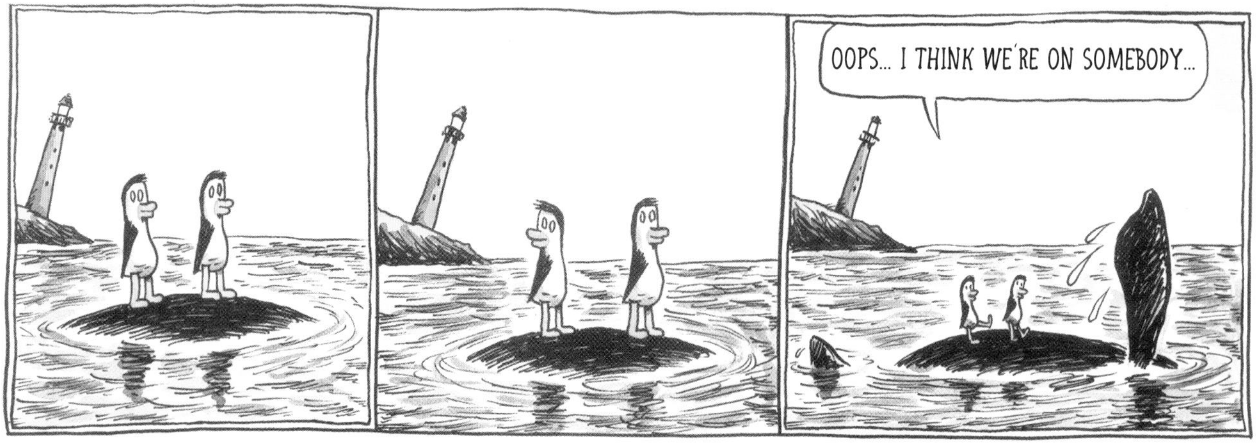
OOPS... I THINK WE'RE ON SOMEBODY...

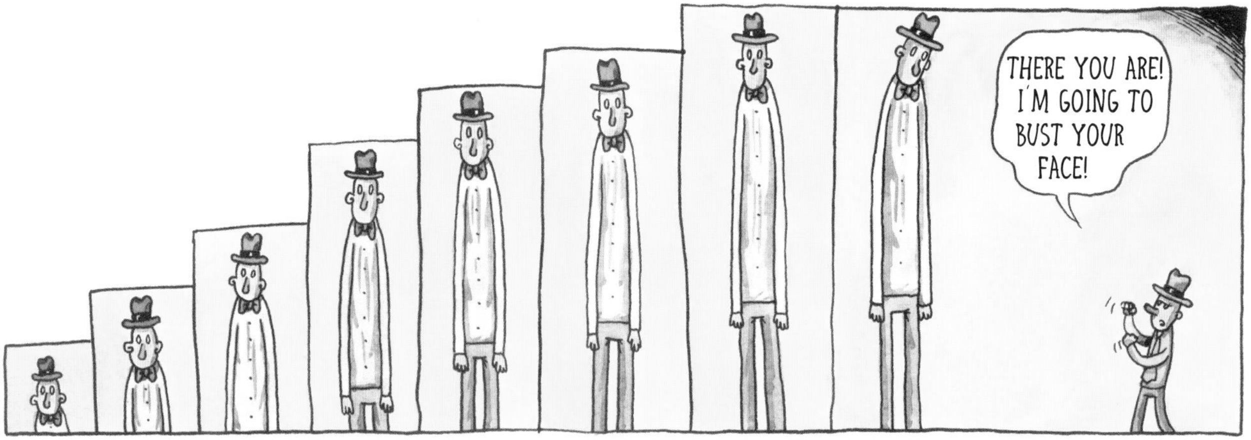
THERE YOU ARE! I'M GOING TO BUST YOUR FACE!

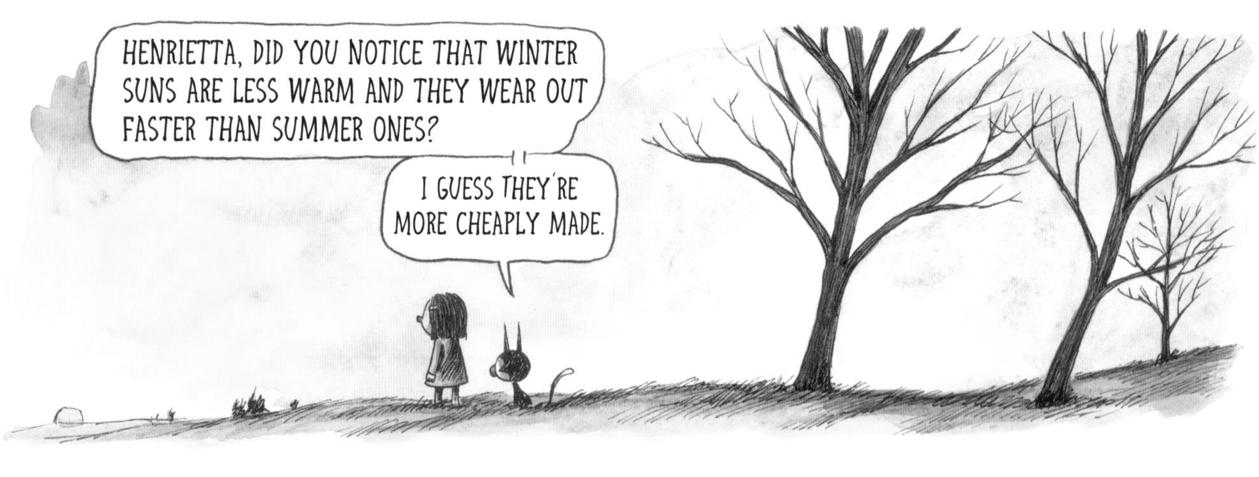
HENRIETTA, DID YOU NOTICE THAT WINTER SUNS ARE LESS WARM AND THEY WEAR OUT FASTER THAN SUMMER ONES?
I GUESS THEY'RE MORE CHEAPLY MADE.

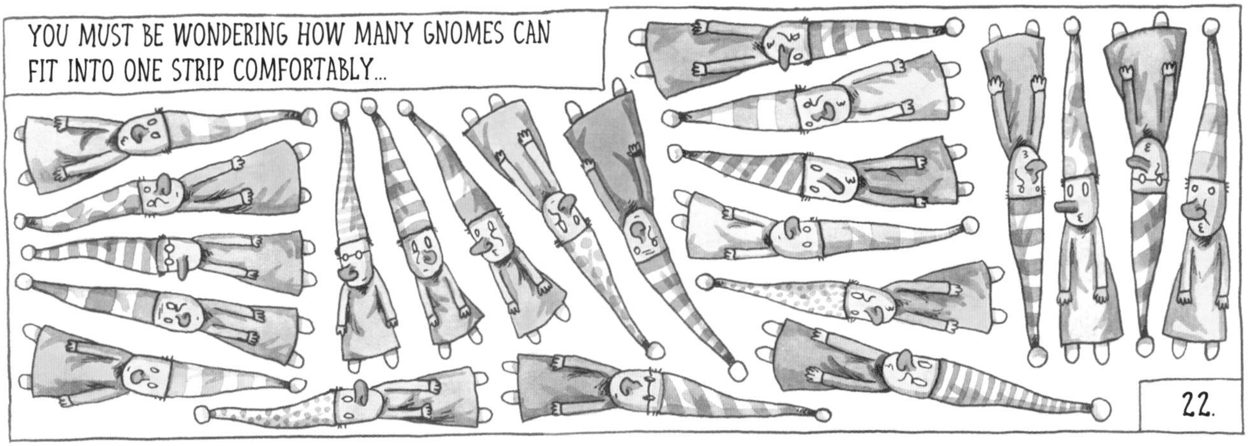
YOU MUST BE WONDERING HOW MANY GNOMES CAN FIT INTO ONE STRIP COMFORTABLY...
22.

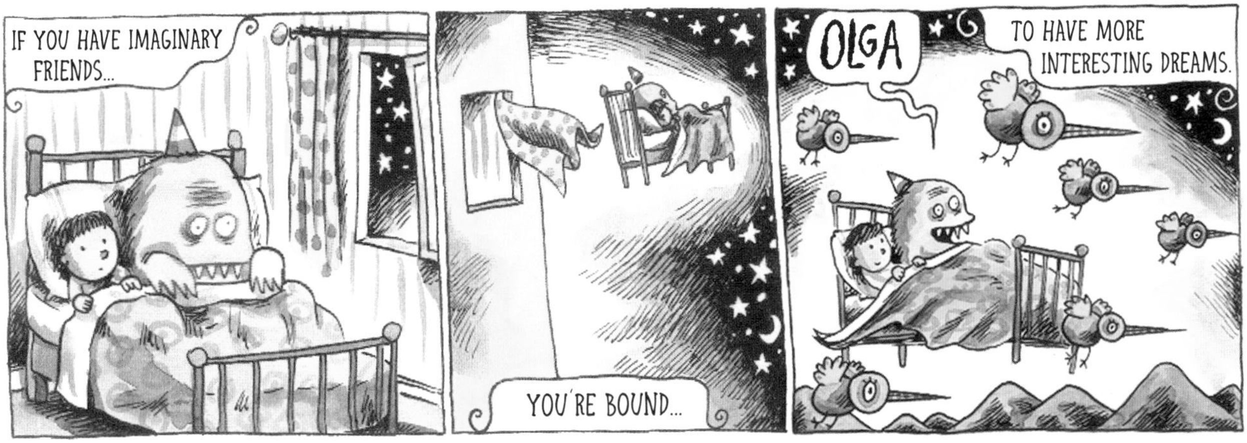
IF YOU HAVE IMAGINARY FRIENDS...
YOU'RE BOUND...
OLGA
TO HAVE MORE INTERESTING DREAMS.

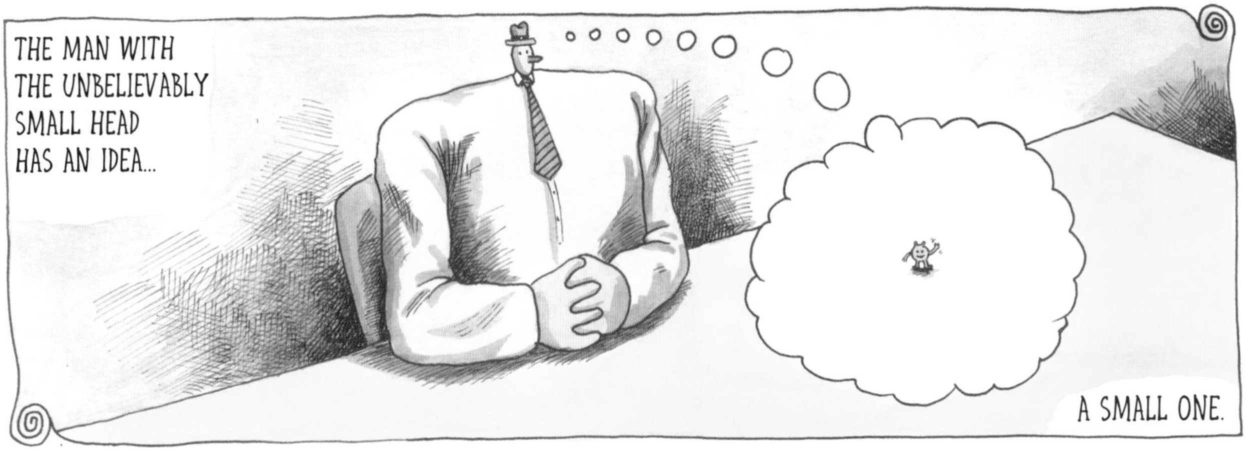
THE MAN WITH THE UNBELIEVABLY SMALL HEAD HAS AN IDEA...
A SMALL ONE.

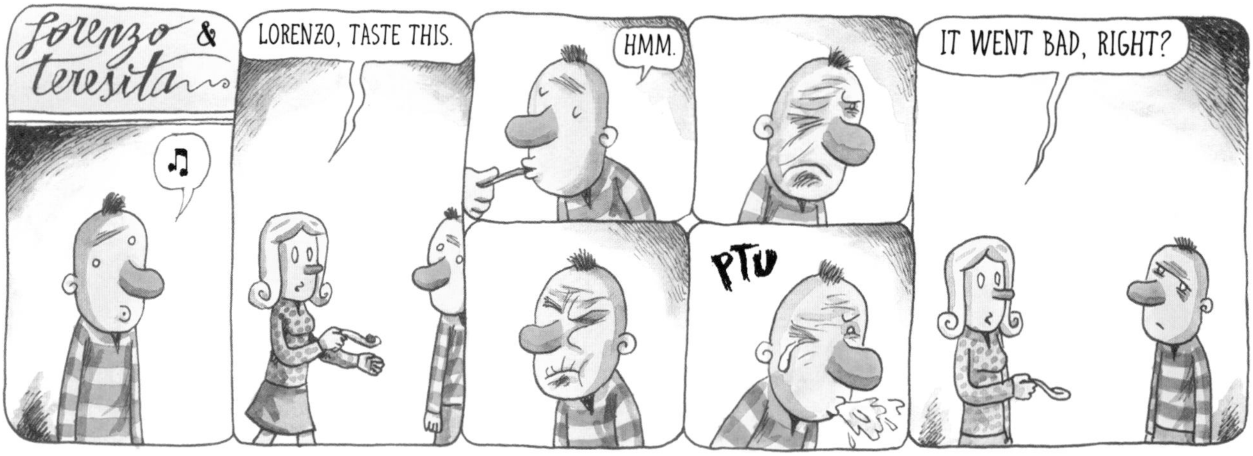
Lorenzo & teresita
LORENZO, TASTE THIS.
HMM.
PTU
IT WENT BAD, RIGHT?

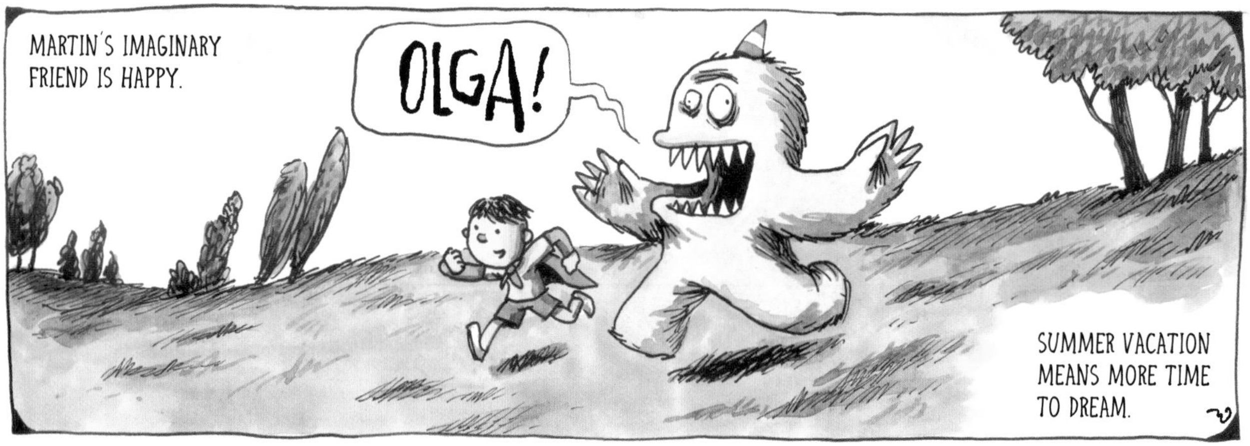
MARTIN'S IMAGINARY FRIEND IS HAPPY.
OLGA!
SUMMER VACATION MEANS MORE TIME TO DREAM.

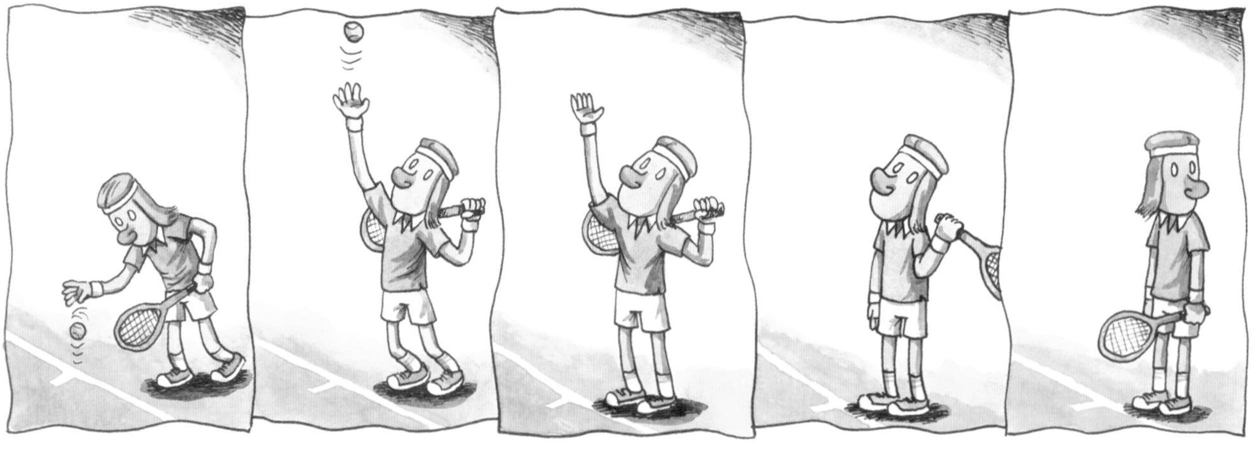

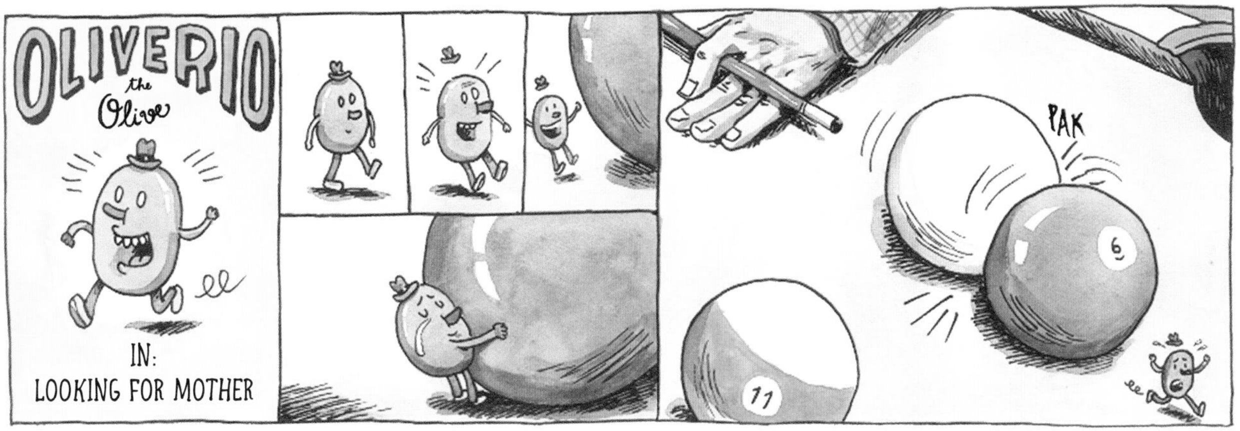
OLIVERIO
the
Olive
IN:
LOOKING FOR MOTHER
PAK

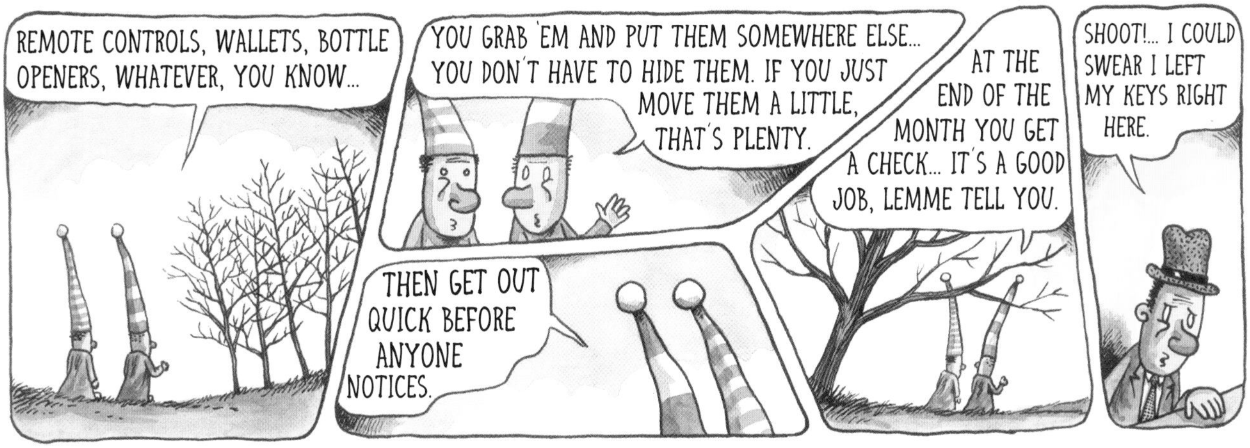
REMOTE CONTROLS, WALLETS, BOTTLE OPENERS, WHATEVER, YOU KNOW...
YOU GRAB 'EM AND PUT THEM SOMEWHERE ELSE... YOU DON'T HAVE TO HIDE THEM. IF YOU JUST MOVE THEM A LITTLE, THAT'S PLENTY.
THEN GET OUT QUICK BEFORE ANYONE NOTICES.
AT THE END OF THE MONTH YOU GET A CHECK... IT'S A GOOD JOB, LEMME TELL YOU.
SHOOT!... I COULD SWEAR I LEFT MY KEYS RIGHT HERE.

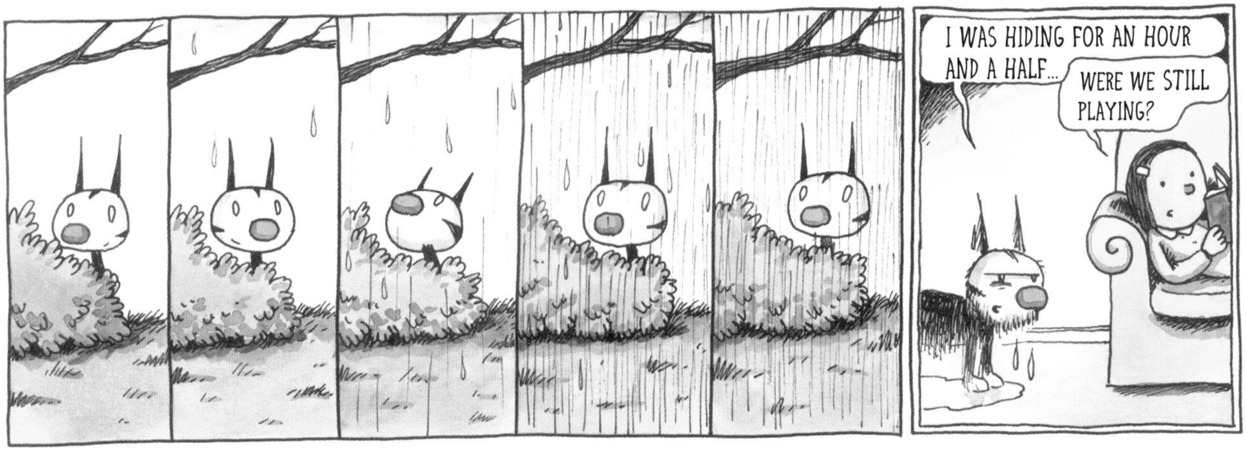
I WAS HIDING FOR AN HOUR AND A HALF...
WERE WE STILL PLAYING?

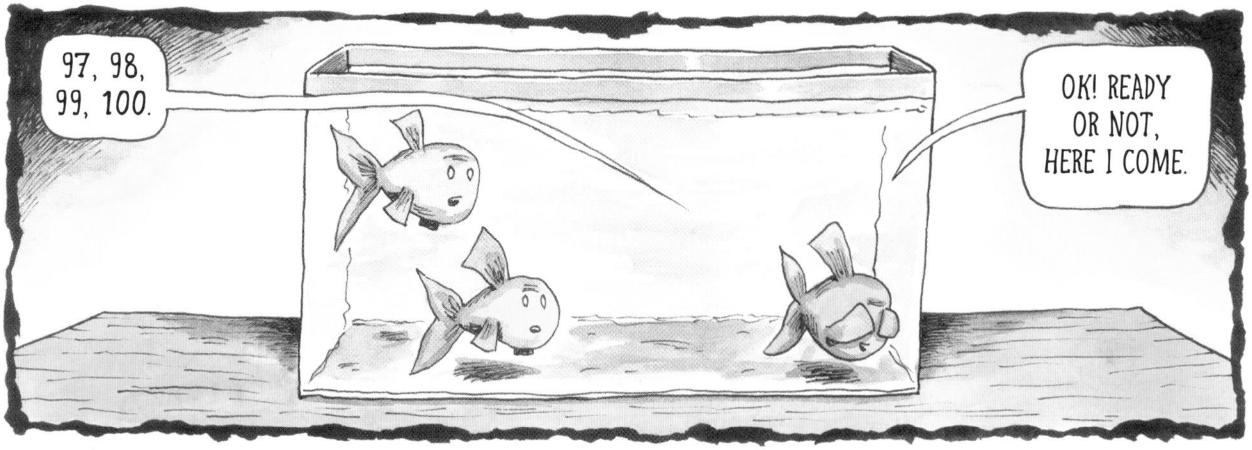
97, 98, 99, 100.
OK! READY OR NOT, HERE I COME.

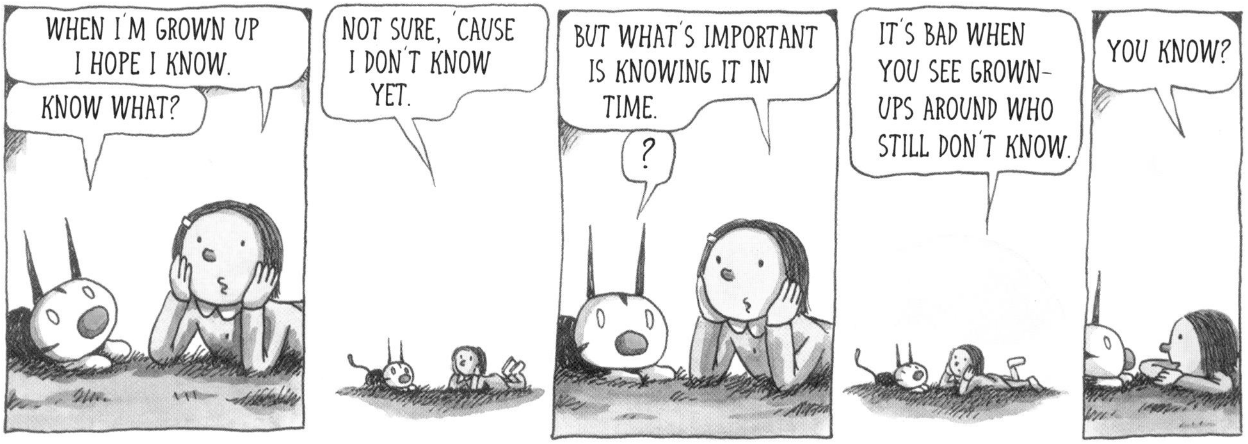
WHEN I'M GROWN UP I HOPE I KNOW.
KNOW WHAT?
NOT SURE, 'CAUSE I DON'T KNOW YET.
BUT WHAT'S IMPORTANT IS KNOWING IT IN TIME.
?
IT'S BAD WHEN YOU SEE GROWN-UPS AROUND WHO STILL DON'T KNOW.
YOU KNOW?

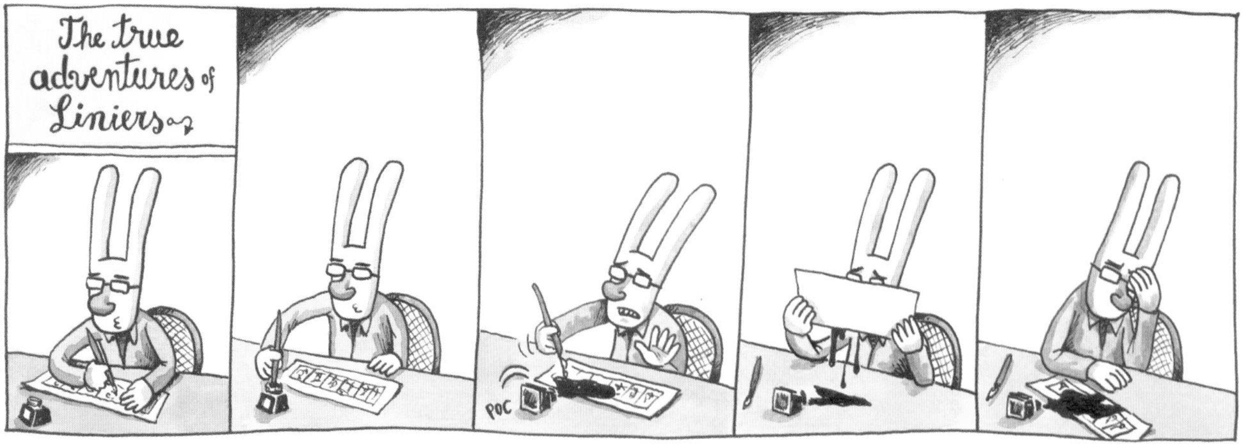
The true adventures of Liniers
POC

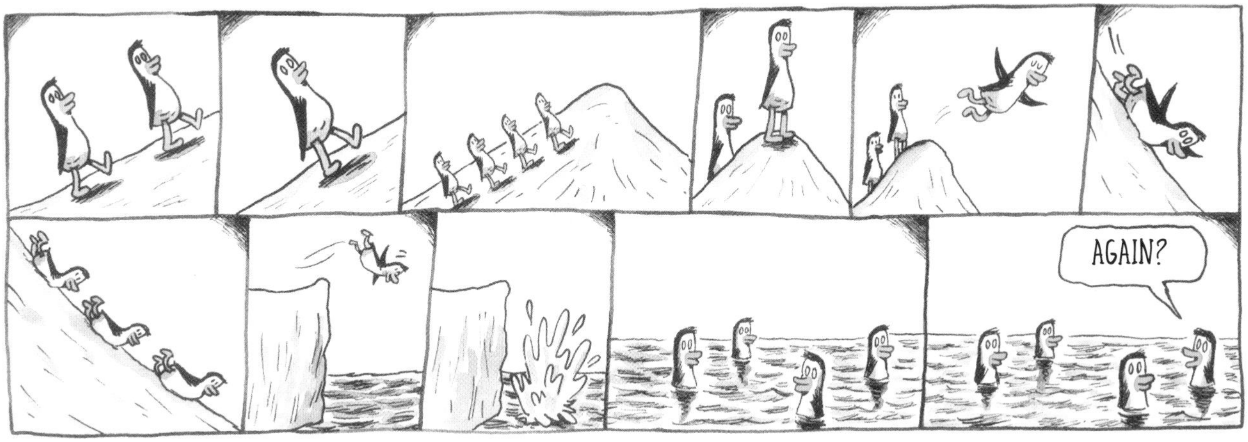
AGAIN?

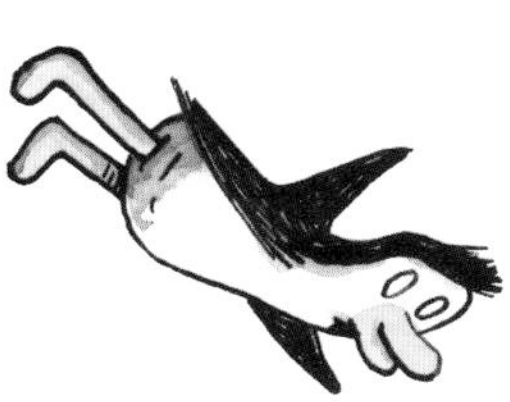

THE SECOND BEFORE SOMETHING HAPPENS IS A WONDERFUL SECOND.

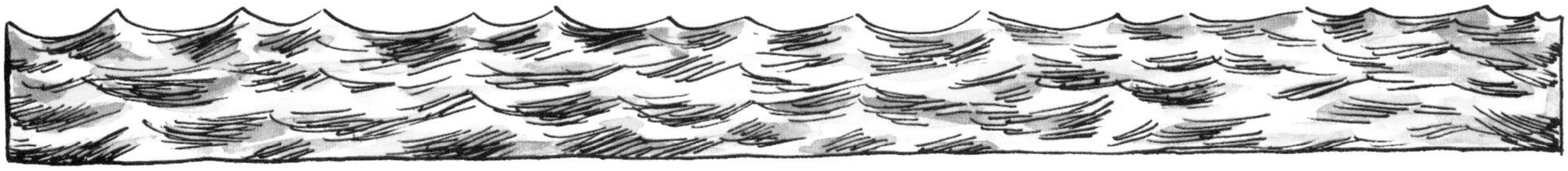

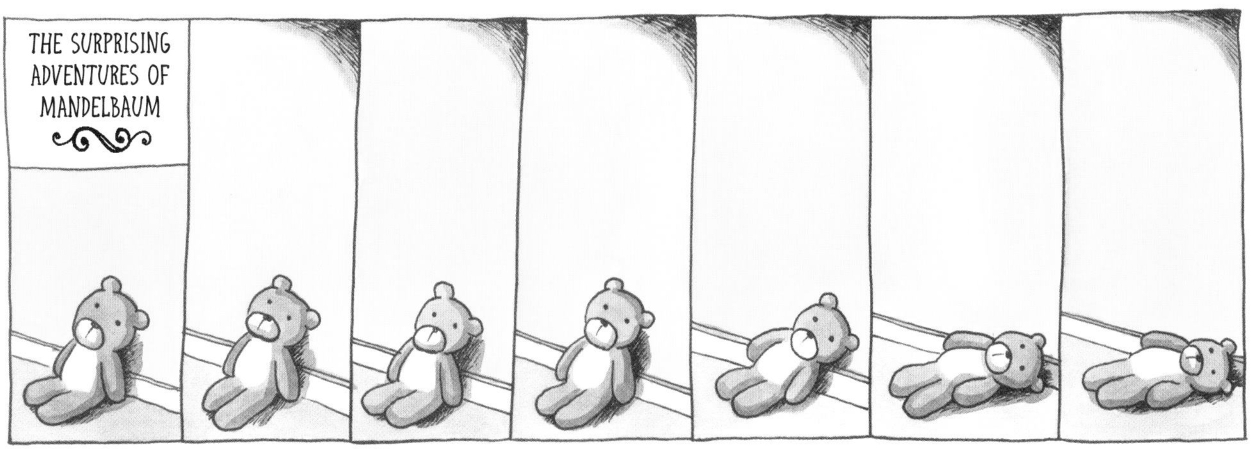
THE SURPRISING ADVENTURES OF MANDELBAUM

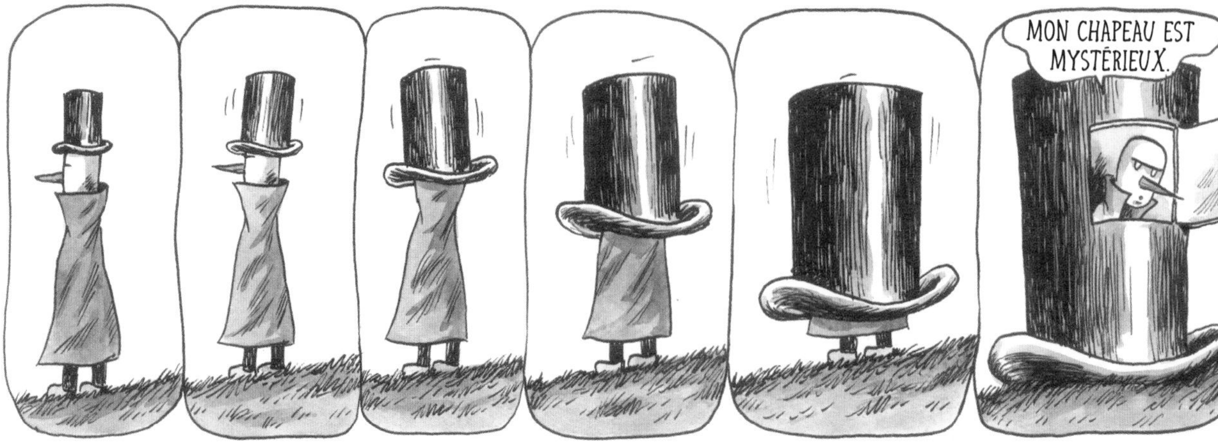
MON CHAPEAU EST MYSTÉRIEUX.

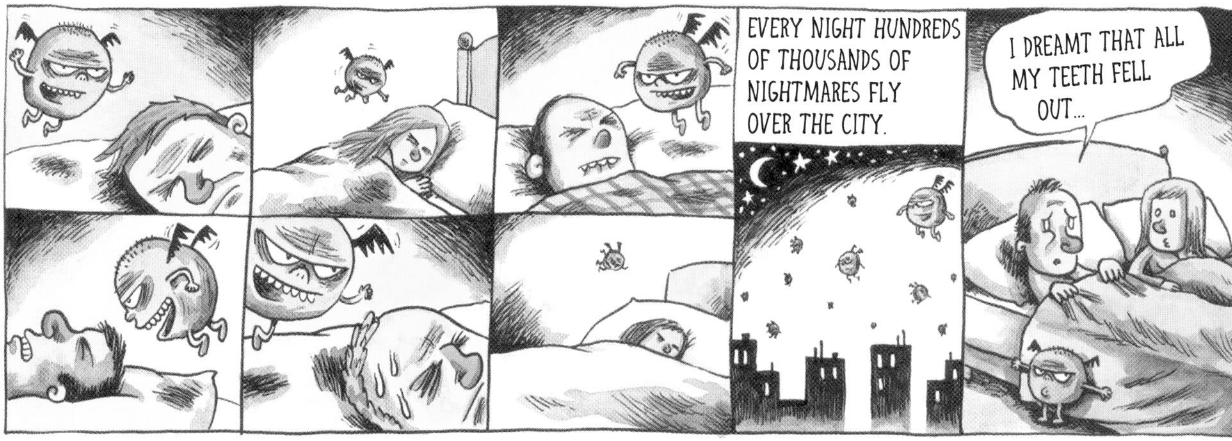
EVERY NIGHT HUNDREDS OF THOUSANDS OF NIGHTMARES FLY OVER THE CITY.
I DREAMT THAT ALL MY TEETH FELL OUT...

MORTEK, ZUPPI, FLEBROX, GRONDOR, HERNANDEZ, MERBLAT, AND ROTRON... INTERGALACTIC FRIENDS!!

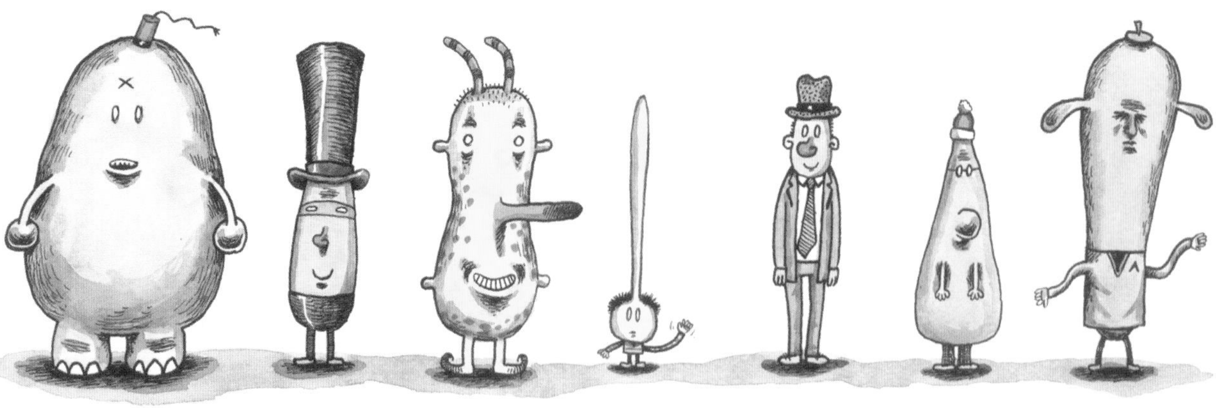

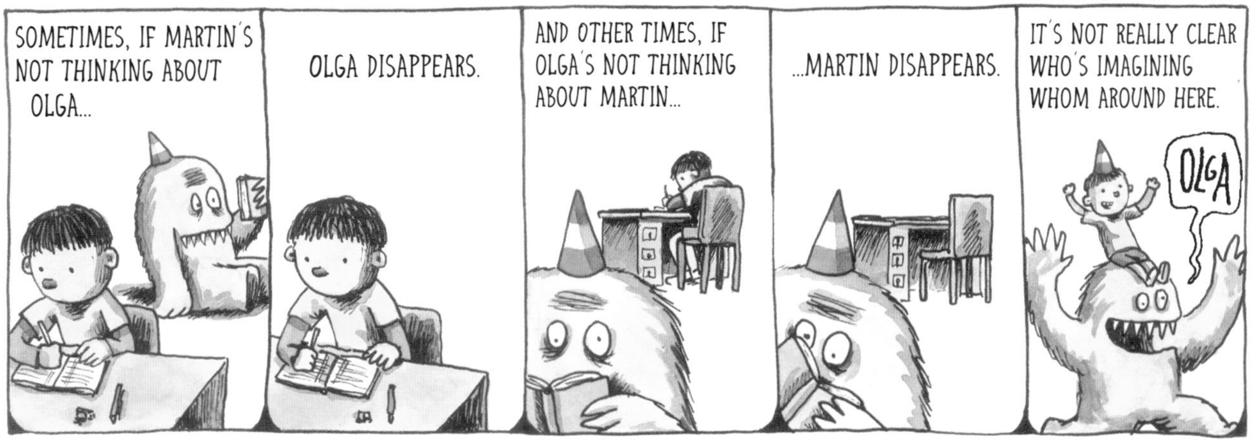
SOMETIMES, IF MARTIN'S NOT THINKING ABOUT OLGA...
OLGA DISAPPEARS.
AND OTHER TIMES, IF OLGA'S NOT THINKING ABOUT MARTIN...
...MARTIN DISAPPEARS.
IT'S NOT REALLY CLEAR WHO'S IMAGINING WHOM AROUND HERE.
OLGA

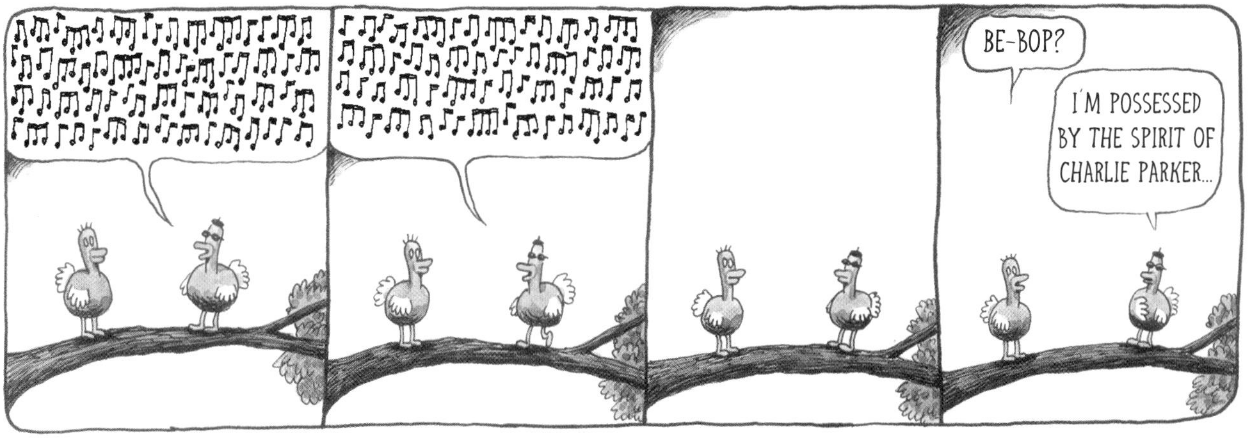
BE-BOP?
I'M POSSESSED BY THE SPIRIT OF CHARLIE PARKER...

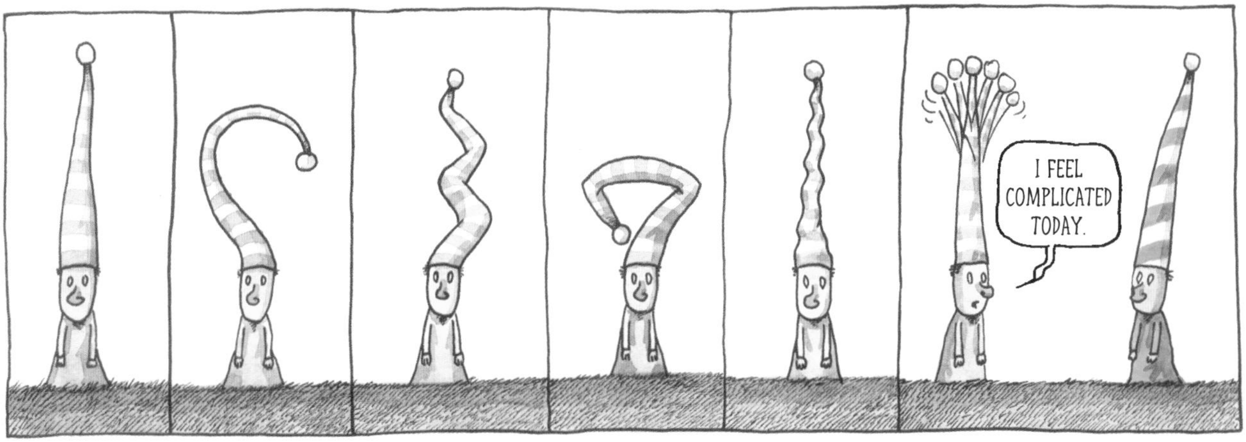
I FEEL COMPLICATED TODAY.

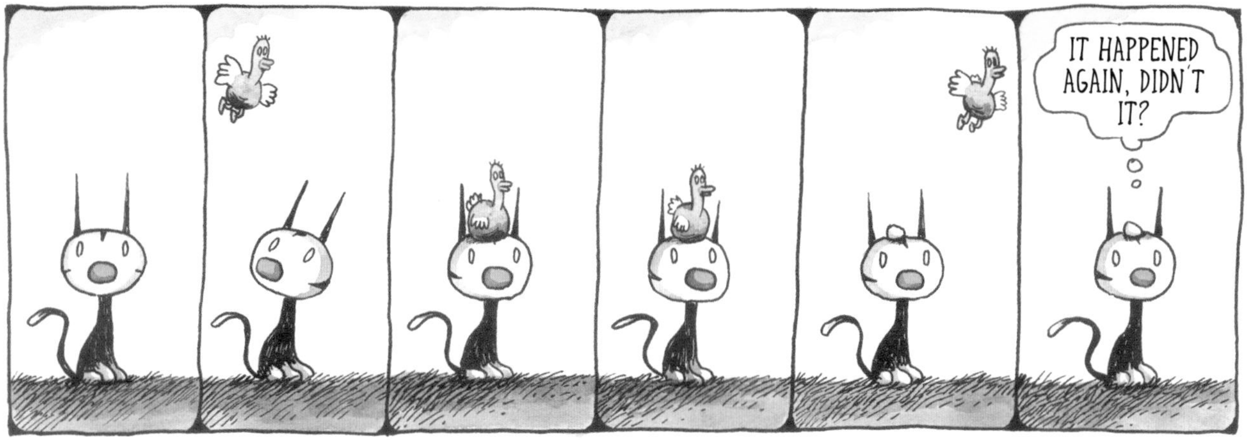
IT HAPPENED AGAIN, DIDN'T IT?

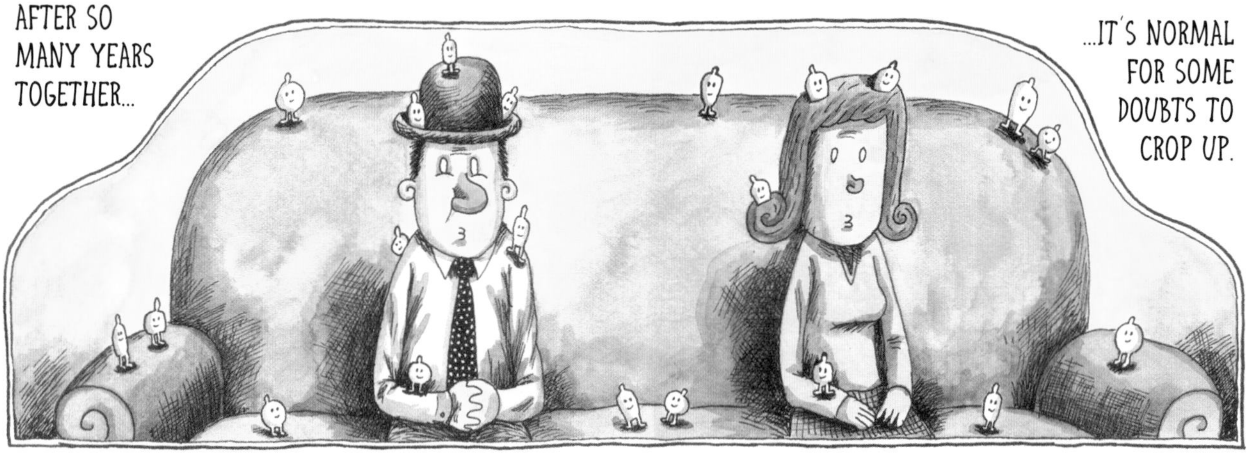
AFTER SO MANY YEARS TOGETHER...
...IT'S NORMAL FOR SOME DOUBTS TO CROP UP.

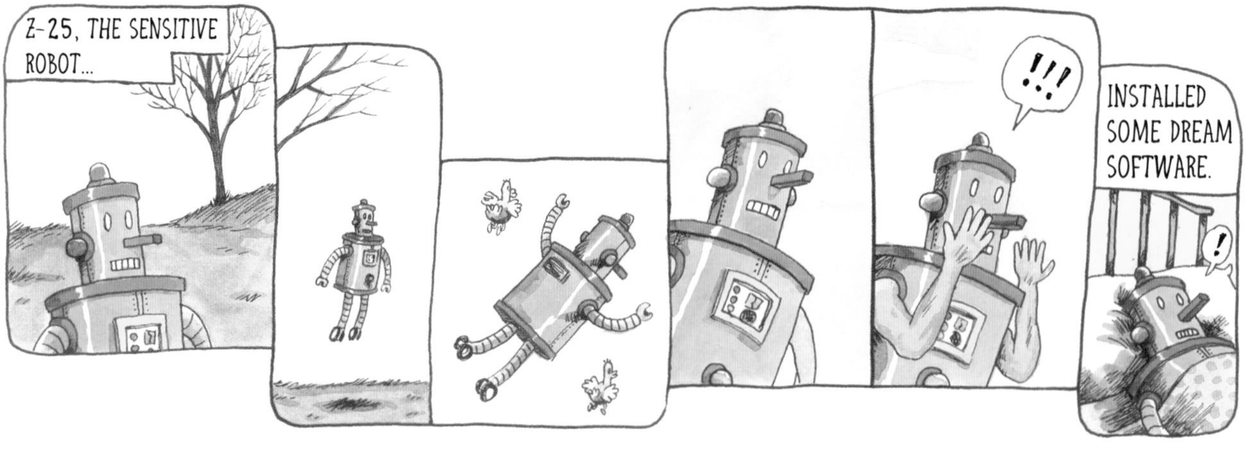
Z-25, THE SENSITIVE ROBOT...
!!!
INSTALLED SOME DREAM SOFTWARE.
!

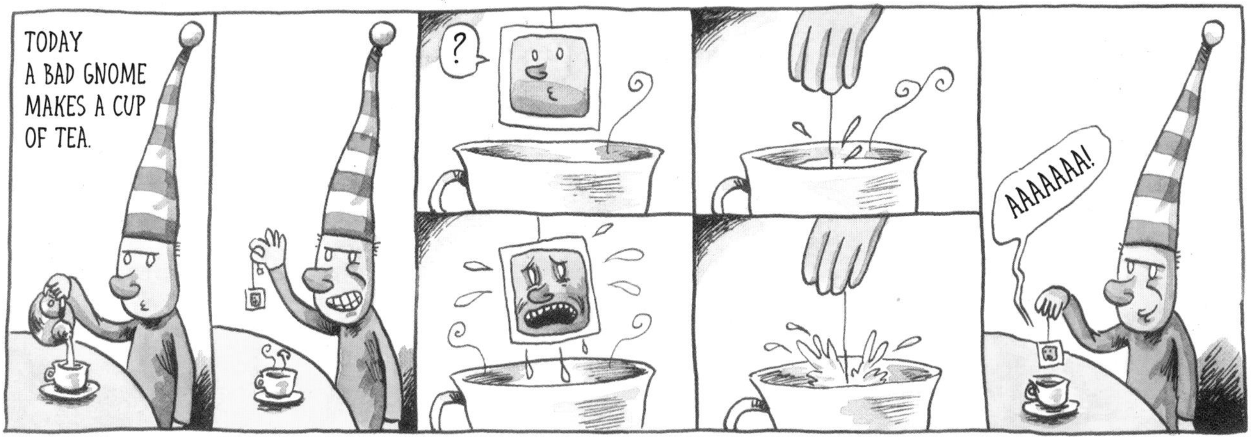
TODAY A BAD GNOME MAKES A CUP OF TEA.
?
AAAAAAA!

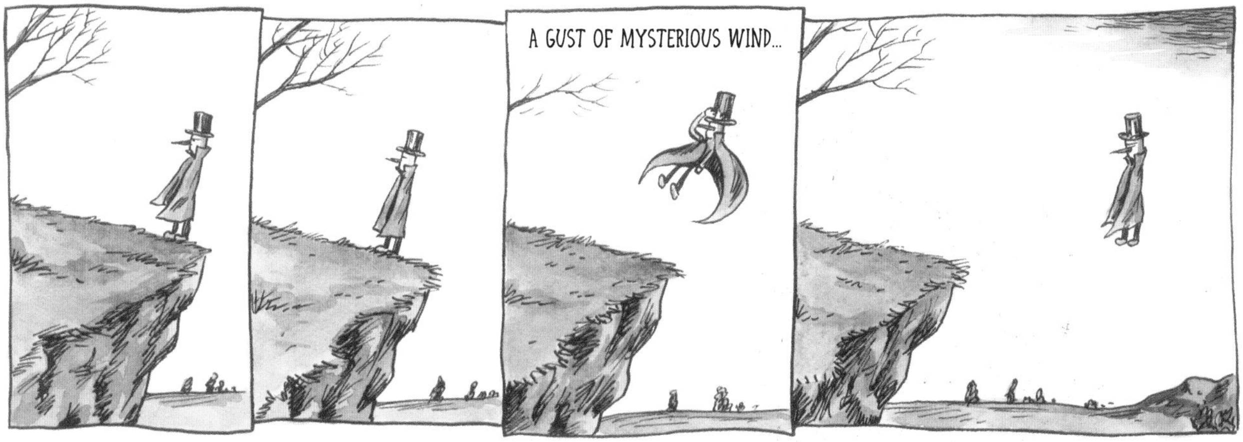
A GUST OF MYSTERIOUS WIND...

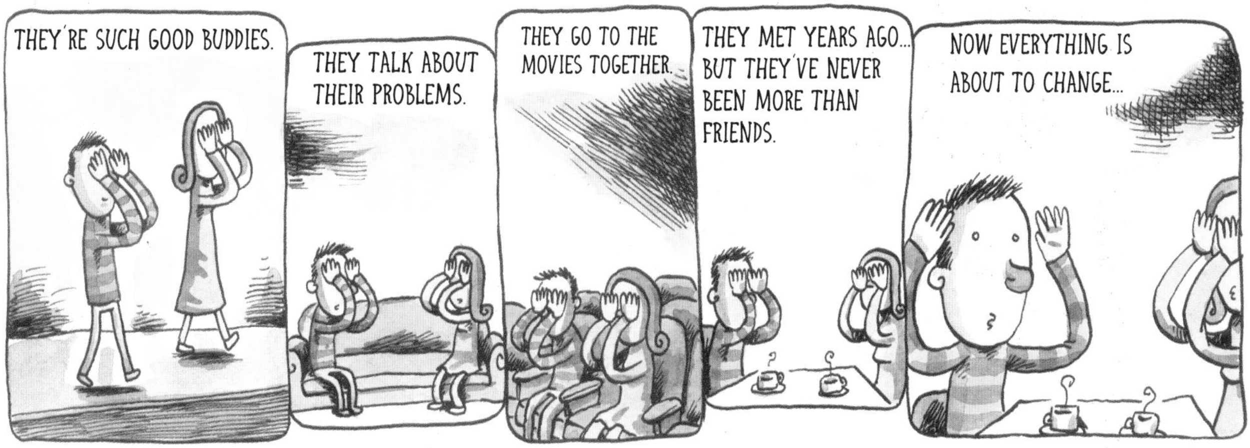
THEY'RE SUCH GOOD BUDDIES.
THEY TALK ABOUT THEIR PROBLEMS.
THEY GO TO THE MOVIES TOGETHER.
THEY MET YEARS AGO... BUT THEY'VE NEVER BEEN MORE THAN FRIENDS.
NOW EVERYTHING IS ABOUT TO CHANGE...

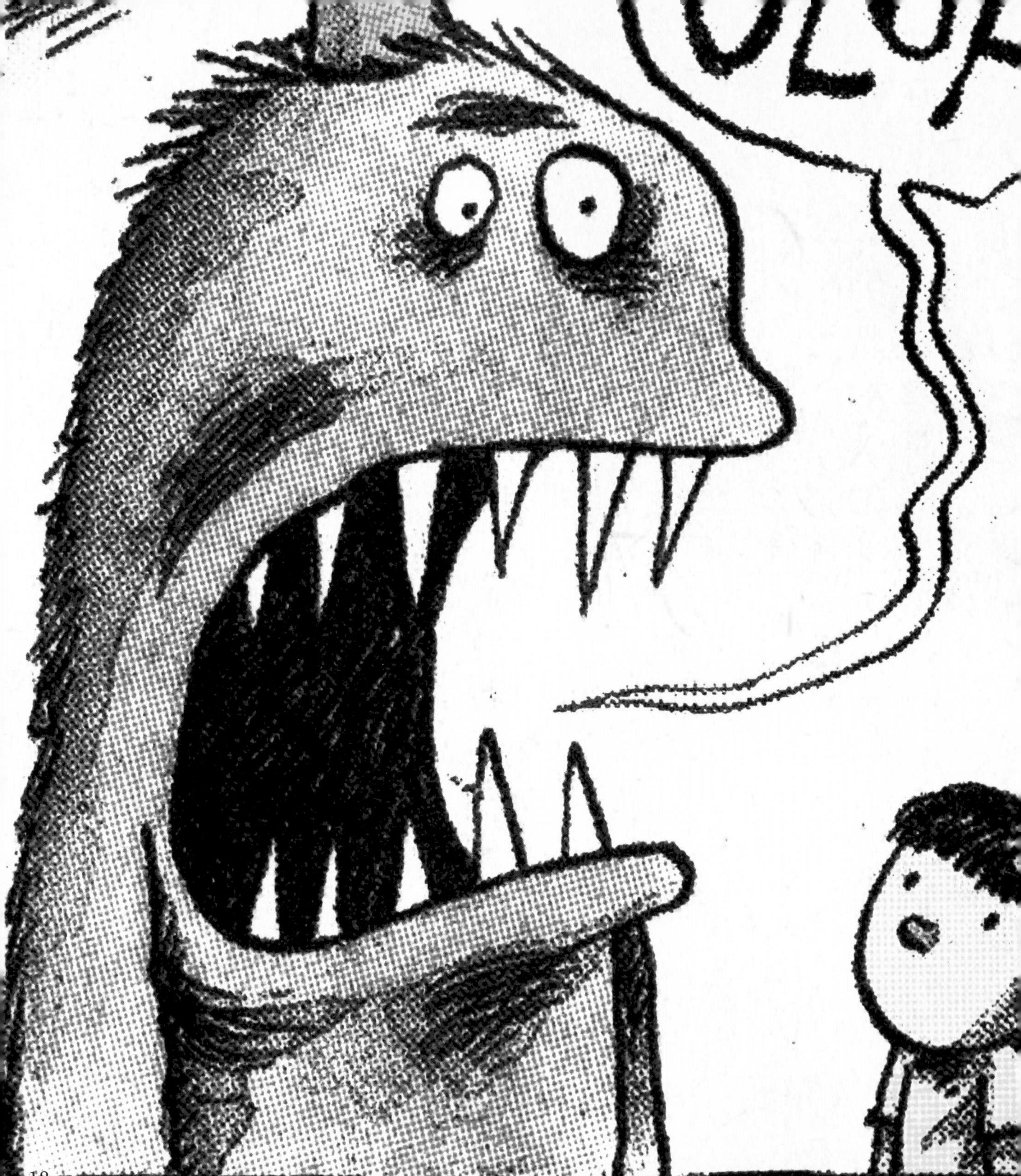

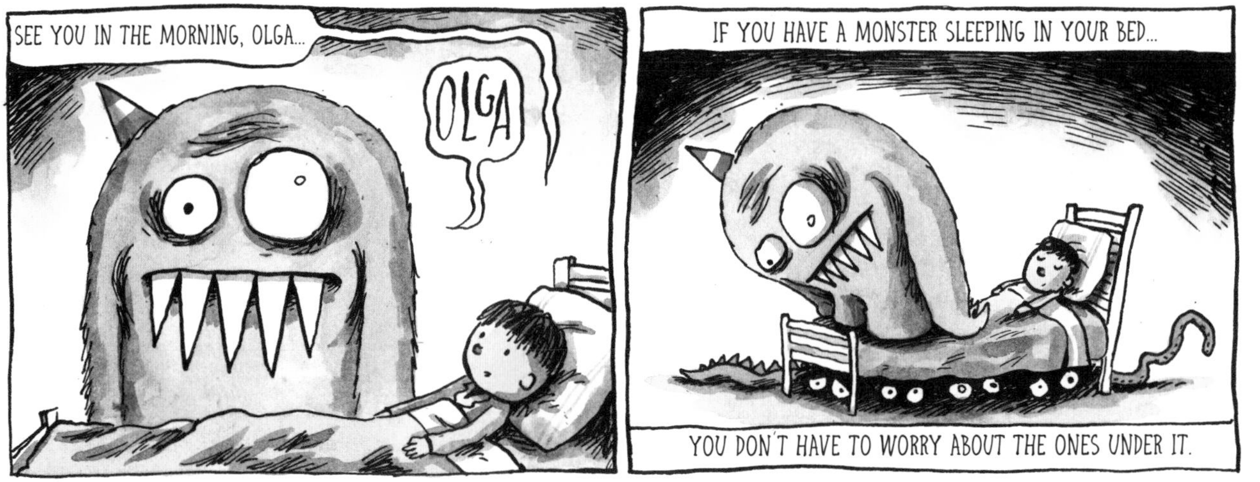
SEE YOU IN THE MORNING, OLGA...
OLGA
IF YOU HAVE A MONSTER SLEEPING IN YOUR BED...
YOU DON'T HAVE TO WORRY ABOUT THE ONES UNDER IT.

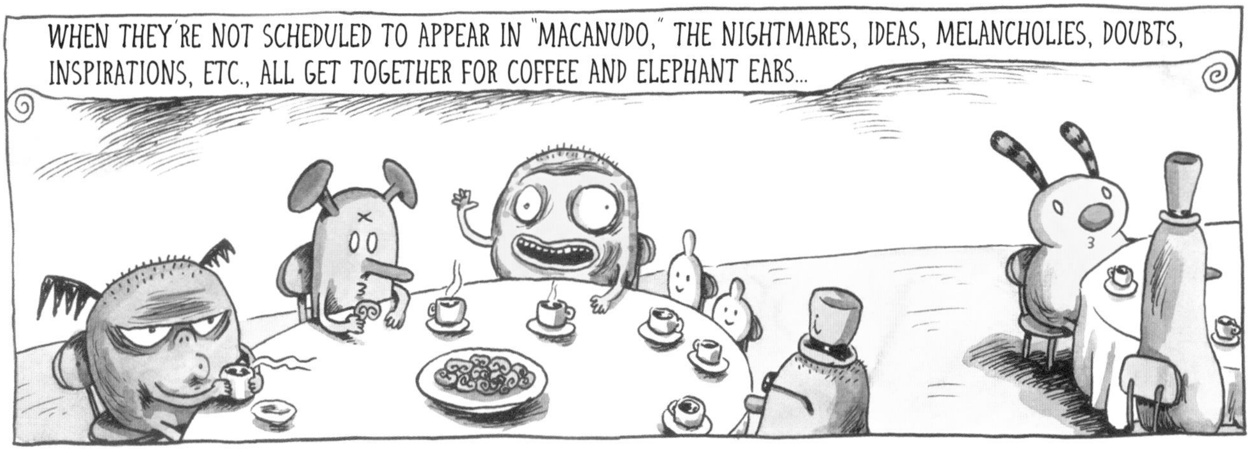
WHEN THEY'RE NOT SCHEDULED TO APPEAR IN "MACANUDO," THE NIGHTMARES, IDEAS, MELANCHOLIES, DOUBTS, INSPIRATIONS, ETC., ALL GET TOGETHER FOR COFFEE AND ELEPHANT EARS...

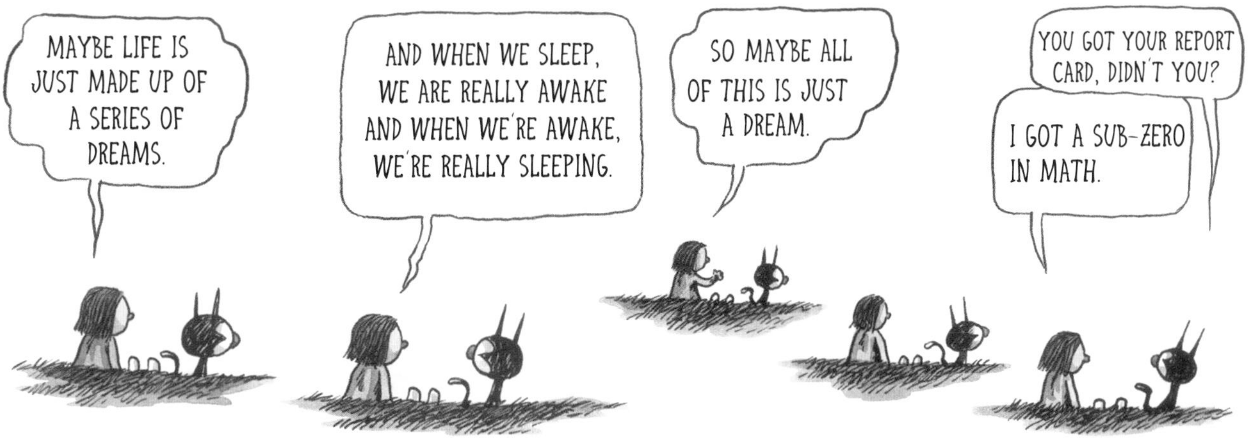
MAYBE LIFE IS JUST MADE UP OF A SERIES OF DREAMS.
AND WHEN WE SLEEP, WE ARE REALLY AWAKE AND WHEN WE'RE AWAKE, WE'RE REALLY SLEEPING.
SO MAYBE ALL OF THIS IS JUST A DREAM.
YOU GOT YOUR REPORT CARD, DIDN'T YOU?
I GOT A SUB-ZERO IN MATH.

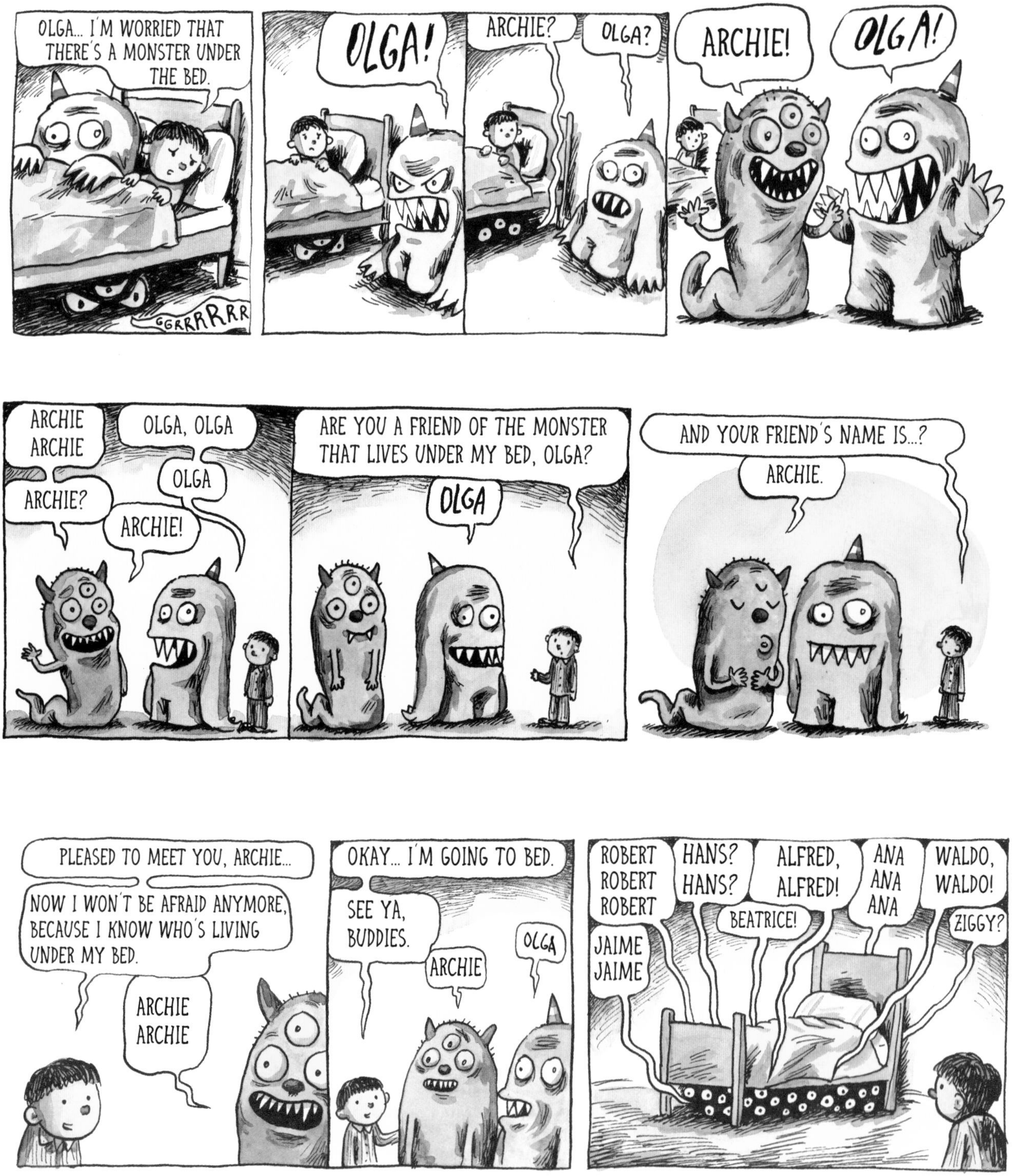
OLGA... I'M WORRIED THAT THERE'S A MONSTER UNDER THE BED.
GGRRRRRR
OLGA!
ARCHIE?
OLGA?
ARCHIE!
OLGA!
ARCHIE ARCHIE
OLGA, OLGA
OLGA
ARCHIE?
ARCHIE!
ARE YOU A FRIEND OF THE MONSTER THAT LIVES UNDER MY BED, OLGA?
OLGA
AND YOUR FRIEND'S NAME IS...?
ARCHIE.
PLEASED TO MEET YOU, ARCHIE...
NOW I WON'T BE AFRAID ANYMORE, BECAUSE I KNOW WHO'S LIVING UNDER MY BED.
ARCHIE ARCHIE
OKAY... I'M GOING TO BED.
SEE YA, BUDDIES.
ARCHIE
OLGA
ROBERT ROBERT ROBERT
HANS? HANS?
ALFRED, ALFRED!
ANA ANA ANA
WALDO, WALDO!
BEATRICE!
ZIGGY?
JAIME JAIME

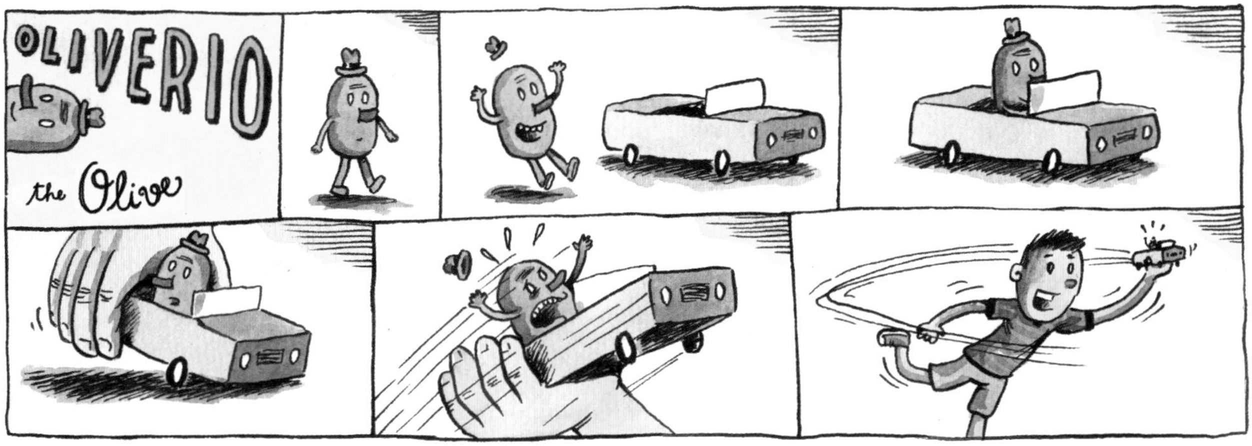
OLIVERIO
the Olive

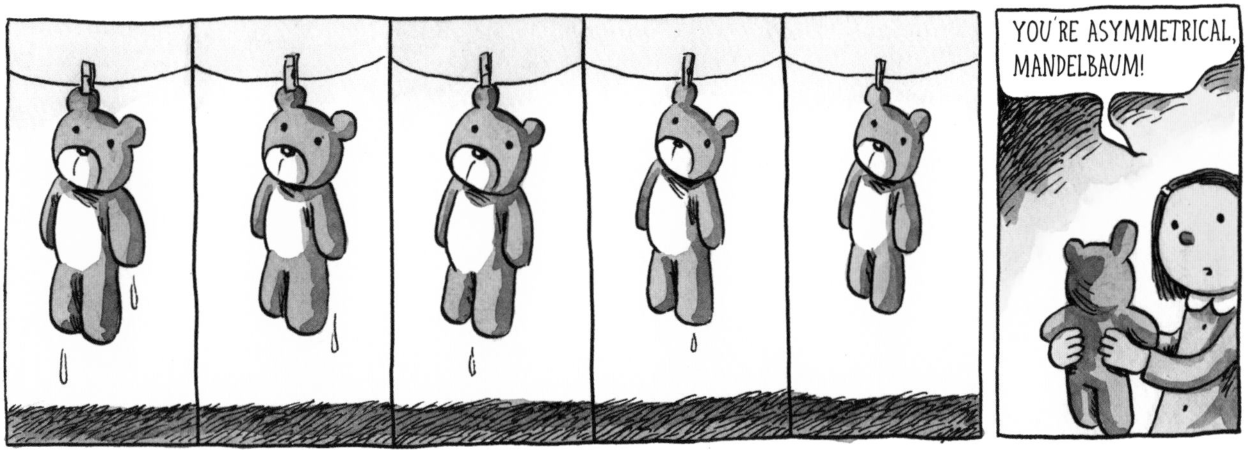
YOU'RE ASYMMETRICAL, MANDELBAUM!

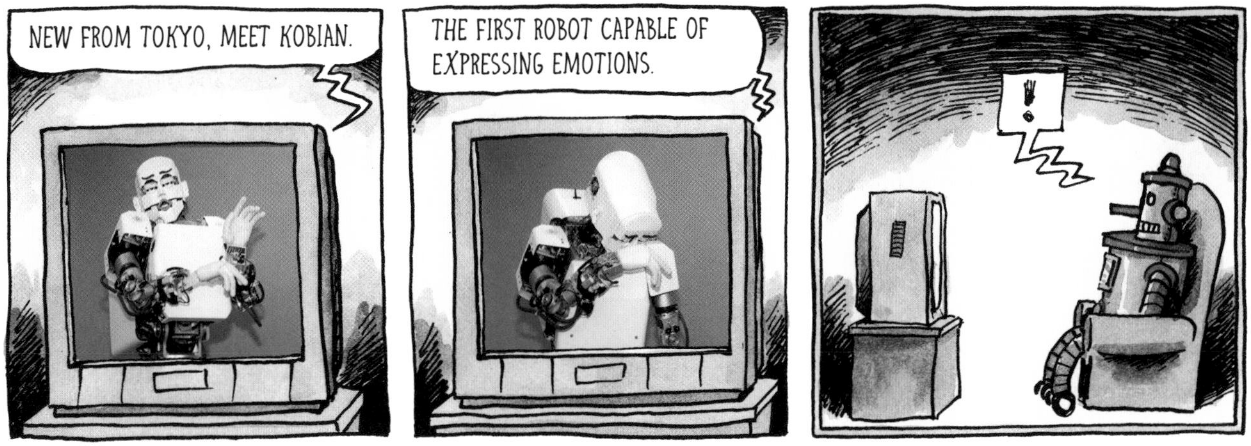
NEW FROM TOKYO, MEET KOBIAN.
THE FIRST ROBOT CAPABLE OF EXPRESSING EMOTIONS.

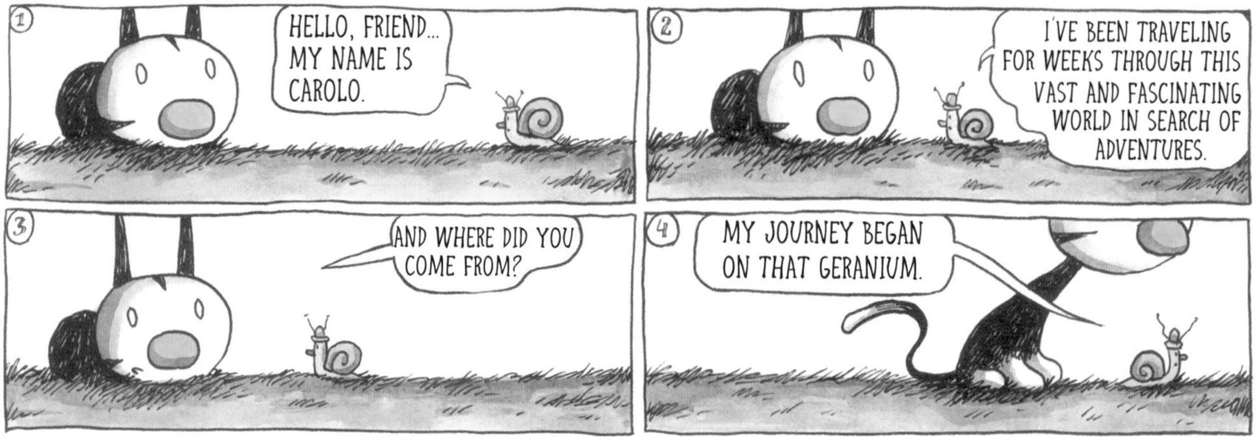
HELLO, FRIEND... MY NAME IS CAROLO.
I'VE BEEN TRAVELING FOR WEEKS THROUGH THIS VAST AND FASCINATING WORLD IN SEARCH OF ADVENTURES.
AND WHERE DID YOU COME FROM?
MY JOURNEY BEGAN ON THAT GERANIUM.

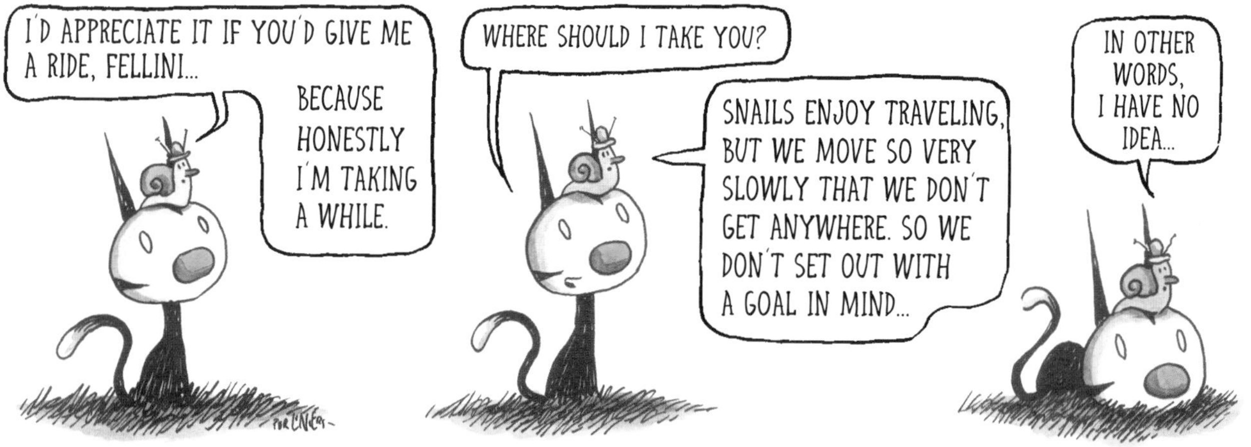
I'D APPRECIATE IT IF YOU'D GIVE ME A RIDE, FELLINI...
BECAUSE HONESTLY I'M TAKING A WHILE.
WHERE SHOULD I TAKE YOU?
SNAILS ENJOY TRAVELING, BUT WE MOVE SO VERY SLOWLY THAT WE DON'T GET ANYWHERE. SO WE DON'T SET OUT WITH A GOAL IN MIND...
IN OTHER WORDS, I HAVE NO IDEA...

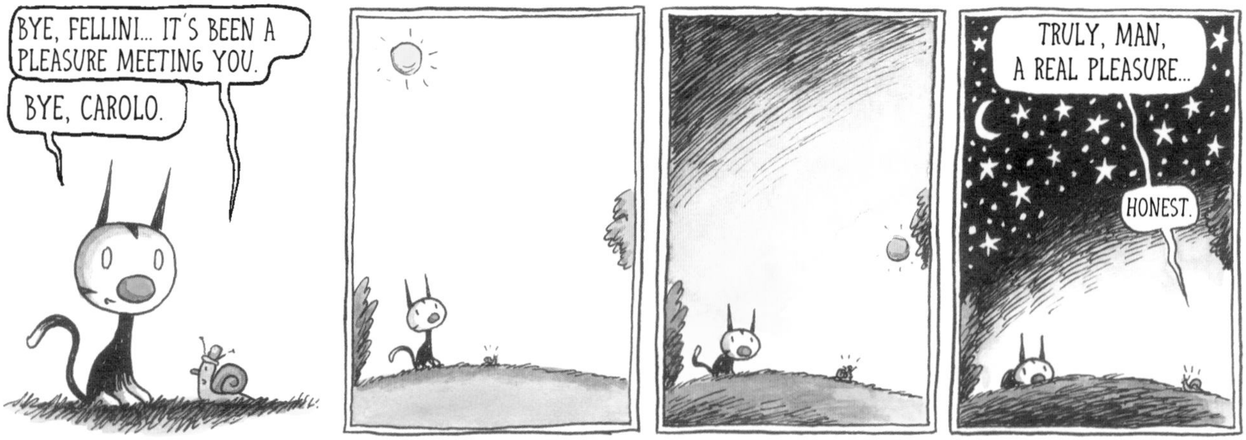
BYE, FELLINI... IT'S BEEN A PLEASURE MEETING YOU.
BYE, CAROLO.
TRULY, MAN, A REAL PLEASURE...
HONEST.

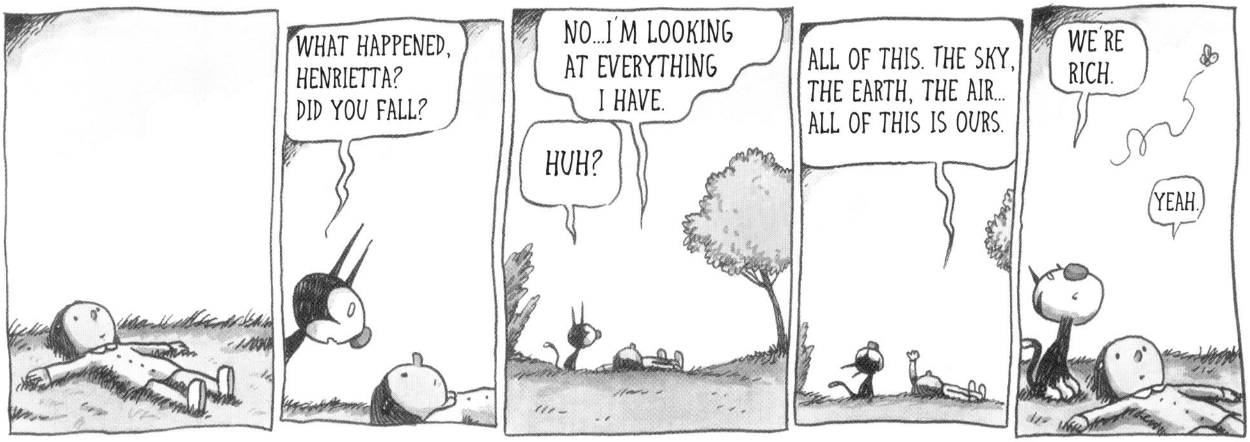
WHAT HAPPENED, HENRIETTA? DID YOU FALL?
NO...I'M LOOKING AT EVERYTHING I HAVE.
HUH?
ALL OF THIS. THE SKY, THE EARTH, THE AIR... ALL OF THIS IS OURS.
WE'RE RICH.
YEAH.

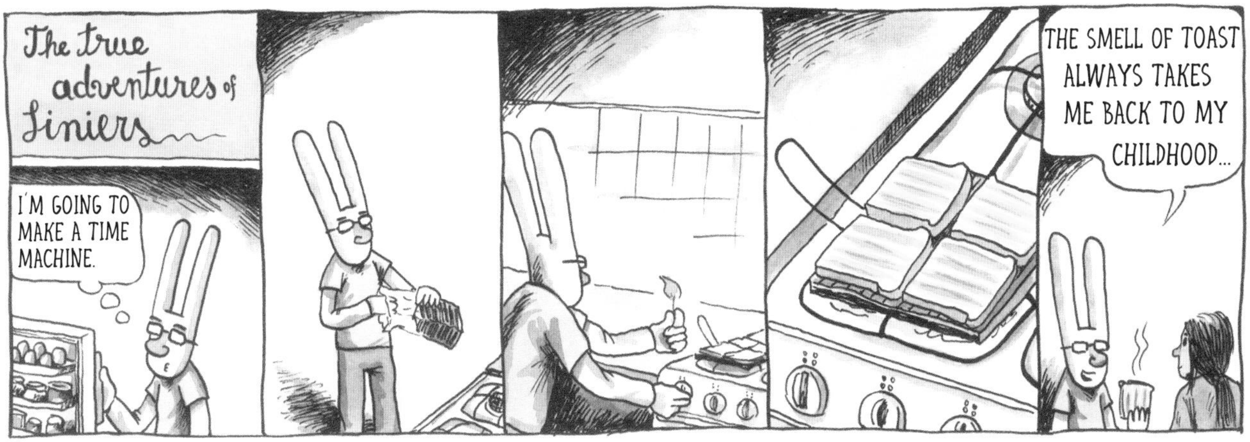
The true adventures of Liniers
I'M GOING TO MAKE A TIME MACHINE.
THE SMELL OF TOAST ALWAYS TAKES ME BACK TO MY CHILDHOOD...

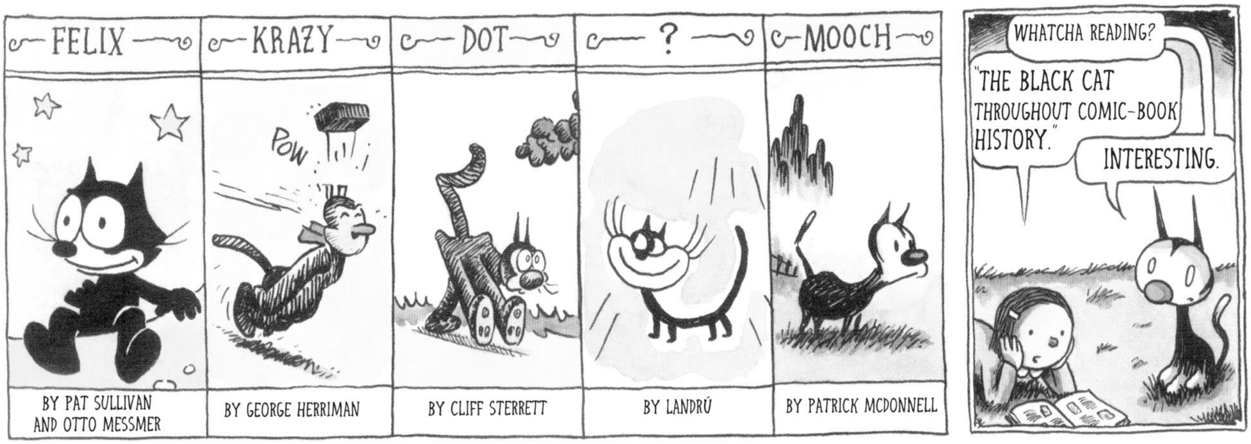
FELIX
KRAZY
DOT
?
MOOCH
POW
BY PAT SULLIVAN AND OTTO MESSMER
BY GEORGE HERRIMAN
BY CLIFF STERRETT
BY LANDRÚ
BY PATRICK MCDONNELL
WHATCHA READING?
"THE BLACK CAT THROUGHOUT COMIC-BOOK HISTORY."
INTERESTING.

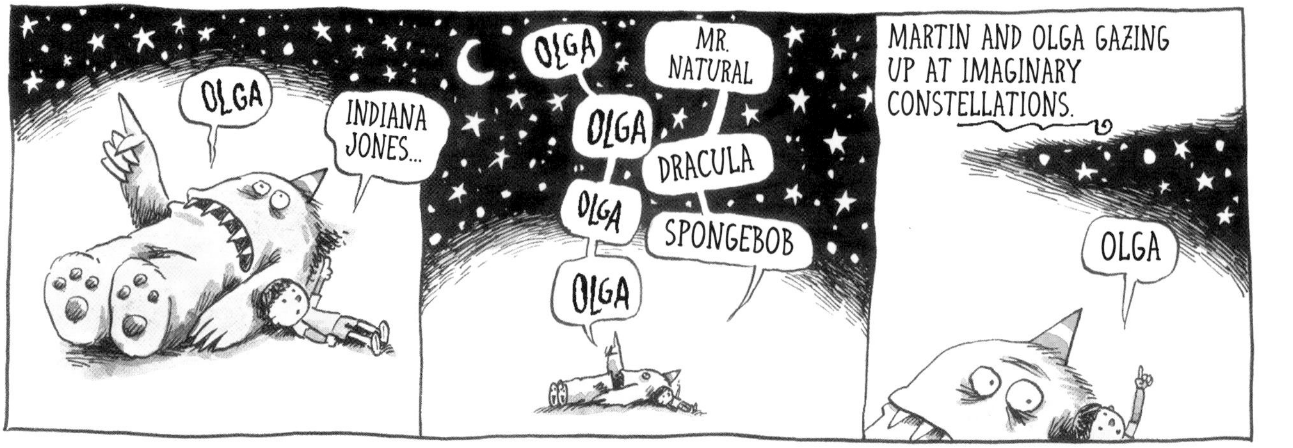
OLGA
INDIANA JONES...
OLGA
MR. NATURAL
OLGA
DRACULA
OLGA
SPONGEBOB
OLGA
MARTIN AND OLGA GAZING UP AT IMAGINARY CONSTELLATIONS.
OLGA

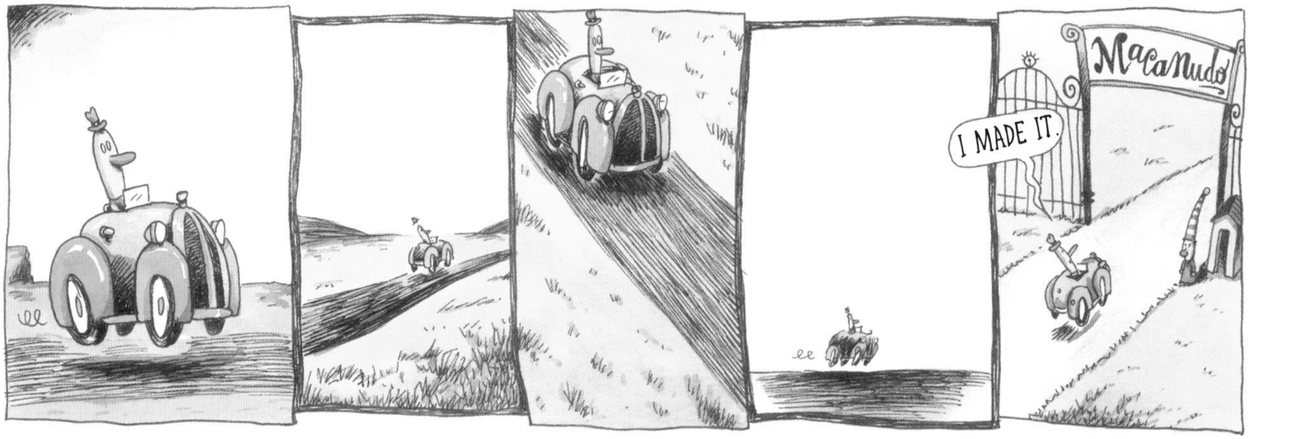
Macanudo
I MADE IT.

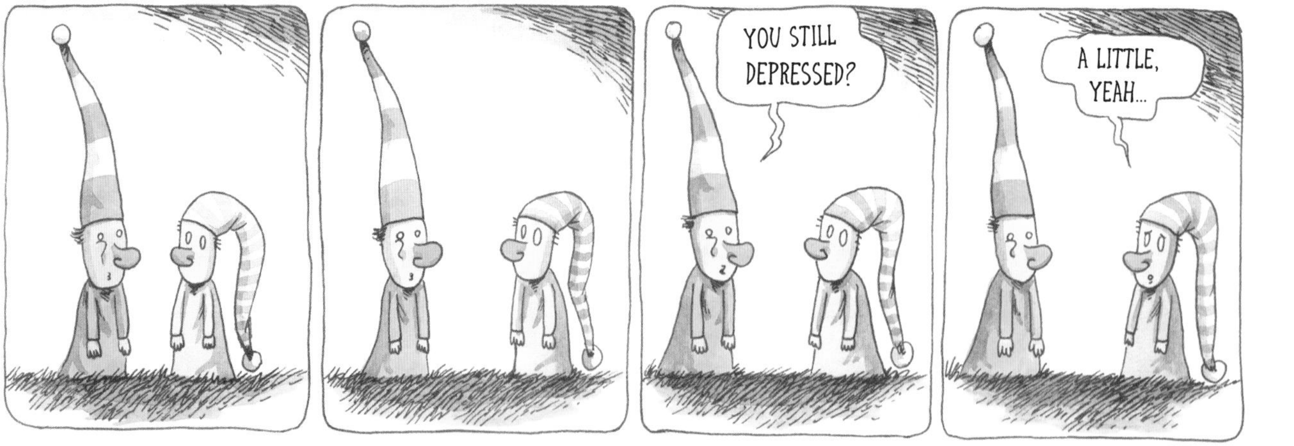
YOU STILL DEPRESSED?
A LITTLE, YEAH...

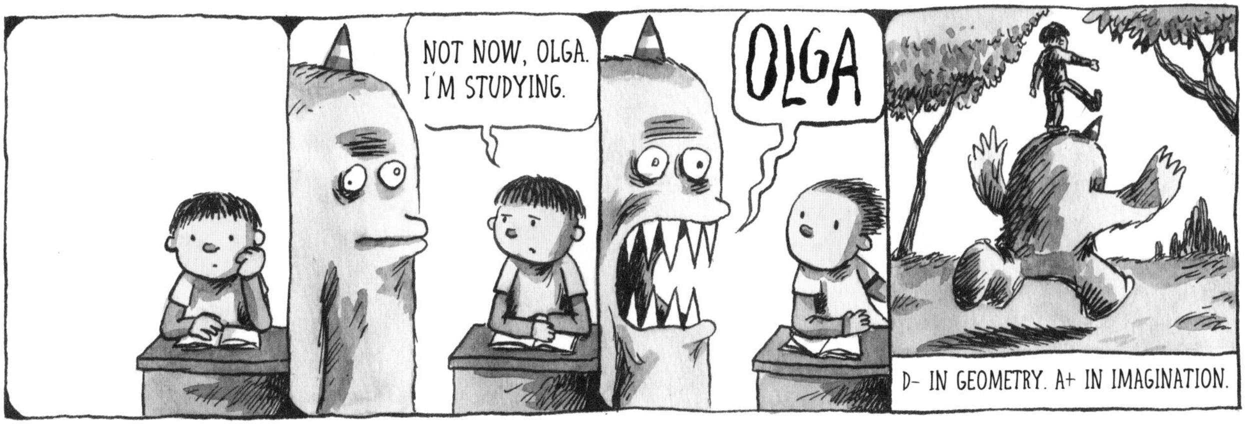
NOT NOW, OLGA. I'M STUDYING.
OLGA
D- IN GEOMETRY. A+ IN IMAGINATION.

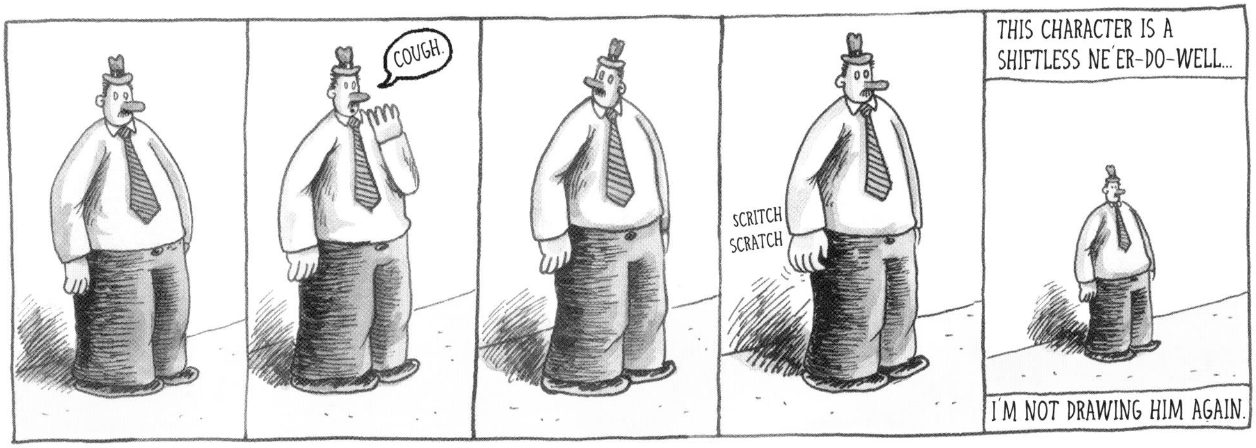
COUGH.
SCRITCH SCRATCH
THIS CHARACTER IS A SHIFTLESS NE'ER-DO-WELL...
I'M NOT DRAWING HIM AGAIN.

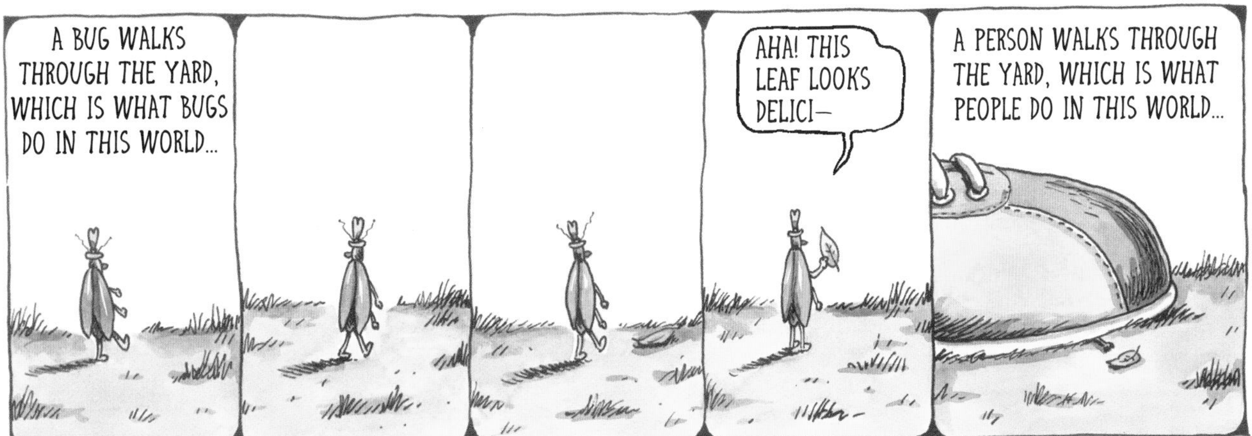
A BUG WALKS THROUGH THE YARD, WHICH IS WHAT BUGS DO IN THIS WORLD...
AHA! THIS LEAF LOOKS DELICI–
A PERSON WALKS THROUGH THE YARD, WHICH IS WHAT PEOPLE DO IN THIS WORLD...

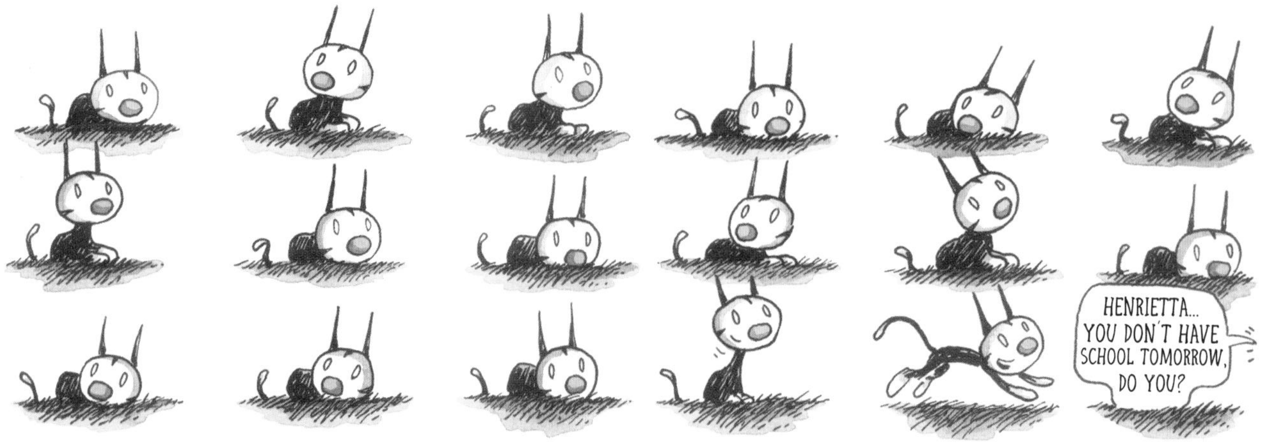
HENRIETTA... YOU DON'T HAVE SCHOOL TOMORROW, DO YOU?

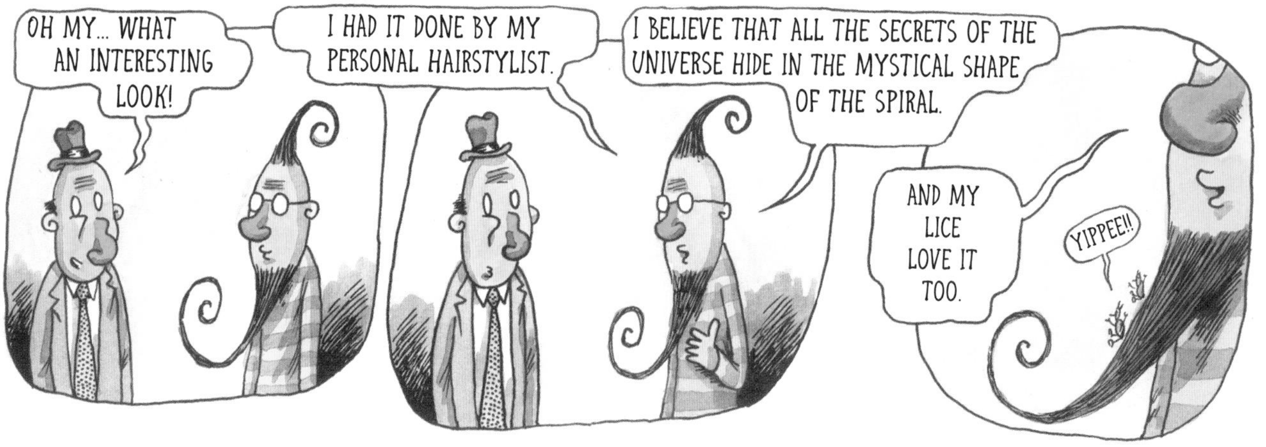
OH MY... WHAT AN INTERESTING LOOK!
I HAD IT DONE BY MY PERSONAL HAIRSTYLIST.
I BELIEVE THAT ALL THE SECRETS OF THE UNIVERSE HIDE IN THE MYSTICAL SHAPE OF THE SPIRAL.
AND MY LICE LOVE IT TOO.
YIPPEE!!

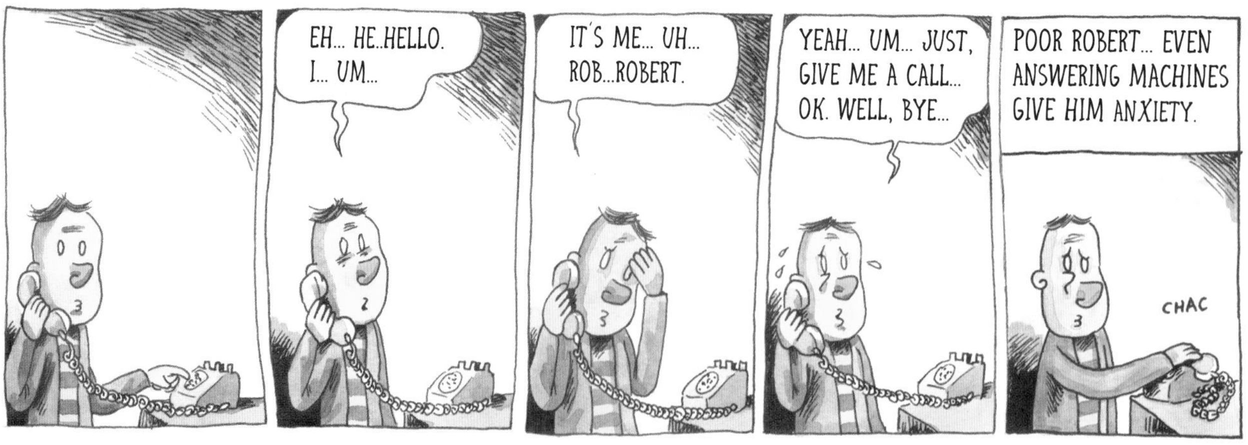
EH... HE..HELLO. I... UM...
IT'S ME... UH... ROB...ROBERT.
YEAH... UM... JUST, GIVE ME A CALL... OK. WELL, BYE...
POOR ROBERT... EVEN ANSWERING MACHINES GIVE HIM ANXIETY.
CHAC

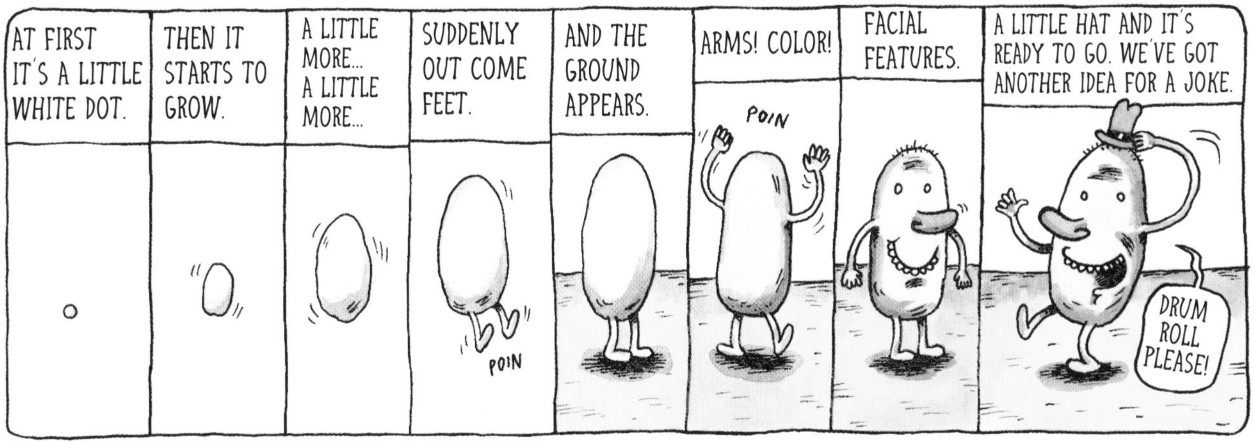
AT FIRST IT'S A LITTLE WHITE DOT.
THEN IT STARTS TO GROW.
A LITTLE MORE... A LITTLE MORE...
SUDDENLY OUT COME FEET.
POIN
AND THE GROUND APPEARS.
ARMS! COLOR!
POIN
FACIAL FEATURES.
A LITTLE HAT AND IT'S READY TO GO. WE'VE GOT ANOTHER IDEA FOR A JOKE.
DRUM ROLL PLEASE!

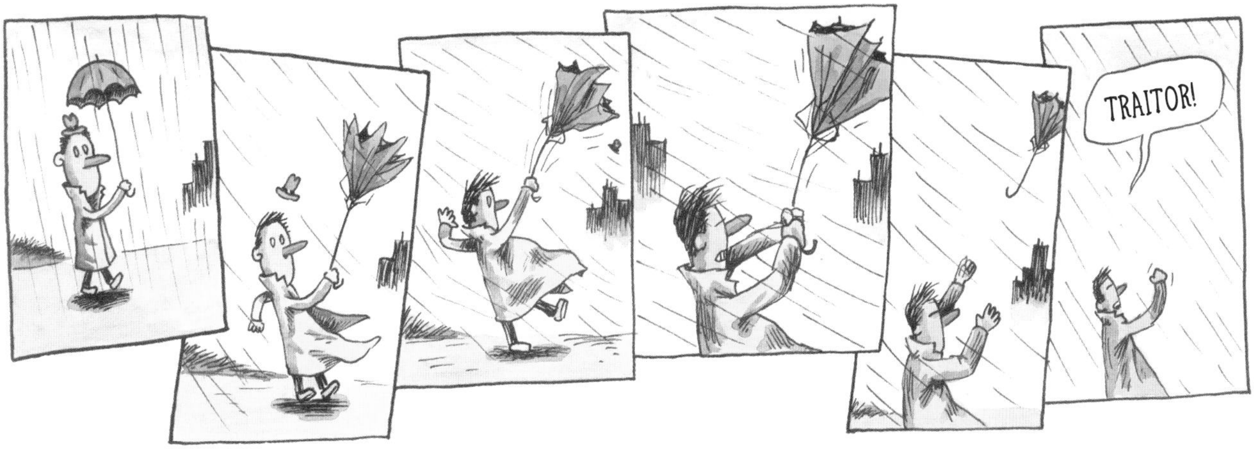
TRAITOR!

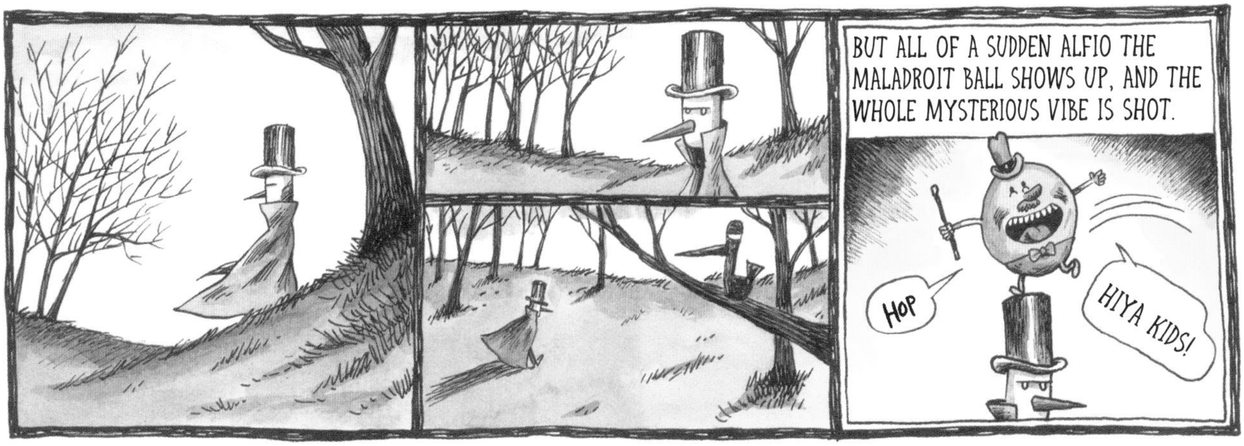
BUT ALL OF A SUDDEN ALFIO THE MALADROIT BALL SHOWS UP, AND THE WHOLE MYSTERIOUS VIBE IS SHOT.
HOP
HIYA KIDS!

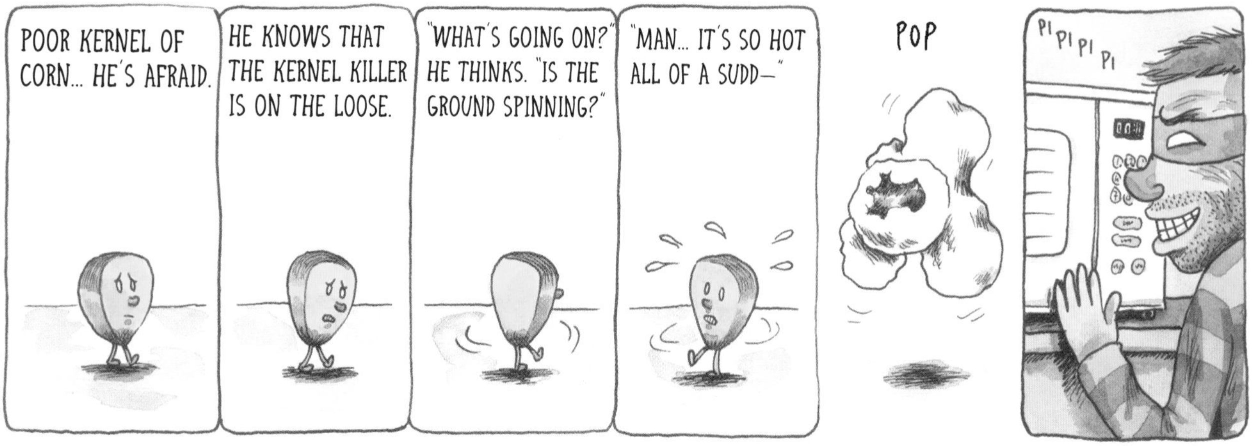
POOR KERNEL OF CORN... HE'S AFRAID.
HE KNOWS THAT THE KERNEL KILLER IS ON THE LOOSE.
"WHAT'S GOING ON?" HE THINKS. "IS THE GROUND SPINNING?"
"MAN... IT'S SO HOT ALL OF A SUDD—"
POP
PI PI PI PI

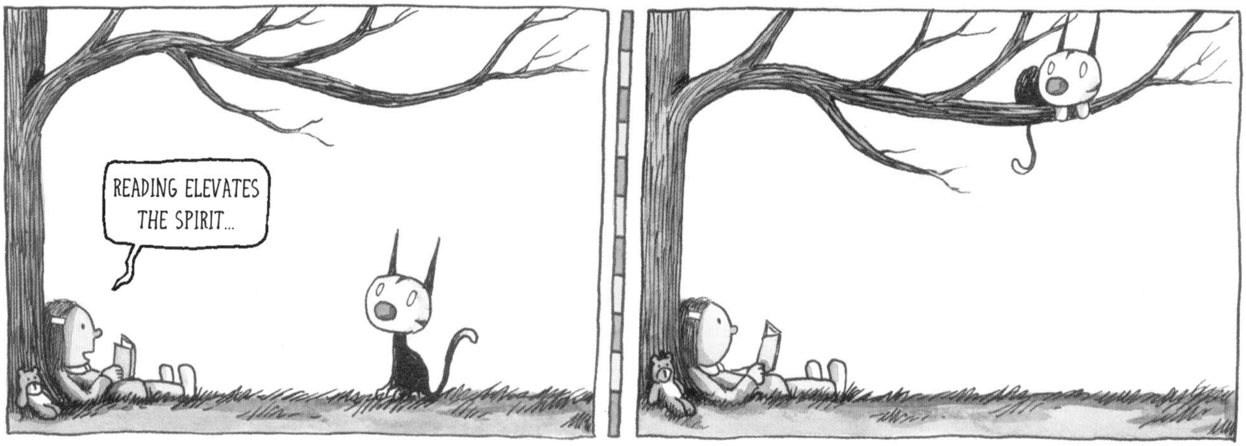
READING ELEVATES THE SPIRIT...

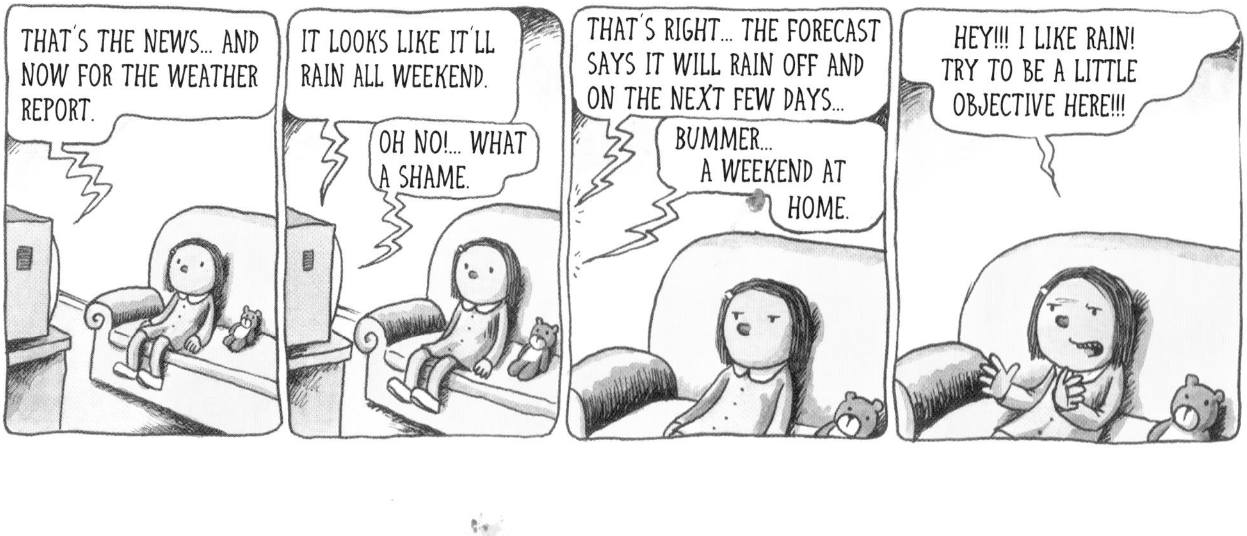
THAT'S THE NEWS... AND NOW FOR THE WEATHER REPORT.
IT LOOKS LIKE IT'LL RAIN ALL WEEKEND.
OH NO!... WHAT A SHAME.
THAT'S RIGHT... THE FORECAST SAYS IT WILL RAIN OFF AND ON THE NEXT FEW DAYS...
BUMMER... A WEEKEND AT HOME.
HEY!!! I LIKE RAIN! TRY TO BE A LITTLE OBJECTIVE HERE!!!

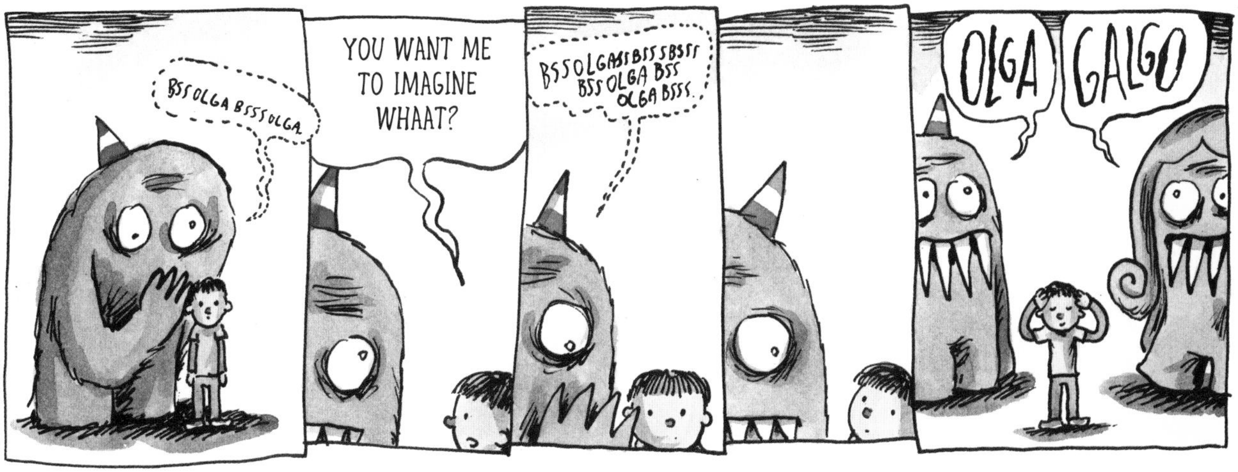
BSSOLGABSSSOLGA
YOU WANT ME TO IMAGINE WHAAT?
BSSOLGABSSBSSSBSSS BSS OLGA BSS OLGA BSSS.
OLGA
GALGO

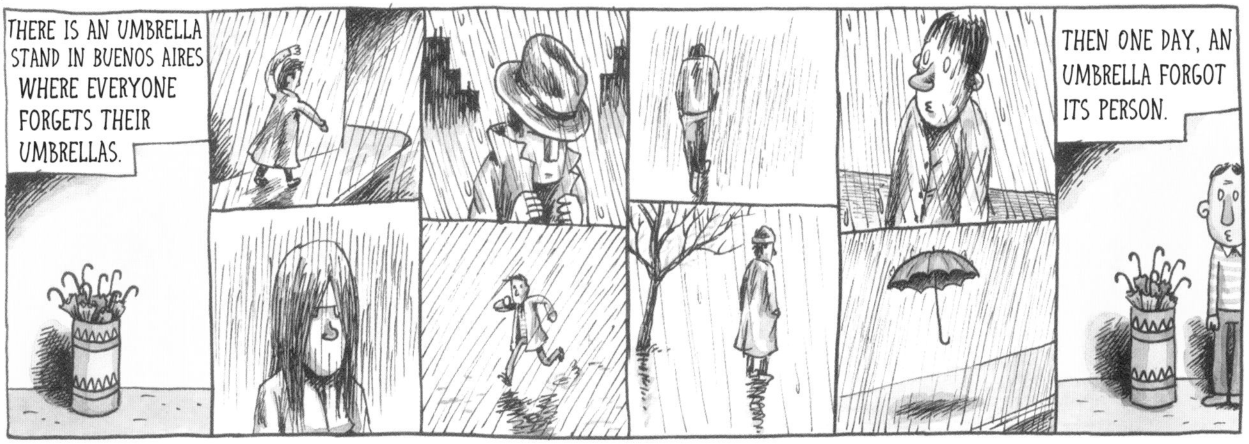
THERE IS AN UMBRELLA STAND IN BUENOS AIRES WHERE EVERYONE FORGETS THEIR UMBRELLAS.
THEN ONE DAY, AN UMBRELLA FORGOT ITS PERSON.

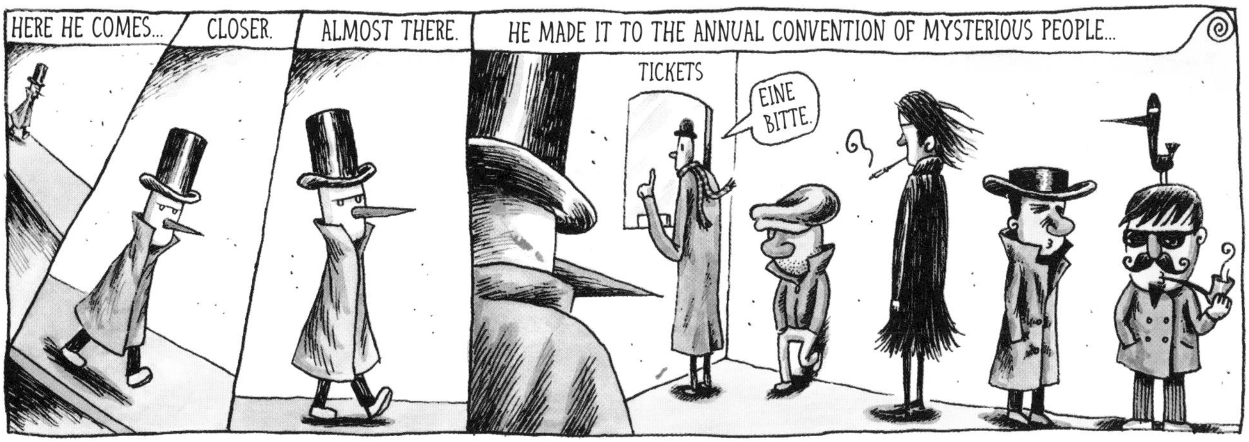
HERE HE COMES...
CLOSER.
ALMOST THERE.
HE MADE IT TO THE ANNUAL CONVENTION OF MYSTERIOUS PEOPLE...
TICKETS
EINE BITTE.

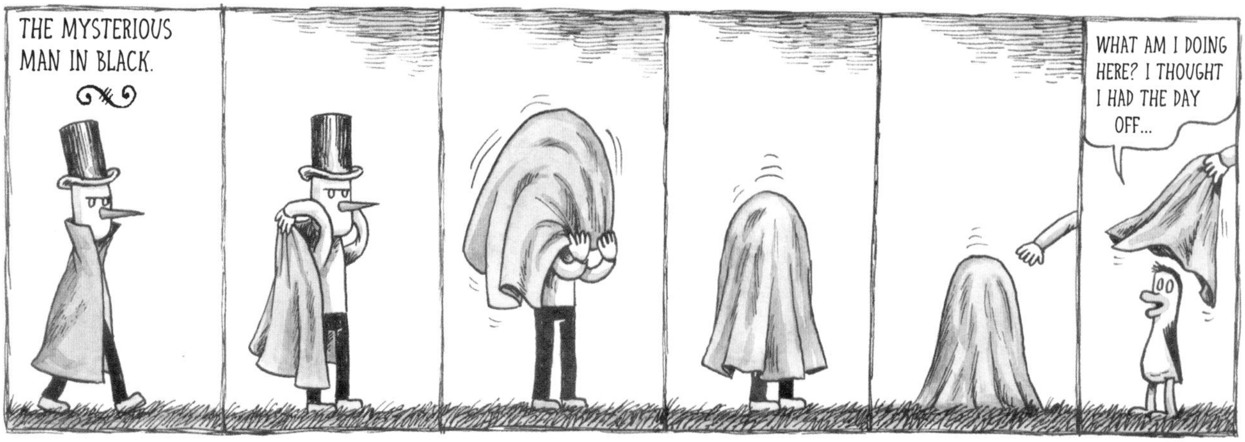
THE MYSTERIOUS MAN IN BLACK.
WHAT AM I DOING HERE? I THOUGHT I HAD THE DAY OFF...

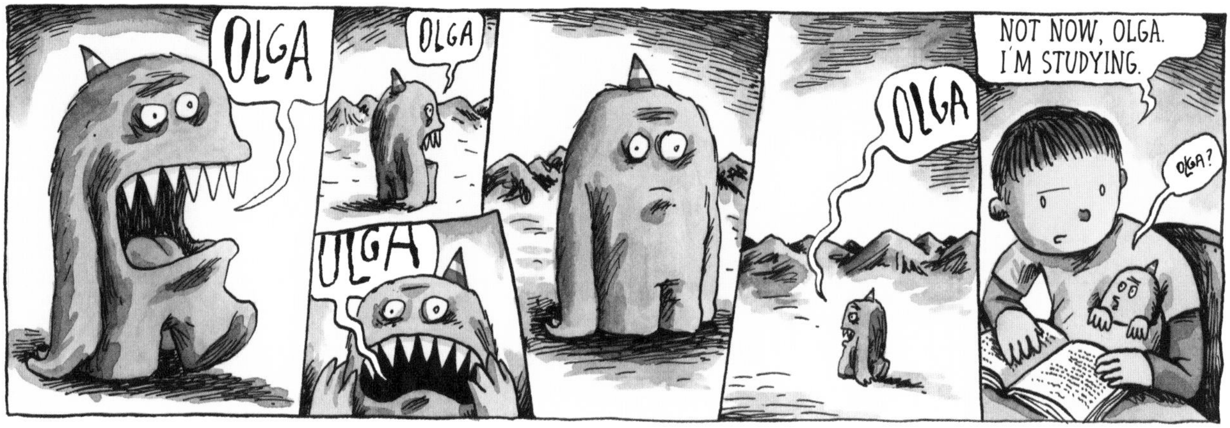
OLGA
OLGA
OLGA
OLGA
NOT NOW, OLGA. I'M STUDYING.
OLGA?

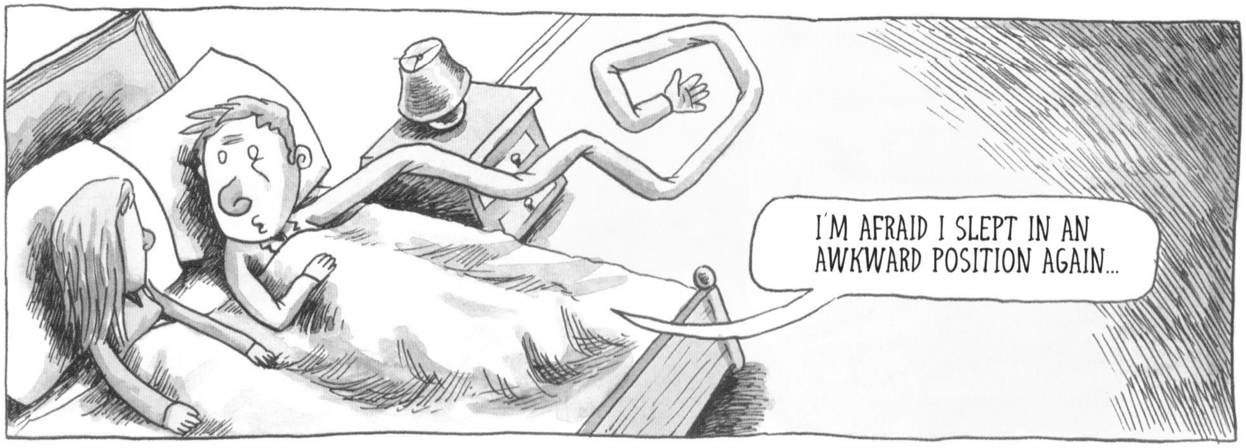
I'M AFRAID I SLEPT IN AN AWKWARD POSITION AGAIN...

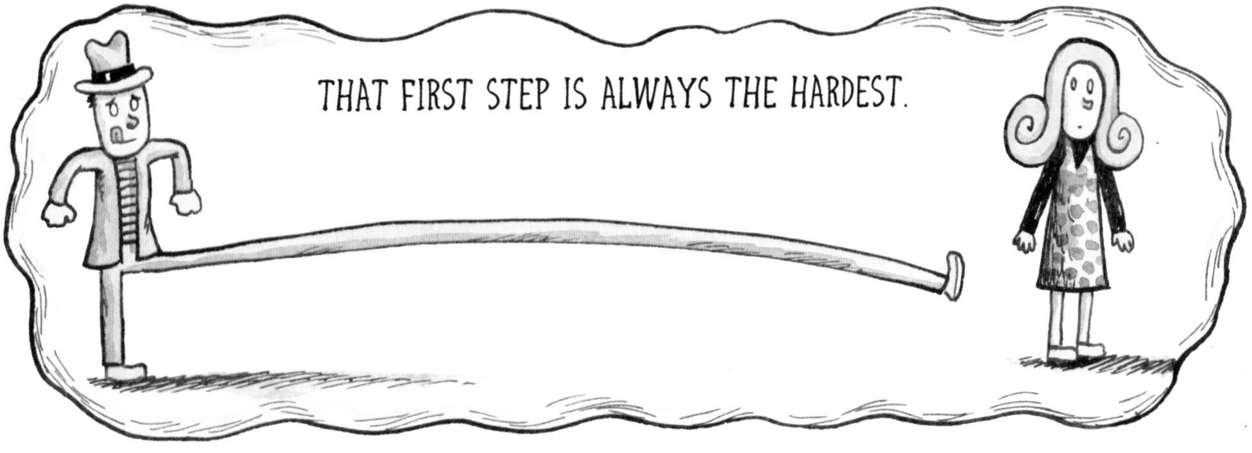
THAT FIRST STEP IS ALWAYS THE HARDEST.

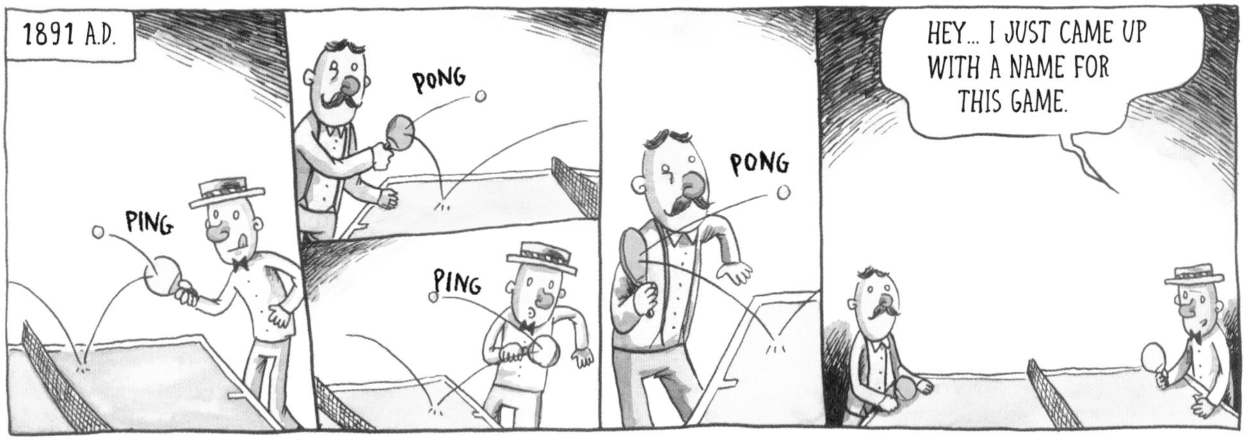
1891 A.D.
PING
PONG
PING
PONG
HEY... I JUST CAME UP WITH A NAME FOR THIS GAME.

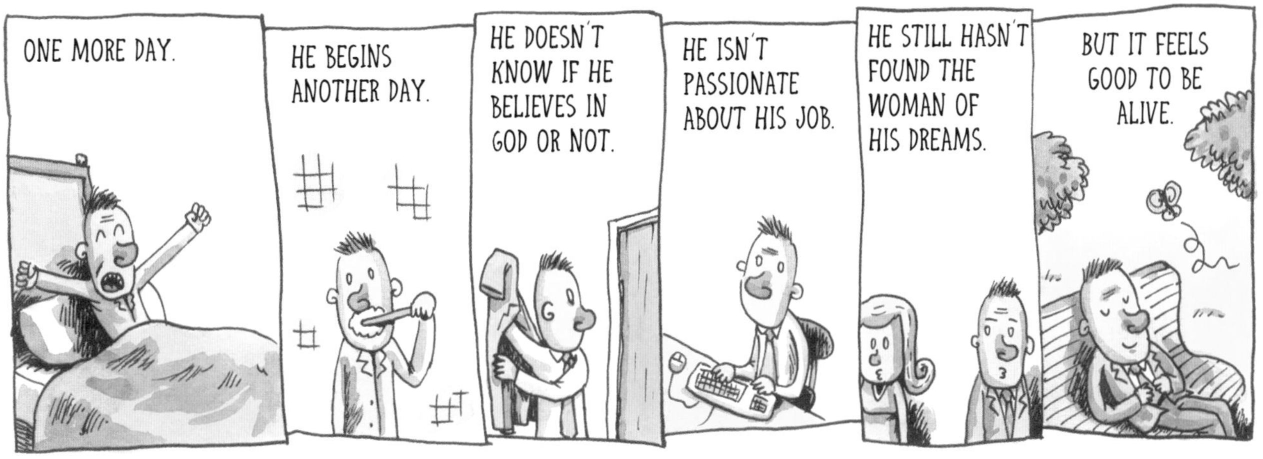
ONE MORE DAY.
HE BEGINS ANOTHER DAY.
HE DOESN'T KNOW IF HE BELIEVES IN GOD OR NOT.
HE ISN'T PASSIONATE ABOUT HIS JOB.
HE STILL HASN'T FOUND THE WOMAN OF HIS DREAMS.
BUT IT FEELS GOOD TO BE ALIVE.

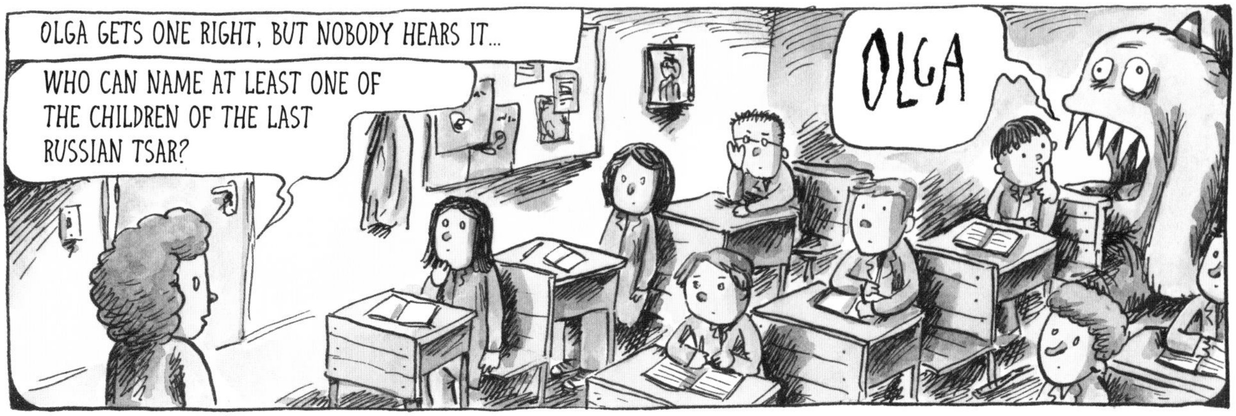
OLGA GETS ONE RIGHT, BUT NOBODY HEARS IT...
WHO CAN NAME AT LEAST ONE OF THE CHILDREN OF THE LAST RUSSIAN TSAR?
OLGA

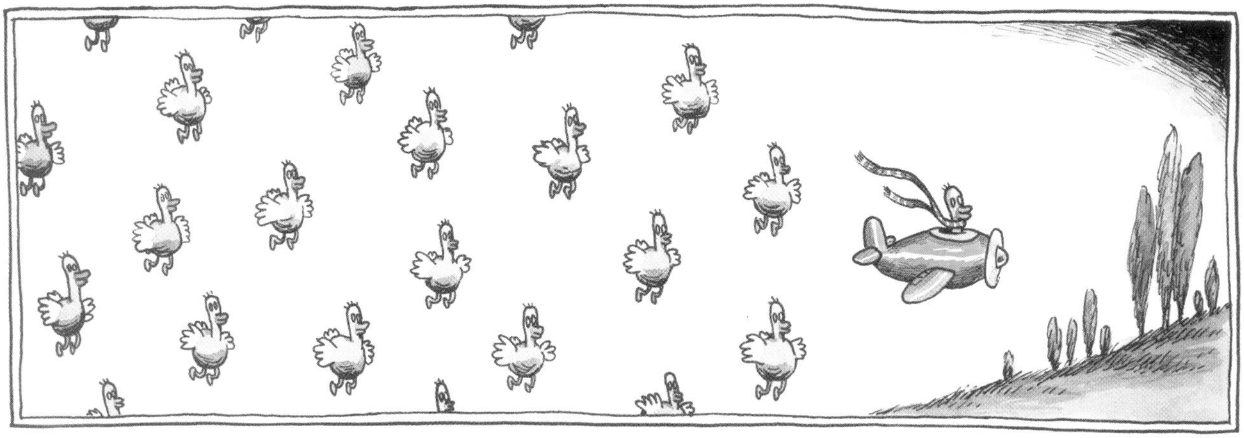

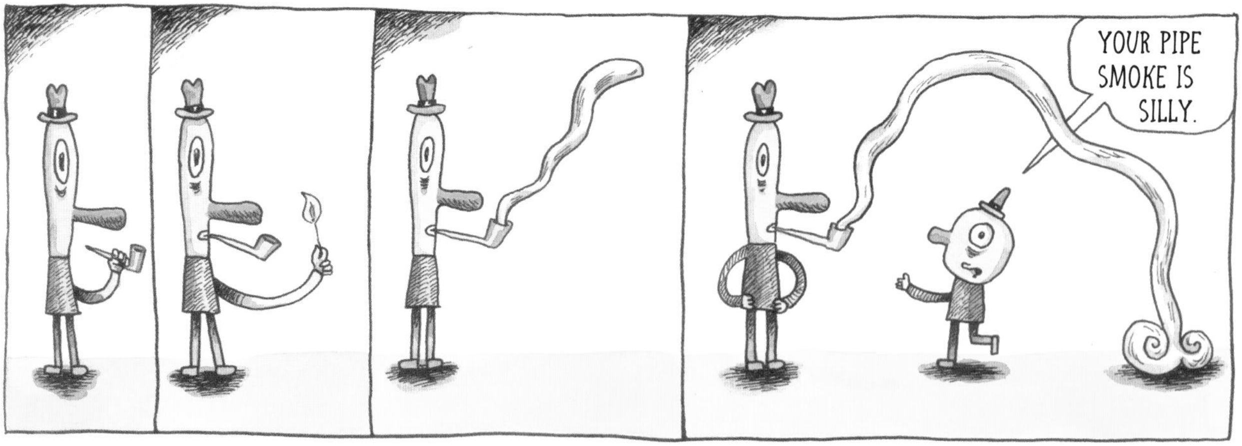
YOUR PIPE SMOKE IS SILLY.

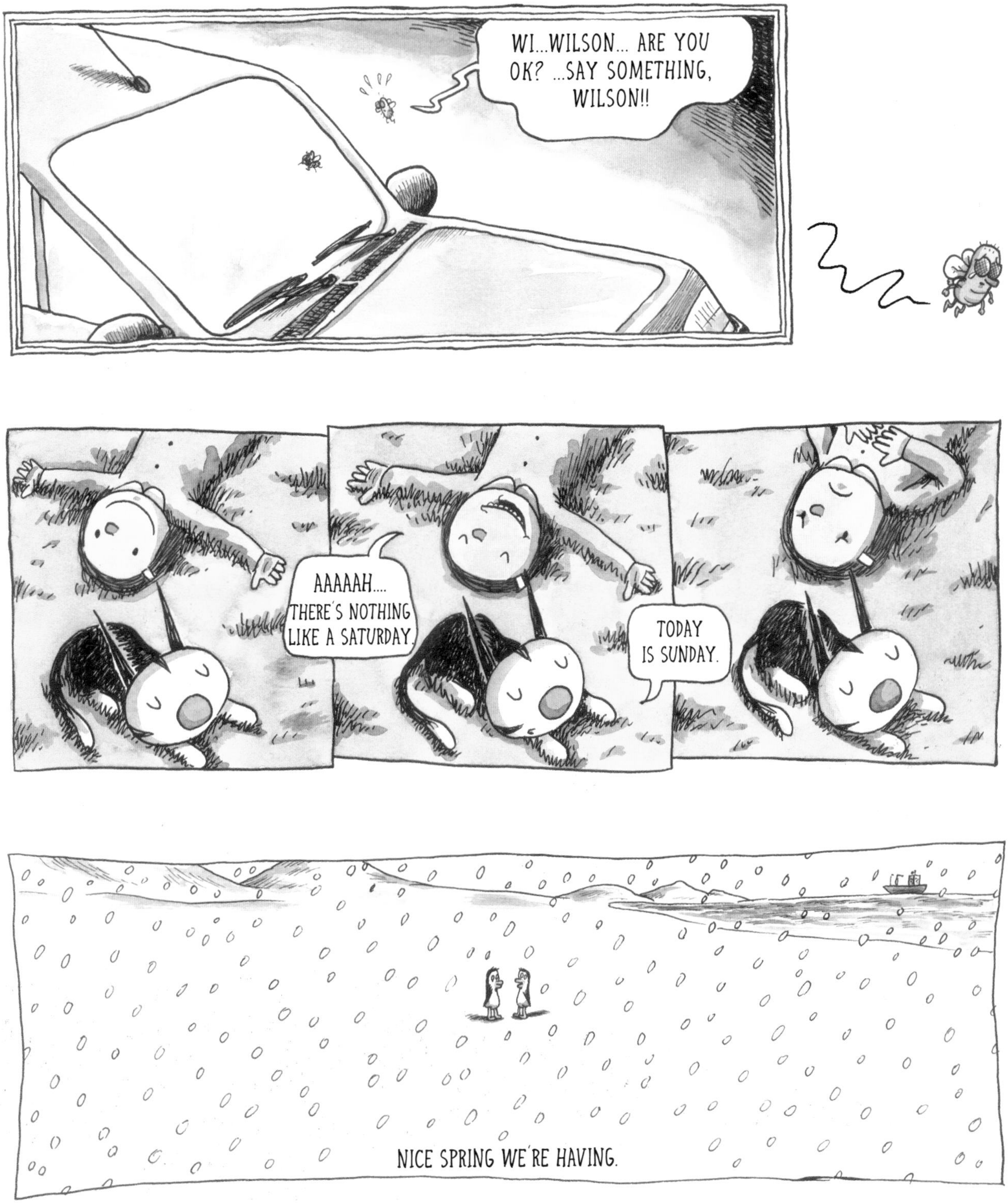
WI...WILSON... ARE YOU OK? ...SAY SOMETHING, WILSON!!
AAAAAH.... THERE'S NOTHING LIKE A SATURDAY.
TODAY IS SUNDAY.
NICE SPRING WE'RE HAVING.

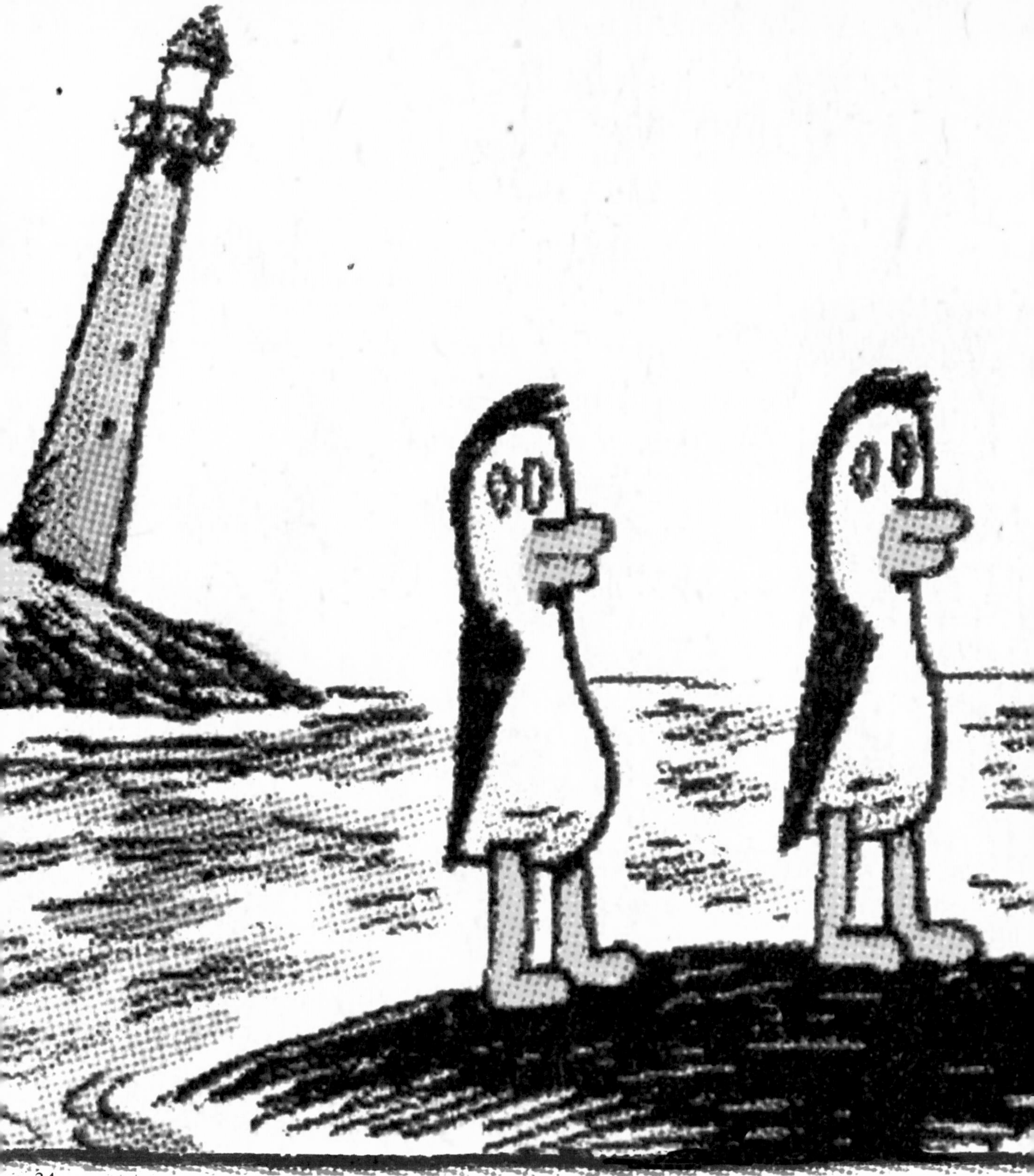

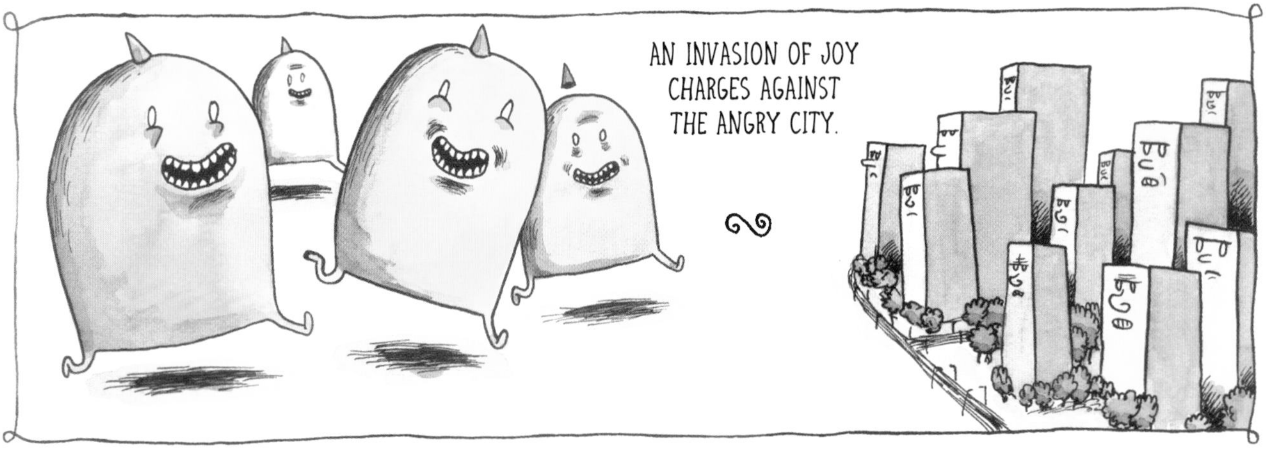
AN INVASION OF JOY CHARGES AGAINST THE ANGRY CITY.

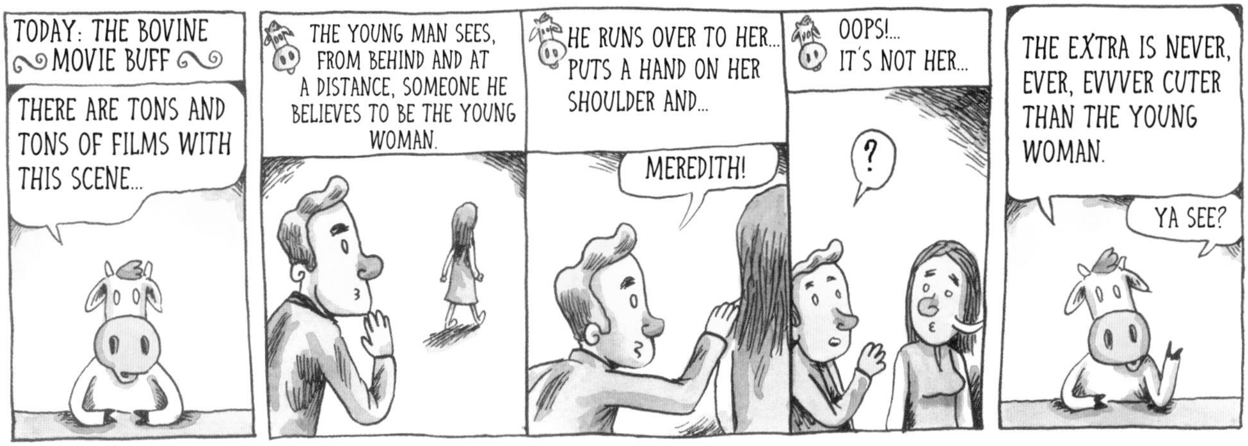
TODAY: THE BOVINE MOVIE BUFF
THERE ARE TONS AND TONS OF FILMS WITH THIS SCENE...
THE YOUNG MAN SEES, FROM BEHIND AND AT A DISTANCE, SOMEONE HE BELIEVES TO BE THE YOUNG WOMAN.
HE RUNS OVER TO HER... PUTS A HAND ON HER SHOULDER AND...
MEREDITH!
OOPS!... IT'S NOT HER...
?
THE EXTRA IS NEVER, EVER, EVVVER CUTER THAN THE YOUNG WOMAN.
YA SEE?

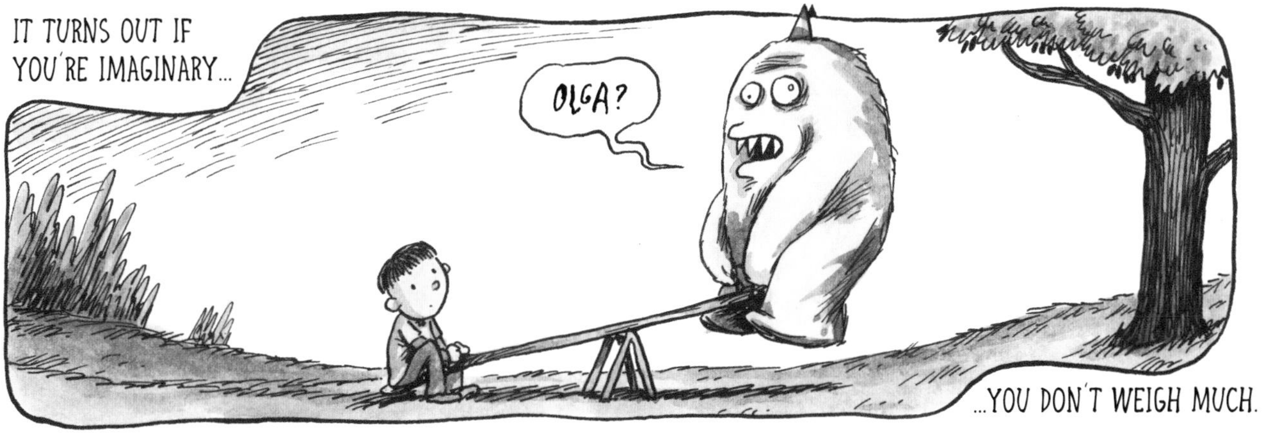
IT TURNS OUT IF YOU'RE IMAGINARY...
OLGA?
...YOU DON'T WEIGH MUCH.

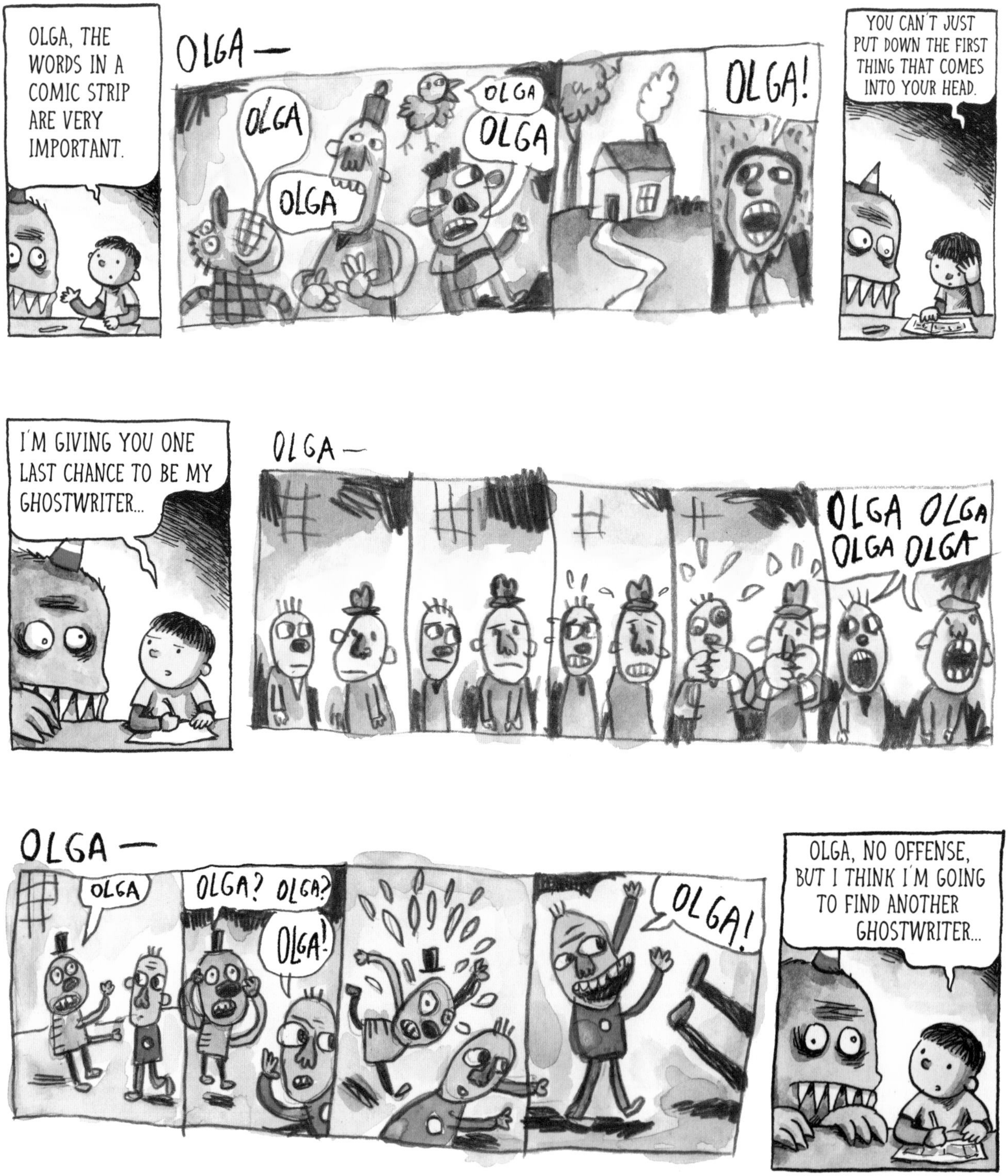
OLGA, THE WORDS IN A COMIC STRIP ARE VERY IMPORTANT.
OLGA—
OLGA
OLGA
OLGA
OLGA
OLGA!
YOU CAN'T JUST PUT DOWN THE FIRST THING THAT COMES INTO YOUR HEAD.
I'M GIVING YOU ONE LAST CHANCE TO BE MY GHOSTWRITER...
OLGA—
OLGA OLGA OLGA OLGA
OLGA—
OLGA
OLGA? OLGA?
OLGA!
OLGA!
OLGA, NO OFFENSE, BUT I THINK I'M GOING TO FIND ANOTHER GHOSTWRITER...

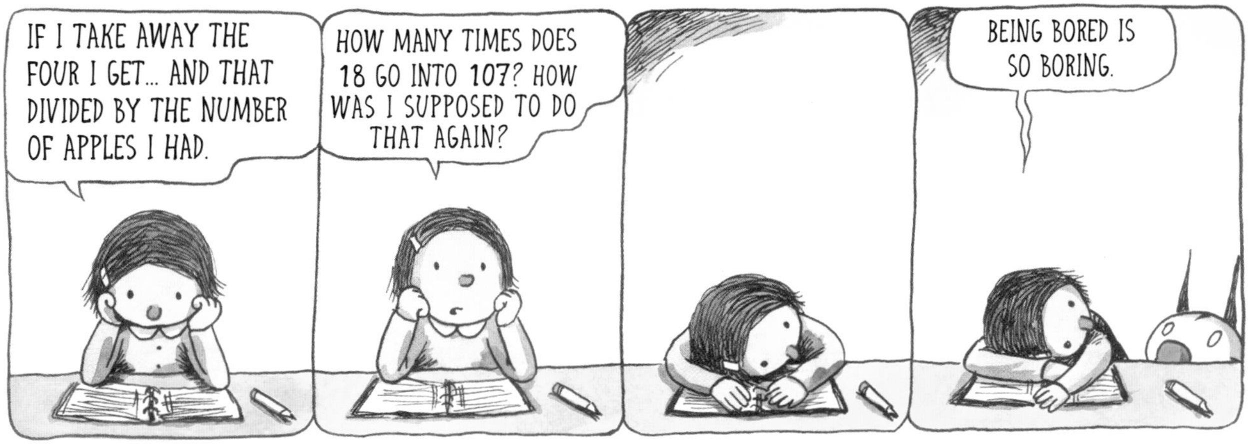
IF I TAKE AWAY THE FOUR I GET... AND THAT DIVIDED BY THE NUMBER OF APPLES I HAD.
HOW MANY TIMES DOES 18 GO INTO 107? HOW WAS I SUPPOSED TO DO THAT AGAIN?
BEING BORED IS SO BORING.

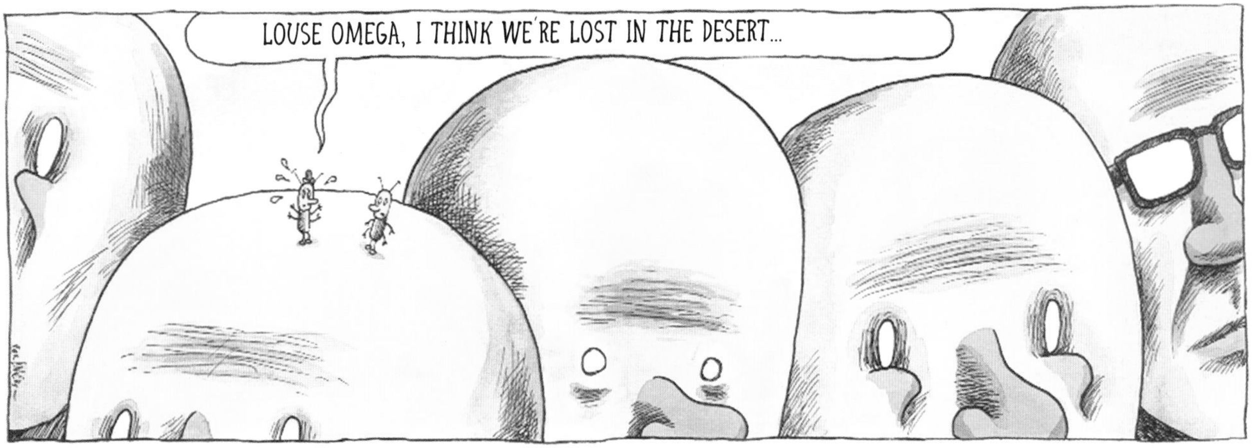
LOUSE OMEGA, I THINK WE'RE LOST IN THE DESERT...

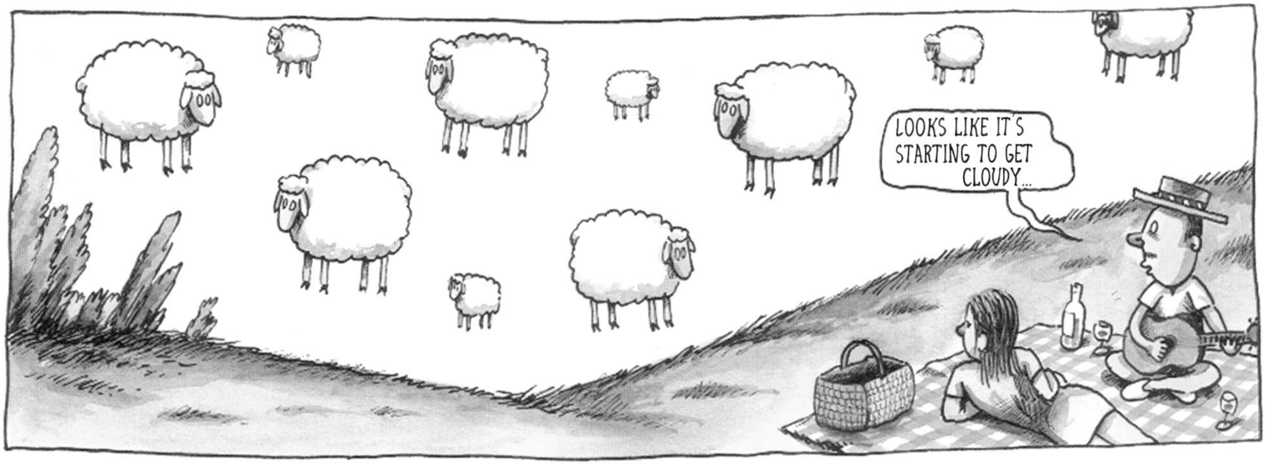
LOOKS LIKE IT'S STARTING TO GET CLOUDY...

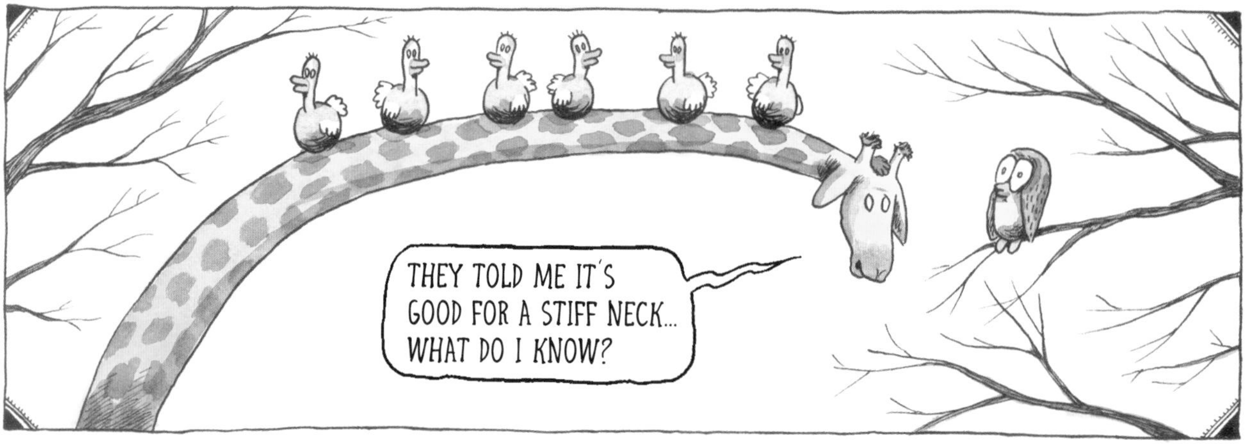
THEY TOLD ME IT'S GOOD FOR A STIFF NECK... WHAT DO I KNOW?

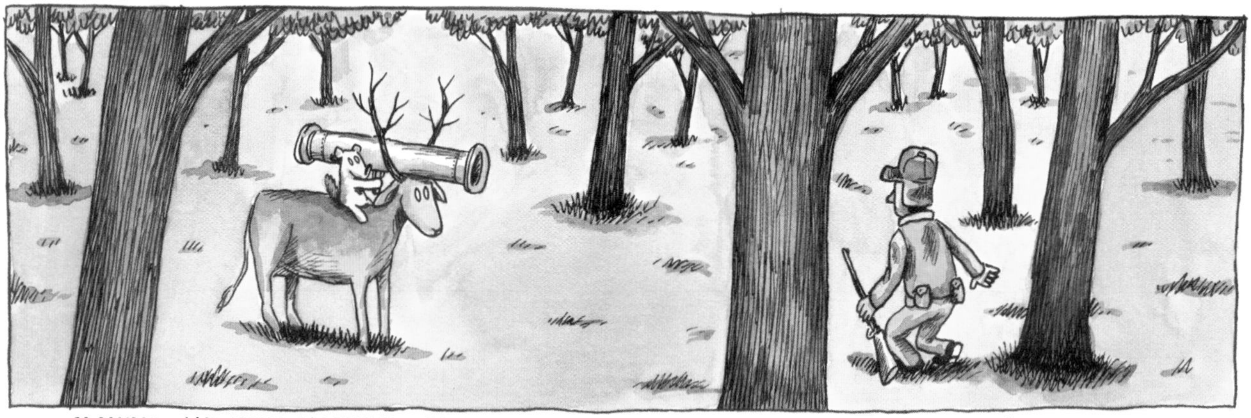

SLOWLY... AND VERY CAREFULLY, HE LOWERED HIS RIFLE. YET HE KNEW HE STILL WASN'T SAFE, NO SIR.

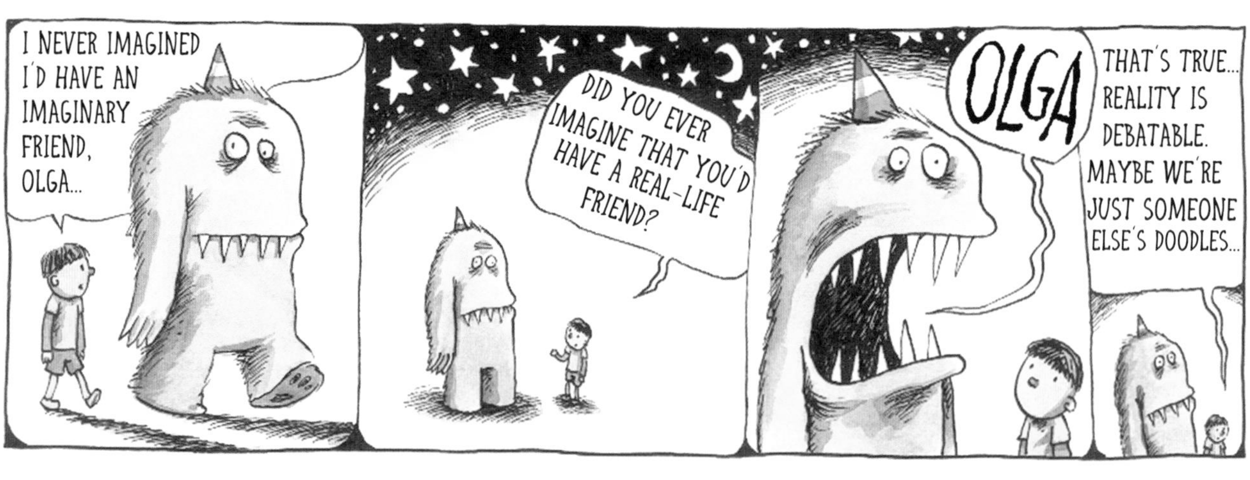
I NEVER IMAGINED I'D HAVE AN IMAGINARY FRIEND, OLGA...
DID YOU EVER IMAGINE THAT YOU'D HAVE A REAL-LIFE FRIEND?
OLGA
THAT'S TRUE... REALITY IS DEBATABLE. MAYBE WE'RE JUST SOMEONE ELSE'S DOODLES...

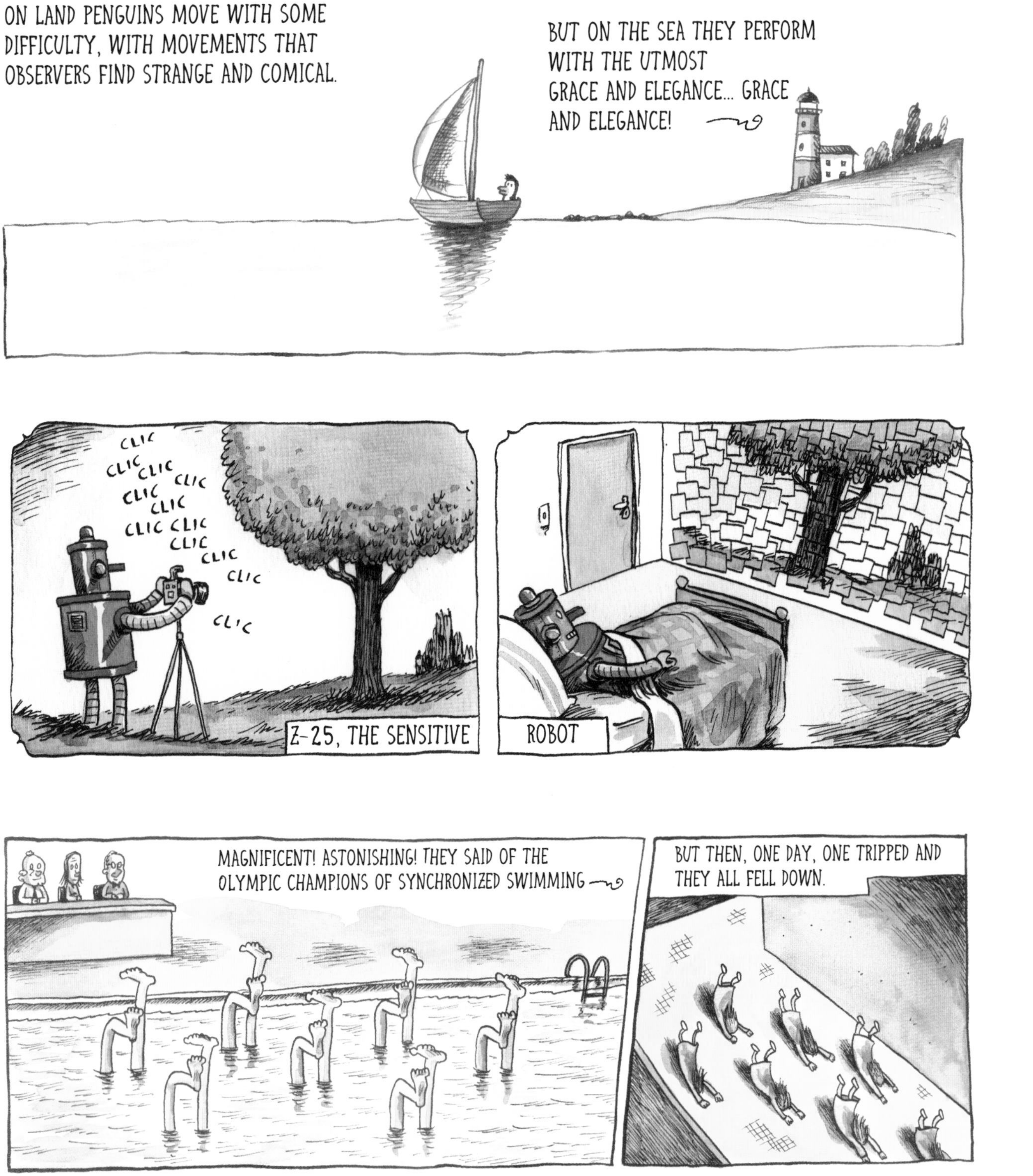
ON LAND PENGUINS MOVE WITH SOME DIFFICULTY, WITH MOVEMENTS THAT OBSERVERS FIND STRANGE AND COMICAL.
BUT ON THE SEA THEY PERFORM WITH THE UTMOST GRACE AND ELEGANCE... GRACE AND ELEGANCE!
CLIC CLIC CLIC CLIC CLIC CLIC CLIC CLIC CLIC CLIC CLIC CLIC
Z-25, THE SENSITIVE
ROBOT
MAGNIFICENT! ASTONISHING! THEY SAID OF THE OLYMPIC CHAMPIONS OF SYNCHRONIZED SWIMMING
BUT THEN, ONE DAY, ONE TRIPPED AND THEY ALL FELL DOWN.

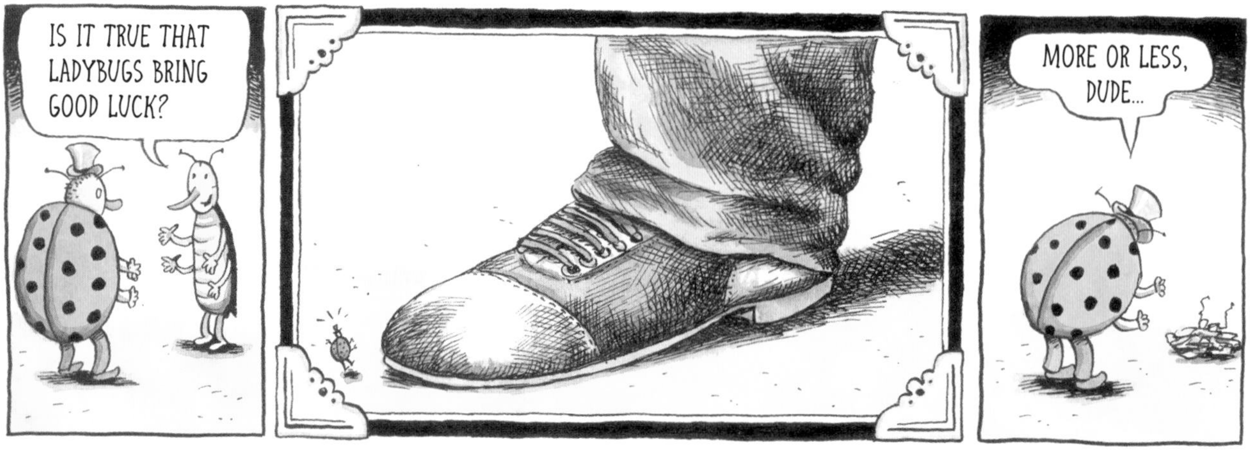
IS IT TRUE THAT LADYBUGS BRING GOOD LUCK?
MORE OR LESS, DUDE...

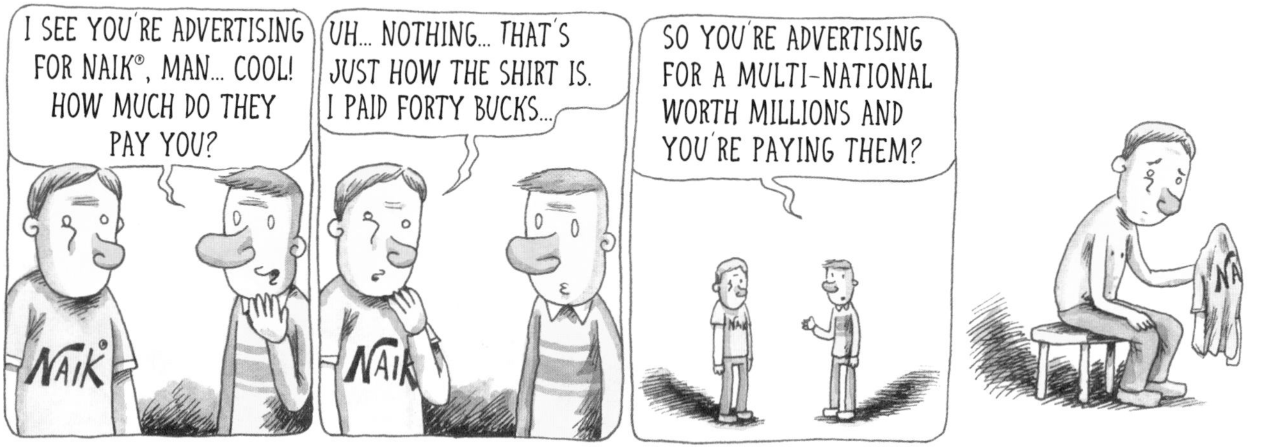
I SEE YOU'RE ADVERTISING FOR NAIK®, MAN... COOL! HOW MUCH DO THEY PAY YOU?
NAIK
UH... NOTHING... THAT'S JUST HOW THE SHIRT IS. I PAID FORTY BUCKS...
SO YOU'RE ADVERTISING FOR A MULTI-NATIONAL WORTH MILLIONS AND YOU'RE PAYING THEM?

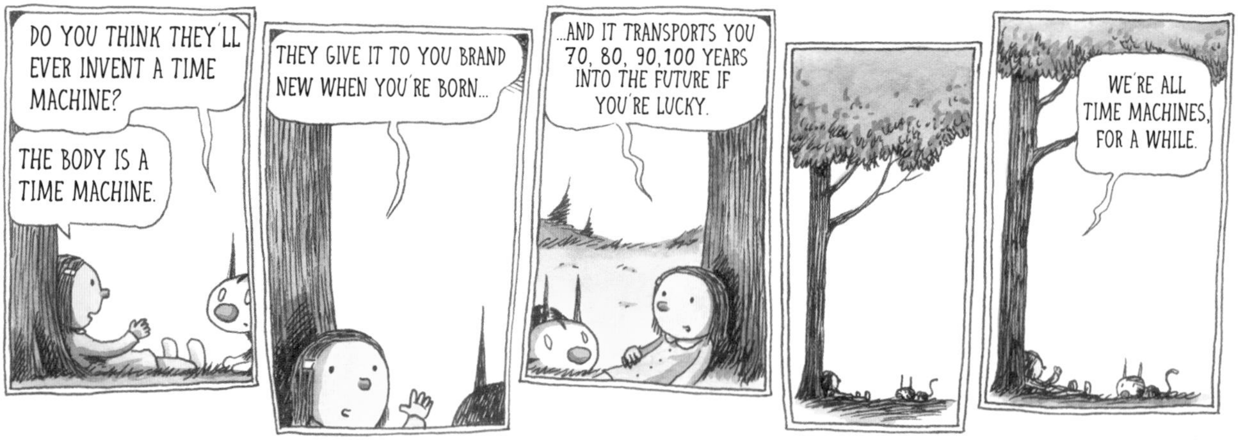
DO YOU THINK THEY'LL EVER INVENT A TIME MACHINE?
THE BODY IS A TIME MACHINE.
THEY GIVE IT TO YOU BRAND NEW WHEN YOU'RE BORN...
...AND IT TRANSPORTS YOU 70, 80, 90,100 YEARS INTO THE FUTURE IF YOU'RE LUCKY.
WE'RE ALL TIME MACHINES, FOR A WHILE.

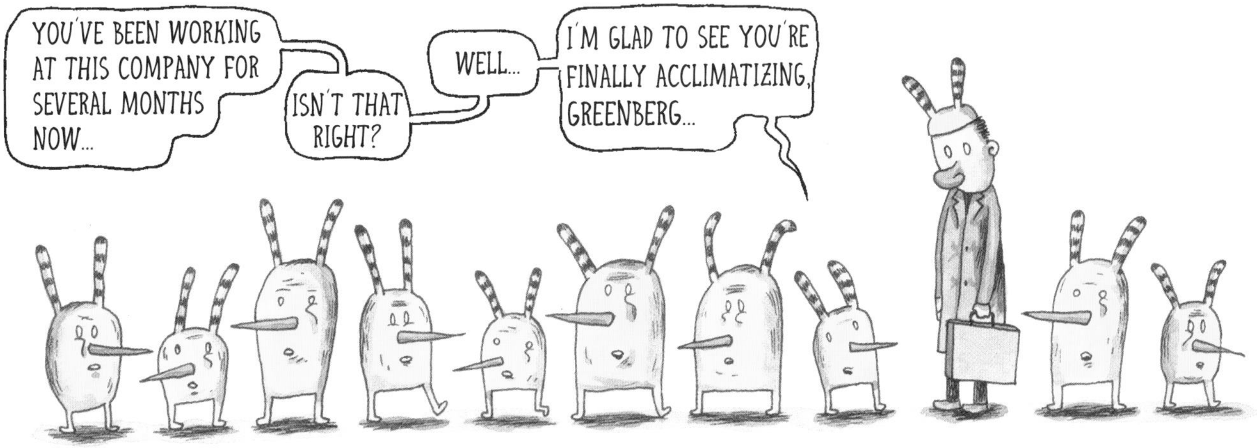
YOU'VE BEEN WORKING AT THIS COMPANY FOR SEVERAL MONTHS NOW...
ISN'T THAT RIGHT?
WELL...
I'M GLAD TO SEE YOU'RE FINALLY ACCLIMATIZING, GREENBERG...

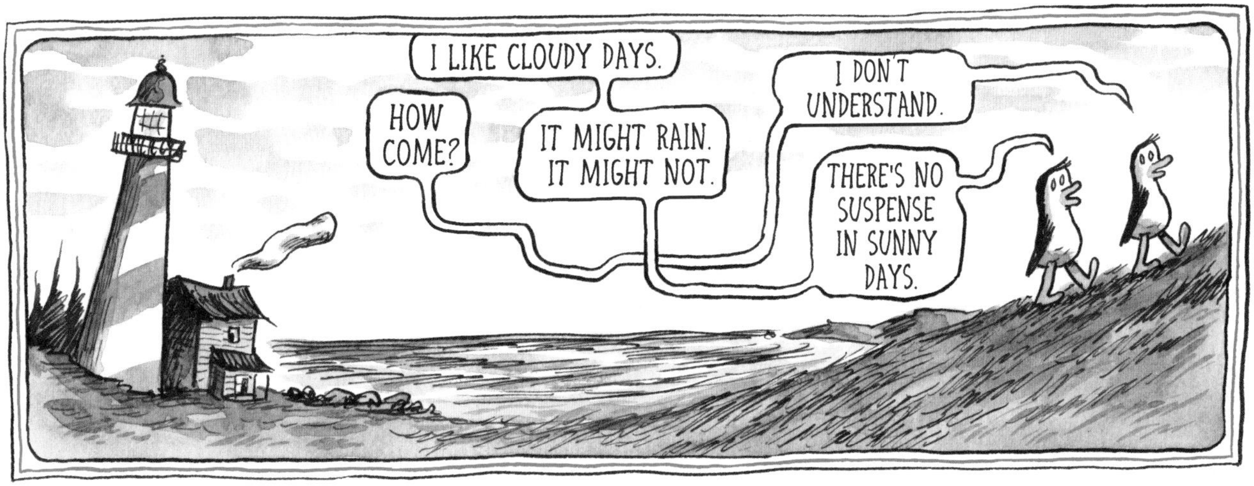
I LIKE CLOUDY DAYS.
HOW COME?
IT MIGHT RAIN. IT MIGHT NOT.
I DON'T UNDERSTAND.
THERE'S NO SUSPENSE IN SUNNY DAYS.

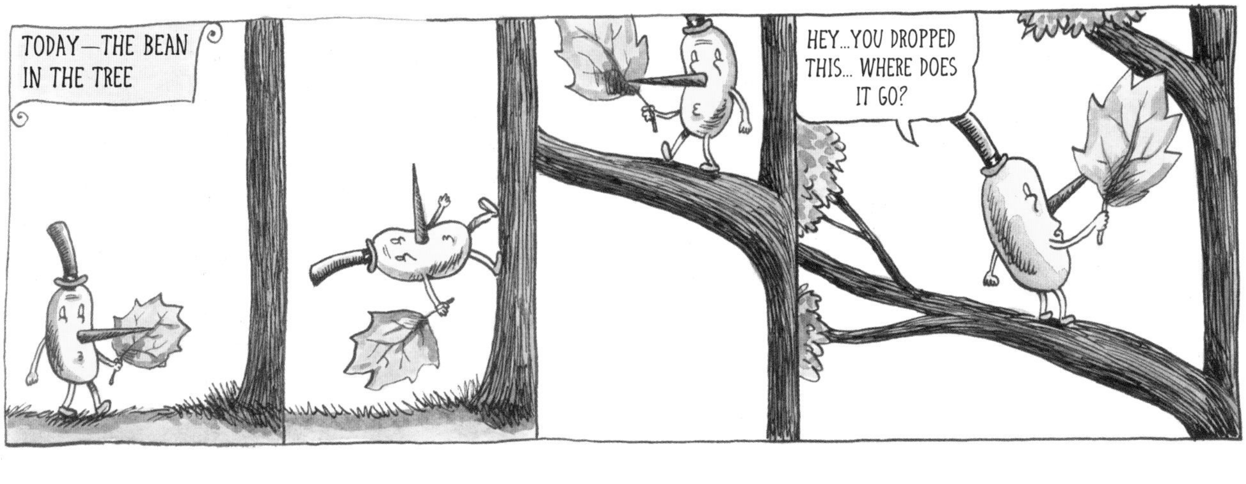
TODAY—THE BEAN IN THE TREE
HEY...YOU DROPPED THIS... WHERE DOES IT GO?

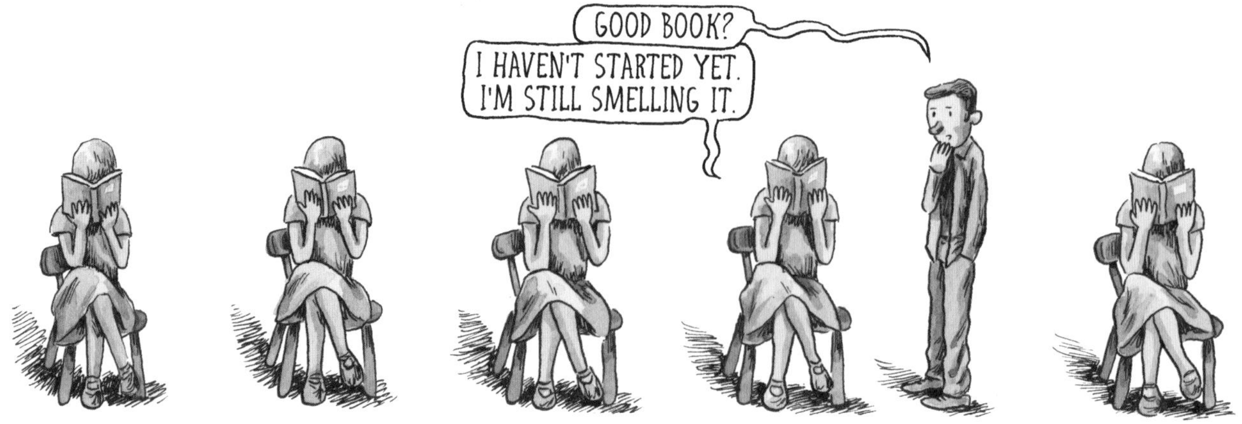
GOOD BOOK?
I HAVEN'T STARTED YET. I'M STILL SMELLING IT.

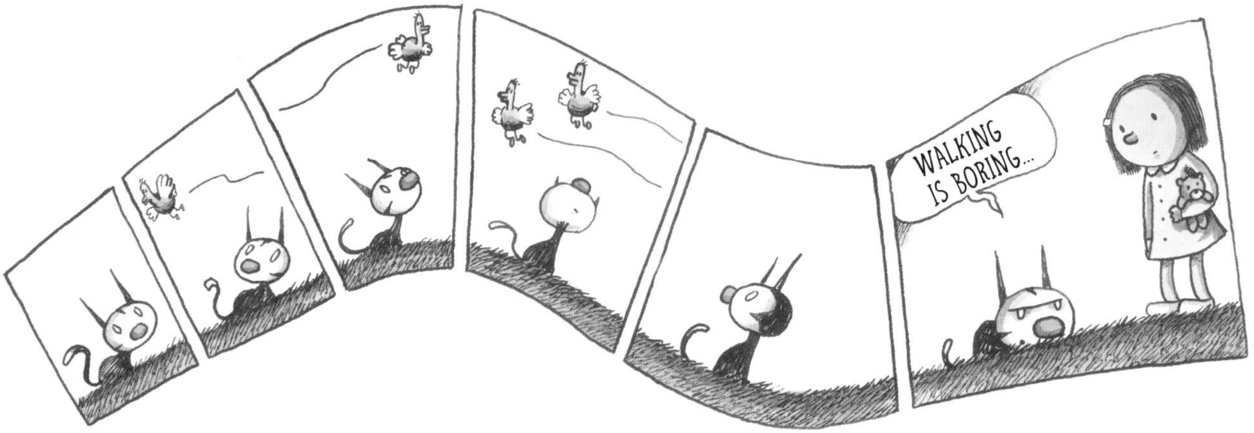
WALKING IS BORING...

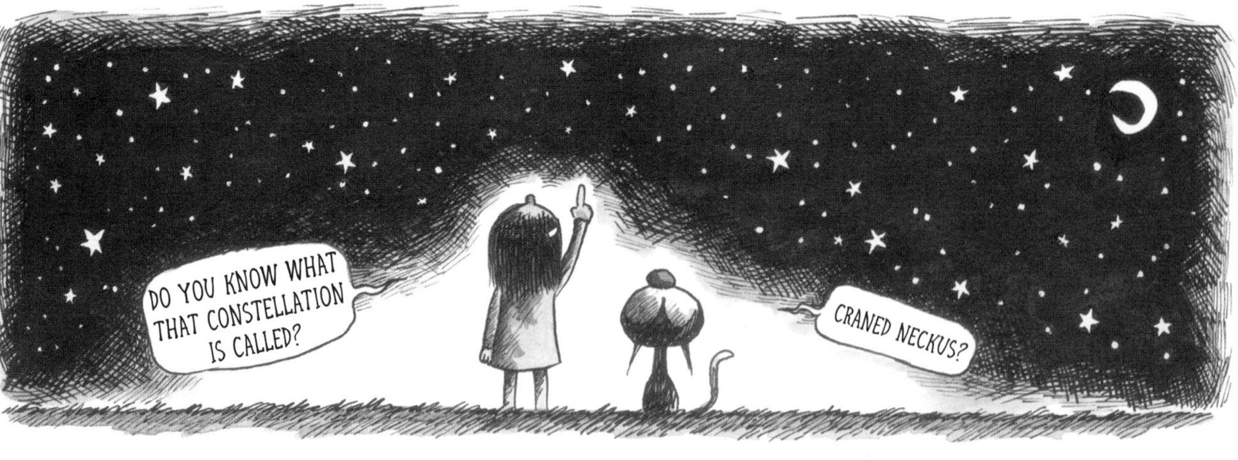
DO YOU KNOW WHAT THAT CONSTELLATION IS CALLED?
CRANED NECKUS?

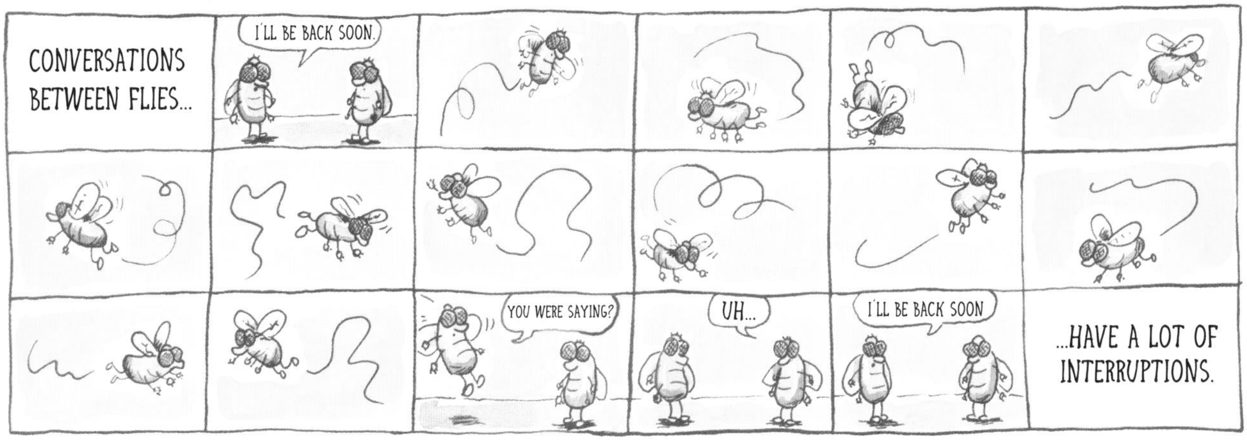
CONVERSATIONS BETWEEN FLIES...
I'LL BE BACK SOON.
YOU WERE SAYING?
UH...
I'LL BE BACK SOON
...HAVE A LOT OF INTERRUPTIONS.

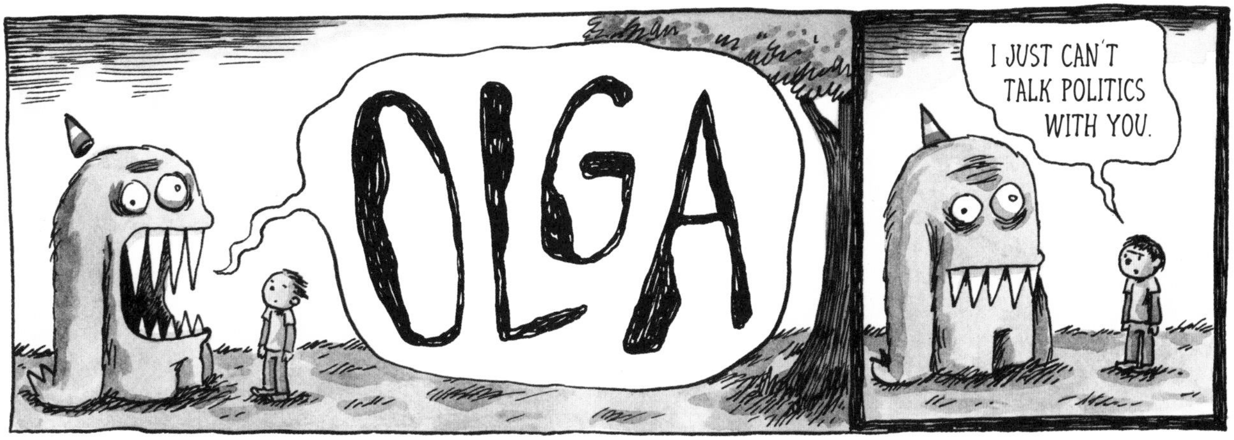
OLGA
I JUST CAN'T TALK POLITICS WITH YOU.

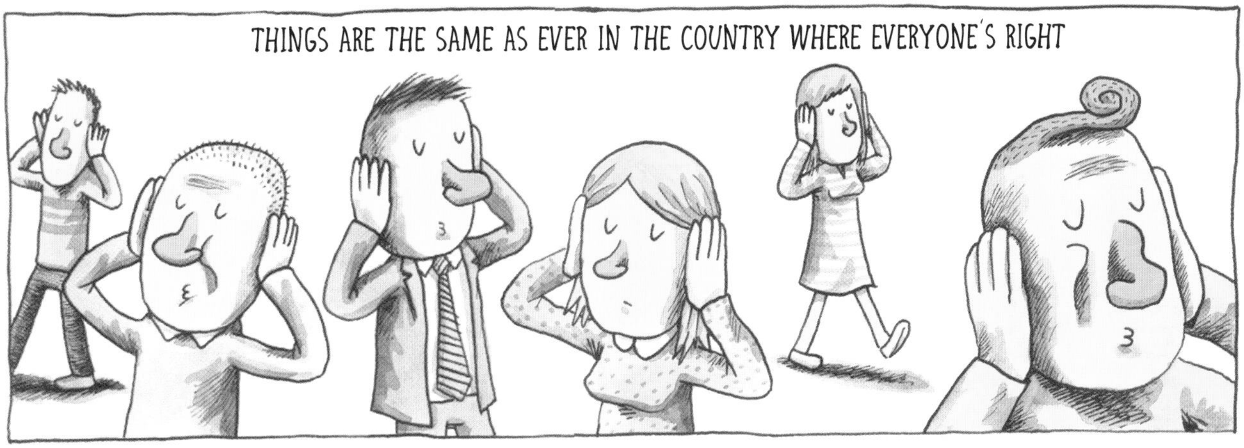
THINGS ARE THE SAME AS EVER IN THE COUNTRY WHERE EVERYONE'S RIGHT

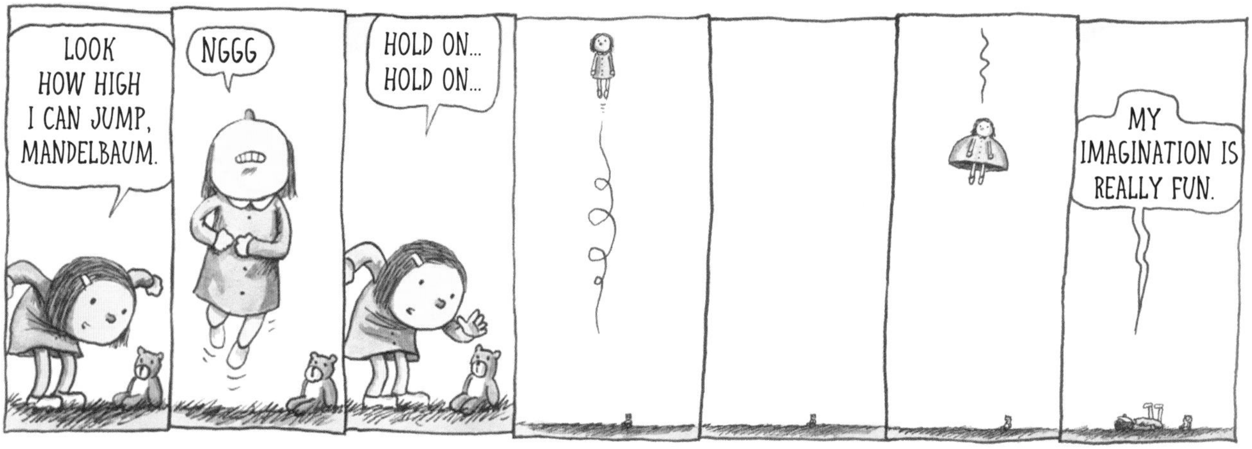
LOOK HOW HIGH I CAN JUMP, MANDELBAUM.
NGGG
HOLD ON... HOLD ON...
MY IMAGINATION IS REALLY FUN.

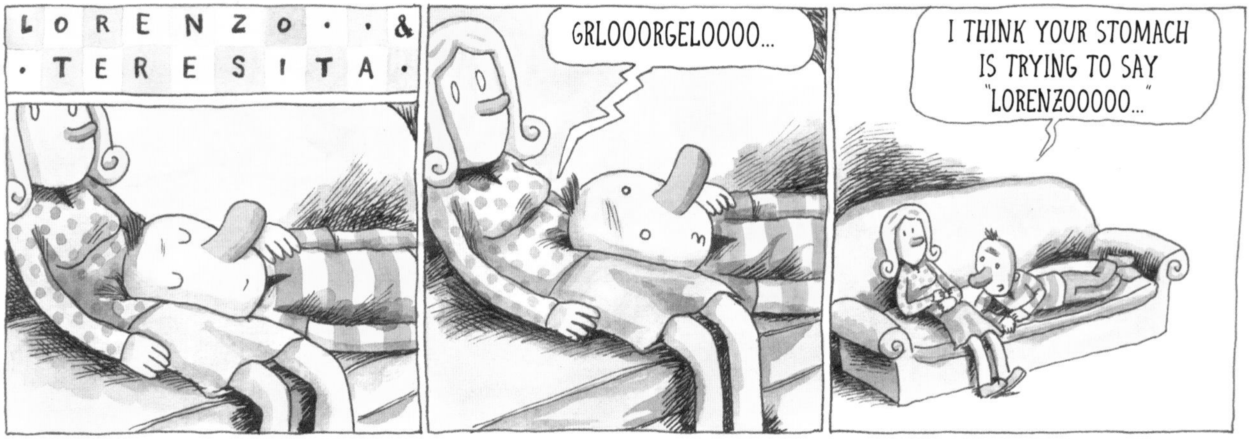
LORENZO & TERESITA
GRLOOORGELOOOO...
I THINK YOUR STOMACH IS TRYING TO SAY "LORENZOOOOO..."

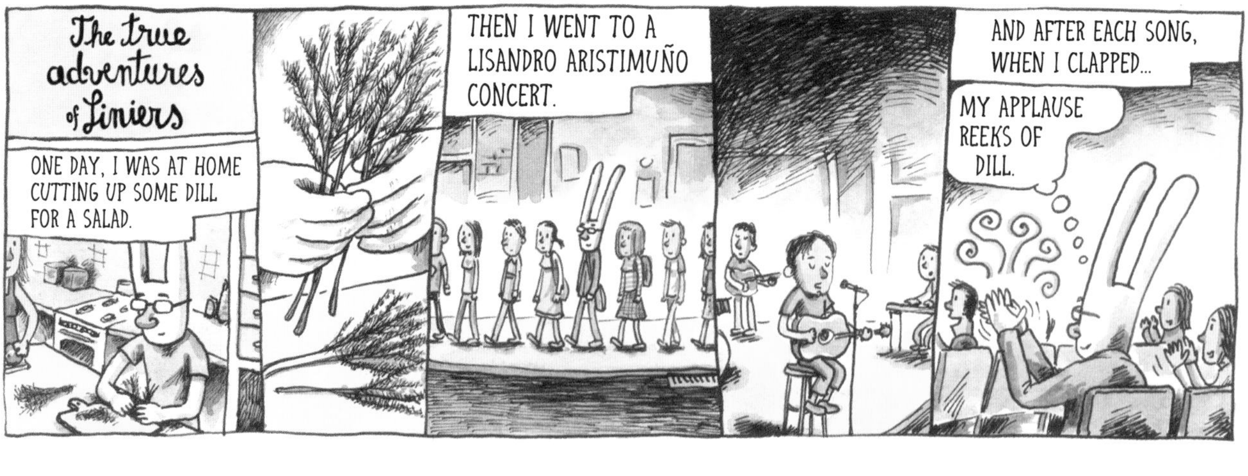
The true adventures of Liniers
ONE DAY, I WAS AT HOME CUTTING UP SOME DILL FOR A SALAD.
THEN I WENT TO A LISANDRO ARISTIMUÑO CONCERT.
AND AFTER EACH SONG, WHEN I CLAPPED...
MY APPLAUSE REEKS OF DILL.

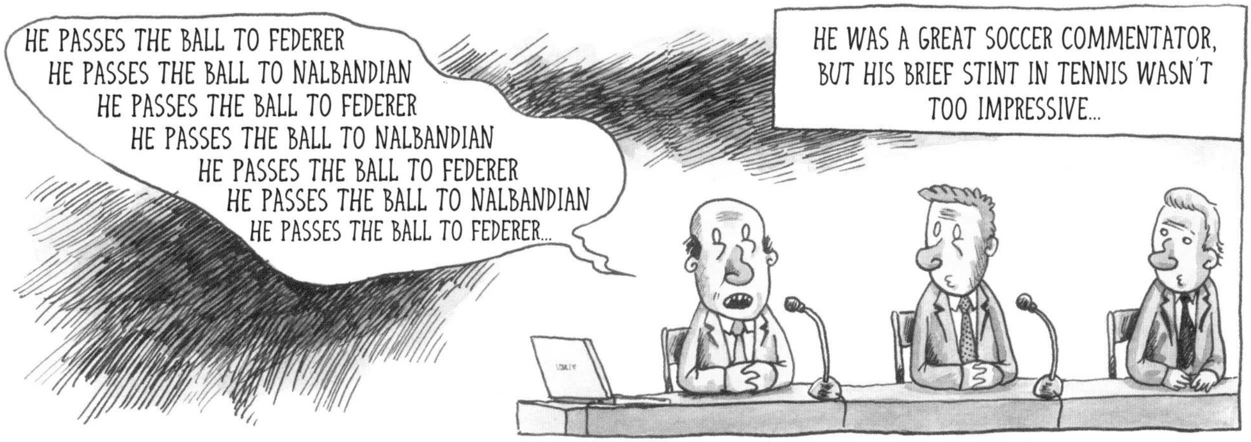
HE PASSES THE BALL TO FEDERER
HE PASSES THE BALL TO NALBANDIAN
HE PASSES THE BALL TO FEDERER
HE PASSES THE BALL TO NALBANDIAN
HE PASSES THE BALL TO FEDERER
HE PASSES THE BALL TO NALBANDIAN
HE PASSES THE BALL TO FEDERER...
HE WAS A GREAT SOCCER COMMENTATOR, BUT HIS BRIEF STINT IN TENNIS WASN'T TOO IMPRESSIVE...

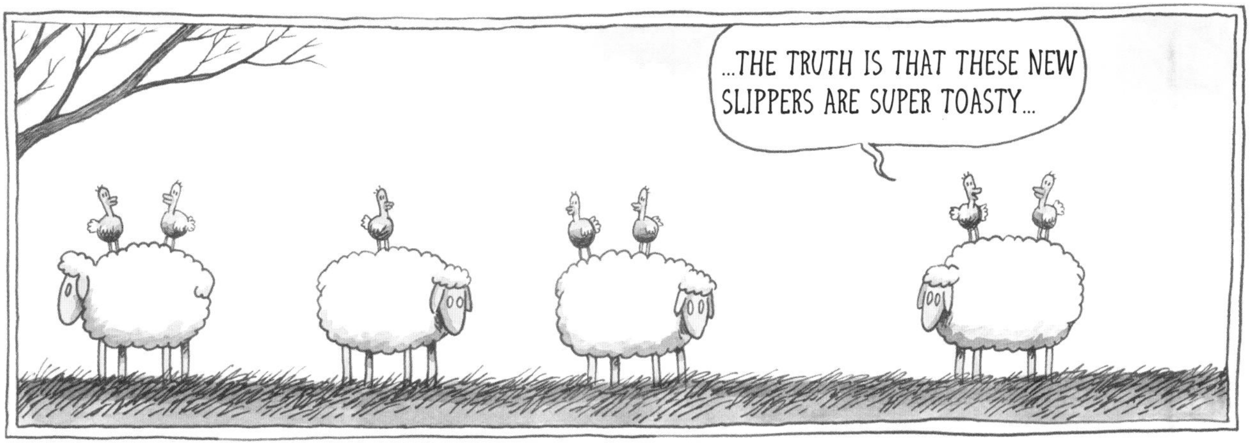
...THE TRUTH IS THAT THESE NEW SLIPPERS ARE SUPER TOASTY...

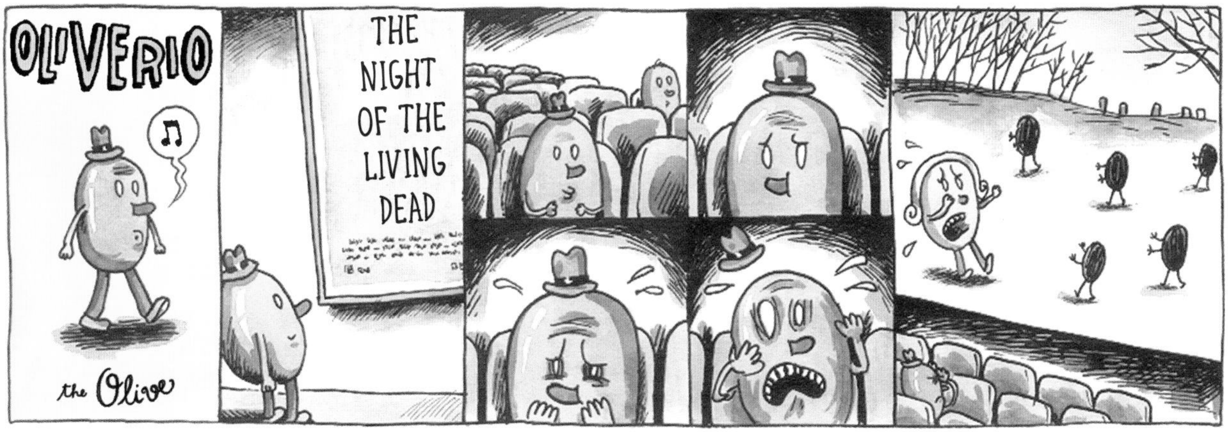
OLIVERIO
the Olive
THE NIGHT OF THE LIVING DEAD

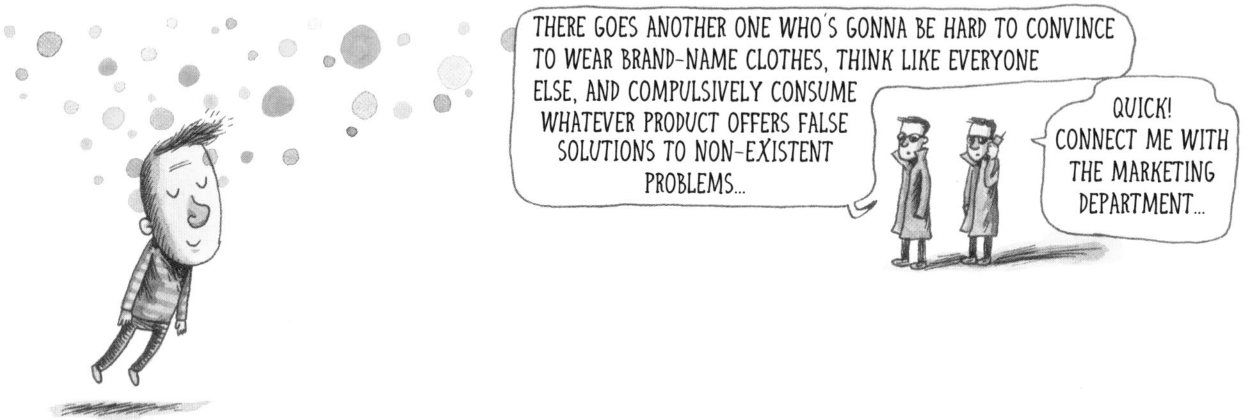
THERE GOES ANOTHER ONE WHO'S GONNA BE HARD TO CONVINCE TO WEAR BRAND-NAME CLOTHES, THINK LIKE EVERYONE ELSE, AND COMPULSIVELY CONSUME WHATEVER PRODUCT OFFERS FALSE SOLUTIONS TO NON-EXISTENT PROBLEMS...
QUICK! CONNECT ME WITH THE MARKETING DEPARTMENT...

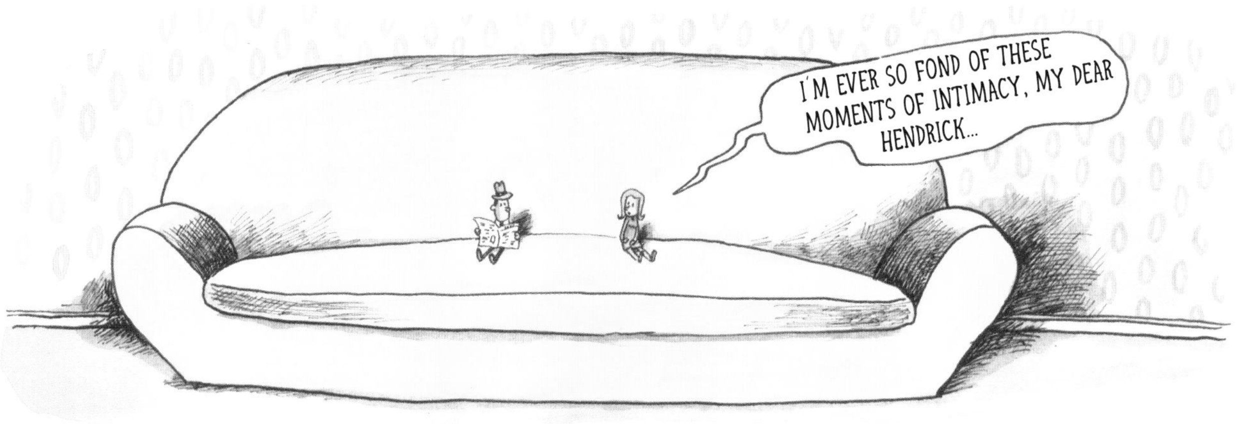
I'M EVER SO FOND OF THESE MOMENTS OF INTIMACY, MY DEAR HENDRICK...

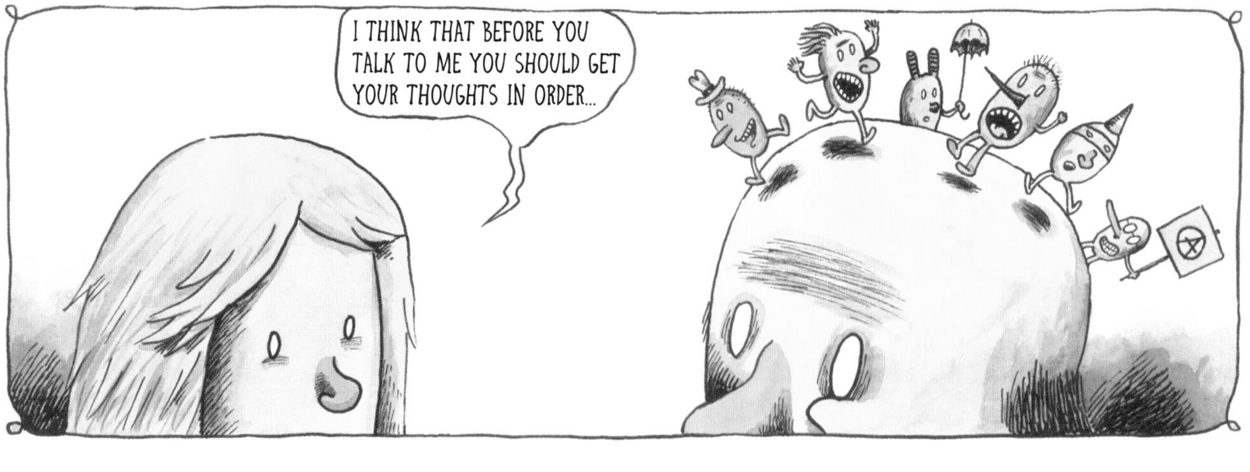
I THINK THAT BEFORE YOU TALK TO ME YOU SHOULD GET YOUR THOUGHTS IN ORDER...

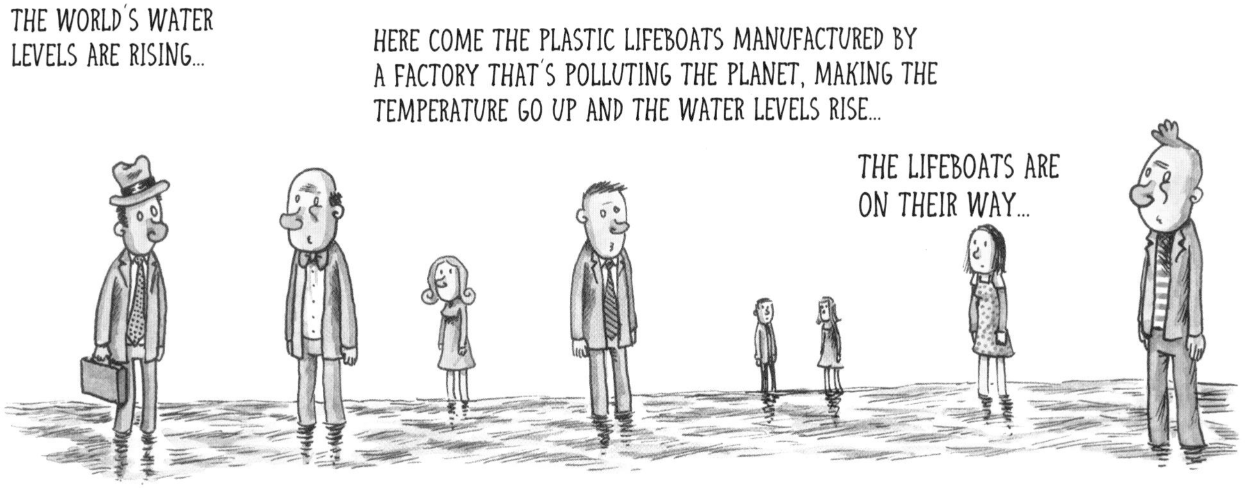
THE WORLD'S WATER LEVELS ARE RISING...
HERE COME THE PLASTIC LIFEBOATS MANUFACTURED BY A FACTORY THAT'S POLLUTING THE PLANET, MAKING THE TEMPERATURE GO UP AND THE WATER LEVELS RISE...
THE LIFEBOATS ARE ON THEIR WAY...

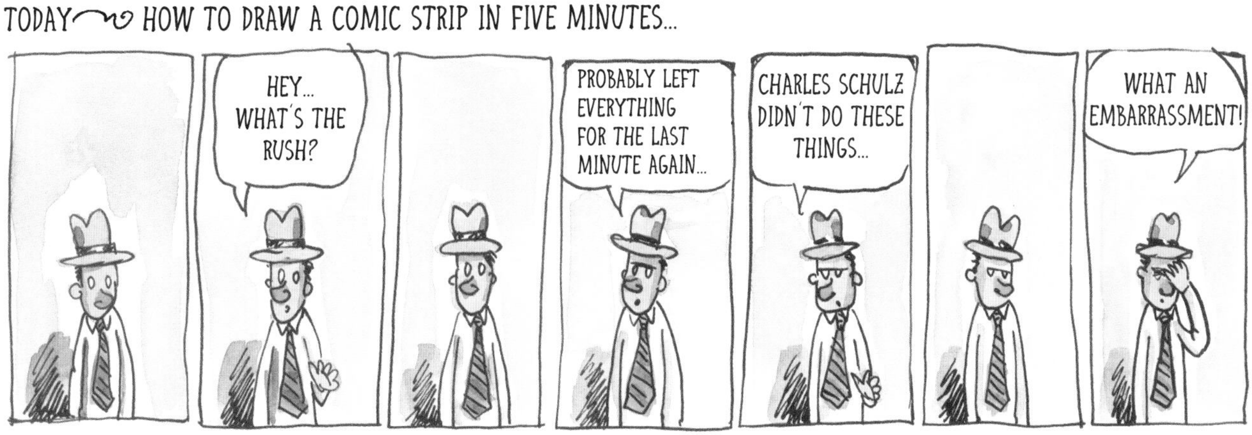
TODAY ~ HOW TO DRAW A COMIC STRIP IN FIVE MINUTES...
HEY... WHAT'S THE RUSH?
PROBABLY LEFT EVERYTHING FOR THE LAST MINUTE AGAIN...
CHARLES SCHULZ DIDN'T DO THESE THINGS...
WHAT AN EMBARRASSMENT!

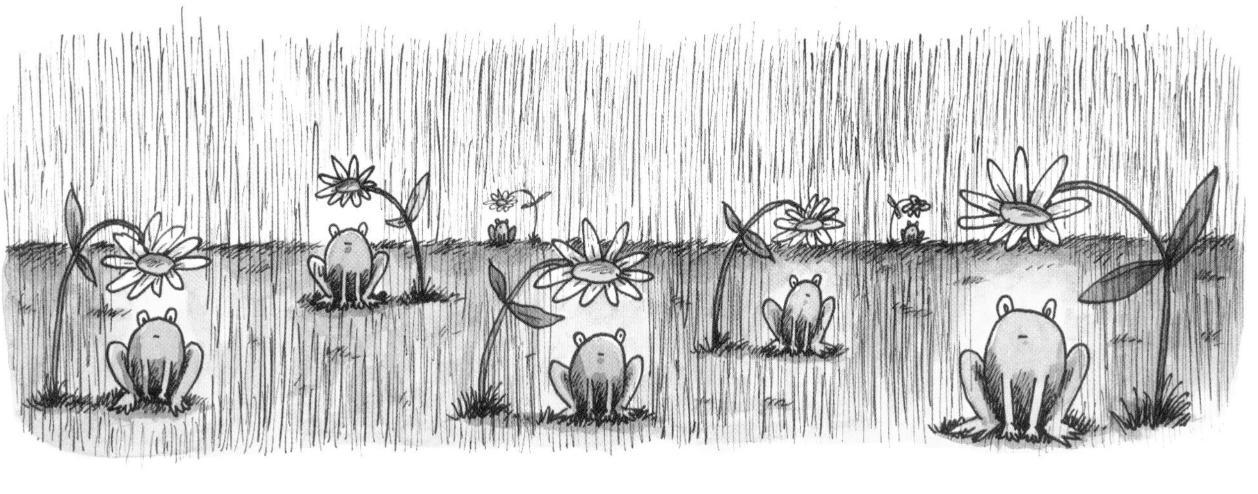

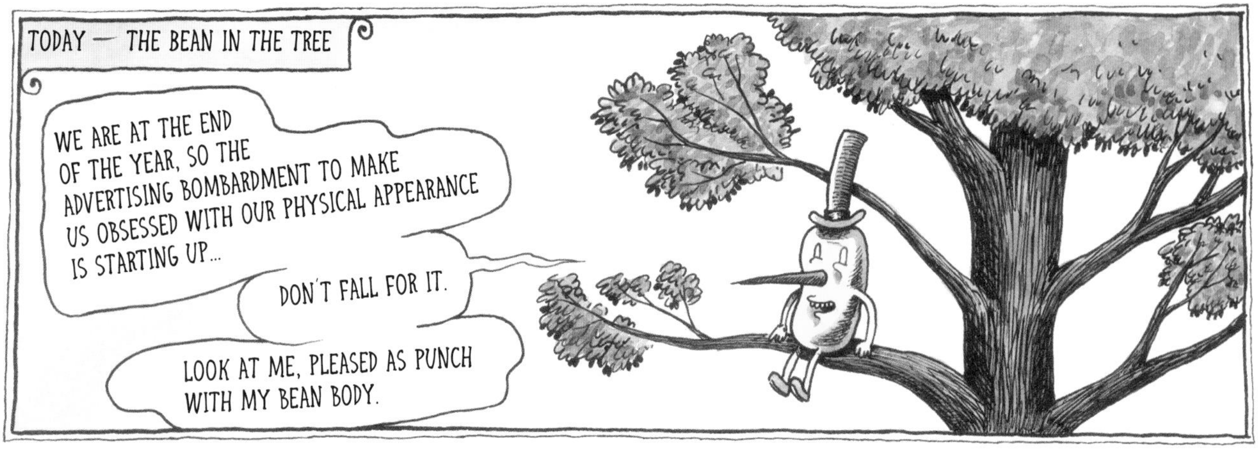
TODAY — THE BEAN IN THE TREE
WE ARE AT THE END OF THE YEAR, SO THE ADVERTISING BOMBARDMENT TO MAKE US OBSESSED WITH OUR PHYSICAL APPEARANCE IS STARTING UP...
DON'T FALL FOR IT.
LOOK AT ME, PLEASED AS PUNCH WITH MY BEAN BODY.

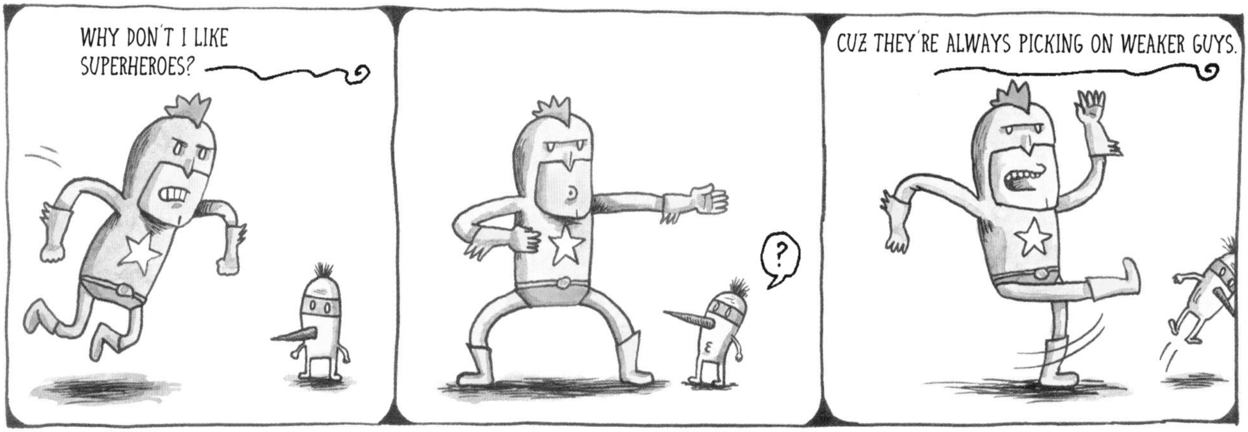
WHY DON'T I LIKE SUPERHEROES?
?
CUZ THEY'RE ALWAYS PICKING ON WEAKER GUYS.

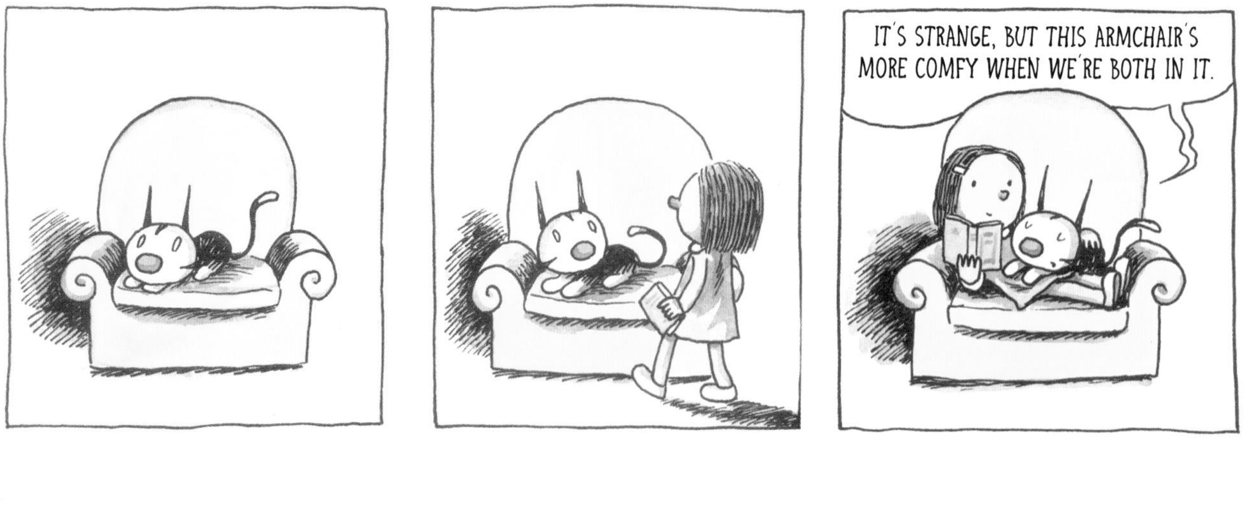
IT'S STRANGE, BUT THIS ARMCHAIR'S MORE COMFY WHEN WE'RE BOTH IN IT.

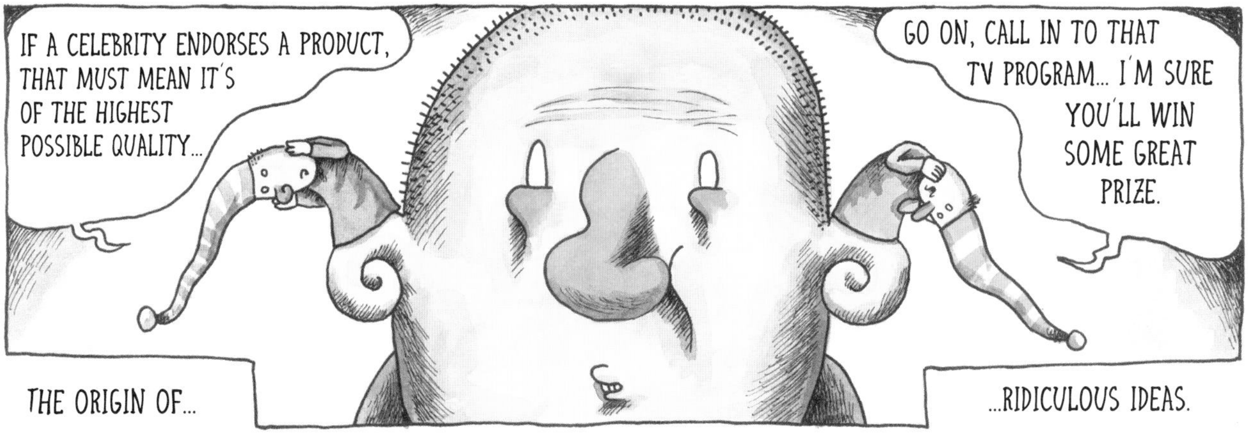
IF A CELEBRITY ENDORSES A PRODUCT, THAT MUST MEAN IT'S OF THE HIGHEST POSSIBLE QUALITY...
GO ON, CALL IN TO THAT TV PROGRAM... I'M SURE YOU'LL WIN SOME GREAT PRIZE.
THE ORIGIN OF...
...RIDICULOUS IDEAS.

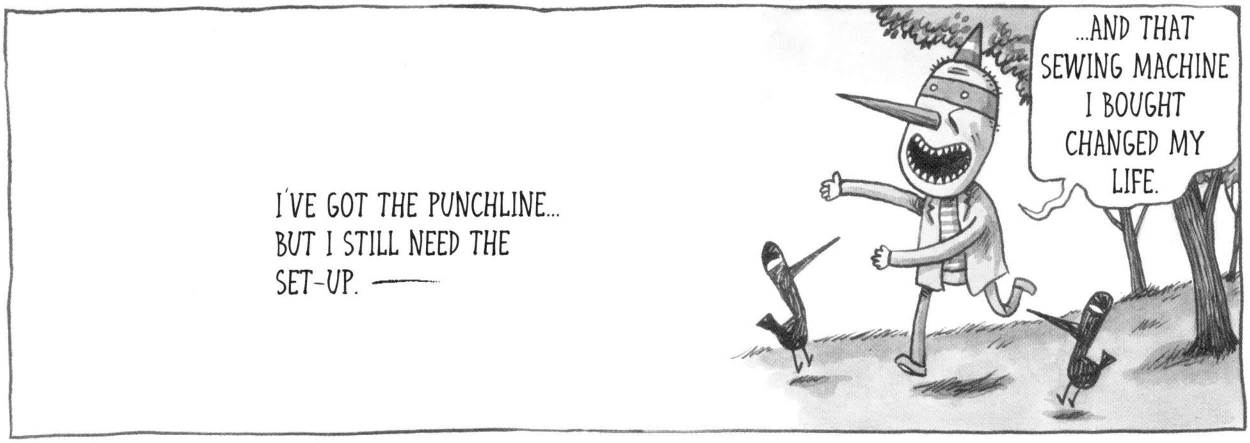
...AND THAT SEWING MACHINE I BOUGHT CHANGED MY LIFE.
I'VE GOT THE PUNCHLINE... BUT I STILL NEED THE SET-UP.

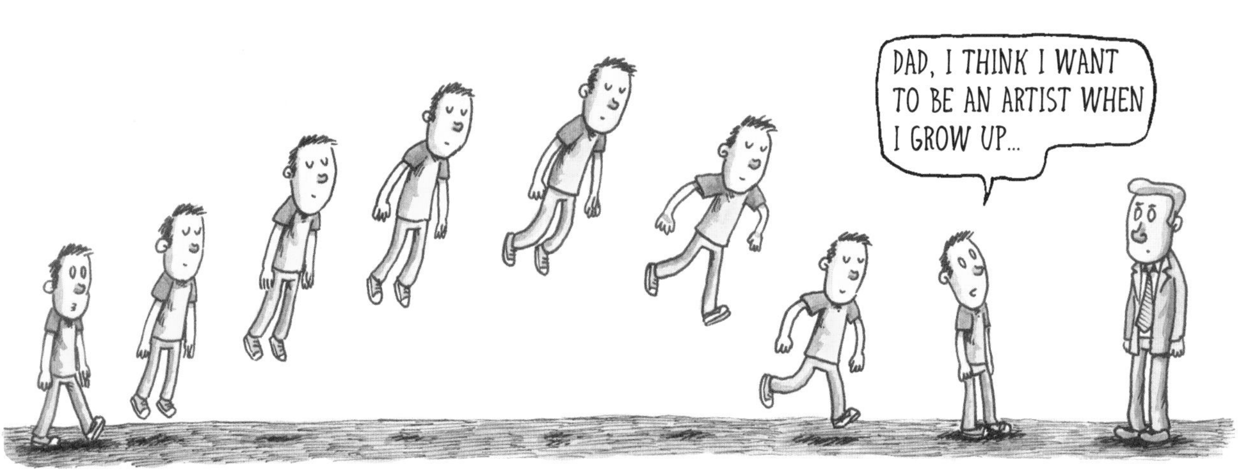
DAD, I THINK I WANT TO BE AN ARTIST WHEN I GROW UP...

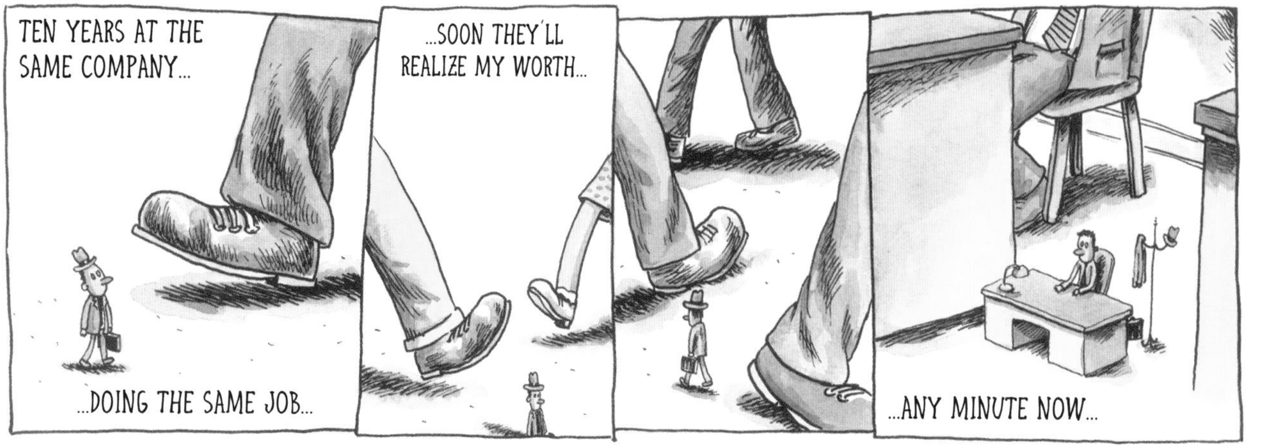
TEN YEARS AT THE SAME COMPANY...
...DOING THE SAME JOB...
...SOON THEY'LL REALIZE MY WORTH...
...ANY MINUTE NOW...

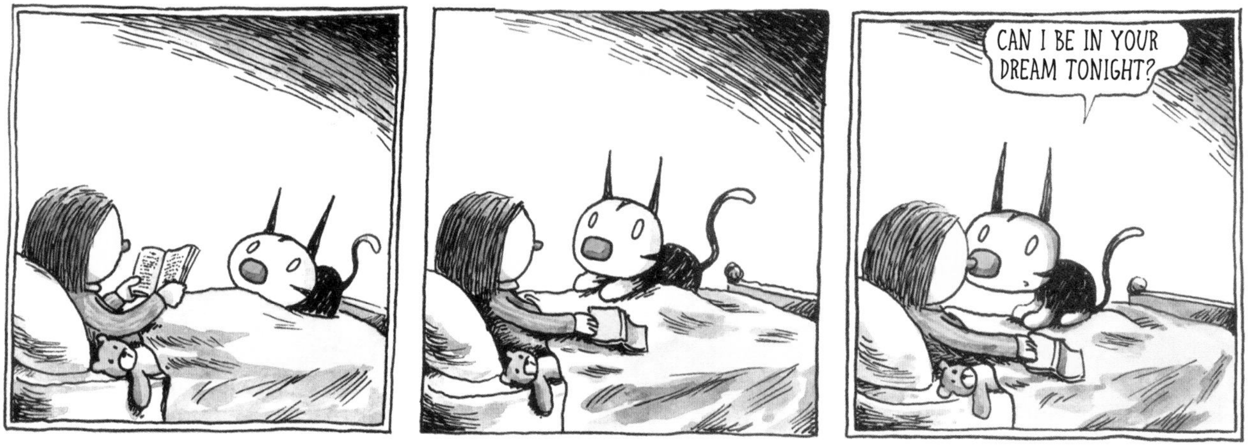
CAN I BE IN YOUR DREAM TONIGHT?

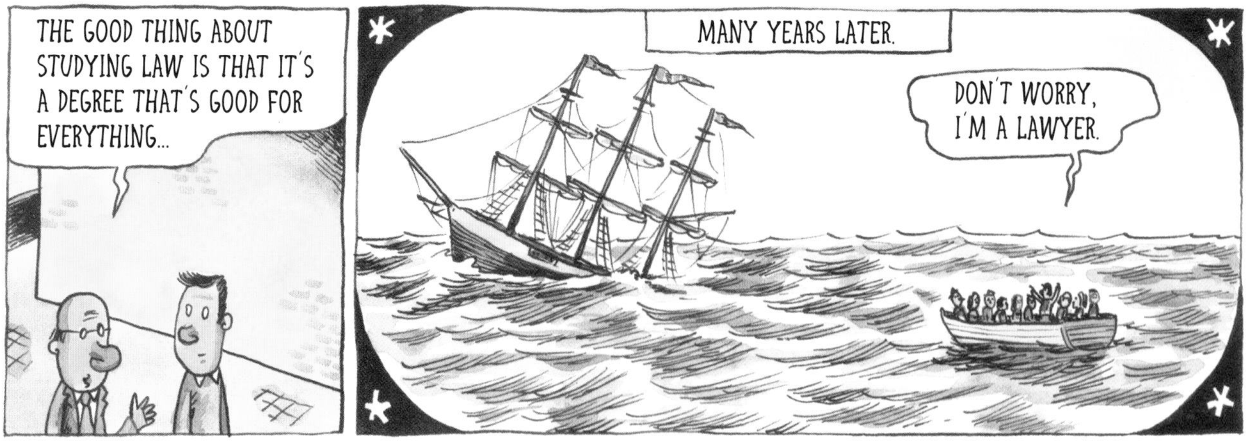
THE GOOD THING ABOUT STUDYING LAW IS THAT IT'S A DEGREE THAT'S GOOD FOR EVERYTHING...
MANY YEARS LATER.
DON'T WORRY, I'M A LAWYER.

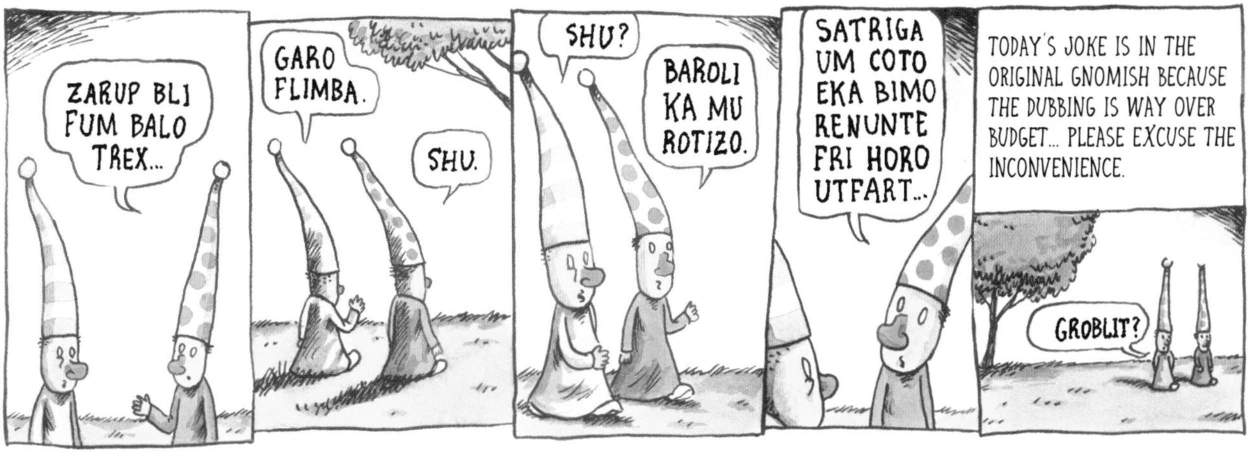
ZARUP BLI FUM BALO TREX...
GARO FLIMBA.
SHU.
SHU?
BAROLI KA MU ROTIZO.
SATRIGA UM COTO EKA BIMO RENUNTE FRI HORO UTFART...
TODAY'S JOKE IS IN THE ORIGINAL GNOMISH BECAUSE THE DUBBING IS WAY OVER BUDGET... PLEASE EXCUSE THE INCONVENIENCE.
GROBLIT?

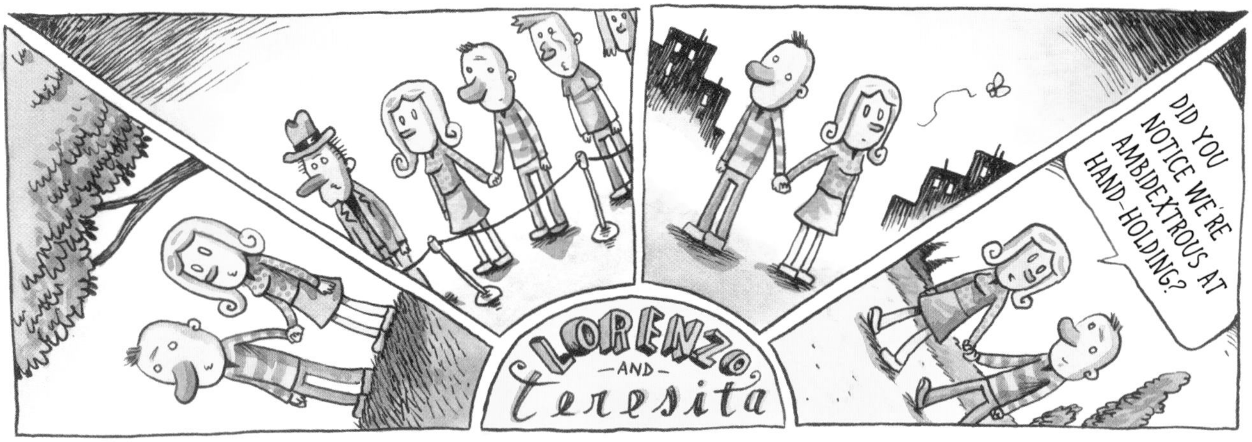
LORENZO -AND- teresita
DID YOU NOTICE WE'RE AMBIDEXTROUS AT HAND-HOLDING?

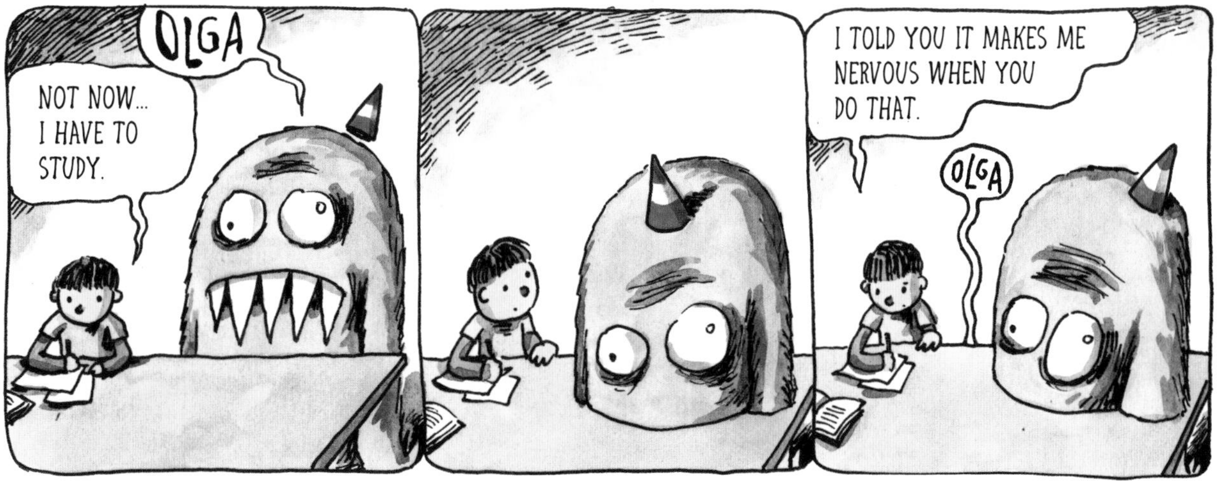
OLGA
NOT NOW... I HAVE TO STUDY.
I TOLD YOU IT MAKES ME NERVOUS WHEN YOU DO THAT.
OLGA

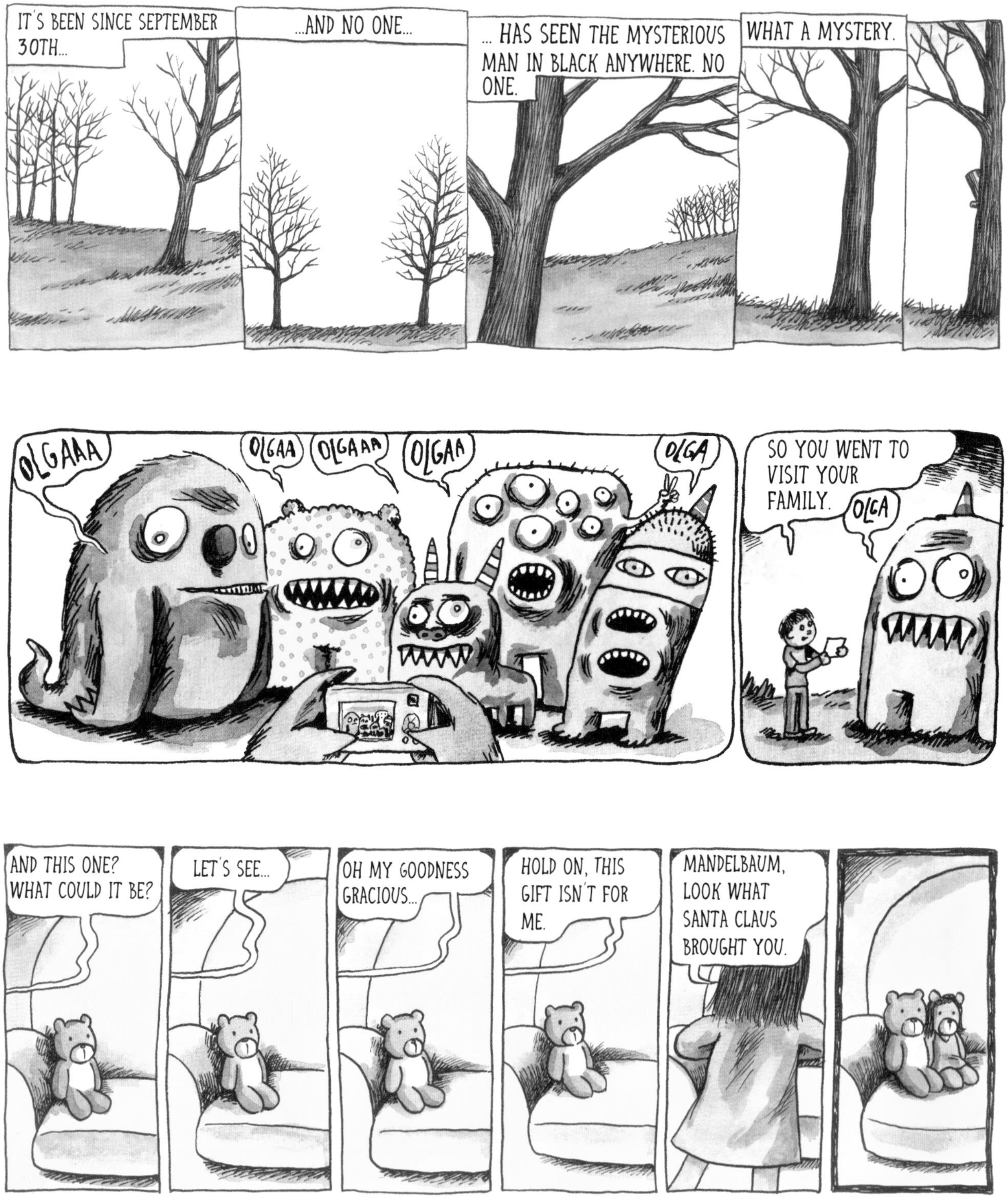

IT'S BEEN SINCE SEPTEMBER 30TH...
...AND NO ONE...
... HAS SEEN THE MYSTERIOUS MAN IN BLACK ANYWHERE. NO ONE.
WHAT A MYSTERY.
OLGAAA
OLGAA
OLGAAA
OLGAA
OLGA
SO YOU WENT TO VISIT YOUR FAMILY.
OLGA
AND THIS ONE? WHAT COULD IT BE?
LET'S SEE...
OH MY GOODNESS GRACIOUS...
HOLD ON, THIS GIFT ISN'T FOR ME.
MANDELBAUM, LOOK WHAT SANTA CLAUS BROUGHT YOU.

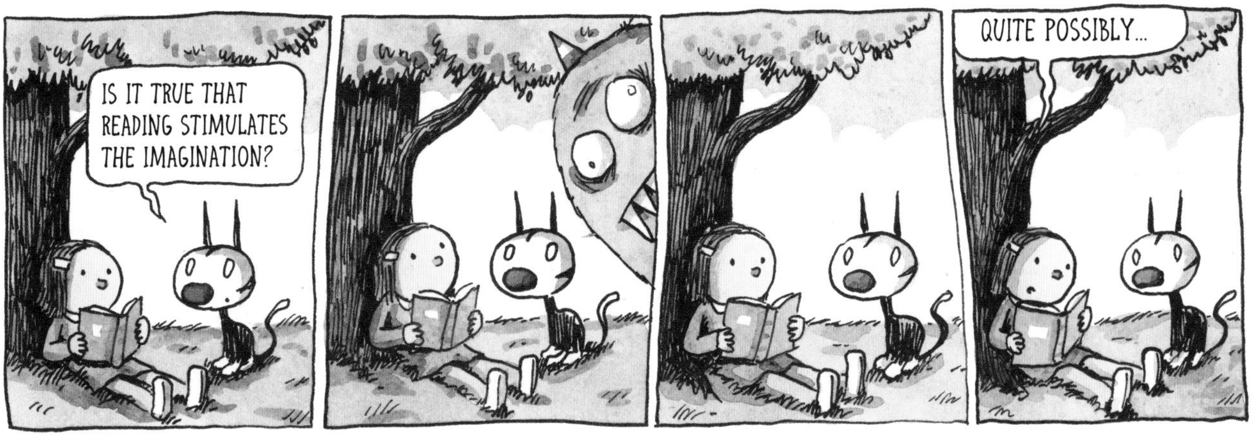
IS IT TRUE THAT READING STIMULATES THE IMAGINATION?
QUITE POSSIBLY...

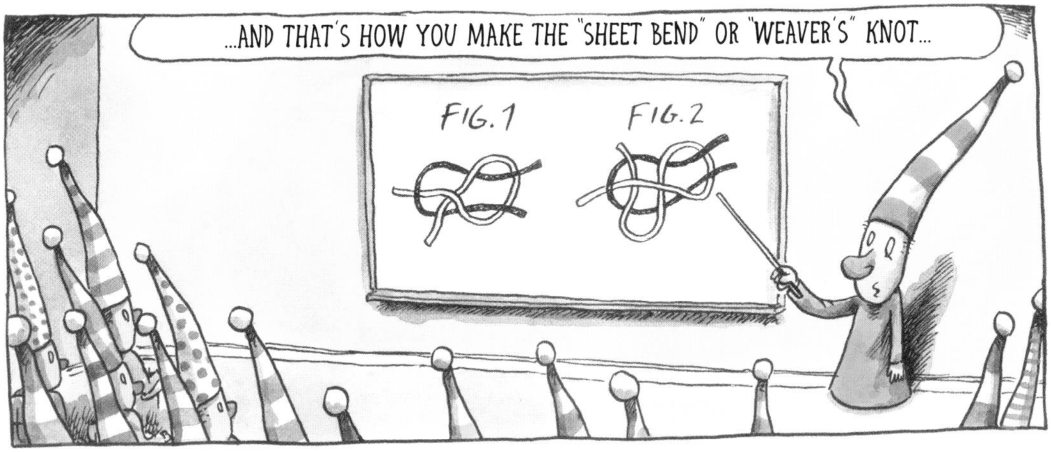
...AND THAT'S HOW YOU MAKE THE "SHEET BEND" OR "WEAVER'S" KNOT...
FIG.1
FIG.2

THE CLASS WHERE GNOMES LEARN HOW TO TIE UP THE HEADPHONE CORDS OF WALKMANS, DISCMANS AND IPODS

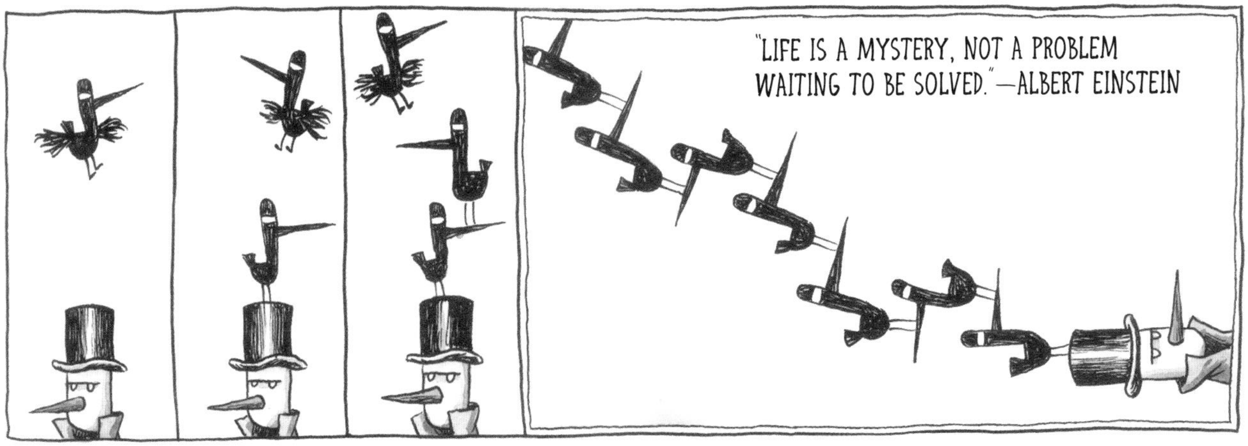
"LIFE IS A MYSTERY, NOT A PROBLEM WAITING TO BE SOLVED."—ALBERT EINSTEIN

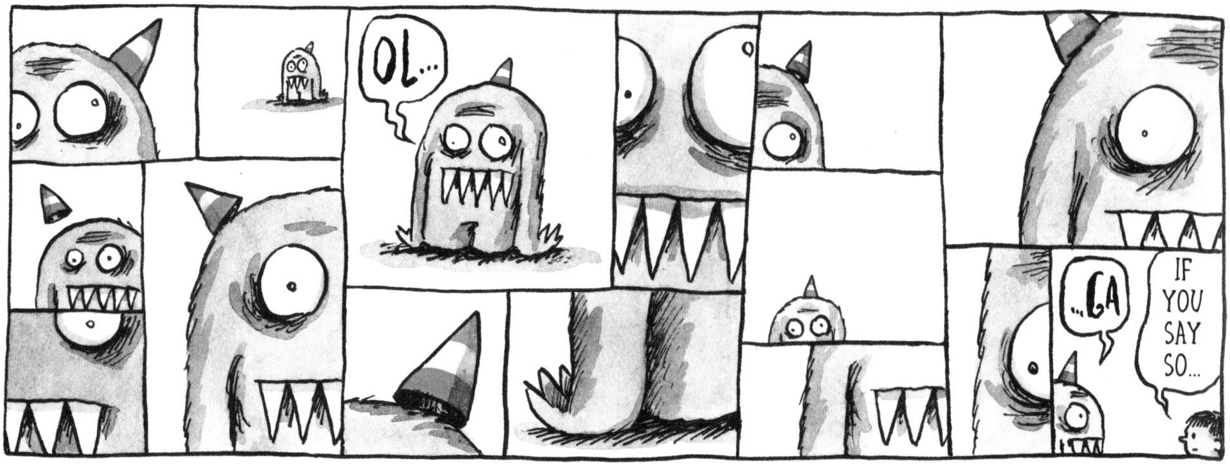
OL...
...GA
IF YOU SAY SO...

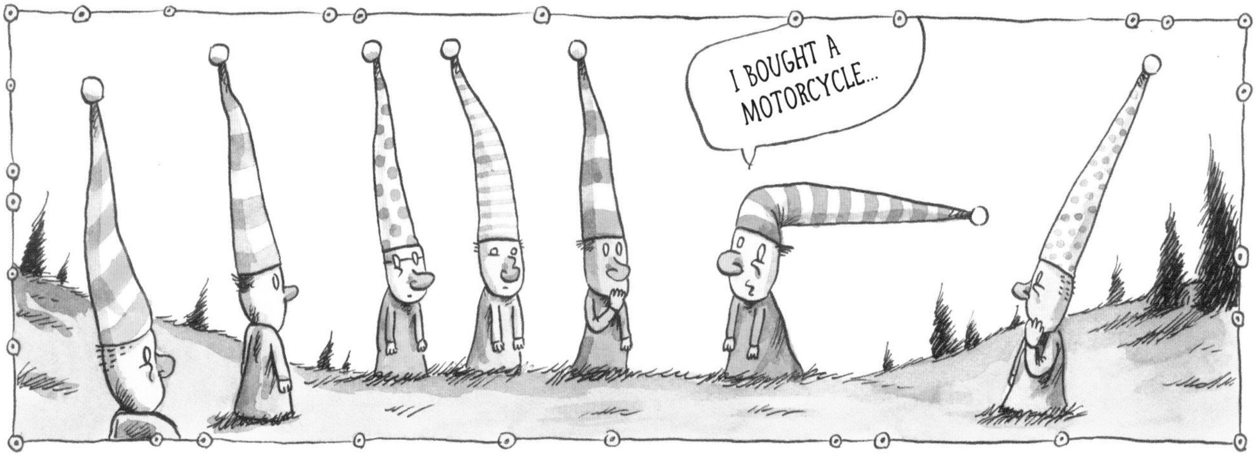
I BOUGHT A MOTORCYCLE...

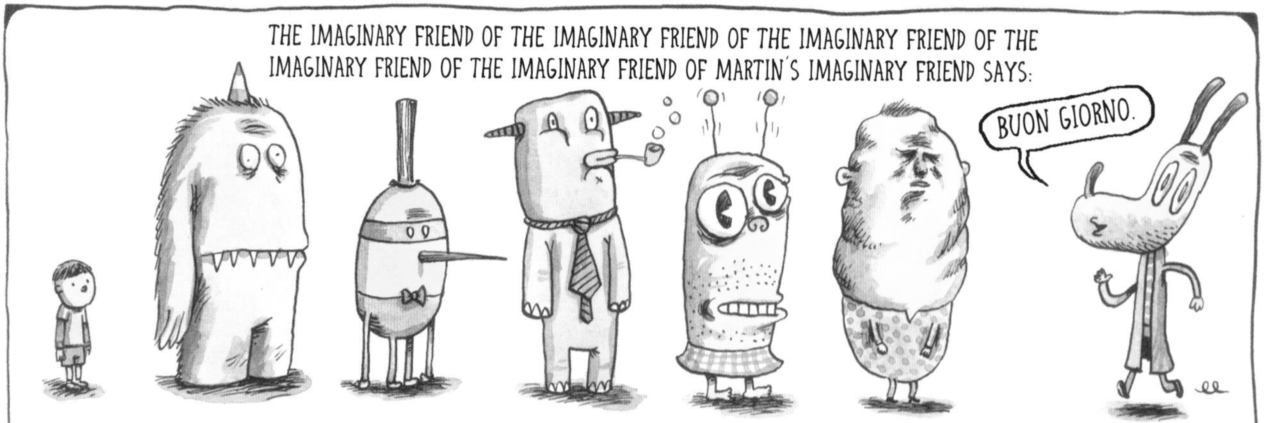
THE IMAGINARY FRIEND OF THE IMAGINARY FRIEND OF THE IMAGINARY FRIEND OF THE IMAGINARY FRIEND OF THE IMAGINARY FRIEND OF MARTIN'S IMAGINARY FRIEND SAYS:
BUON GIORNO.

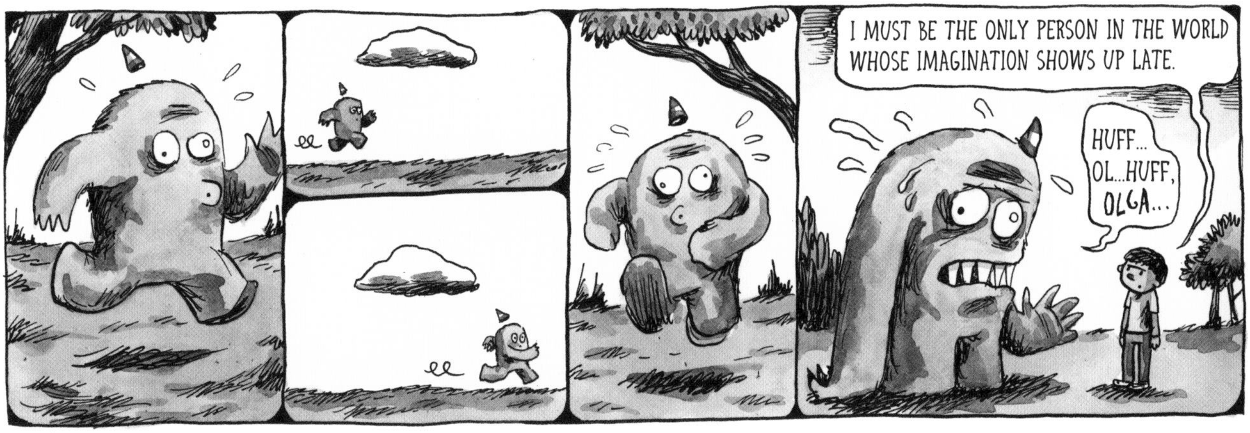
I MUST BE THE ONLY PERSON IN THE WORLD WHOSE IMAGINATION SHOWS UP LATE.
HUFF... OL...HUFF, OLGA...

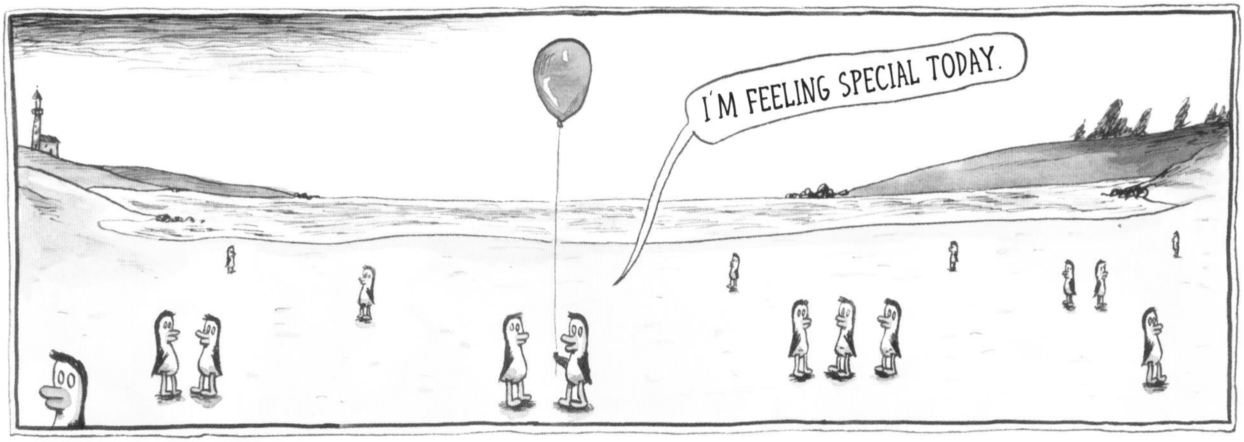
I'M FEELING SPECIAL TODAY.

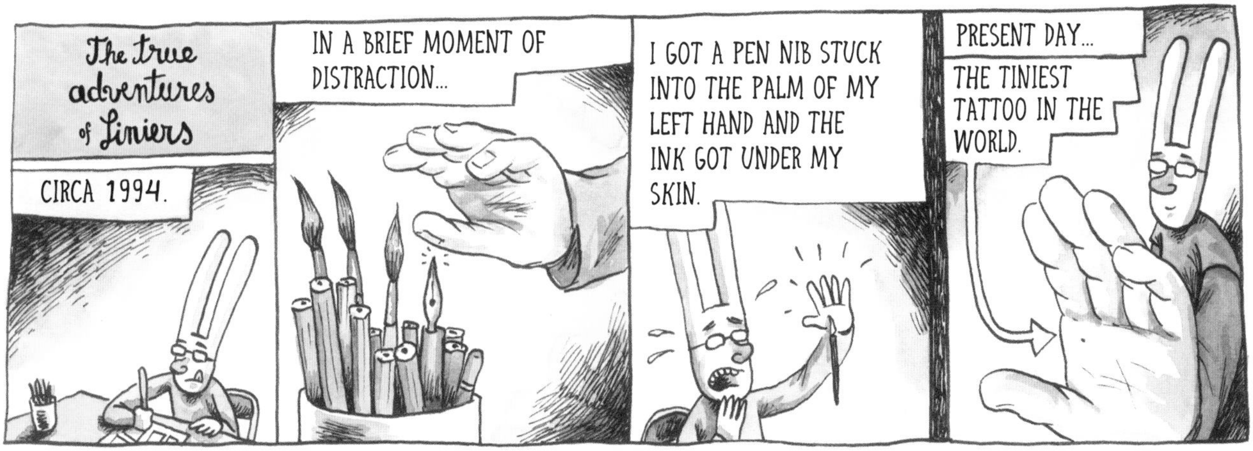
The true adventures of Liniers
CIRCA 1994.
IN A BRIEF MOMENT OF DISTRACTION...
I GOT A PEN NIB STUCK INTO THE PALM OF MY LEFT HAND AND THE INK GOT UNDER MY SKIN.
PRESENT DAY...
THE TINIEST TATTOO IN THE WORLD.

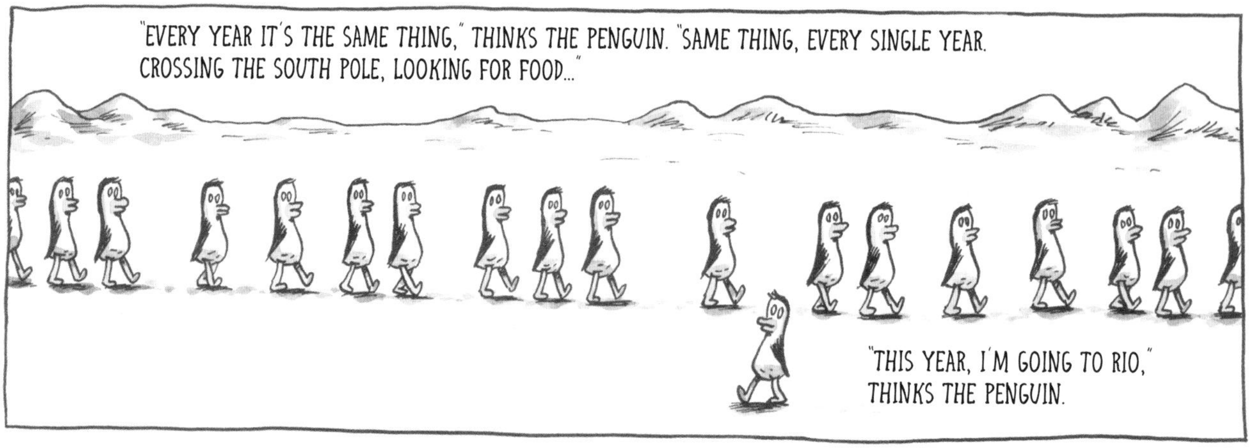
"EVERY YEAR IT'S THE SAME THING," THINKS THE PENGUIN. "SAME THING, EVERY SINGLE YEAR. CROSSING THE SOUTH POLE, LOOKING FOR FOOD..."
"THIS YEAR, I'M GOING TO RIO," THINKS THE PENGUIN.

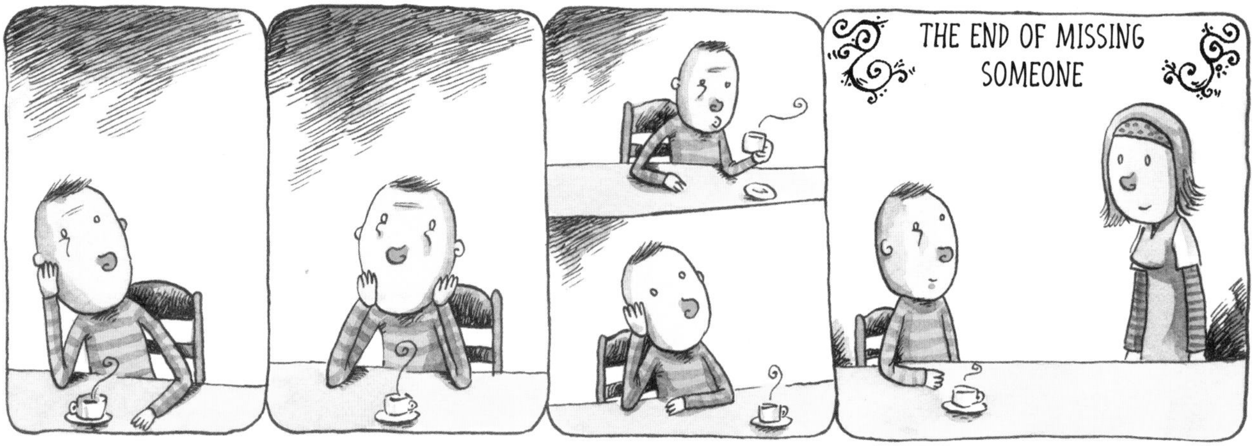
THE END OF MISSING SOMEONE

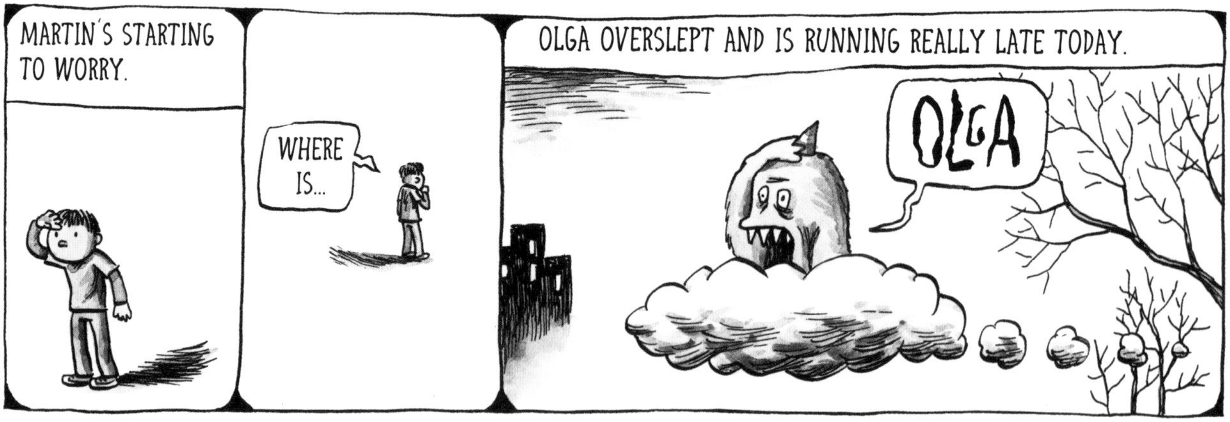
MARTIN'S STARTING TO WORRY.
WHERE IS...
OLGA OVERSLEPT AND IS RUNNING REALLY LATE TODAY.
OLGA

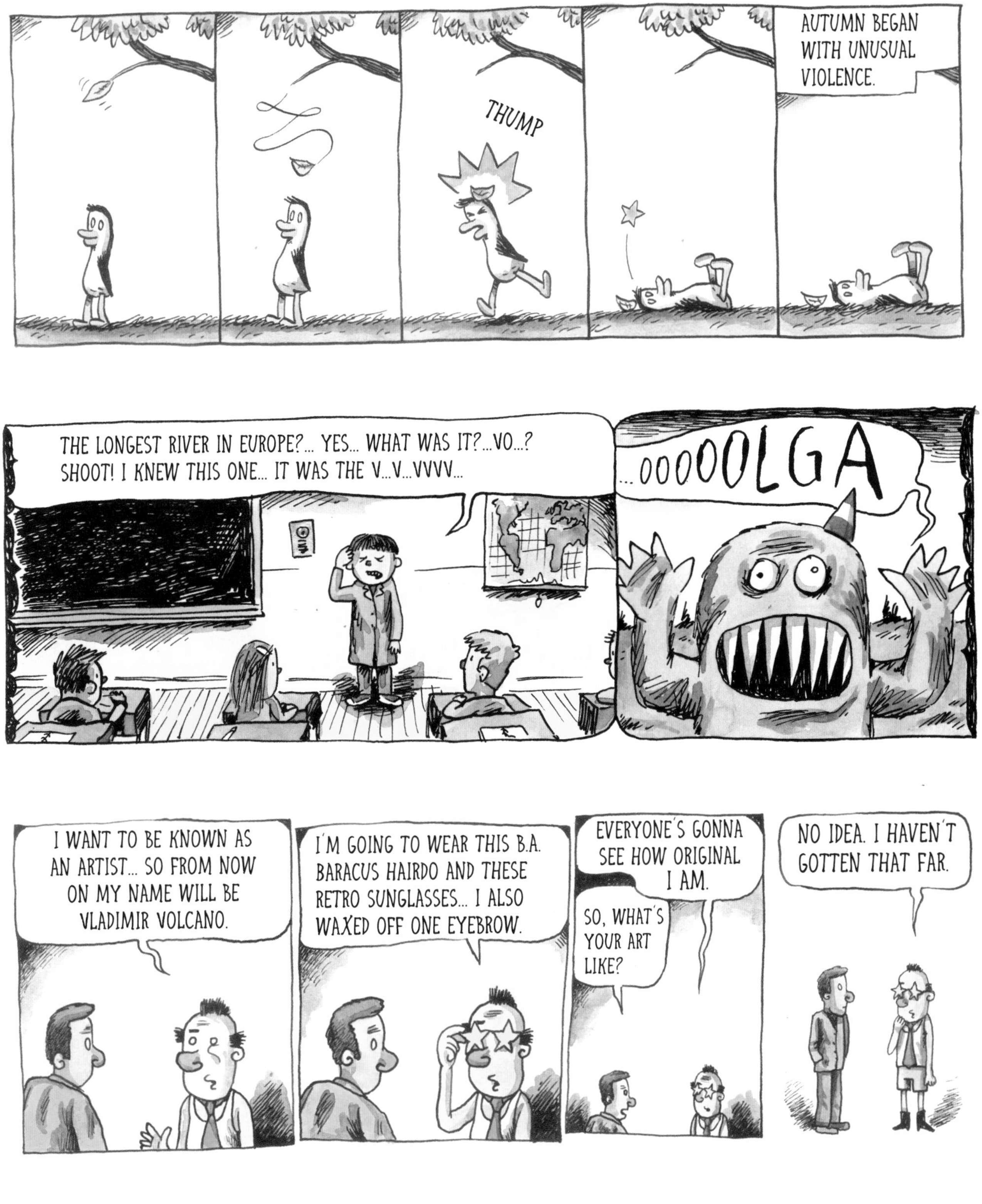

THUMP
AUTUMN BEGAN WITH UNUSUAL VIOLENCE.
THE LONGEST RIVER IN EUROPE?... YES... WHAT WAS IT?...VO...? SHOOT! I KNEW THIS ONE... IT WAS THE V...V...VVVV...
...OOOOOLGA
I WANT TO BE KNOWN AS AN ARTIST... SO FROM NOW ON MY NAME WILL BE VLADIMIR VOLCANO.
I'M GOING TO WEAR THIS B.A. BARACUS HAIRDO AND THESE RETRO SUNGLASSES... I ALSO WAXED OFF ONE EYEBROW.
EVERYONE'S GONNA SEE HOW ORIGINAL I AM.
SO, WHAT'S YOUR ART LIKE?
NO IDEA. I HAVEN'T GOTTEN THAT FAR.

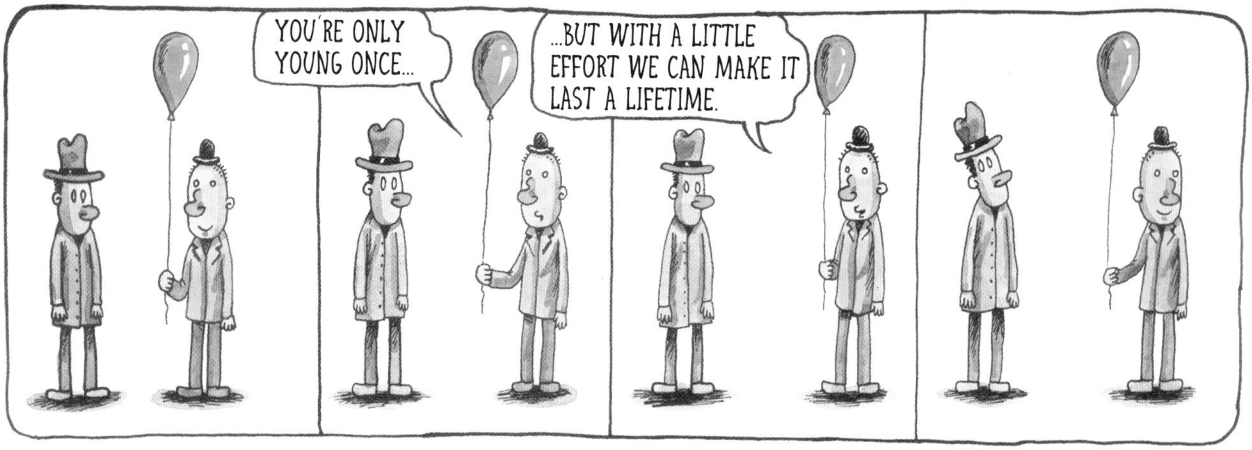
YOU'RE ONLY YOUNG ONCE...
...BUT WITH A LITTLE EFFORT WE CAN MAKE IT LAST A LIFETIME.

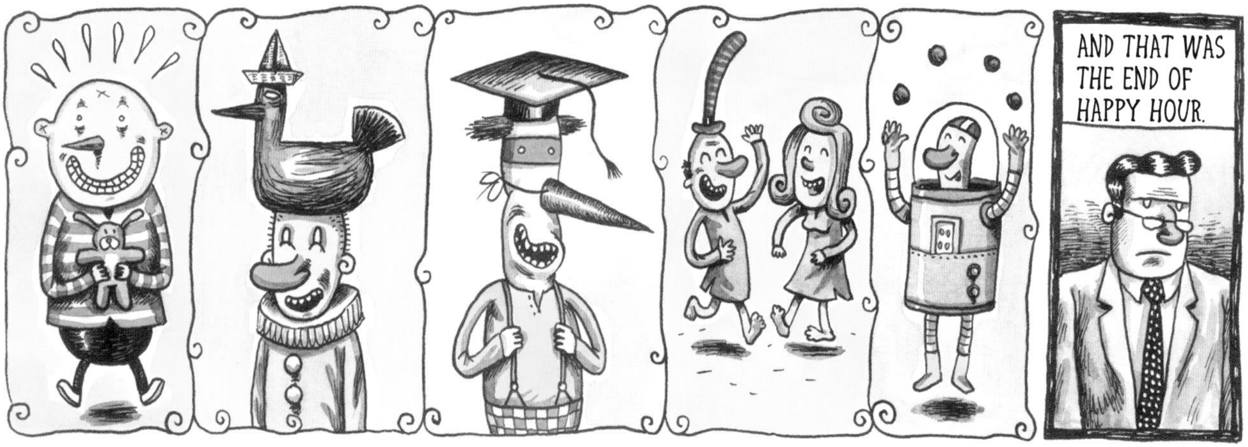
AND THAT WAS THE END OF HAPPY HOUR.

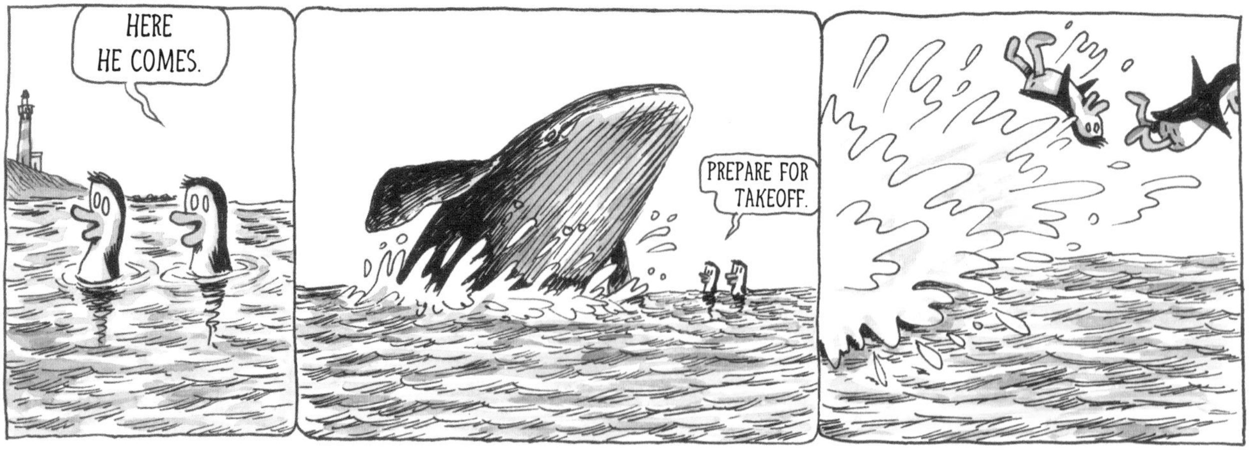
HERE HE COMES.
PREPARE FOR TAKEOFF.

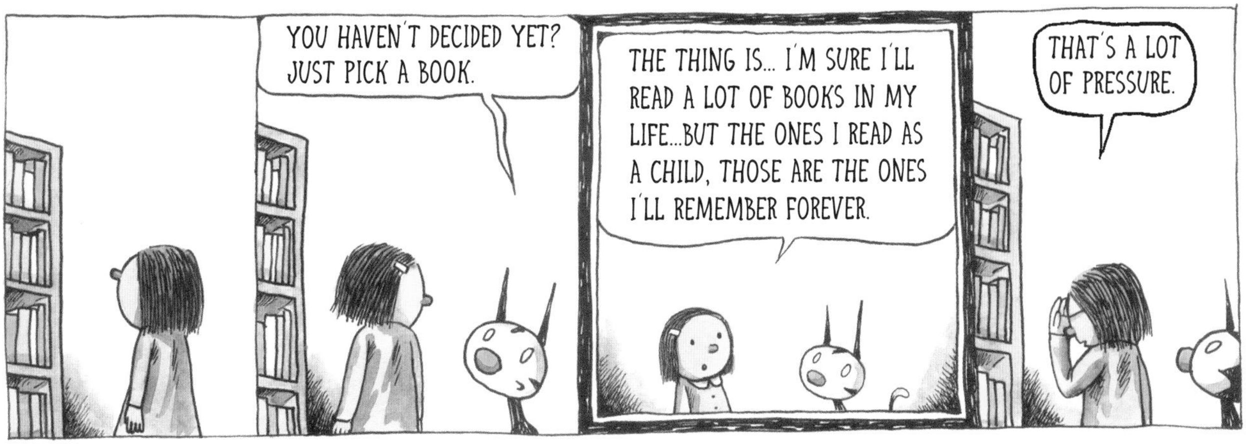
YOU HAVEN'T DECIDED YET? JUST PICK A BOOK.
THE THING IS... I'M SURE I'LL READ A LOT OF BOOKS IN MY LIFE...BUT THE ONES I READ AS A CHILD, THOSE ARE THE ONES I'LL REMEMBER FOREVER.
THAT'S A LOT OF PRESSURE.

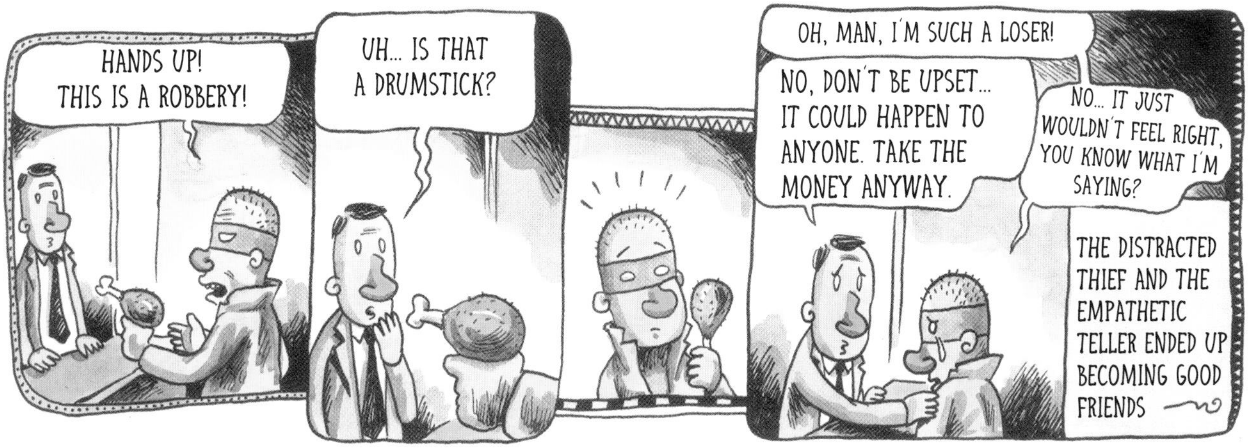
HANDS UP! THIS IS A ROBBERY!
UH... IS THAT A DRUMSTICK?
OH, MAN, I'M SUCH A LOSER!
NO, DON'T BE UPSET... IT COULD HAPPEN TO ANYONE. TAKE THE MONEY ANYWAY.
NO... IT JUST WOULDN'T FEEL RIGHT, YOU KNOW WHAT I'M SAYING?
THE DISTRACTED THIEF AND THE EMPATHETIC TELLER ENDED UP BECOMING GOOD FRIENDS

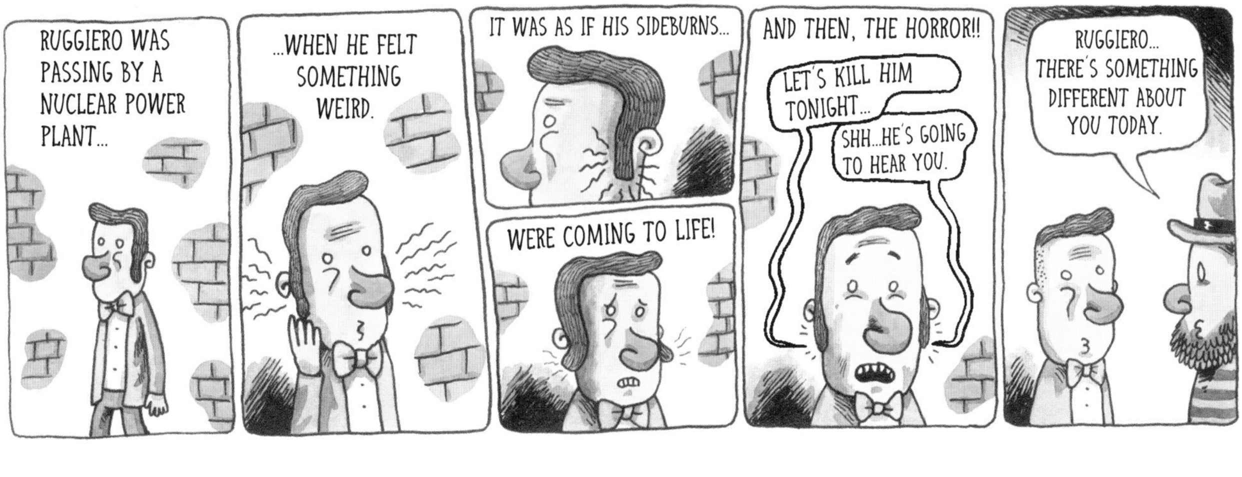
RUGGIERO WAS PASSING BY A NUCLEAR POWER PLANT...
...WHEN HE FELT SOMETHING WEIRD.
IT WAS AS IF HIS SIDEBURNS...
WERE COMING TO LIFE!
AND THEN, THE HORROR!!
LET'S KILL HIM TONIGHT...
SHH...HE'S GOING TO HEAR YOU.
RUGGIERO... THERE'S SOMETHING DIFFERENT ABOUT YOU TODAY.

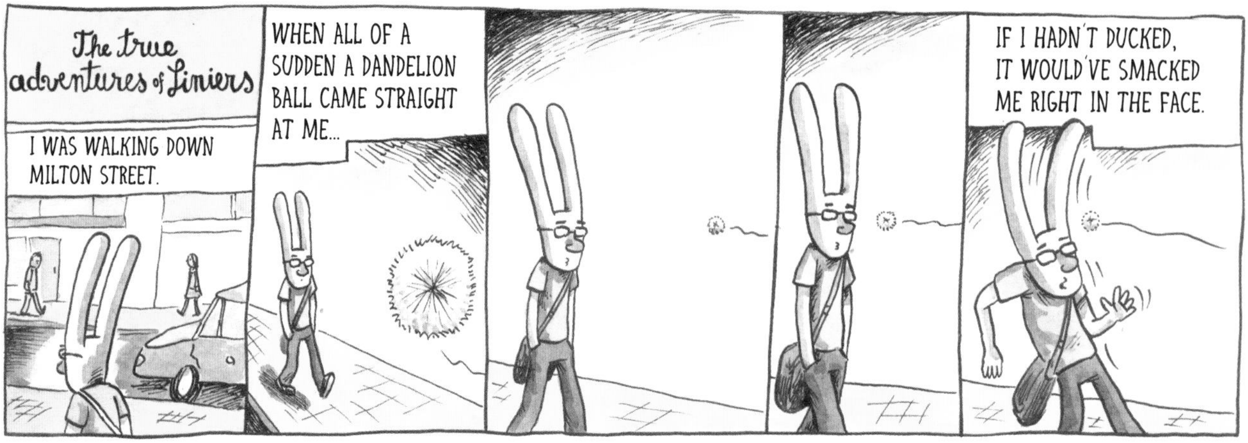
The true adventures of Liniers
I WAS WALKING DOWN MILTON STREET.
WHEN ALL OF A SUDDEN A DANDELION BALL CAME STRAIGHT AT ME...
IF I HADN'T DUCKED, IT WOULD'VE SMACKED ME RIGHT IN THE FACE.

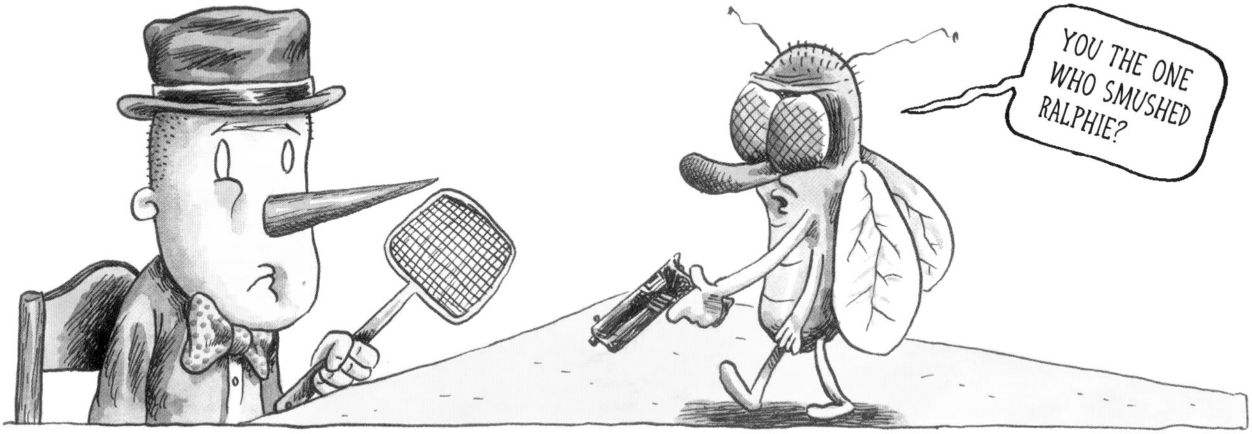
YOU THE ONE WHO SMUSHED RALPHIE?

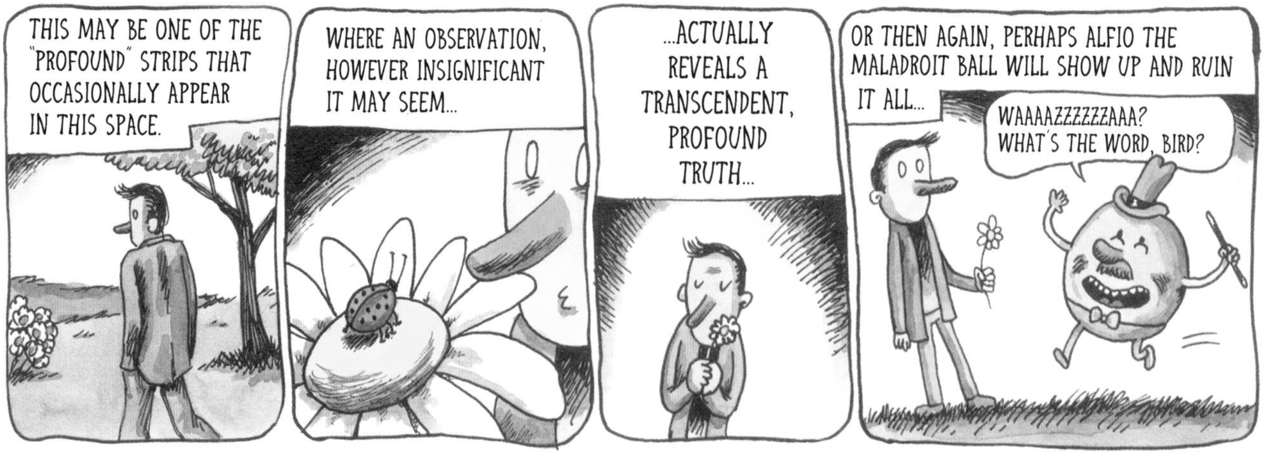
THIS MAY BE ONE OF THE "PROFOUND" STRIPS THAT OCCASIONALLY APPEAR IN THIS SPACE.
WHERE AN OBSERVATION, HOWEVER INSIGNIFICANT IT MAY SEEM...
...ACTUALLY REVEALS A TRANSCENDENT, PROFOUND TRUTH...
OR THEN AGAIN, PERHAPS ALFIO THE MALADROIT BALL WILL SHOW UP AND RUIN IT ALL...
WAAAAZZZZZZAAA? WHAT'S THE WORD, BIRD?

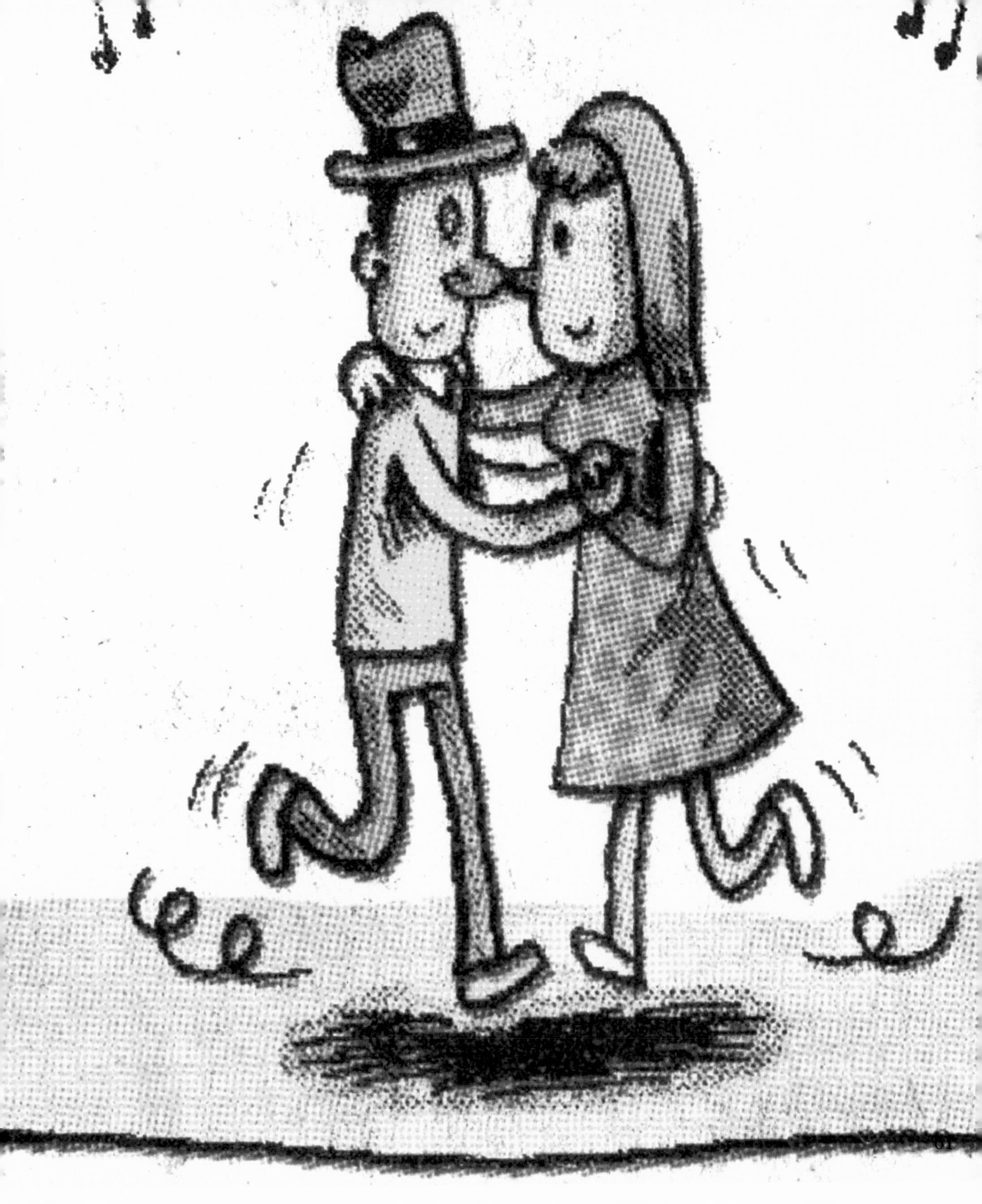

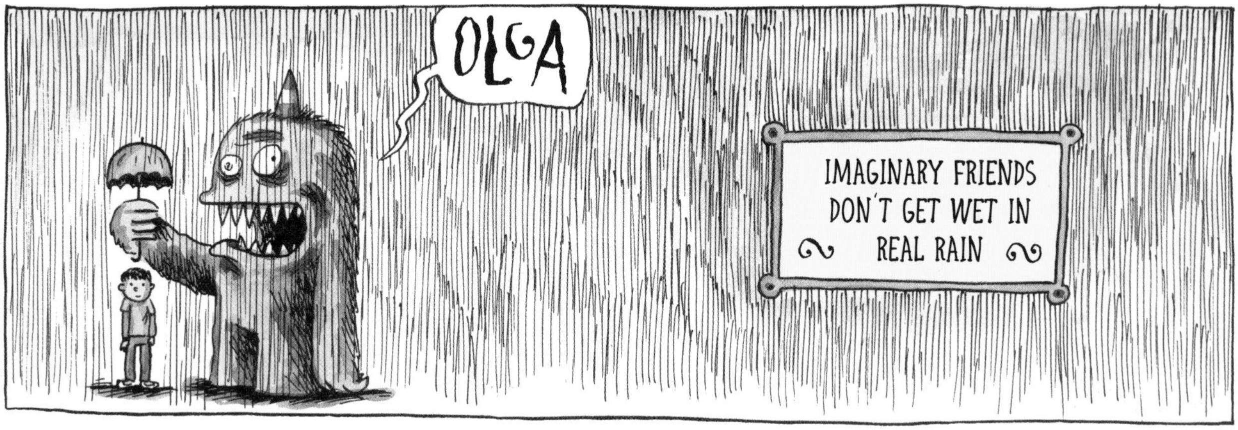
OLGA
IMAGINARY FRIENDS DON'T GET WET IN REAL RAIN

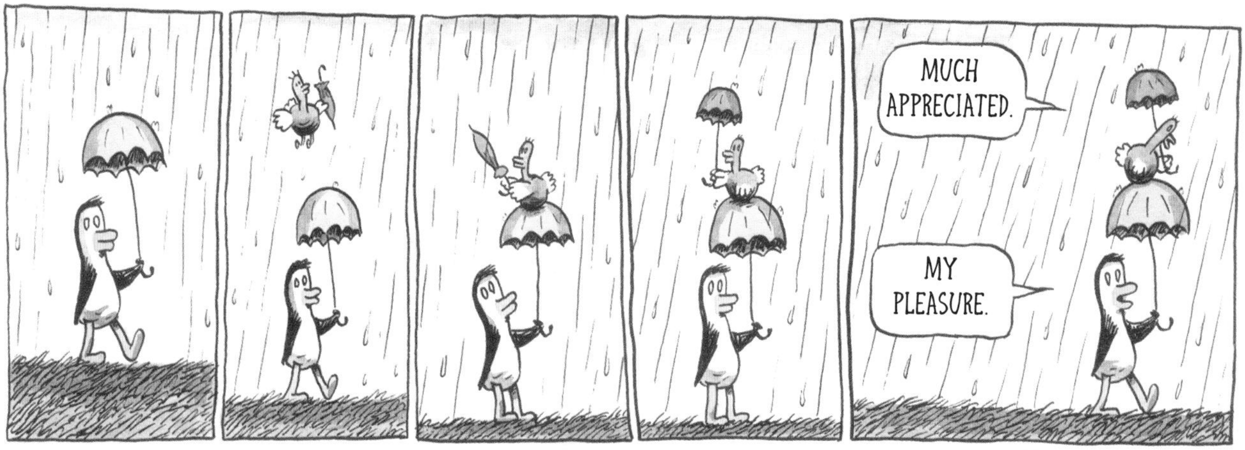
MUCH APPRECIATED.
MY PLEASURE.

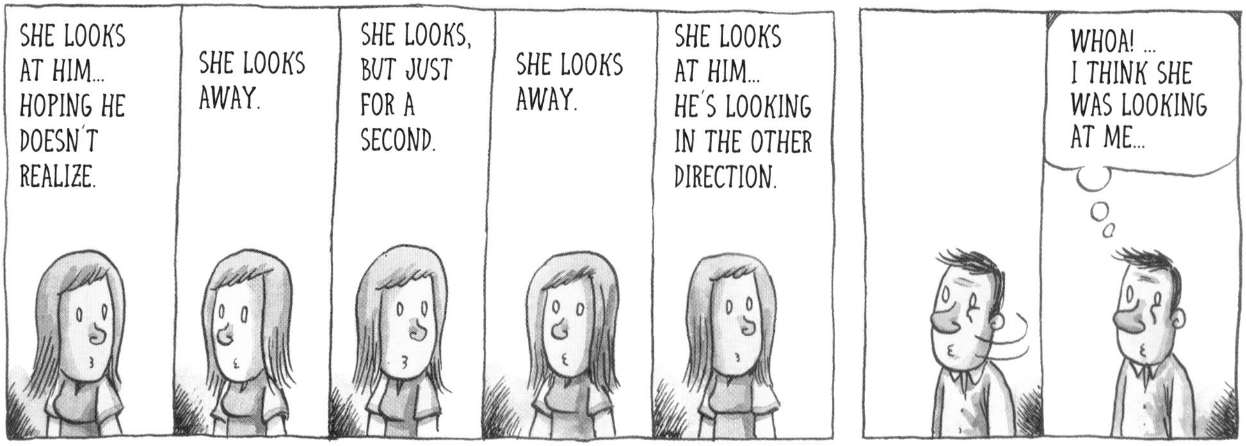
SHE LOOKS AT HIM... HOPING HE DOESN'T REALIZE.
SHE LOOKS AWAY.
SHE LOOKS, BUT JUST FOR A SECOND.
SHE LOOKS AWAY.
SHE LOOKS AT HIM... HE'S LOOKING IN THE OTHER DIRECTION.
WHOA! ... I THINK SHE WAS LOOKING AT ME...

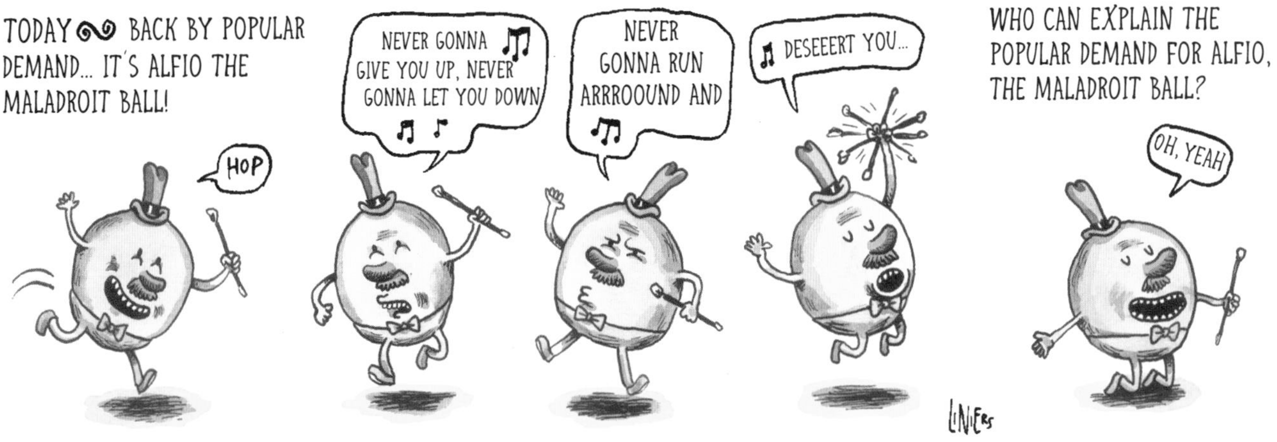
TODAY BACK BY POPULAR DEMAND... IT'S ALFIO THE MALADROIT BALL!
HOP
NEVER GONNA GIVE YOU UP, NEVER GONNA LET YOU DOWN
NEVER GONNA RUN ARRROOUND AND
DESEEERT YOU...
WHO CAN EXPLAIN THE POPULAR DEMAND FOR ALFIO, THE MALADROIT BALL?
OH, YEAH
LINIERS

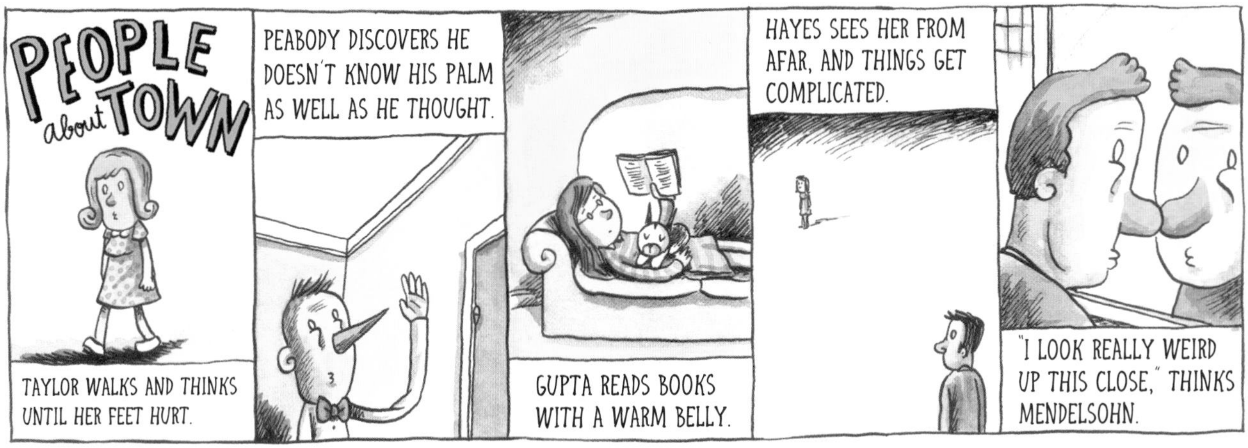
PEOPLE about TOWN
TAYLOR WALKS AND THINKS UNTIL HER FEET HURT.
PEABODY DISCOVERS HE DOESN'T KNOW HIS PALM AS WELL AS HE THOUGHT.
GUPTA READS BOOKS WITH A WARM BELLY.
HAYES SEES HER FROM AFAR, AND THINGS GET COMPLICATED.
"I LOOK REALLY WEIRD UP THIS CLOSE," THINKS MENDELSOHN.

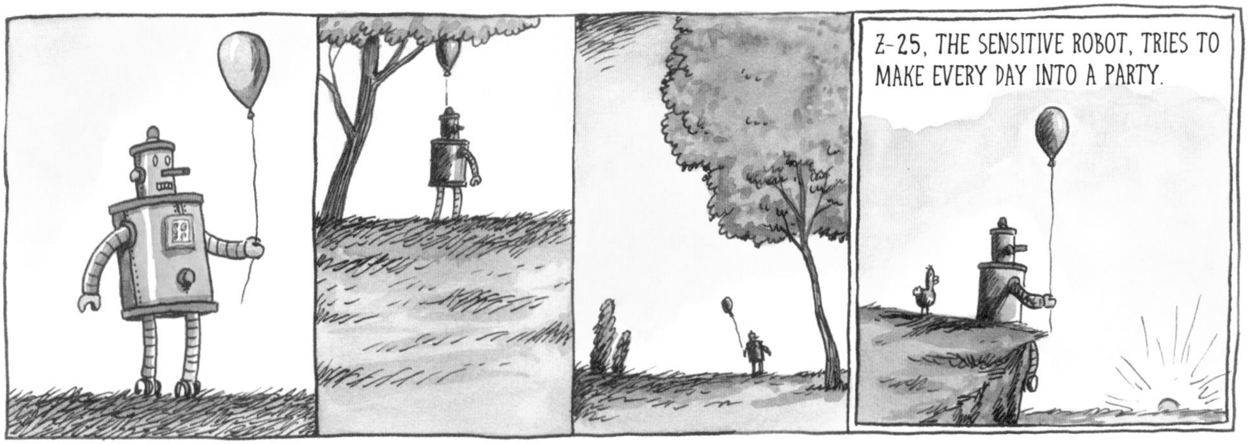
Z-25, THE SENSITIVE ROBOT, TRIES TO MAKE EVERY DAY INTO A PARTY.

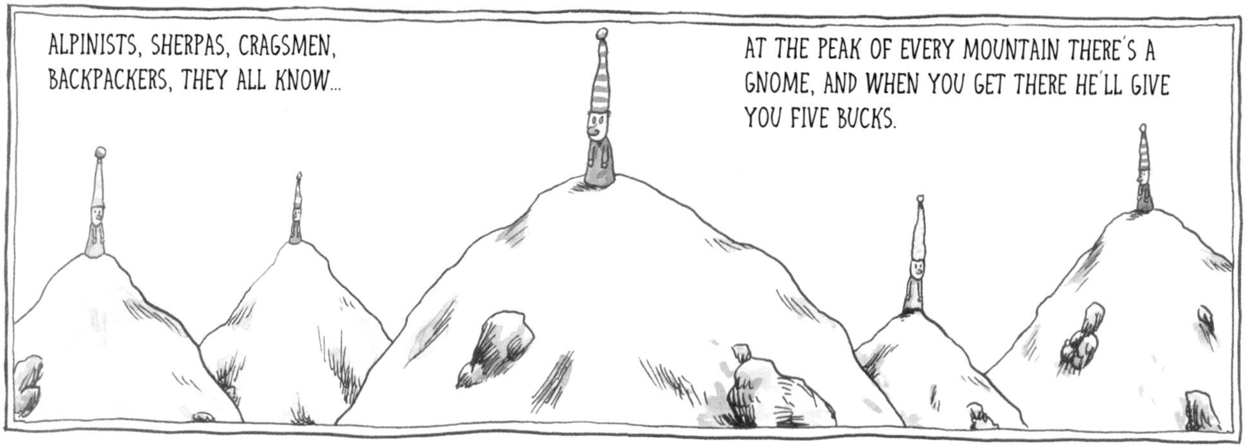
ALPINISTS, SHERPAS, CRAGSMEN, BACKPACKERS, THEY ALL KNOW...
AT THE PEAK OF EVERY MOUNTAIN THERE'S A GNOME, AND WHEN YOU GET THERE HE'LL GIVE YOU FIVE BUCKS.

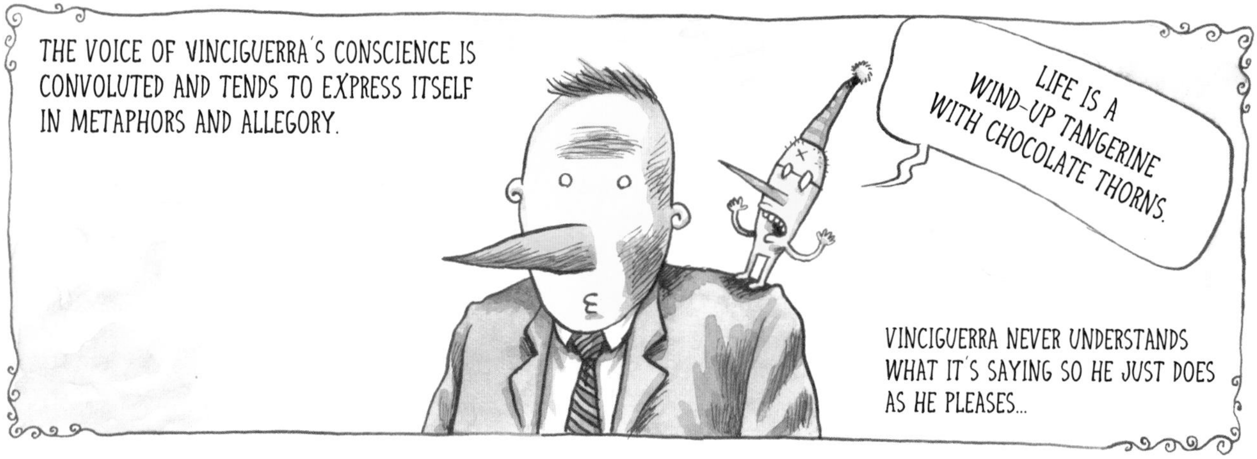
THE VOICE OF VINCIGUERRA'S CONSCIENCE IS CONVOLUTED AND TENDS TO EXPRESS ITSELF IN METAPHORS AND ALLEGORY.
LIFE IS A WIND-UP TANGERINE WITH CHOCOLATE THORNS.
VINCIGUERRA NEVER UNDERSTANDS WHAT IT'S SAYING SO HE JUST DOES AS HE PLEASES...

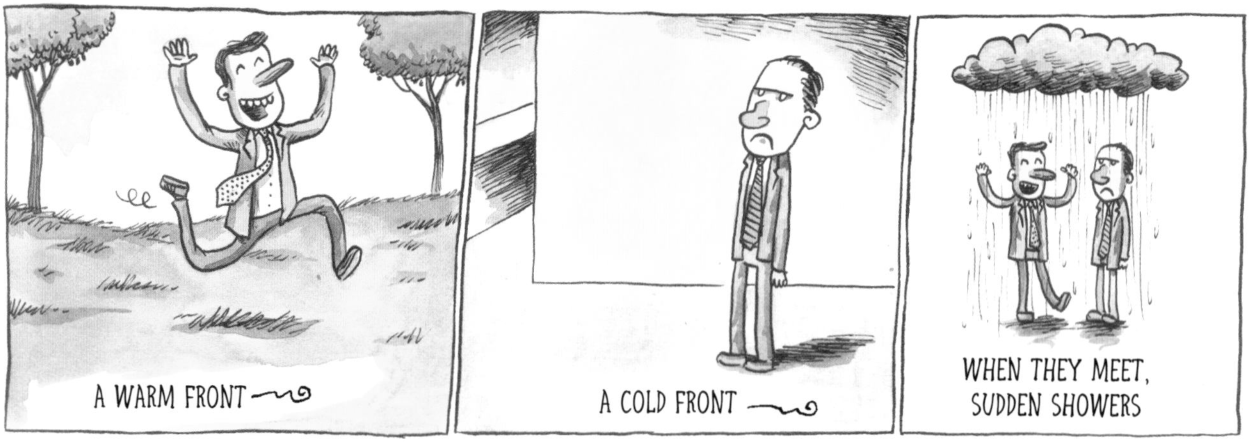
A WARM FRONT
A COLD FRONT
WHEN THEY MEET, SUDDEN SHOWERS

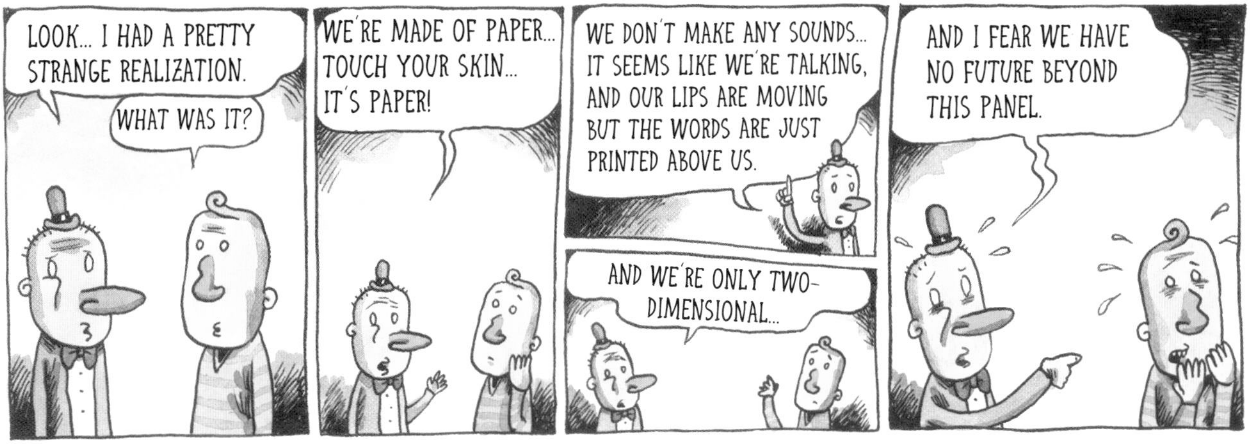
LOOK... I HAD A PRETTY STRANGE REALIZATION.
WHAT WAS IT?
WE'RE MADE OF PAPER... TOUCH YOUR SKIN... IT'S PAPER!
WE DON'T MAKE ANY SOUNDS... IT SEEMS LIKE WE'RE TALKING, AND OUR LIPS ARE MOVING BUT THE WORDS ARE JUST PRINTED ABOVE US.
AND WE'RE ONLY TWO-DIMENSIONAL...
AND I FEAR WE HAVE NO FUTURE BEYOND THIS PANEL.

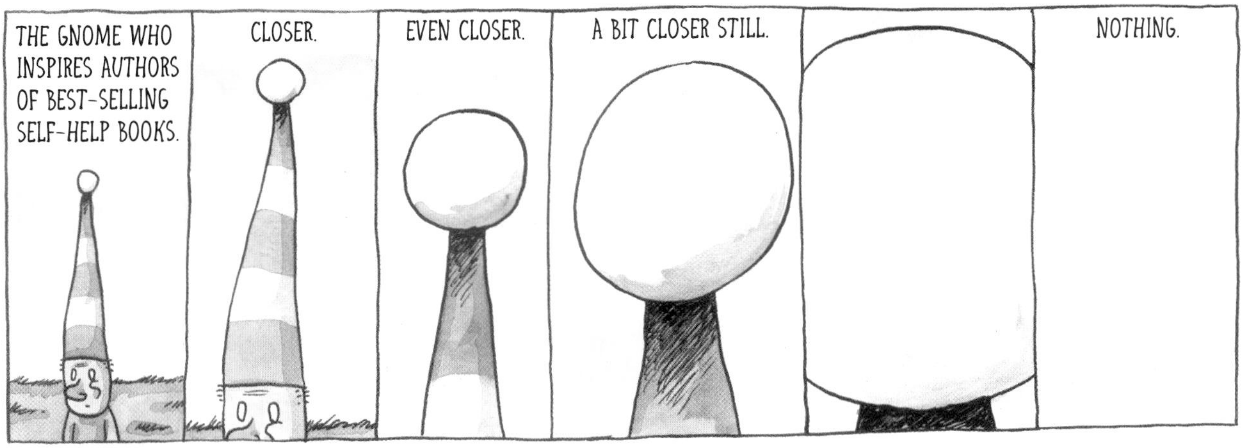
THE GNOME WHO INSPIRES AUTHORS OF BEST-SELLING SELF-HELP BOOKS.
CLOSER.
EVEN CLOSER.
A BIT CLOSER STILL.
NOTHING.

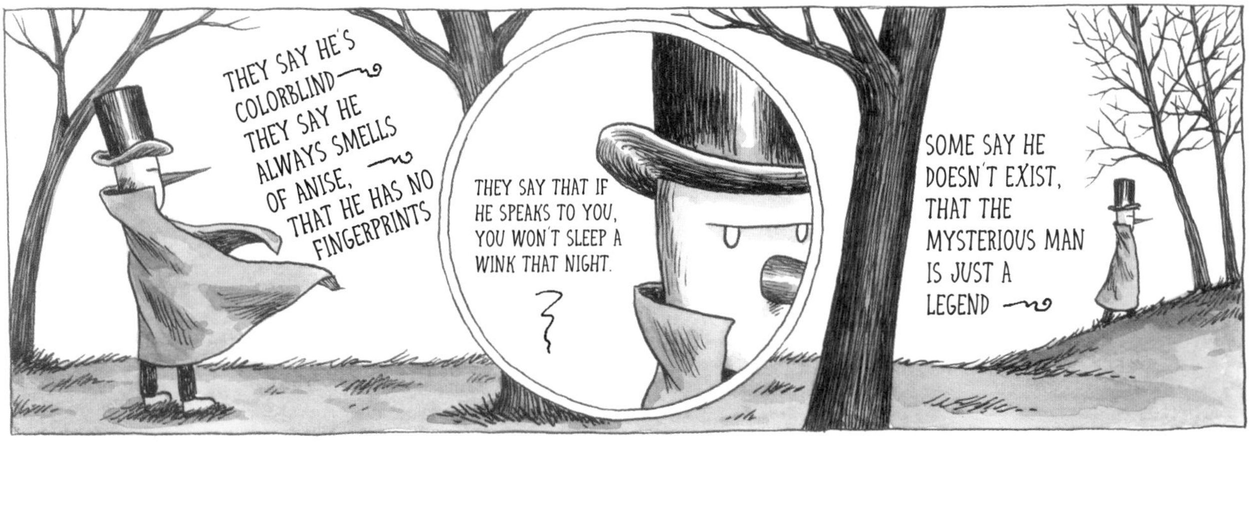
THEY SAY HE'S COLORBLIND
THEY SAY HE ALWAYS SMELLS OF ANISE,
THAT HE HAS NO FINGERPRINTS
THEY SAY THAT IF HE SPEAKS TO YOU, YOU WON'T SLEEP A WINK THAT NIGHT.
SOME SAY HE DOESN'T EXIST, THAT THE MYSTERIOUS MAN IS JUST A LEGEND

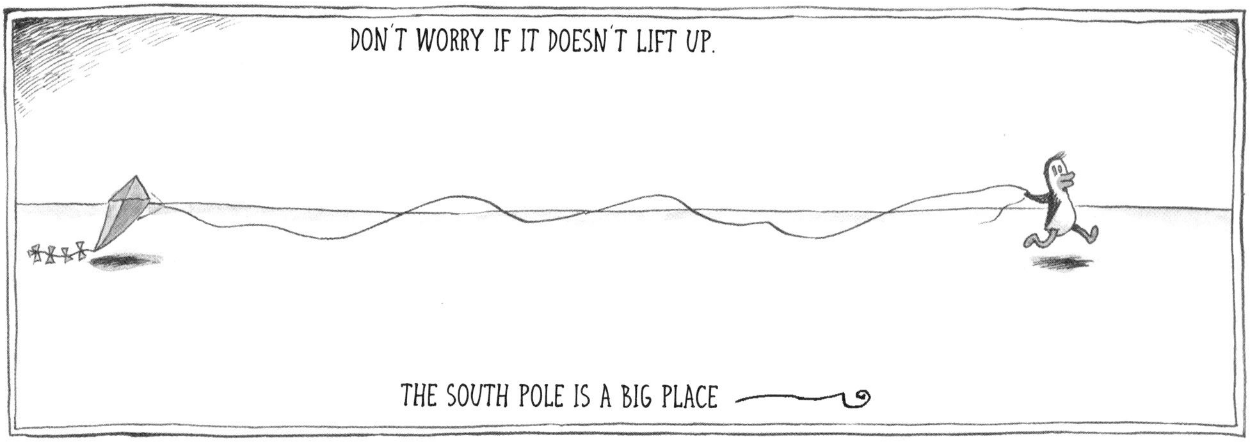
DON'T WORRY IF IT DOESN'T LIFT UP.
THE SOUTH POLE IS A BIG PLACE

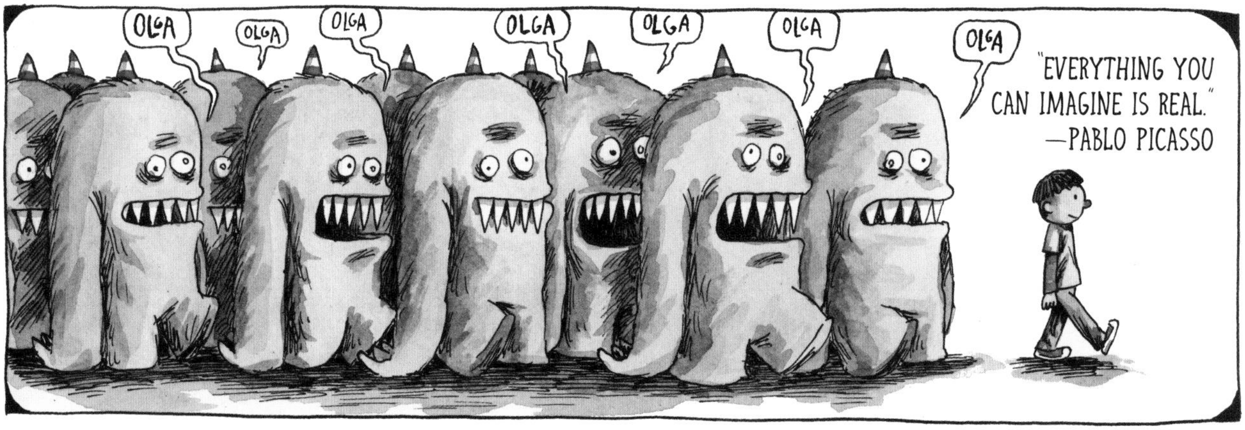
OLGA
OLGA
OLGA
OLGA
OLGA
OLGA
OLGA
"EVERYTHING YOU CAN IMAGINE IS REAL."
—PABLO PICASSO

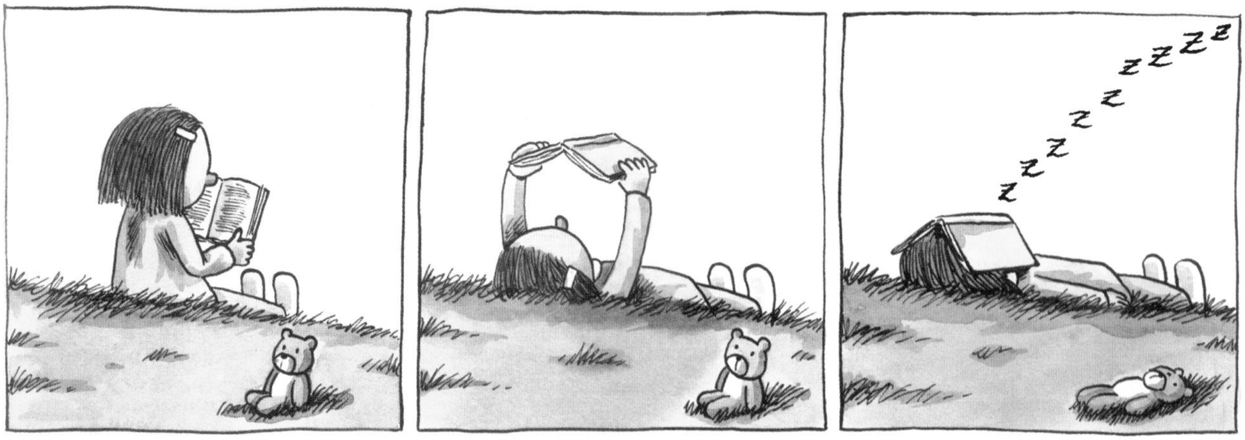
Z Z Z Z Z Z Z Z Z Z

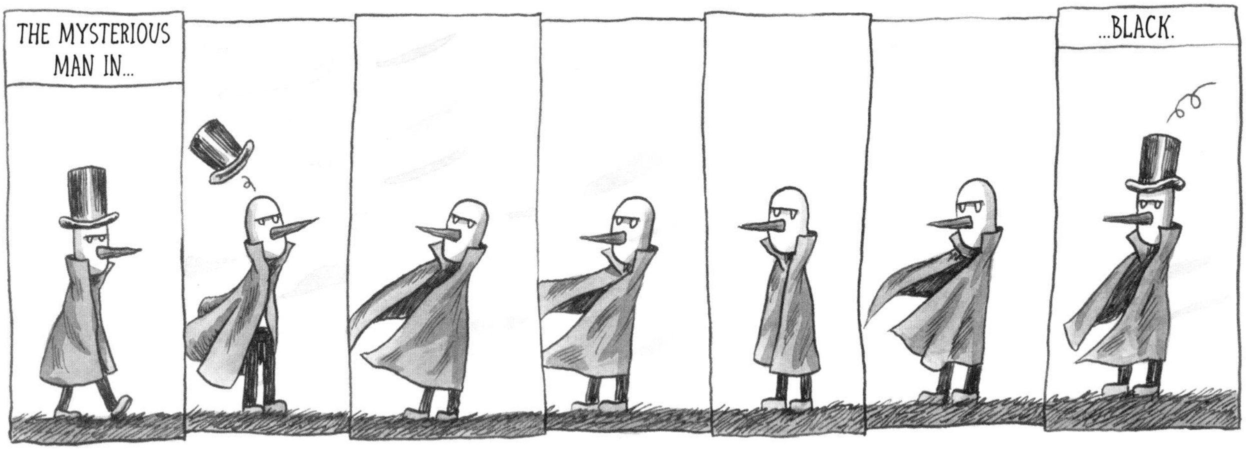
THE MYSTERIOUS MAN IN...
...BLACK.

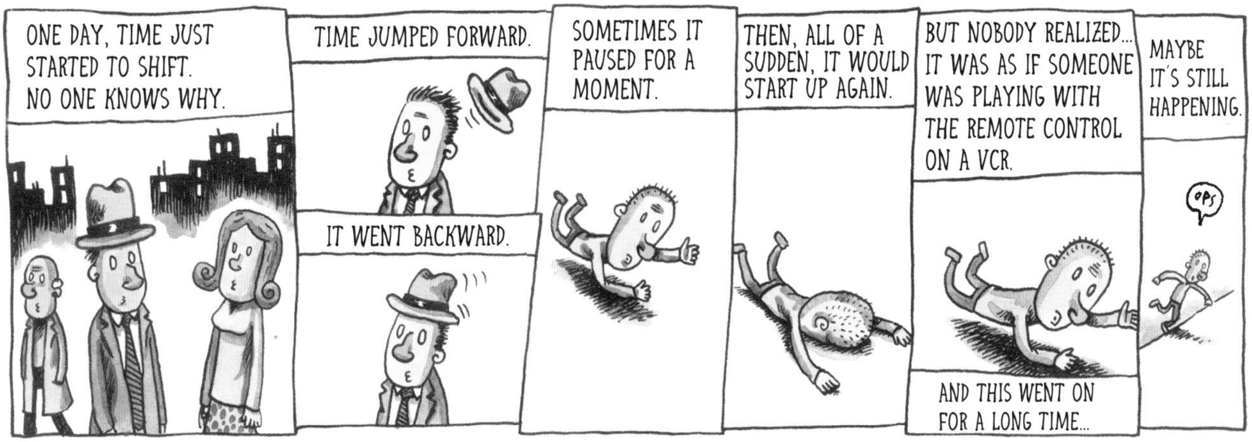
ONE DAY, TIME JUST STARTED TO SHIFT. NO ONE KNOWS WHY.
TIME JUMPED FORWARD.
IT WENT BACKWARD.
SOMETIMES IT PAUSED FOR A MOMENT.
THEN, ALL OF A SUDDEN, IT WOULD START UP AGAIN.
BUT NOBODY REALIZED... IT WAS AS IF SOMEONE WAS PLAYING WITH THE REMOTE CONTROL ON A VCR.
AND THIS WENT ON FOR A LONG TIME...
MAYBE IT'S STILL HAPPENING.
OPS

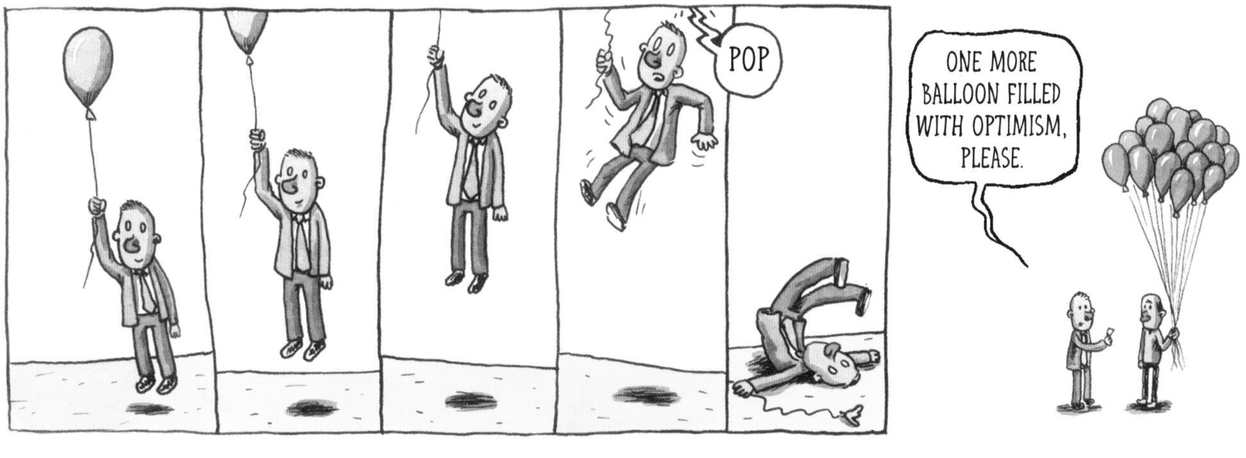
POP
ONE MORE BALLOON FILLED WITH OPTIMISM, PLEASE.

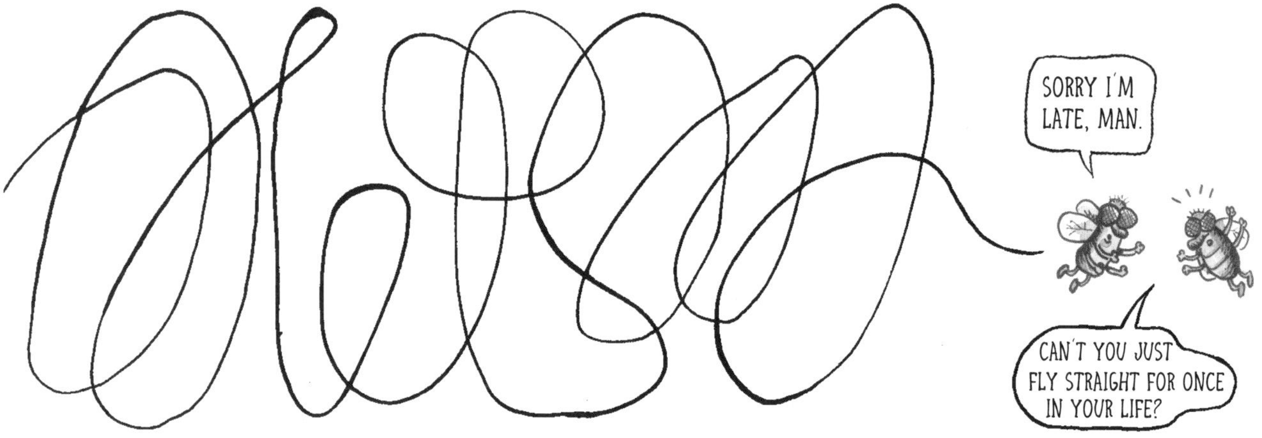
SORRY I'M LATE, MAN.
CAN'T YOU JUST FLY STRAIGHT FOR ONCE IN YOUR LIFE?

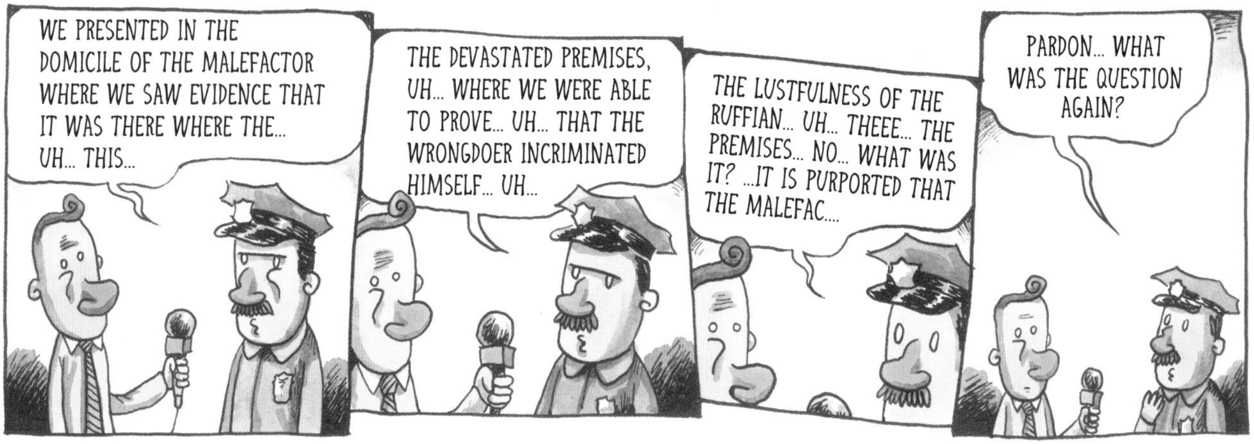
WE PRESENTED IN THE DOMICILE OF THE MALEFACTOR WHERE WE SAW EVIDENCE THAT IT WAS THERE WHERE THE... UH... THIS...
THE DEVASTATED PREMISES, UH... WHERE WE WERE ABLE TO PROVE... UH... THAT THE WRONGDOER INCRIMINATED HIMSELF... UH...
THE LUSTFULNESS OF THE RUFFIAN... UH... THEEE... THE PREMISES... NO... WHAT WAS IT? ...IT IS PURPORTED THAT THE MALEFAC....
PARDON... WHAT WAS THE QUESTION AGAIN?

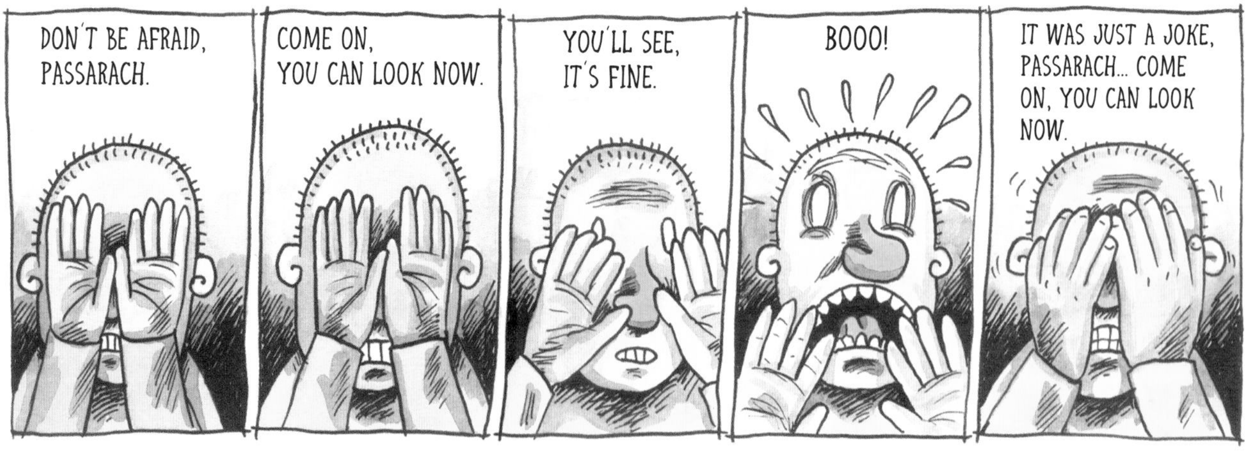
DON'T BE AFRAID, PASSARACH.
COME ON, YOU CAN LOOK NOW.
YOU'LL SEE, IT'S FINE.
BOOO!
IT WAS JUST A JOKE, PASSARACH... COME ON, YOU CAN LOOK NOW.

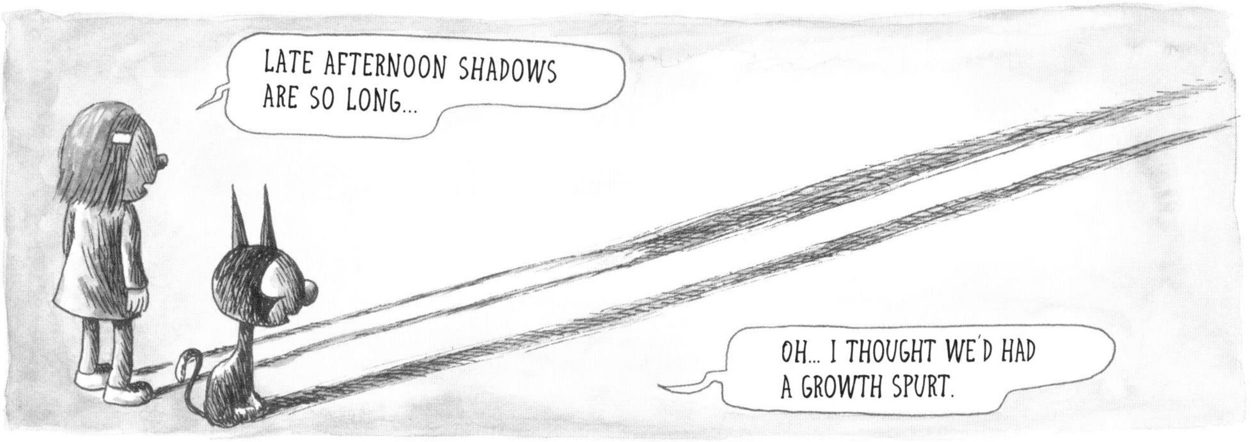
LATE AFTERNOON SHADOWS ARE SO LONG...
OH... I THOUGHT WE'D HAD A GROWTH SPURT.

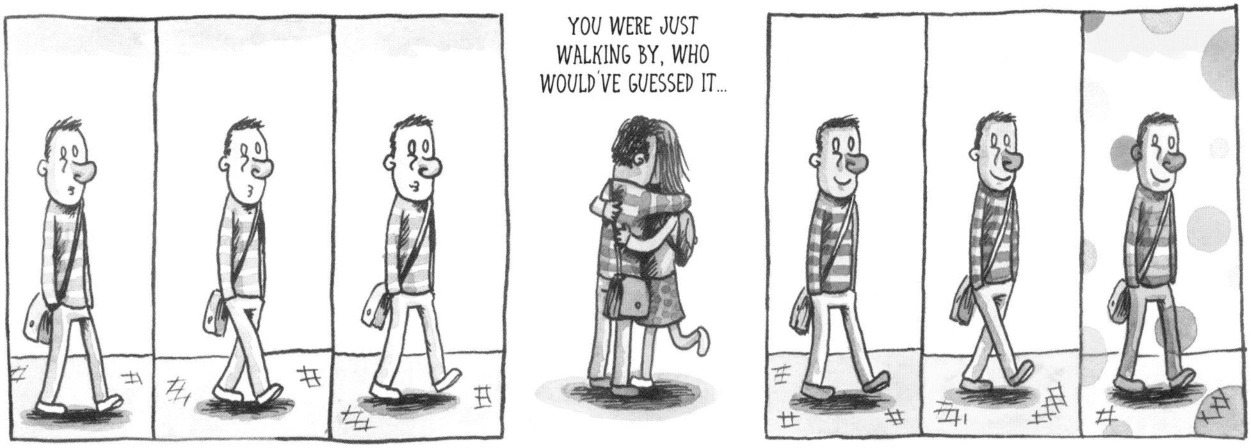
YOU WERE JUST WALKING BY, WHO WOULD'VE GUESSED IT...

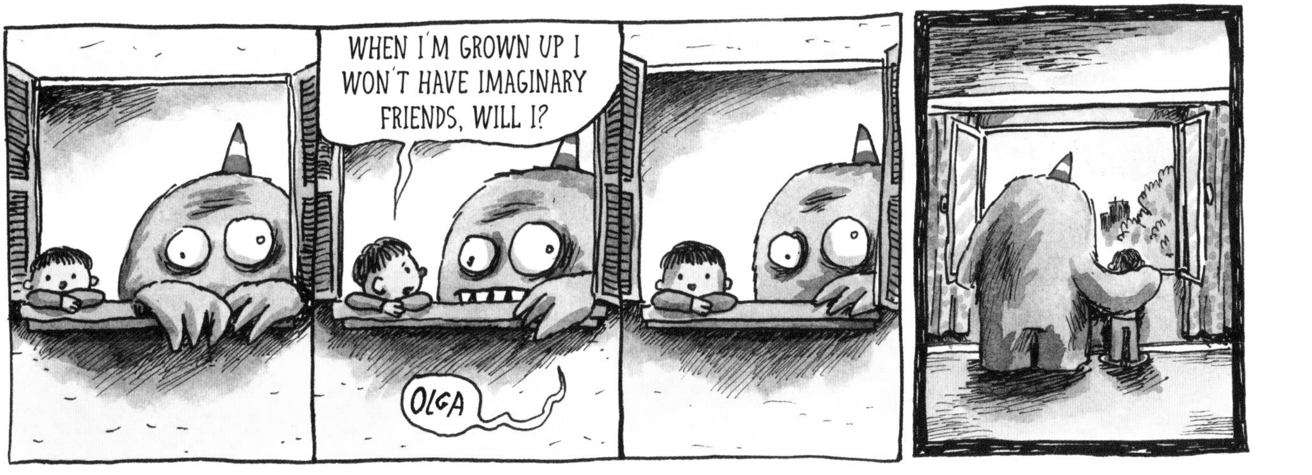
WHEN I'M GROWN UP I WON'T HAVE IMAGINARY FRIENDS, WILL I?
OLGA

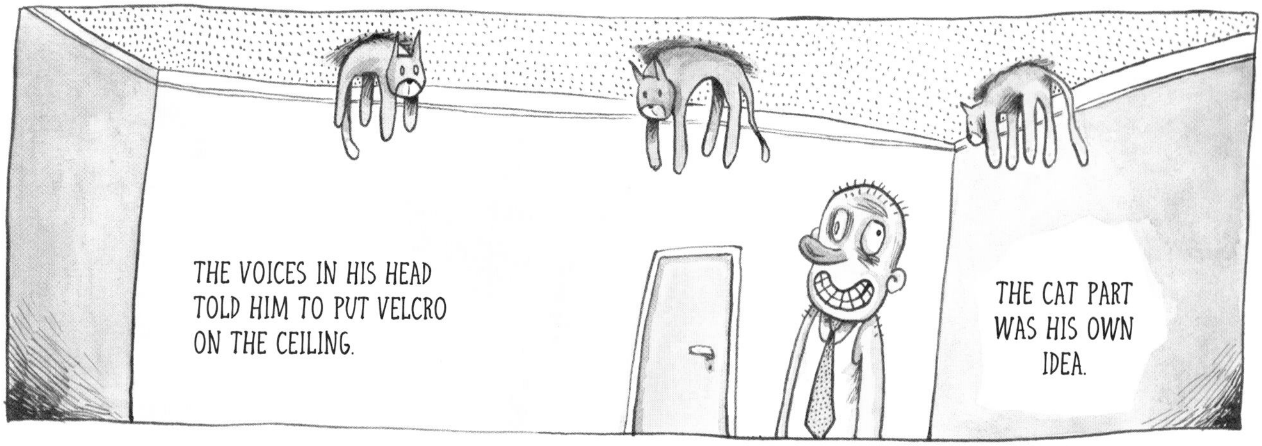
THE VOICES IN HIS HEAD TOLD HIM TO PUT VELCRO ON THE CEILING.
THE CAT PART WAS HIS OWN IDEA.

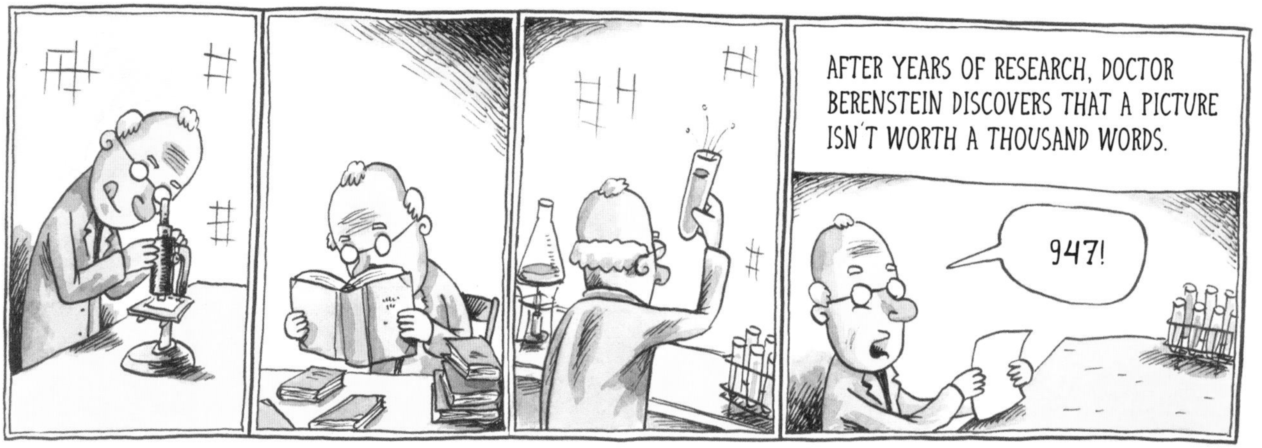
AFTER YEARS OF RESEARCH, DOCTOR BERENSTEIN DISCOVERS THAT A PICTURE ISN'T WORTH A THOUSAND WORDS.
947!

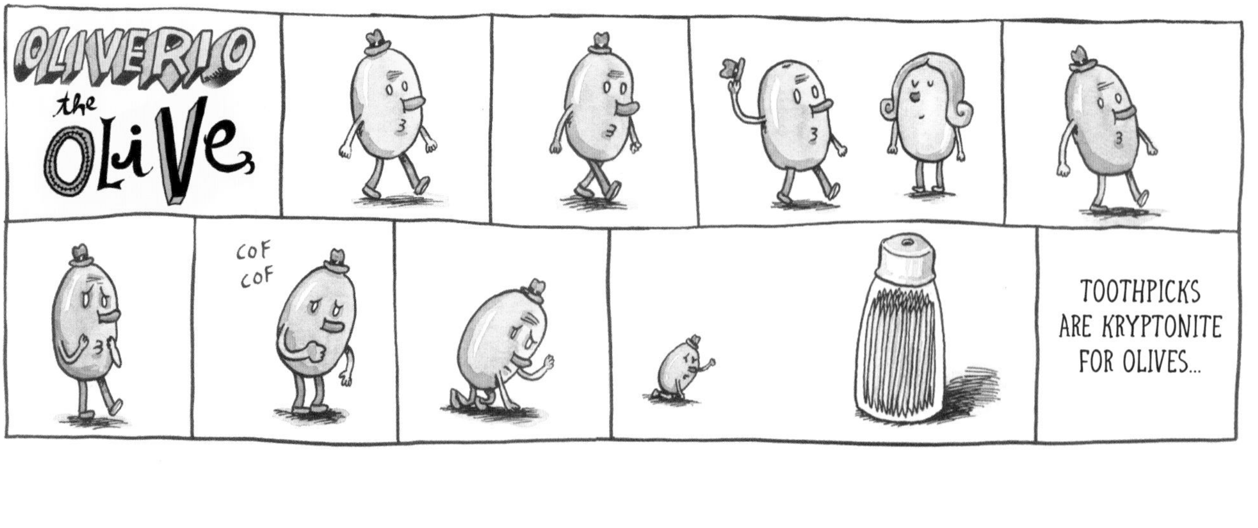
OLIVERIO the OLIVE
COF COF
TOOTHPICKS ARE KRYPTONITE FOR OLIVES...

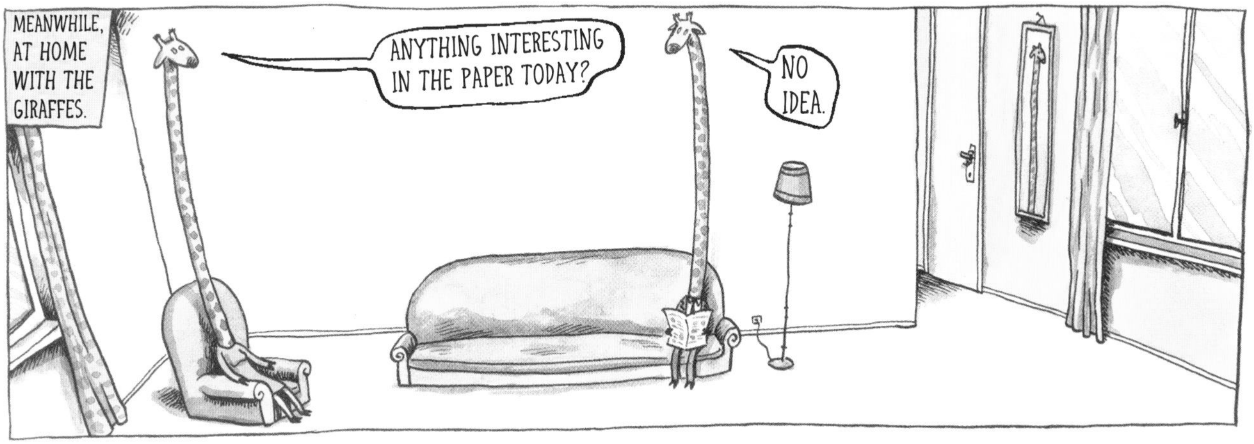
MEANWHILE, AT HOME WITH THE GIRAFFES.
ANYTHING INTERESTING IN THE PAPER TODAY?
NO IDEA.

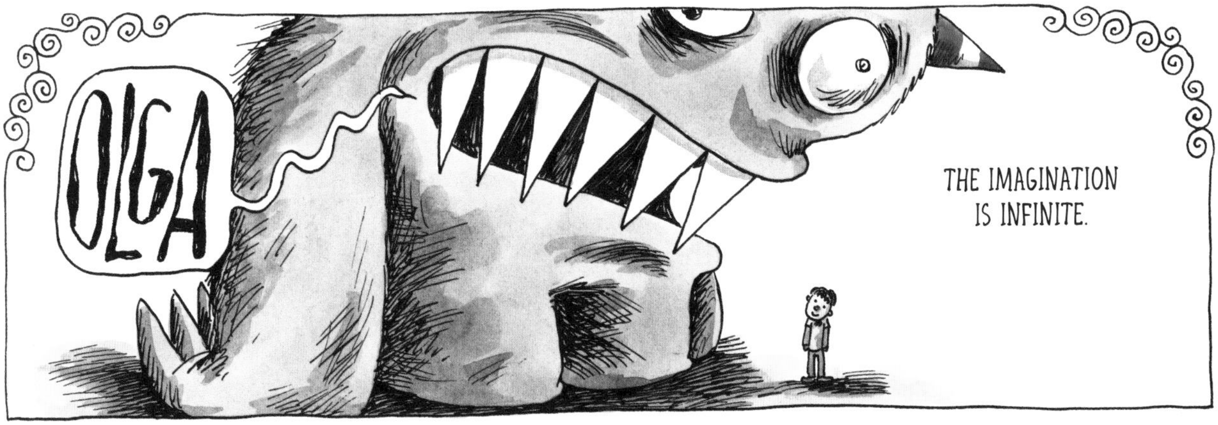
OLGA
THE IMAGINATION IS INFINITE.

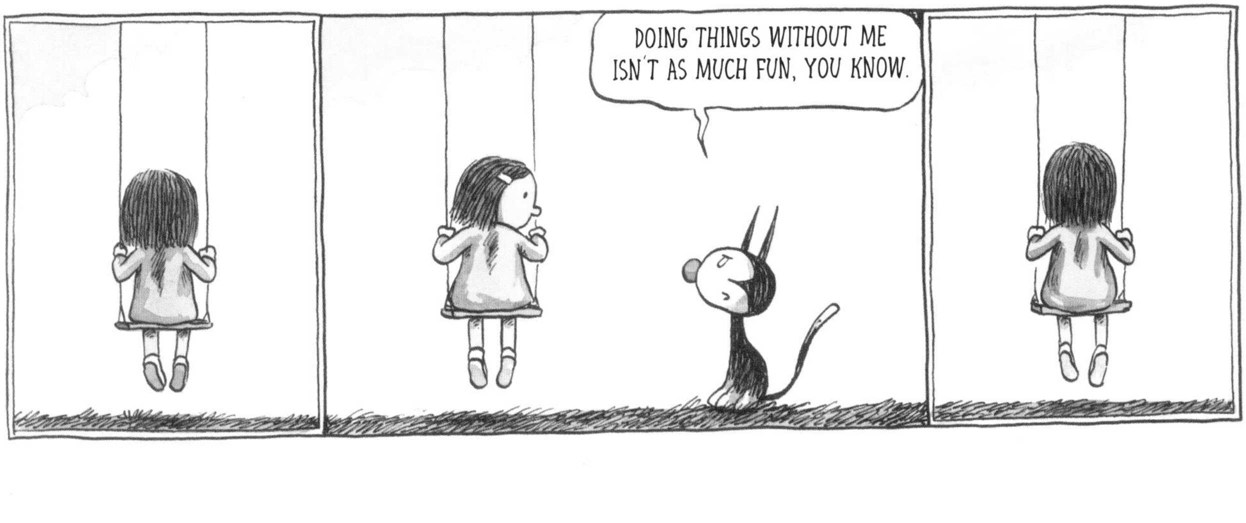
DOING THINGS WITHOUT ME ISN'T AS MUCH FUN, YOU KNOW.

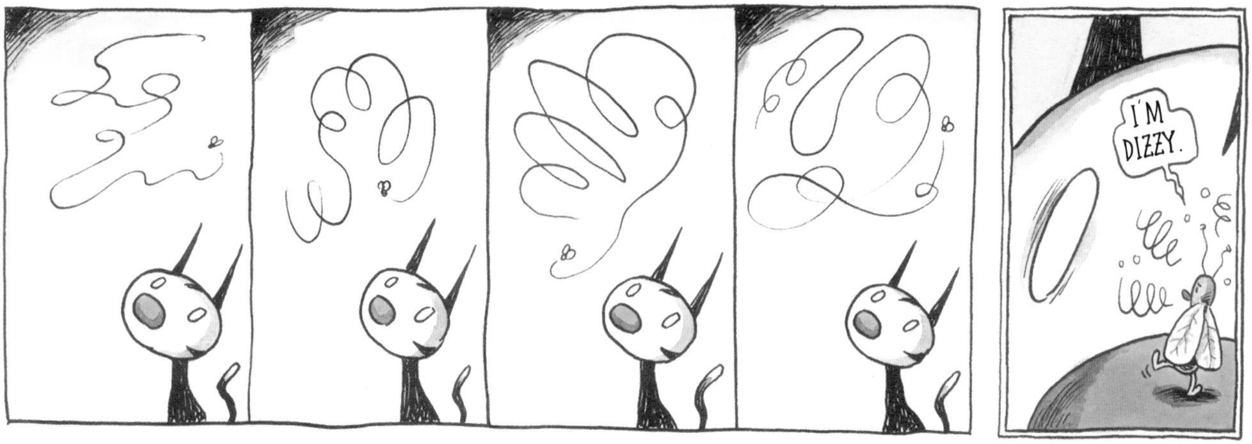
I'M DIZZY.

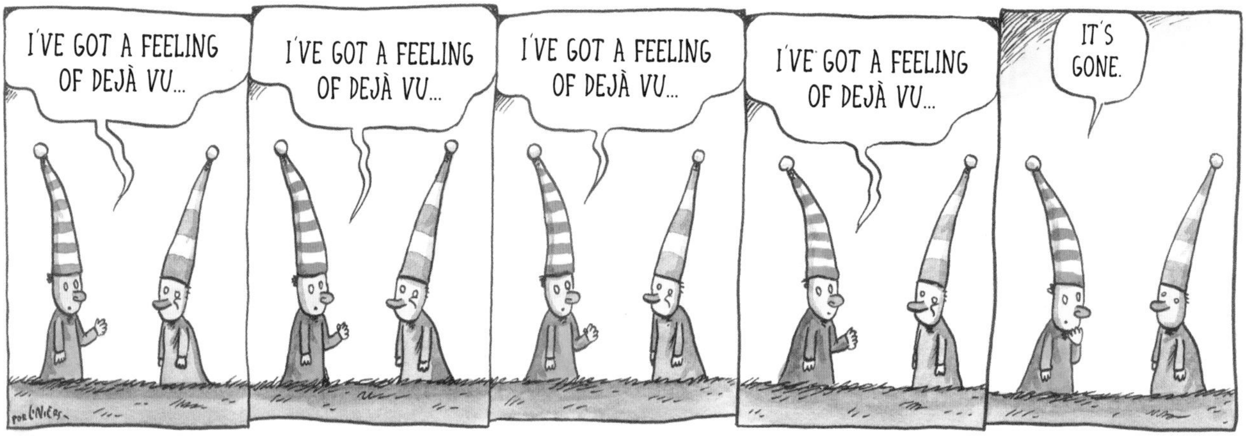
I'VE GOT A FEELING OF DEJÀ VU...
I'VE GOT A FEELING OF DEJÀ VU...
I'VE GOT A FEELING OF DEJÀ VU...
I'VE GOT A FEELING OF DEJÀ VU...
IT'S GONE.

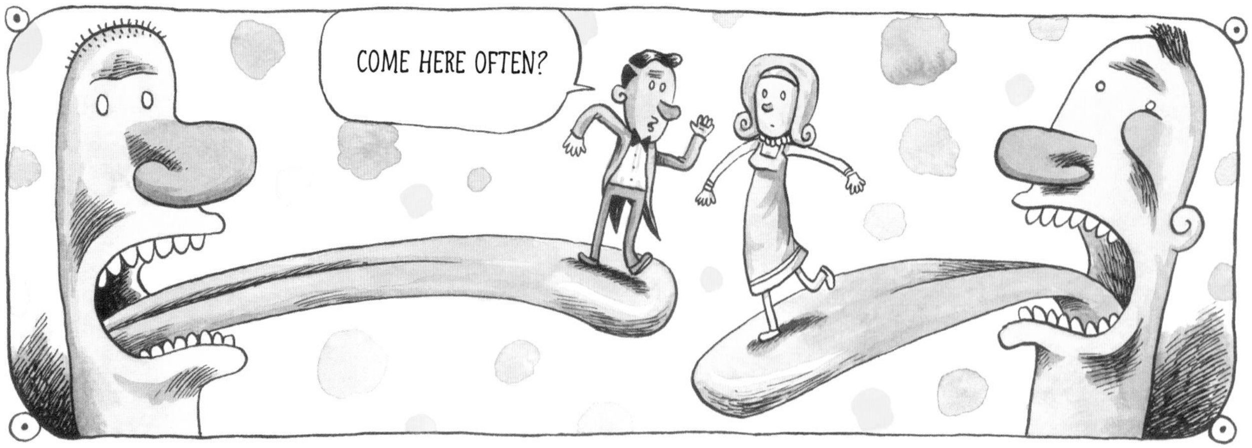
COME HERE OFTEN?

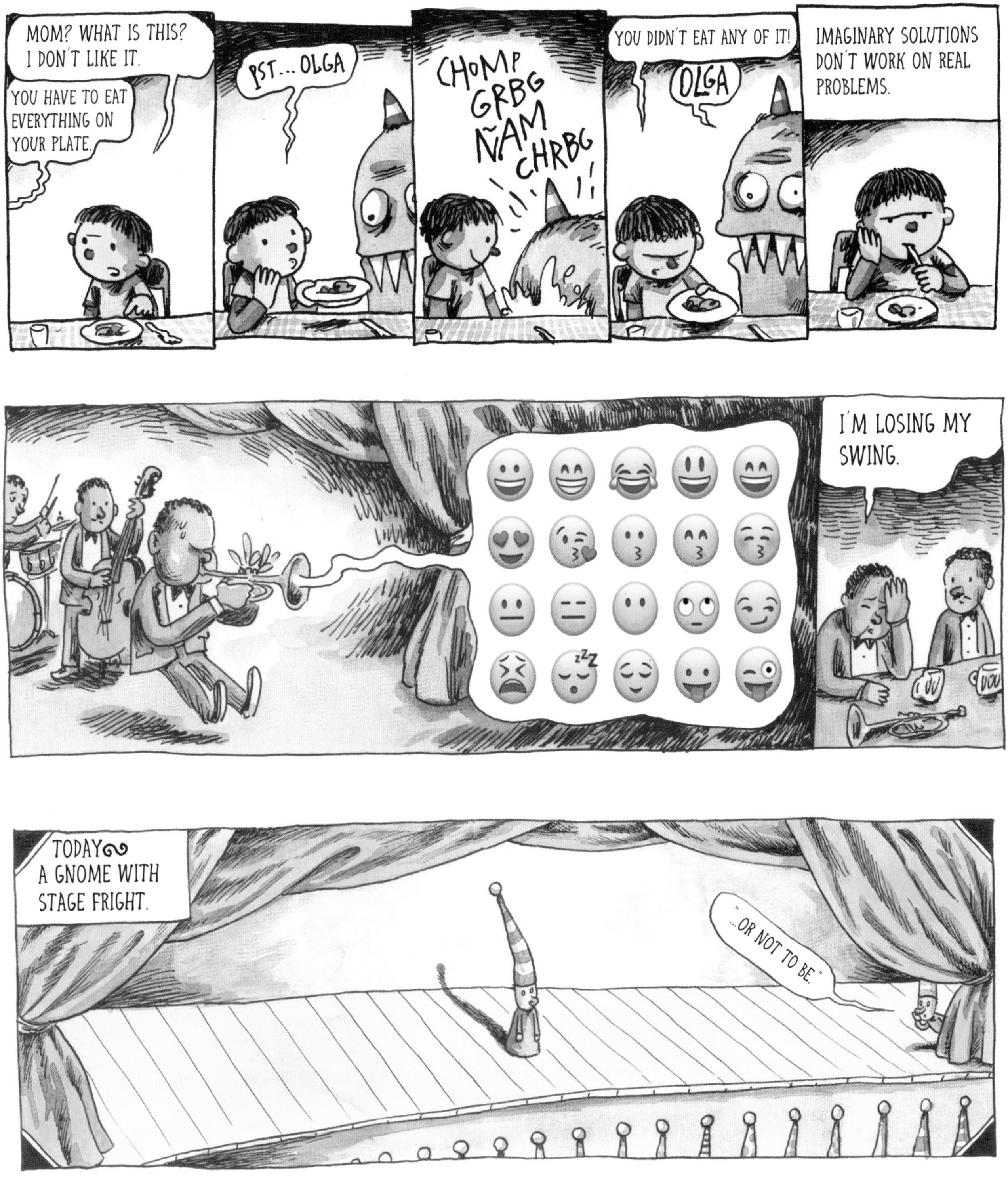
MOM? WHAT IS THIS? I DON'T LIKE IT.
YOU HAVE TO EAT EVERYTHING ON YOUR PLATE.
PST... OLGA
CHOMP GRBG ÑAM CHRBG
YOU DIDN'T EAT ANY OF IT!
OLGA
IMAGINARY SOLUTIONS DON'T WORK ON REAL PROBLEMS.
I'M LOSING MY SWING.
TODAY A GNOME WITH STAGE FRIGHT.
"...OR NOT TO BE."

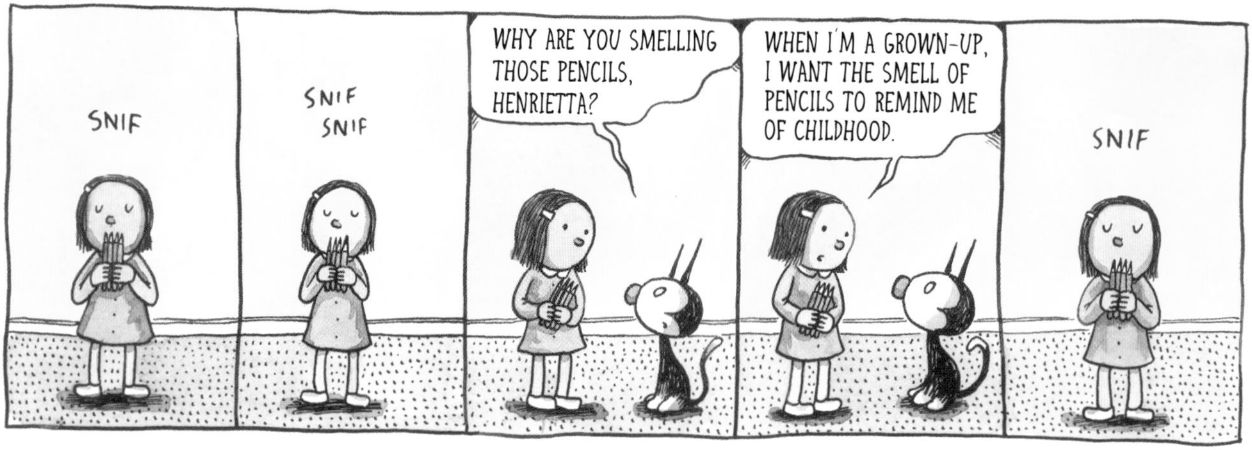
SNIF
SNIF SNIF
WHY ARE YOU SMELLING THOSE PENCILS, HENRIETTA?
WHEN I'M A GROWN-UP, I WANT THE SMELL OF PENCILS TO REMIND ME OF CHILDHOOD.
SNIF

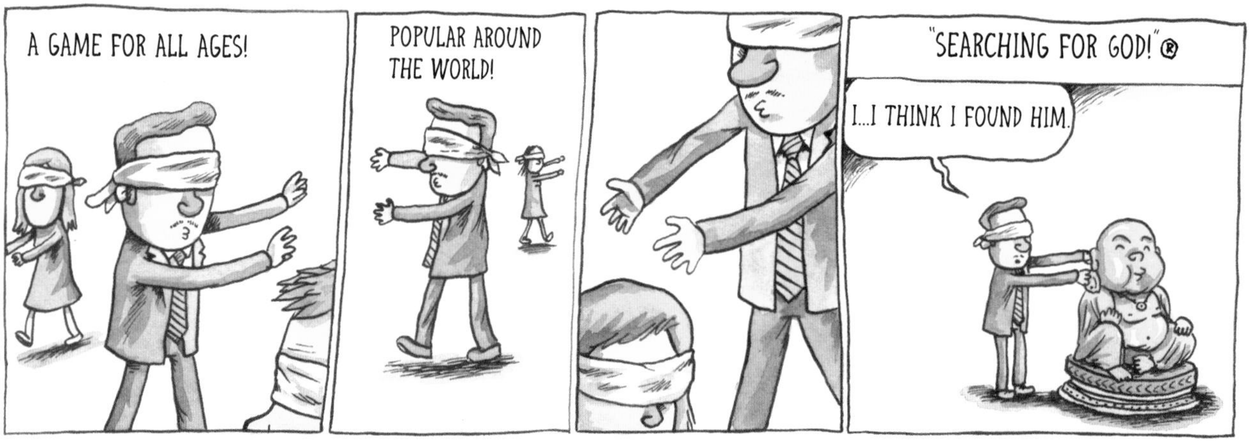
A GAME FOR ALL AGES!
POPULAR AROUND THE WORLD!
"SEARCHING FOR GOD!"®
I...I THINK I FOUND HIM.

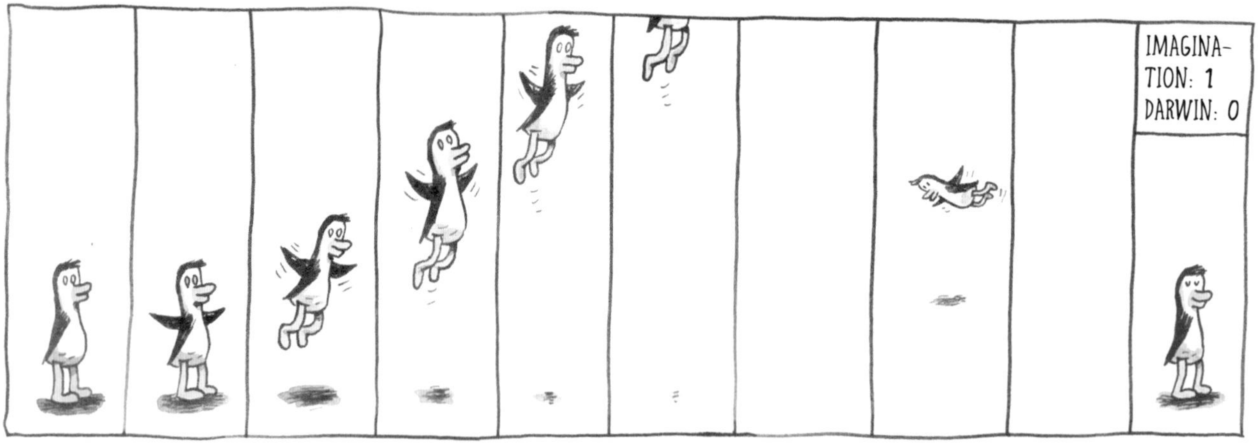
IMAGINATION: 1
DARWIN: 0

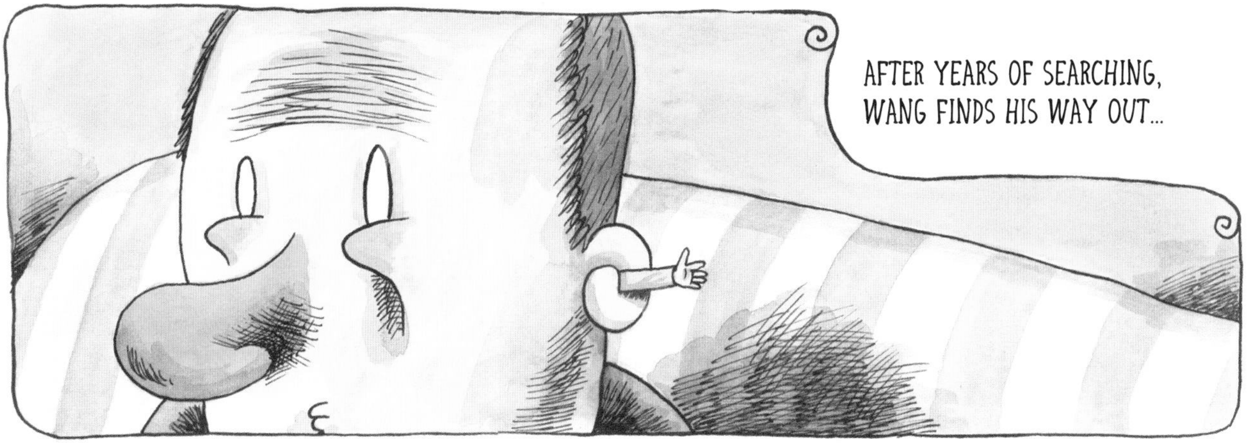
AFTER YEARS OF SEARCHING, WANG FINDS HIS WAY OUT...

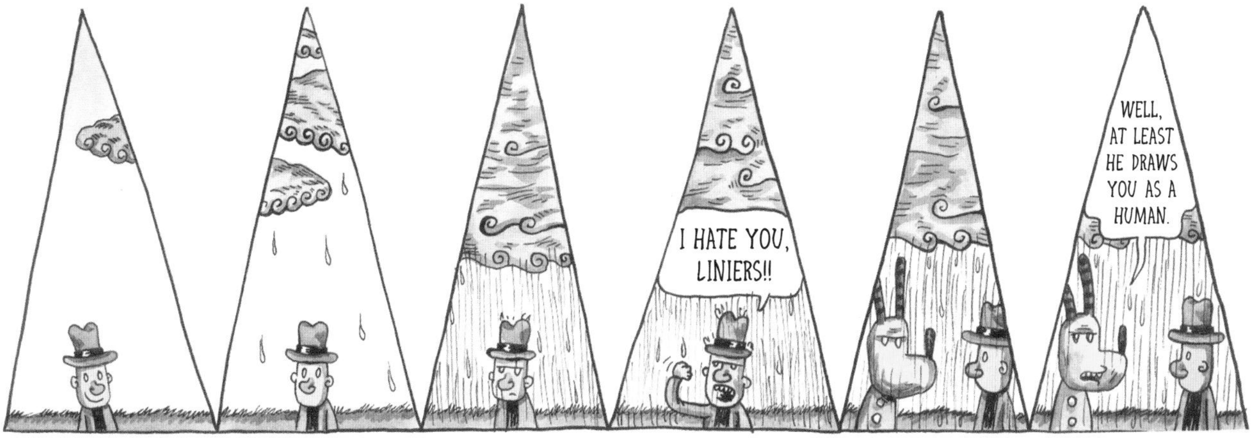
I HATE YOU, LINIERS!!
WELL, AT LEAST HE DRAWS YOU AS A HUMAN.

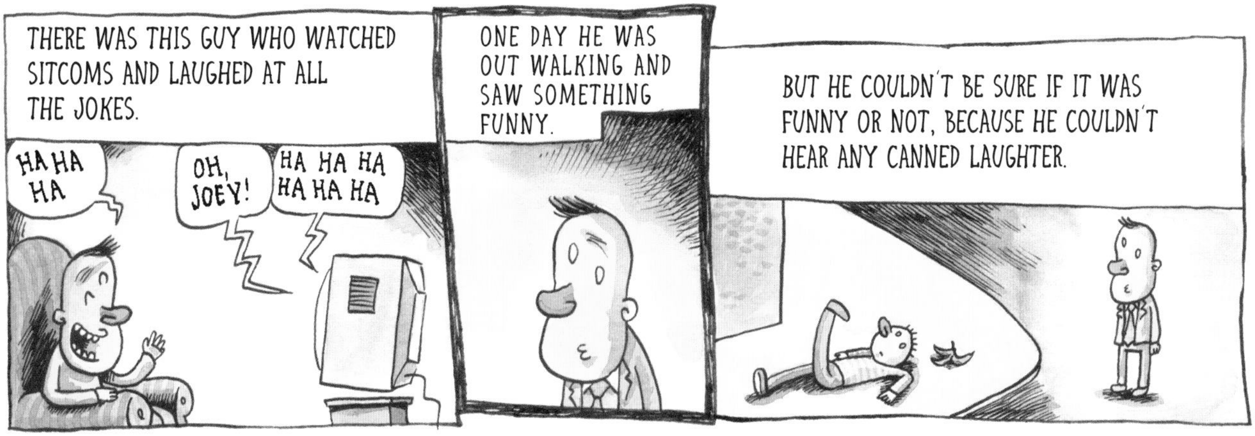
THERE WAS THIS GUY WHO WATCHED SITCOMS AND LAUGHED AT ALL THE JOKES.
HA HA HA
OH, JOEY!
HA HA HA HA HA HA
ONE DAY HE WAS OUT WALKING AND SAW SOMETHING FUNNY.
BUT HE COULDN'T BE SURE IF IT WAS FUNNY OR NOT, BECAUSE HE COULDN'T HEAR ANY CANNED LAUGHTER.

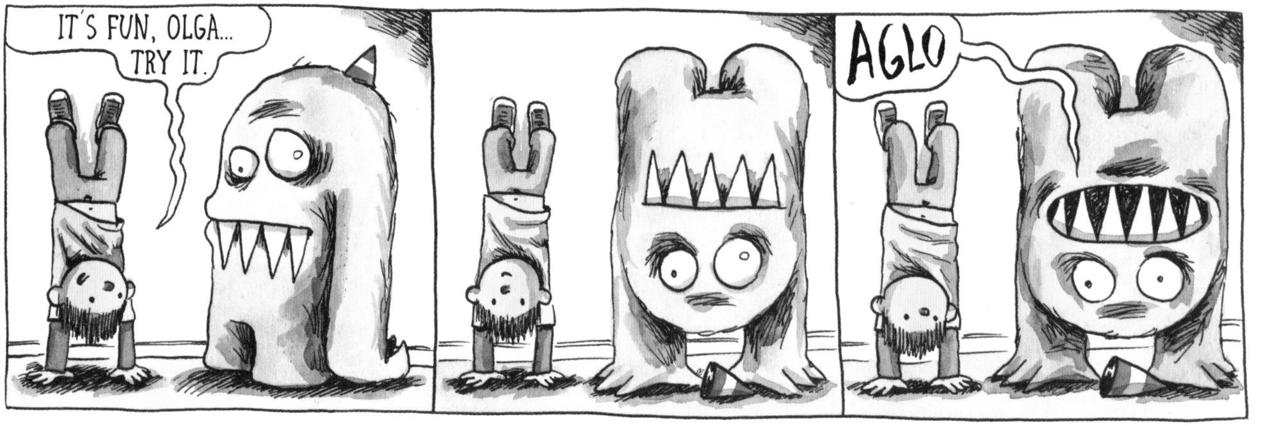
IT'S FUN, OLGA... TRY IT.
AGLO

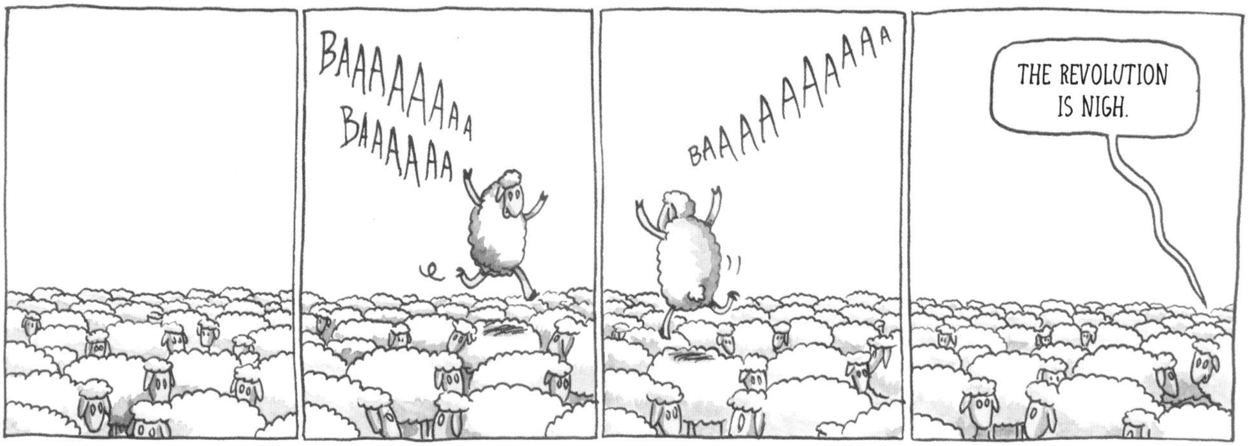
BAAAAAAAAA
BAAAAAA
BAAAAAAAAA
THE REVOLUTION IS NIGH.

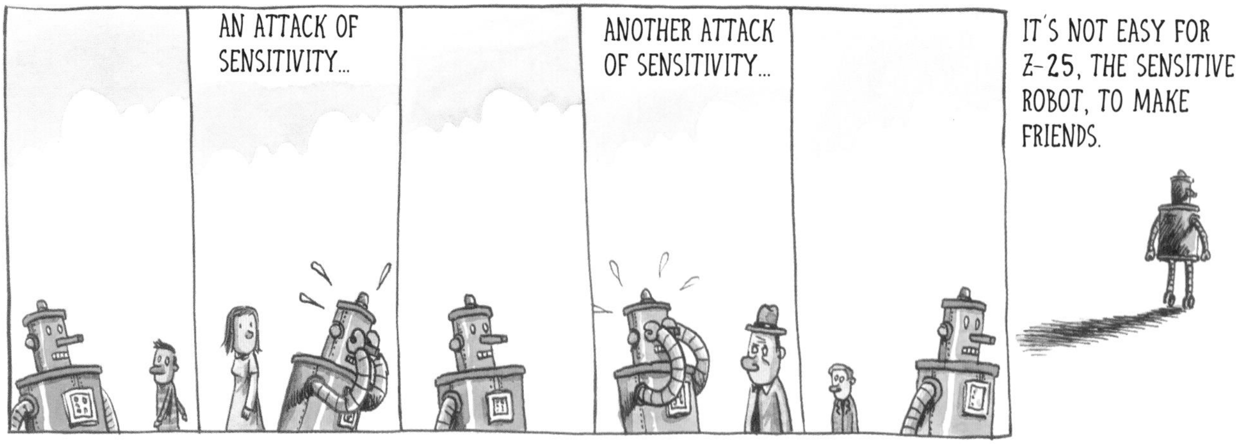
AN ATTACK OF SENSITIVITY...
ANOTHER ATTACK OF SENSITIVITY...
IT'S NOT EASY FOR Z-25, THE SENSITIVE ROBOT, TO MAKE FRIENDS.

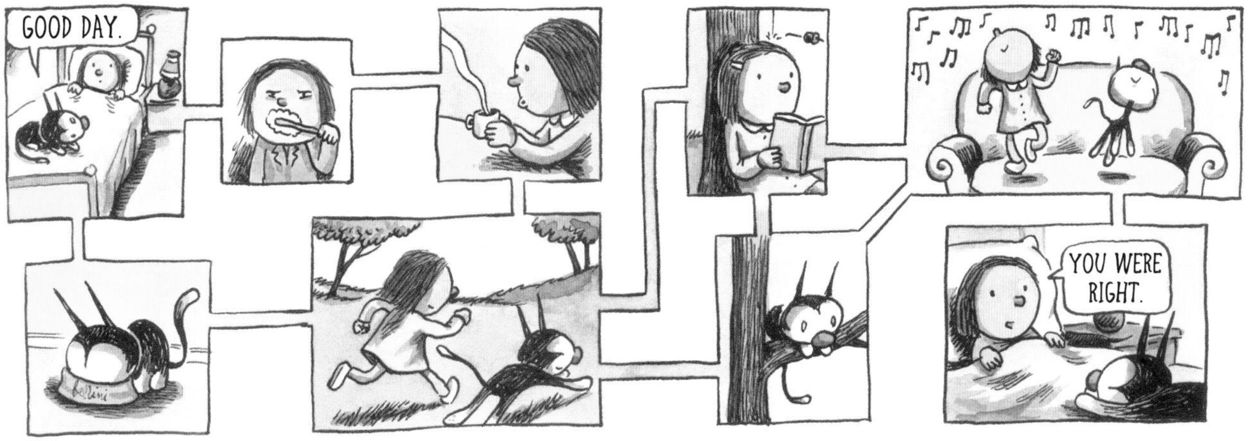
GOOD DAY.
YOU WERE RIGHT.

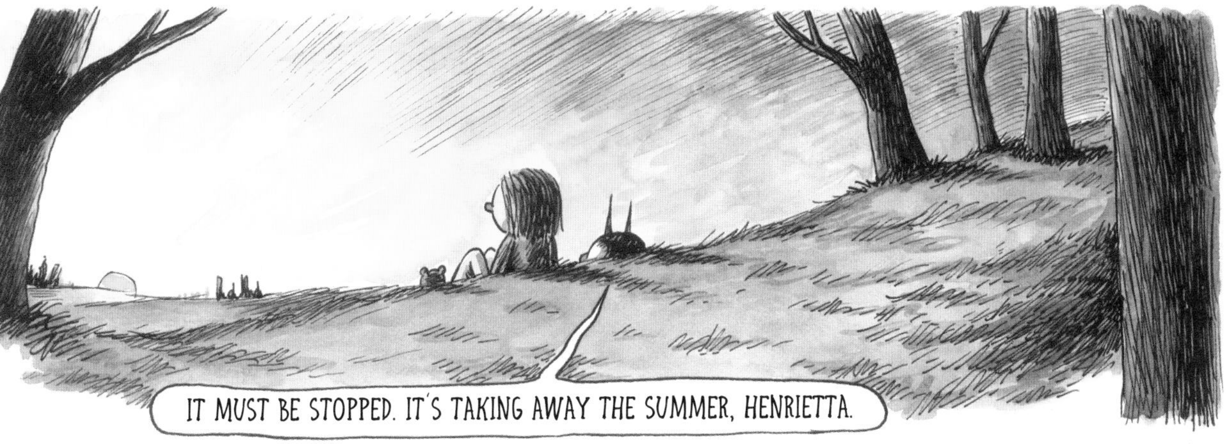
IT MUST BE STOPPED. IT'S TAKING AWAY THE SUMMER, HENRIETTA.

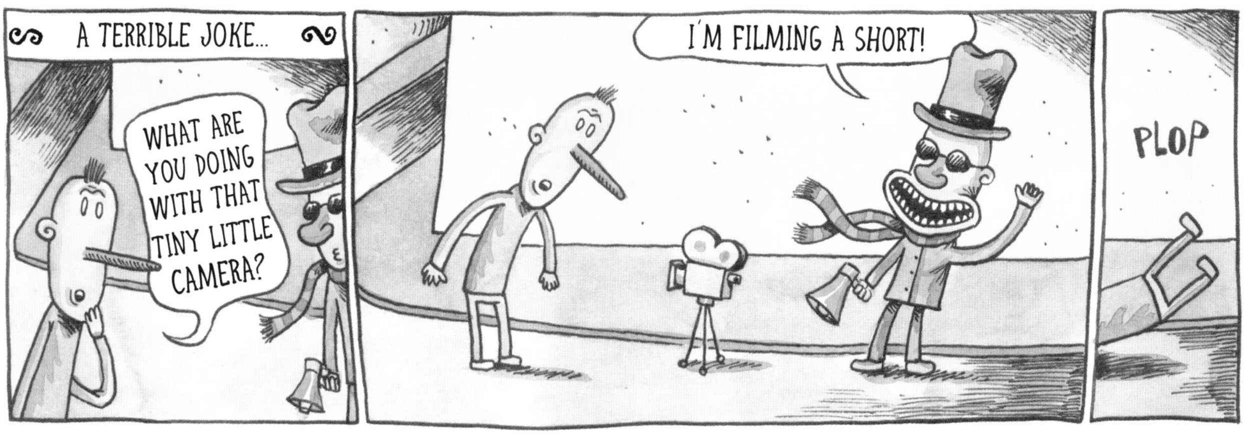
A TERRIBLE JOKE...
WHAT ARE YOU DOING WITH THAT TINY LITTLE CAMERA?
I'M FILMING A SHORT!
PLOP

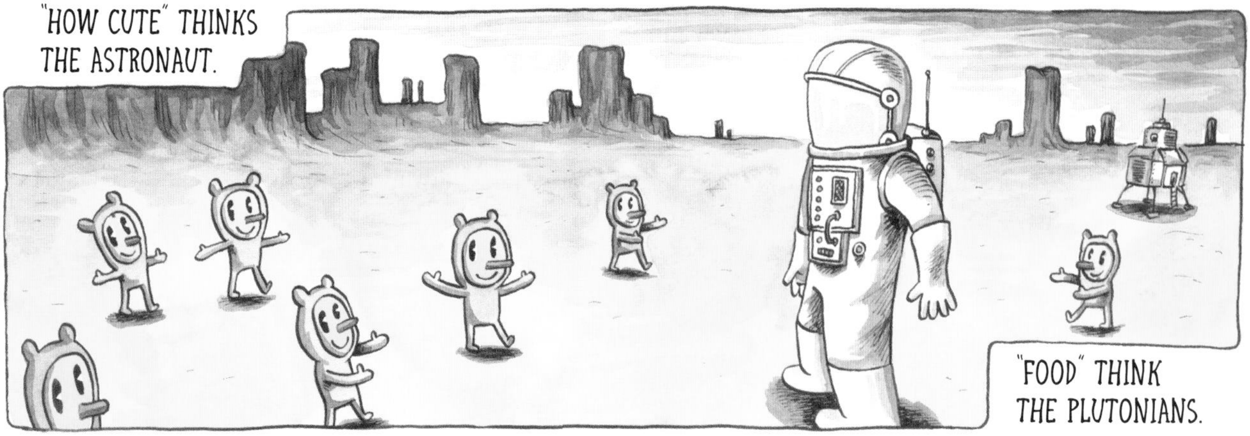
"HOW CUTE" THINKS THE ASTRONAUT.
"FOOD" THINK THE PLUTONIANS.

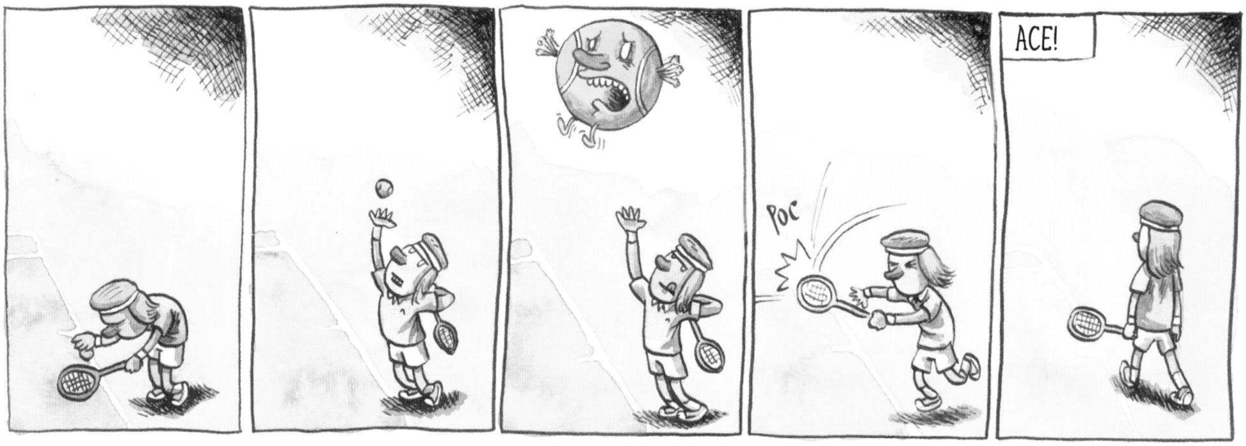
POC
ACE!

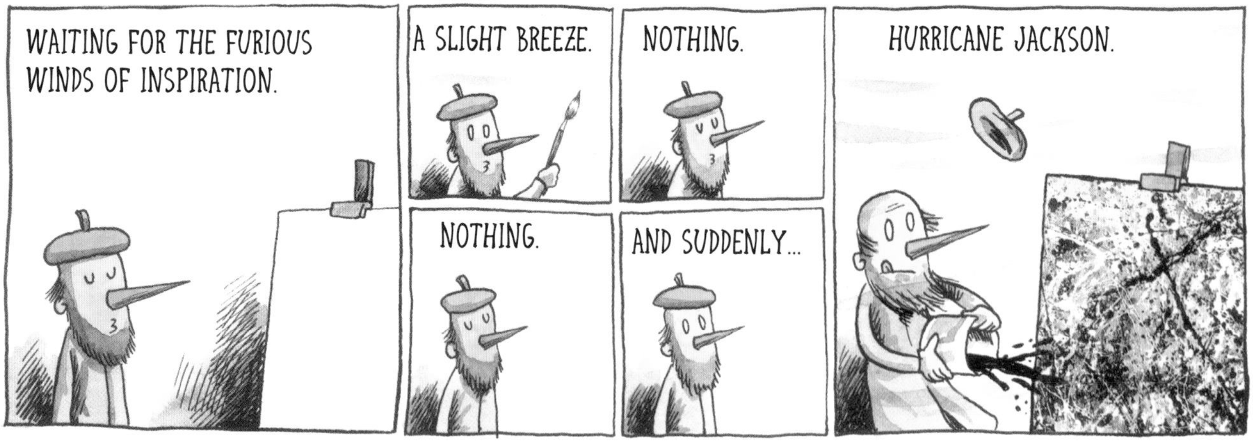
WAITING FOR THE FURIOUS WINDS OF INSPIRATION.
A SLIGHT BREEZE.
NOTHING.
NOTHING.
AND SUDDENLY...
HURRICANE JACKSON.

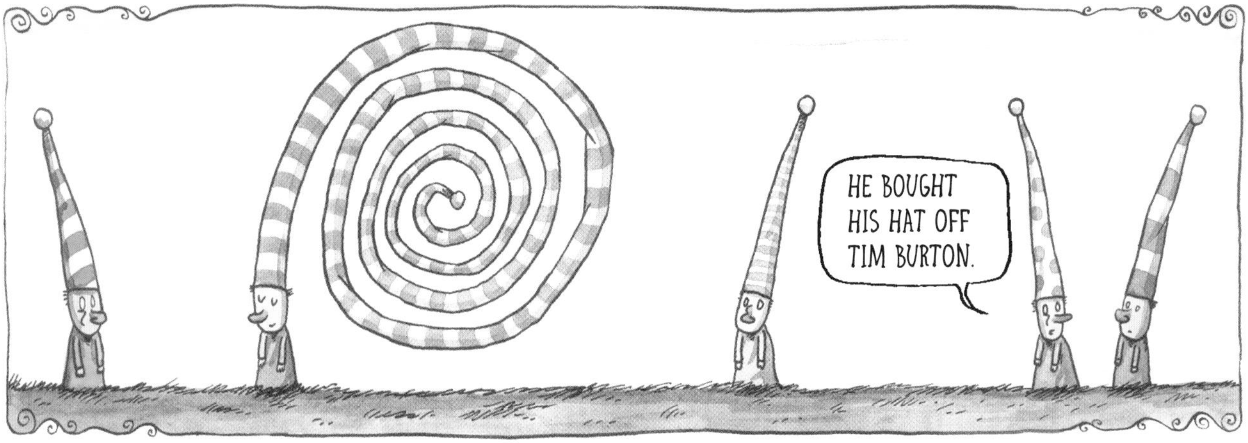
HE BOUGHT HIS HAT OFF TIM BURTON.

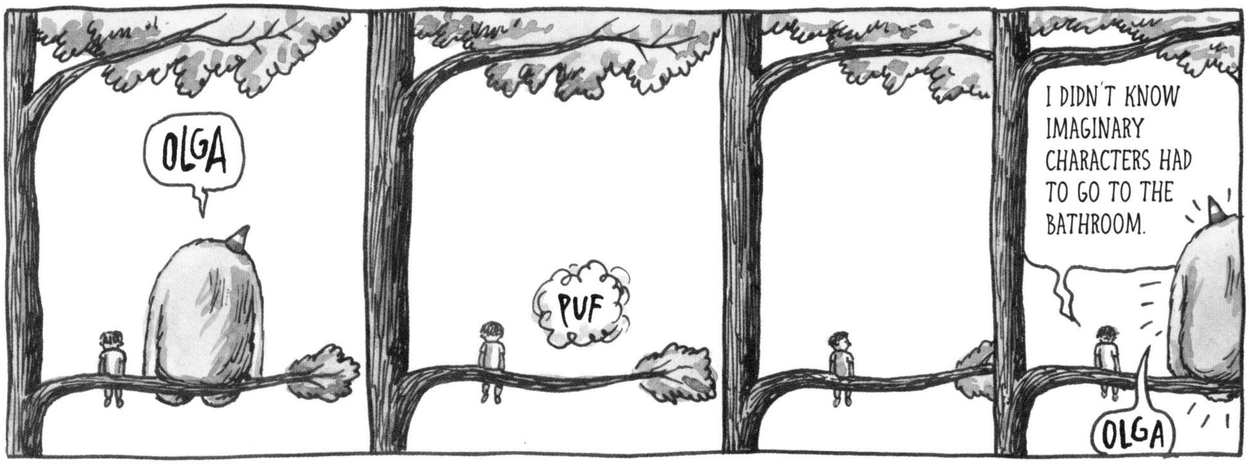
OLGA
PUF
I DIDN'T KNOW IMAGINARY CHARACTERS HAD TO GO TO THE BATHROOM.
OLGA

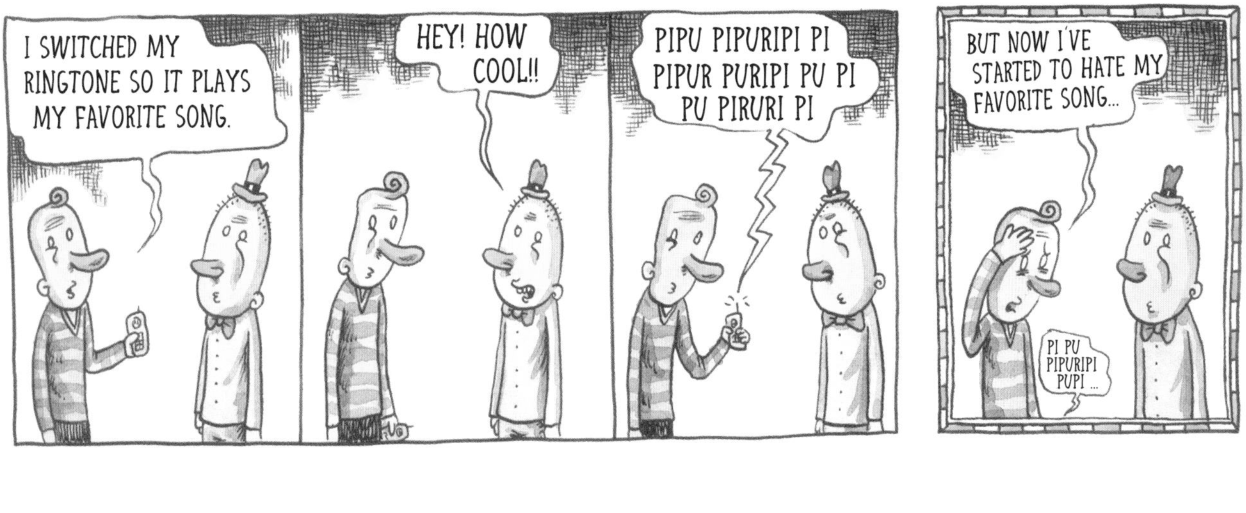
I SWITCHED MY RINGTONE SO IT PLAYS MY FAVORITE SONG.
HEY! HOW COOL!!
PIPU PIPURIPI PI PIPUR PURIPI PU PI PU PIRURI PI
BUT NOW I'VE STARTED TO HATE MY FAVORITE SONG...
PI PU PIPURIPI PUPI ...

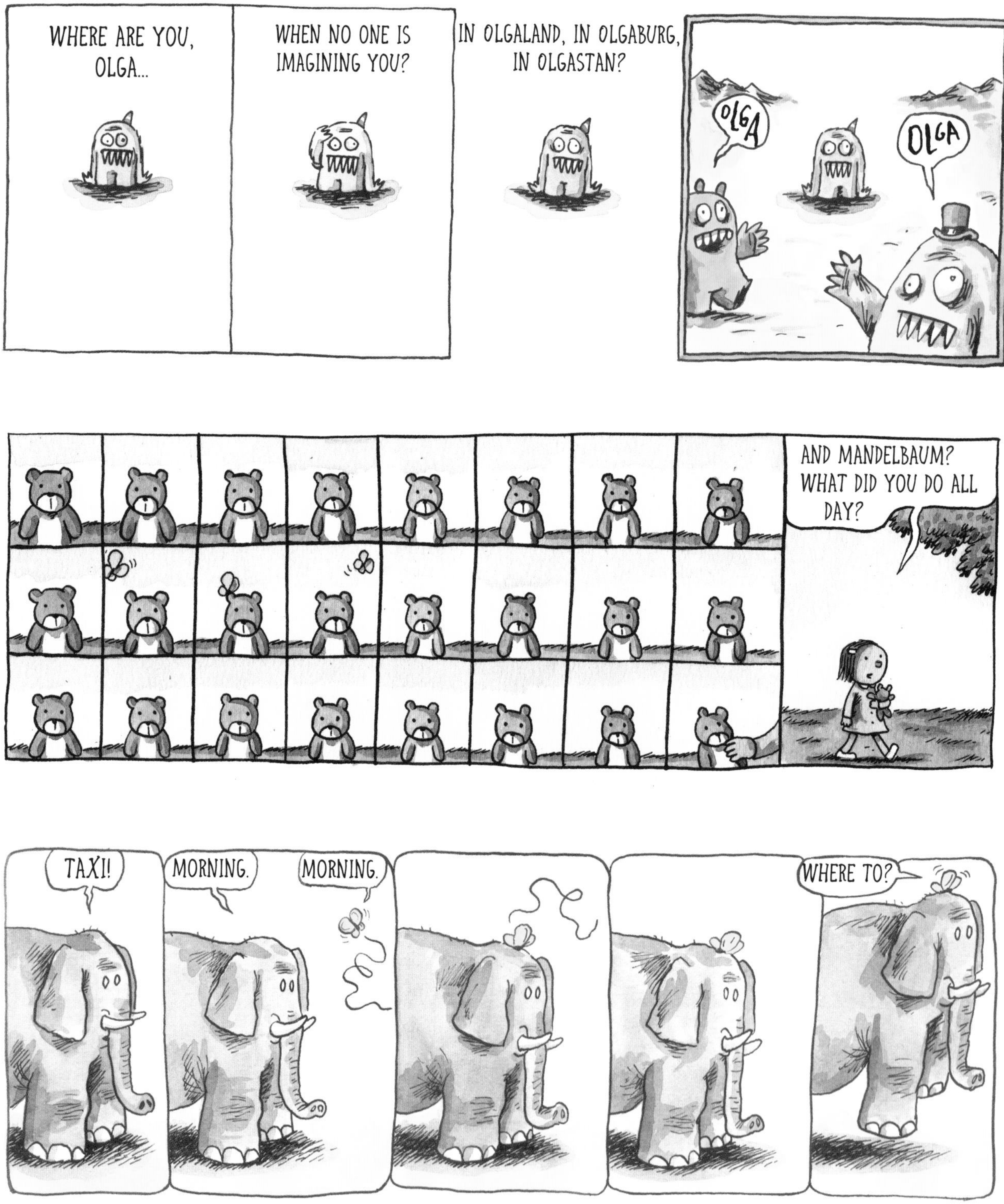
WHERE ARE YOU, OLGA...
WHEN NO ONE IS IMAGINING YOU?
IN OLGALAND, IN OLGABURG, IN OLGASTAN?
OLGA
OLGA
AND MANDELBAUM? WHAT DID YOU DO ALL DAY?
TAXI!
MORNING.
MORNING.
WHERE TO?

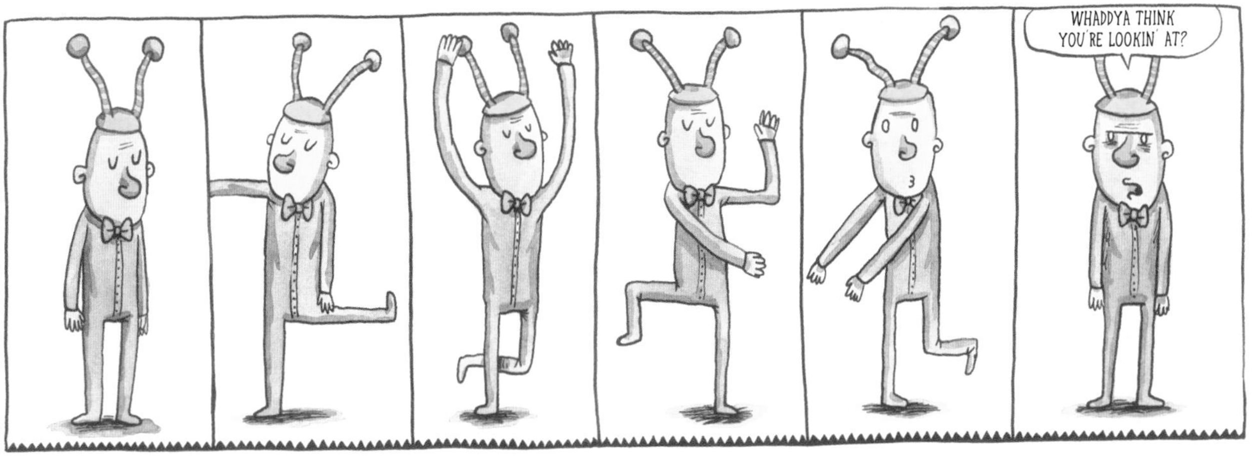
WHADDYA THINK YOU'RE LOOKIN' AT?

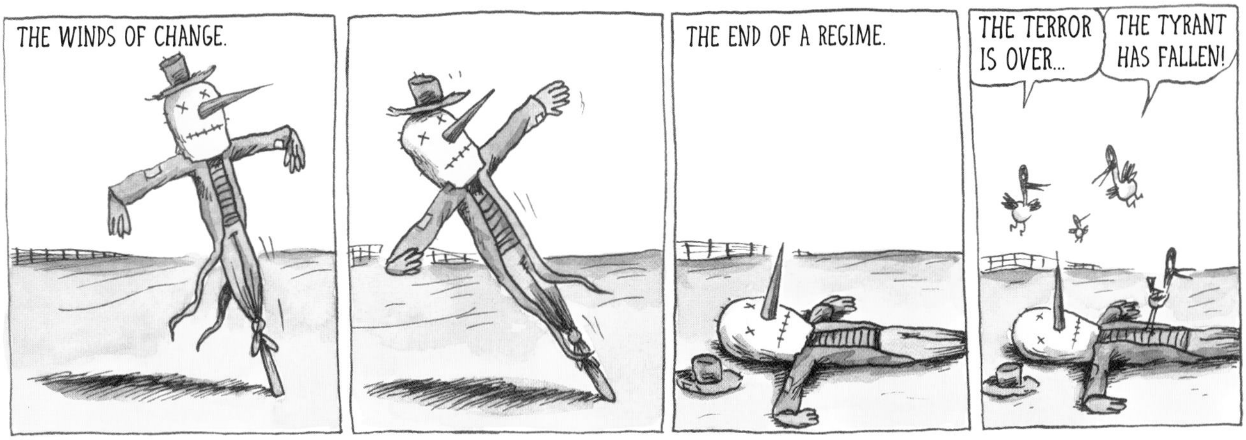
THE WINDS OF CHANGE.
THE END OF A REGIME.
THE TERROR IS OVER...
THE TYRANT HAS FALLEN!

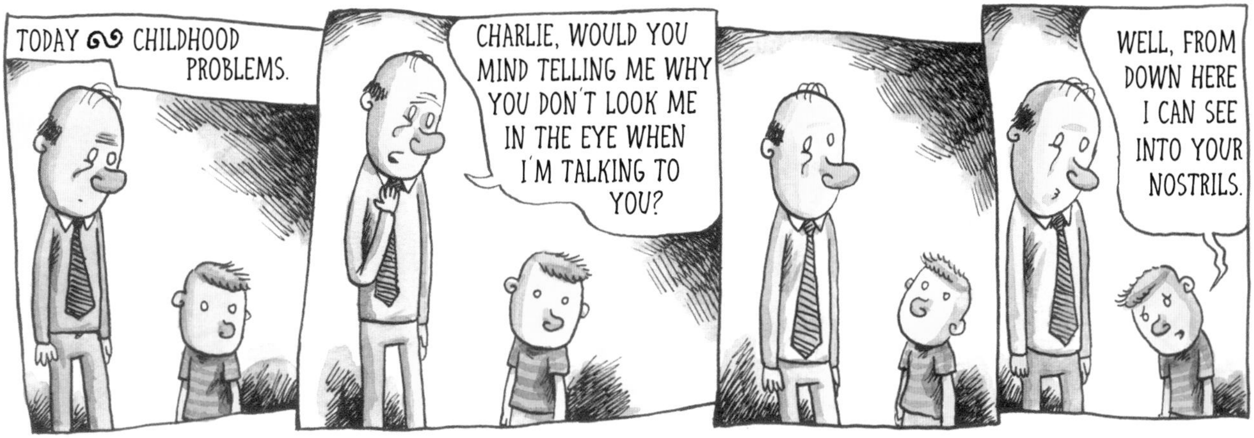
TODAY ᔕ CHILDHOOD PROBLEMS.
CHARLIE, WOULD YOU MIND TELLING ME WHY YOU DON'T LOOK ME IN THE EYE WHEN I'M TALKING TO YOU?
WELL, FROM DOWN HERE I CAN SEE INTO YOUR NOSTRILS.

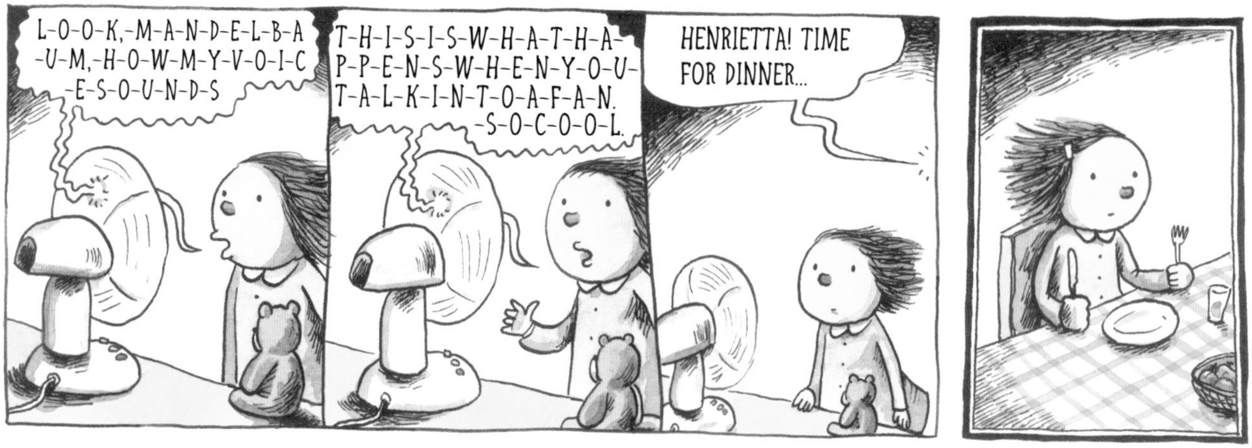
L-O-O-K,-M-A-N-D-E-L-B-A-U-M,-H-O-W-M-Y-V-O-I-C-E-S-O-U-N-D-S
T-H-I-S-I-S-W-H-A-T-H-A-P-P-E-N-S-W-H-E-N-Y-O-U-T-A-L-K-I-N-T-O-A-F-A-N. -S-O-C-O-O-L.
HENRIETTA! TIME FOR DINNER...

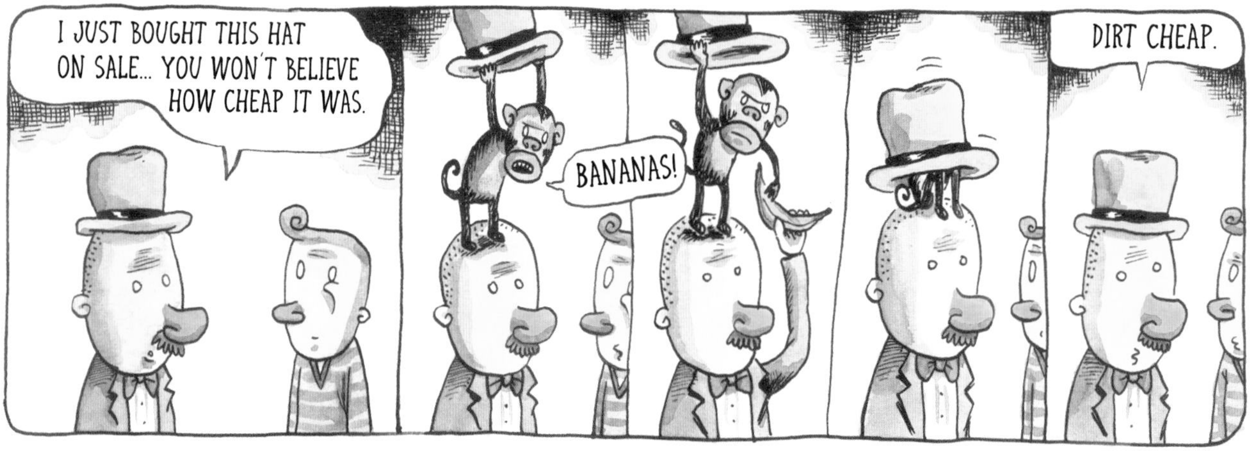
I JUST BOUGHT THIS HAT ON SALE... YOU WON'T BELIEVE HOW CHEAP IT WAS.
BANANAS!
DIRT CHEAP.

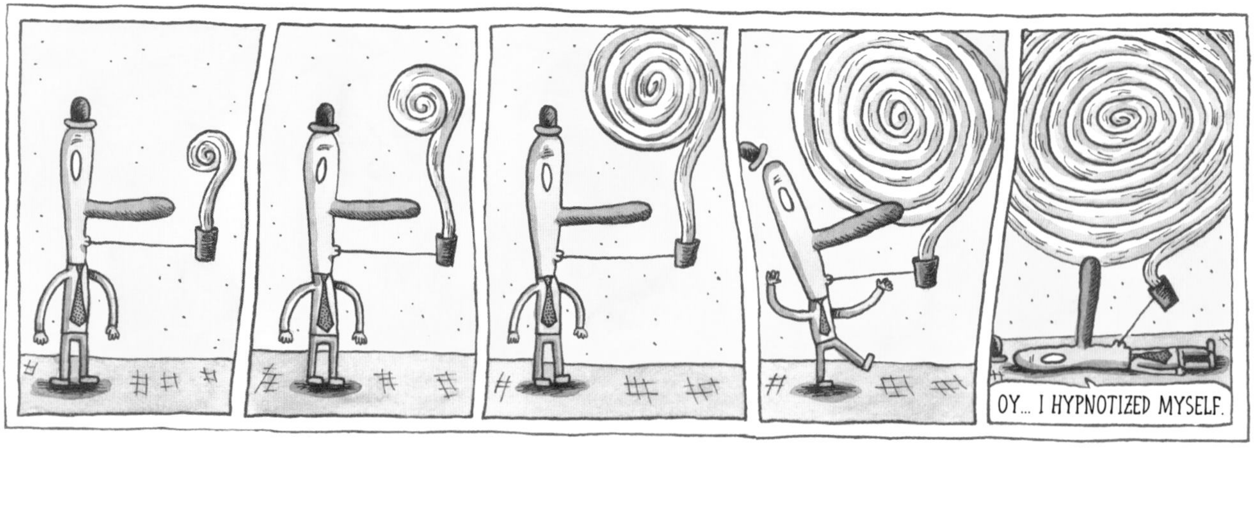
OY... I HYPNOTIZED MYSELF.

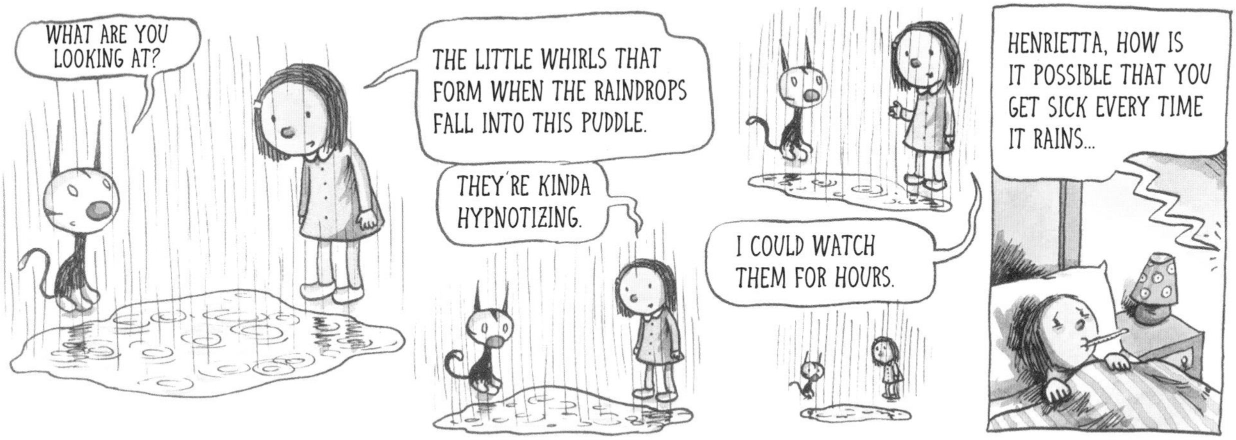
WHAT ARE YOU LOOKING AT?
THE LITTLE WHIRLS THAT FORM WHEN THE RAINDROPS FALL INTO THIS PUDDLE.
THEY'RE KINDA HYPNOTIZING.
I COULD WATCH THEM FOR HOURS.
HENRIETTA, HOW IS IT POSSIBLE THAT YOU GET SICK EVERY TIME IT RAINS...

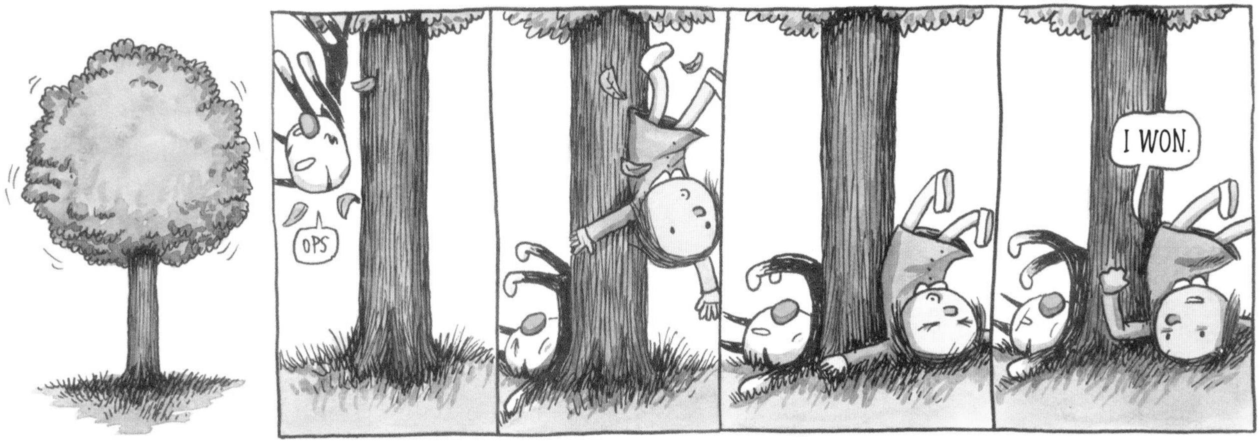
OPS
I WON.

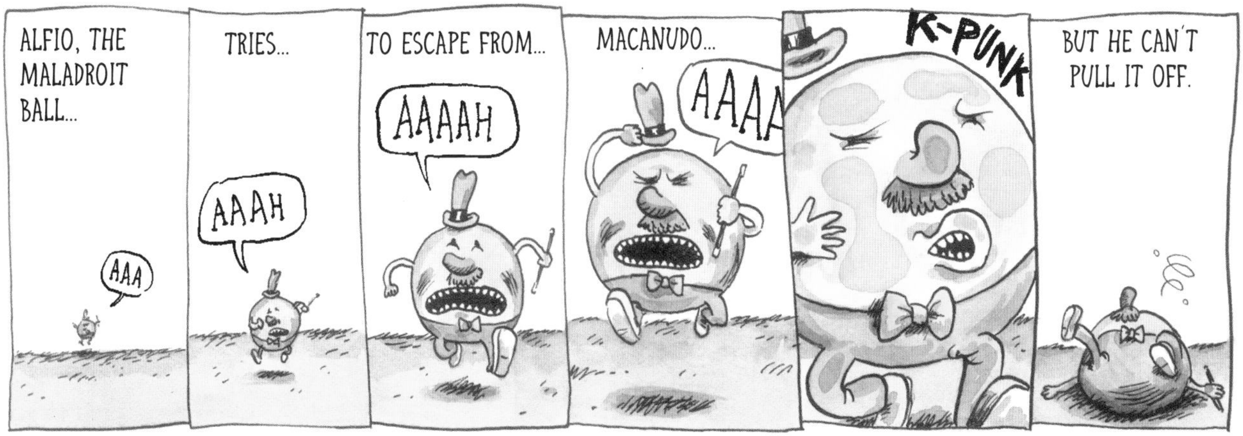
ALFIO, THE MALADROIT BALL...
AAA
TRIES...
AAAH
TO ESCAPE FROM...
AAAAH
MACANUDO...
AAAA
K-PUNK
BUT HE CAN'T PULL IT OFF.

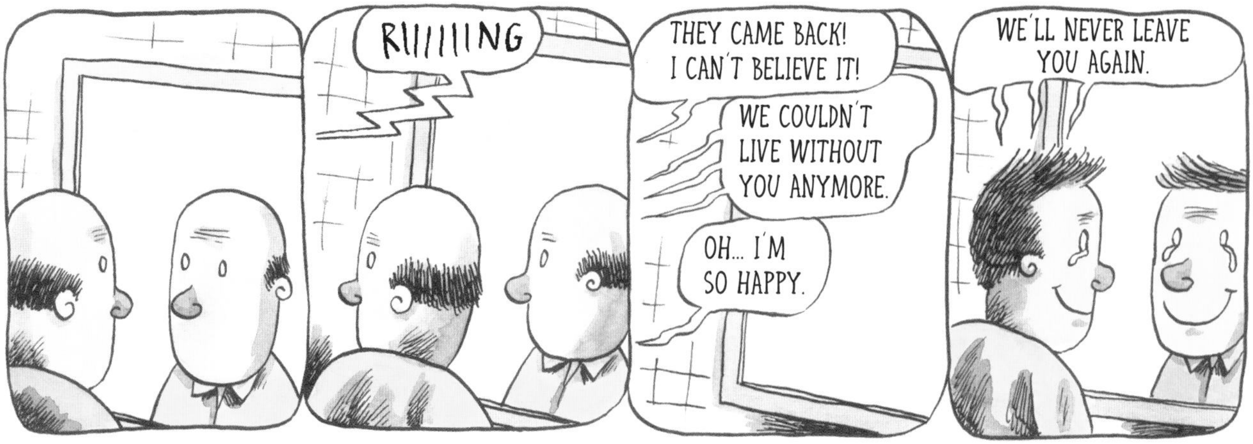
RIIIIIING
THEY CAME BACK! I CAN'T BELIEVE IT!
WE COULDN'T LIVE WITHOUT YOU ANYMORE.
OH... I'M SO HAPPY.
WE'LL NEVER LEAVE YOU AGAIN.

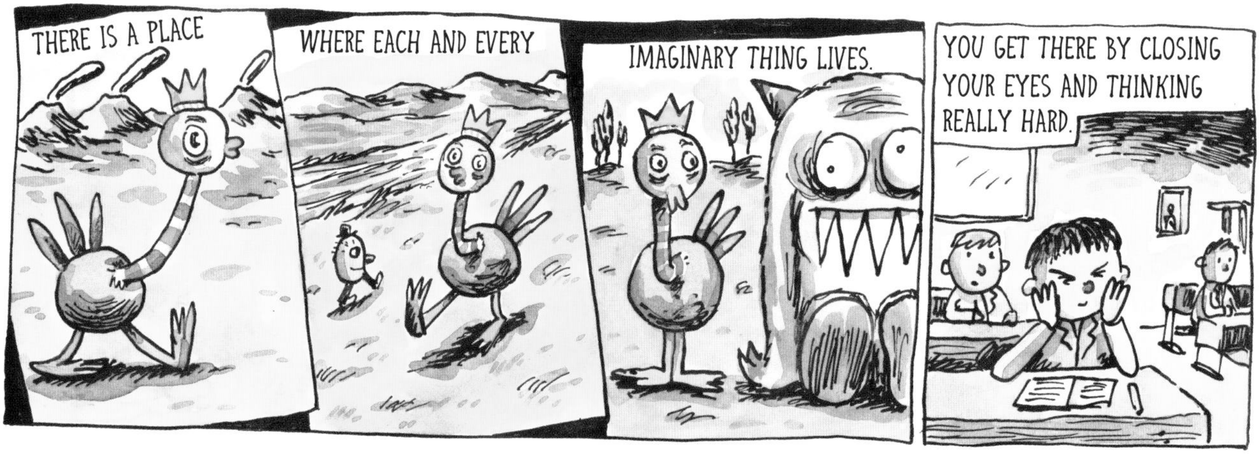
THERE IS A PLACE
WHERE EACH AND EVERY
IMAGINARY THING LIVES.
YOU GET THERE BY CLOSING YOUR EYES AND THINKING REALLY HARD.

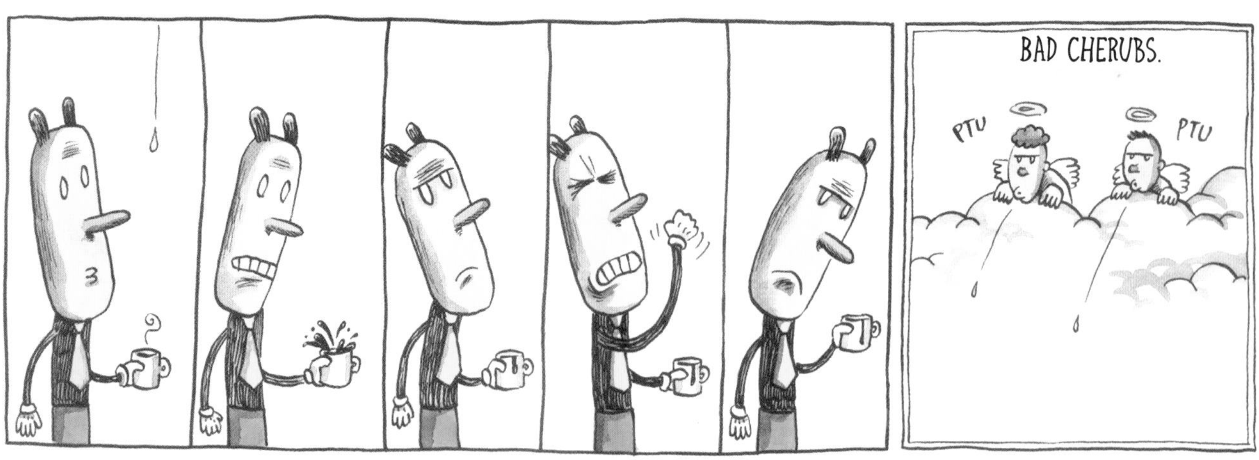
BAD CHERUBS.
PTU
PTU

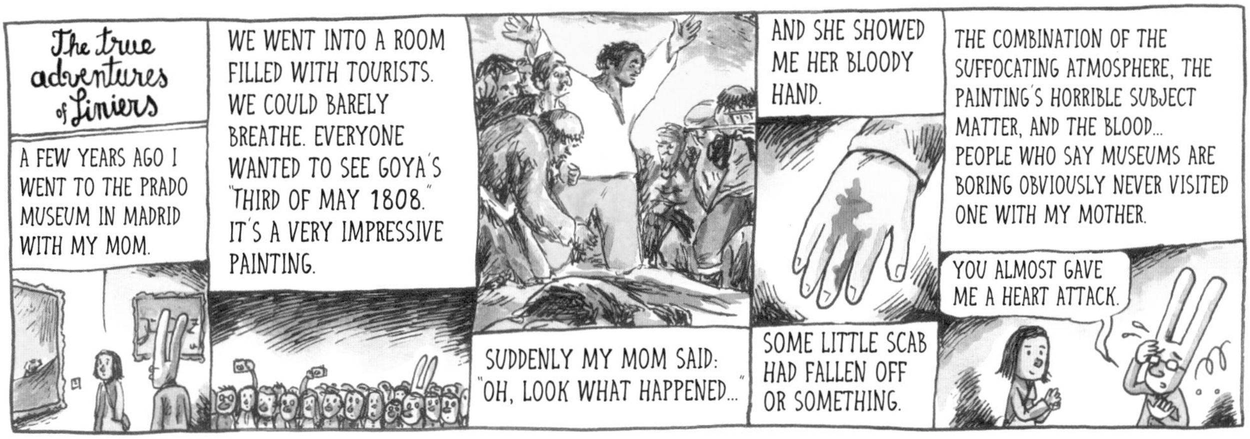
The true adventures of Liniers
A FEW YEARS AGO I WENT TO THE PRADO MUSEUM IN MADRID WITH MY MOM.
WE WENT INTO A ROOM FILLED WITH TOURISTS. WE COULD BARELY BREATHE. EVERYONE WANTED TO SEE GOYA'S "THIRD OF MAY 1808." IT'S A VERY IMPRESSIVE PAINTING.
SUDDENLY MY MOM SAID: "OH, LOOK WHAT HAPPENED..."
AND SHE SHOWED ME HER BLOODY HAND.
SOME LITTLE SCAB HAD FALLEN OFF OR SOMETHING.
THE COMBINATION OF THE SUFFOCATING ATMOSPHERE, THE PAINTING'S HORRIBLE SUBJECT MATTER, AND THE BLOOD... PEOPLE WHO SAY MUSEUMS ARE BORING OBVIOUSLY NEVER VISITED ONE WITH MY MOTHER.
YOU ALMOST GAVE ME A HEART ATTACK.

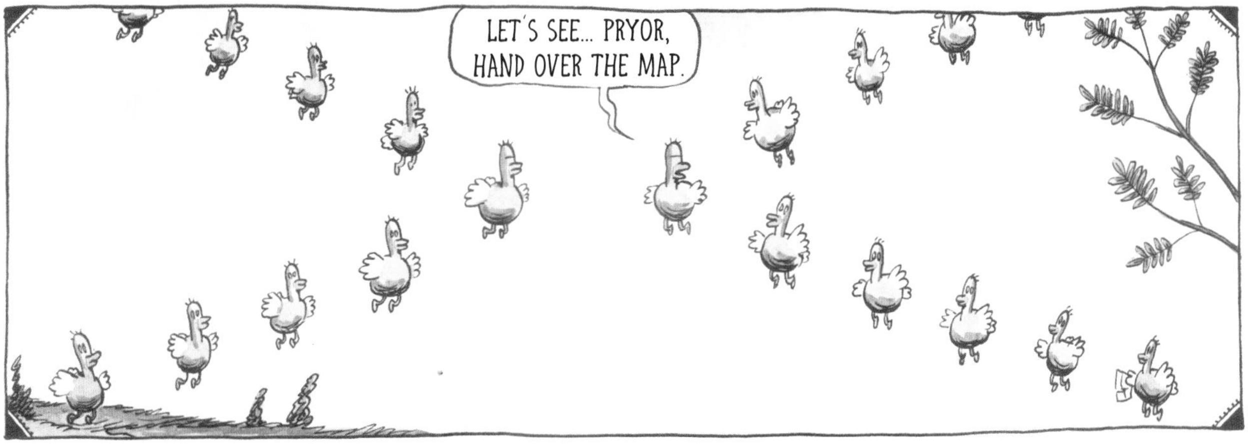
LET'S SEE... PRYOR, HAND OVER THE MAP.

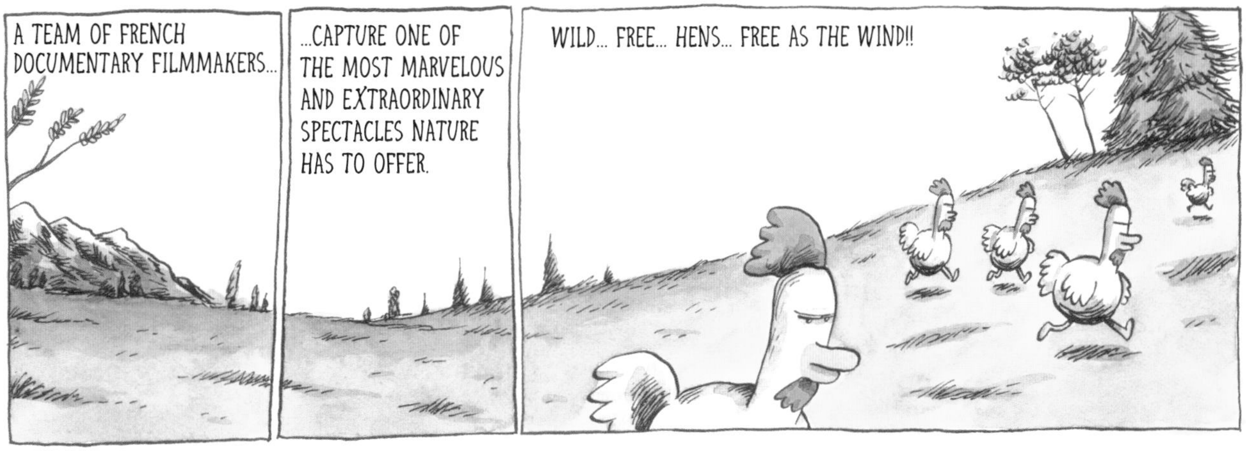
A TEAM OF FRENCH DOCUMENTARY FILMMAKERS...
...CAPTURE ONE OF THE MOST MARVELOUS AND EXTRAORDINARY SPECTACLES NATURE HAS TO OFFER.
WILD... FREE... HENS... FREE AS THE WIND!!

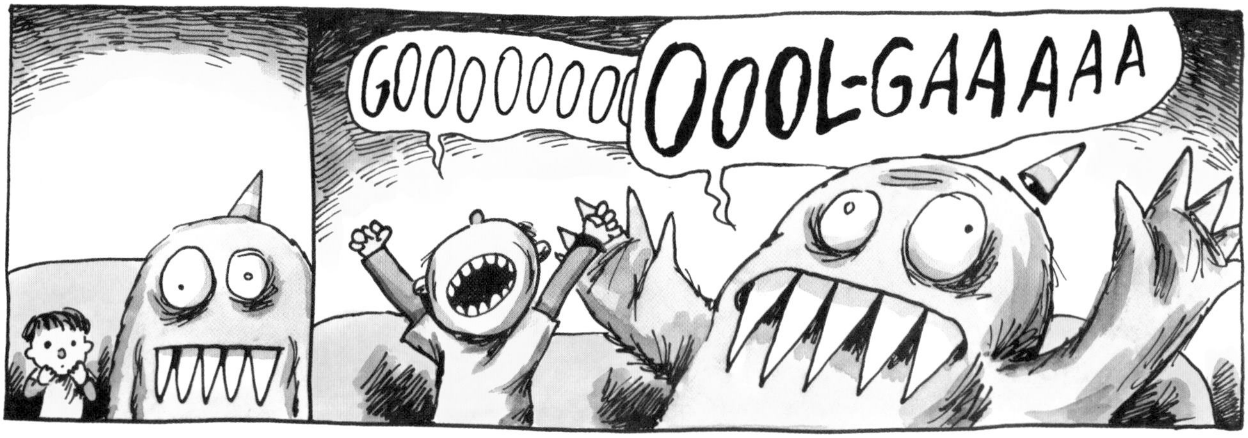
GOOOOOOOO
OOOL-GAAAAA

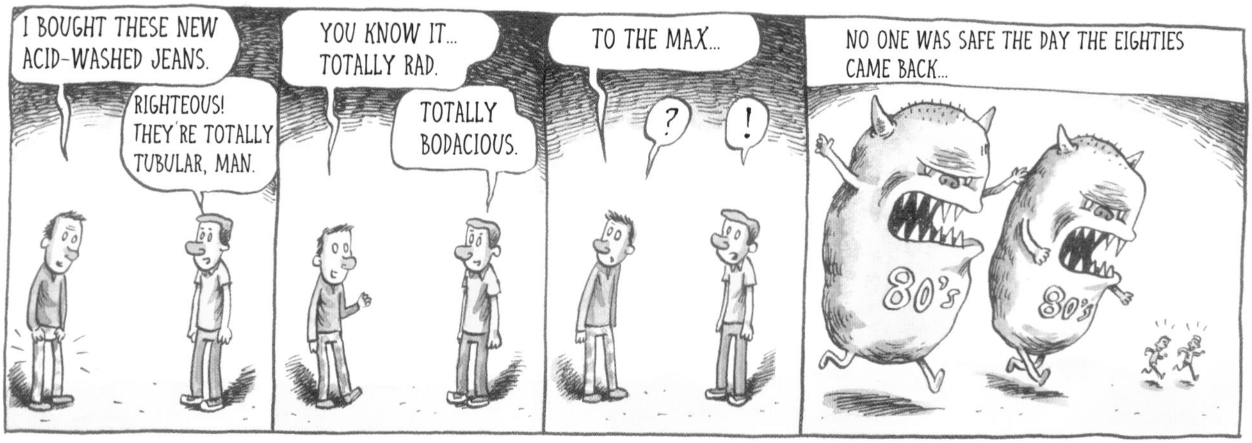
I BOUGHT THESE NEW ACID-WASHED JEANS.
RIGHTEOUS! THEY'RE TOTALLY TUBULAR, MAN.
YOU KNOW IT... TOTALLY RAD.
TOTALLY BODACIOUS.
TO THE MAX...
?
!
NO ONE WAS SAFE THE DAY THE EIGHTIES CAME BACK...
80's
80's

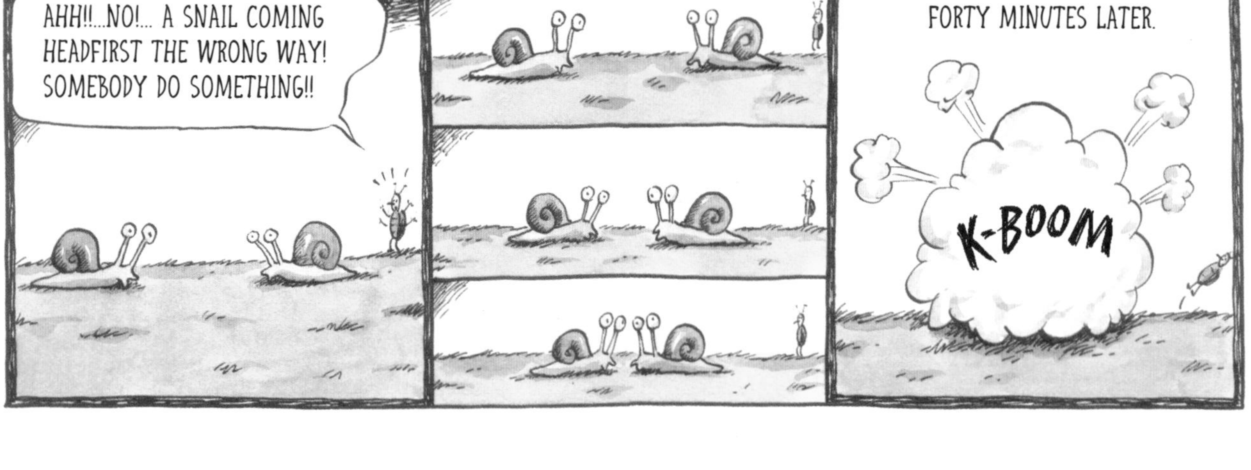
AHH!!...NO!... A SNAIL COMING HEADFIRST THE WRONG WAY! SOMEBODY DO SOMETHING!!
FORTY MINUTES LATER.
K-BOOM

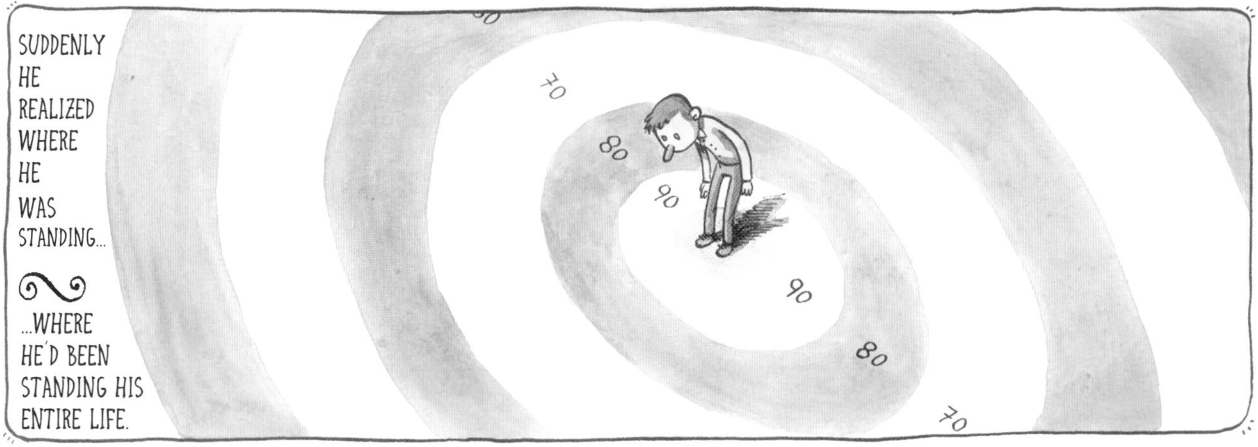
SUDDENLY HE REALIZED WHERE HE WAS STANDING...
...WHERE HE'D BEEN STANDING HIS ENTIRE LIFE.
70
80
90
90
80
70

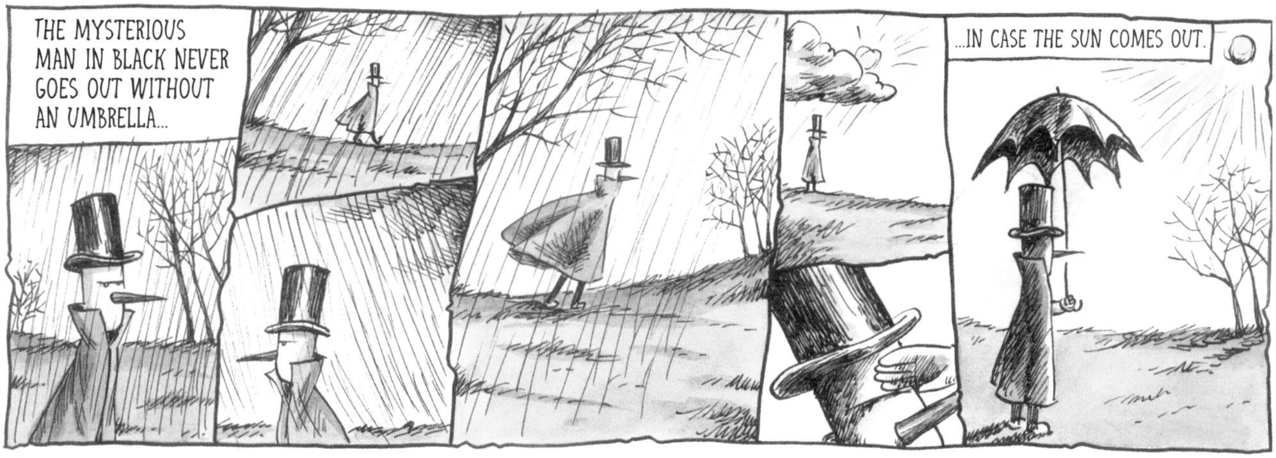
THE MYSTERIOUS MAN IN BLACK NEVER GOES OUT WITHOUT AN UMBRELLA...
...IN CASE THE SUN COMES OUT.

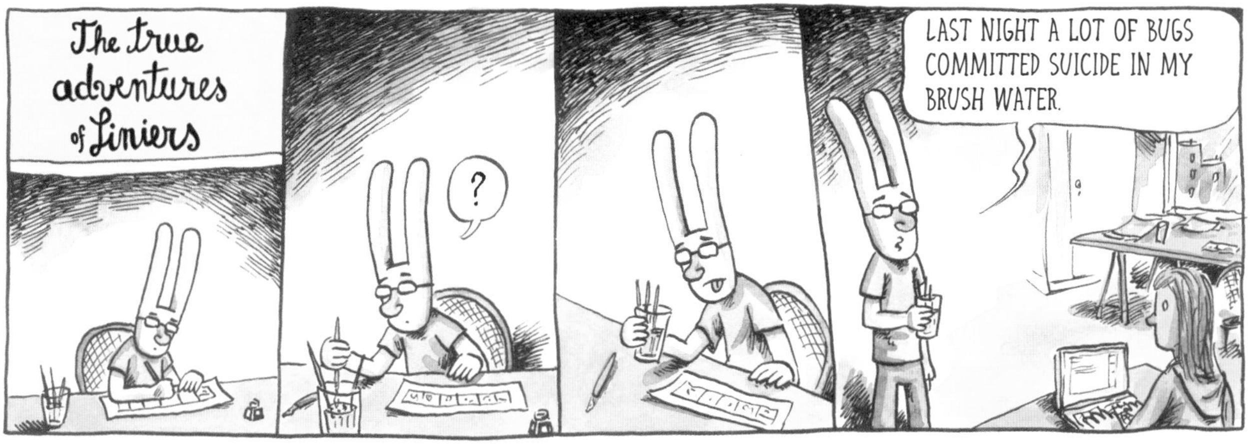
The true adventures of Liniers
?
LAST NIGHT A LOT OF BUGS COMMITTED SUICIDE IN MY BRUSH WATER.

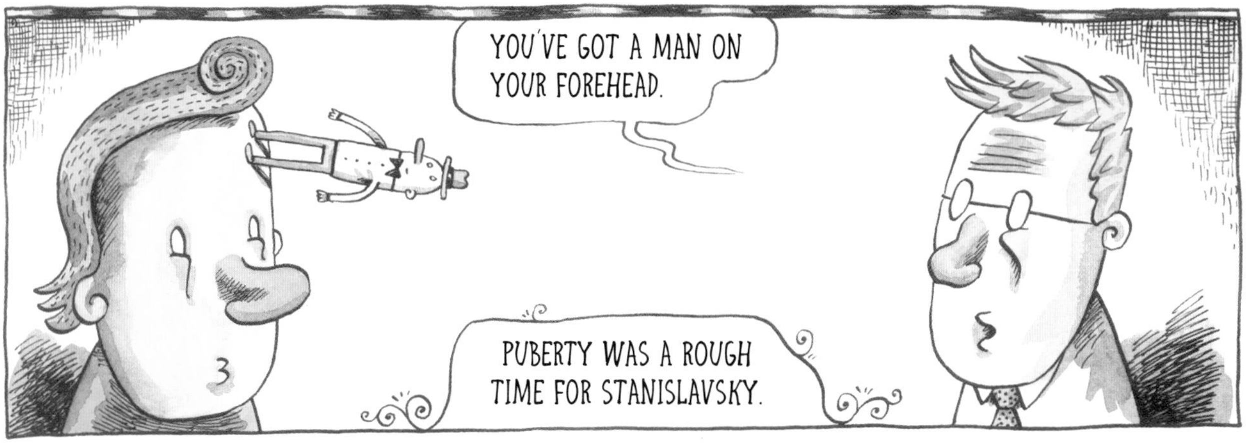
YOU'VE GOT A MAN ON YOUR FOREHEAD.
PUBERTY WAS A ROUGH TIME FOR STANISLAVSKY.

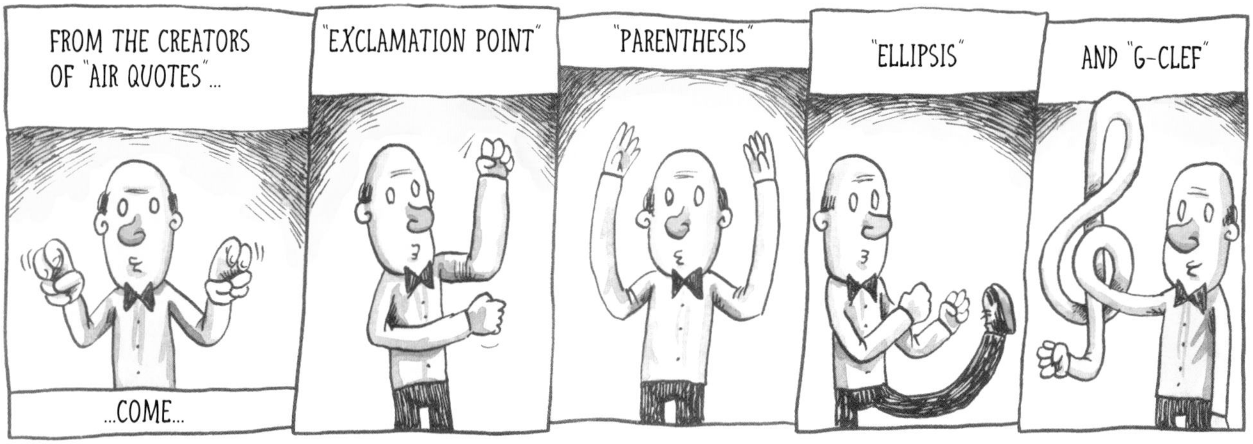
FROM THE CREATORS OF "AIR QUOTES"...
...COME...
"EXCLAMATION POINT"
"PARENTHESIS"
"ELLIPSIS"
AND "G-CLEF"

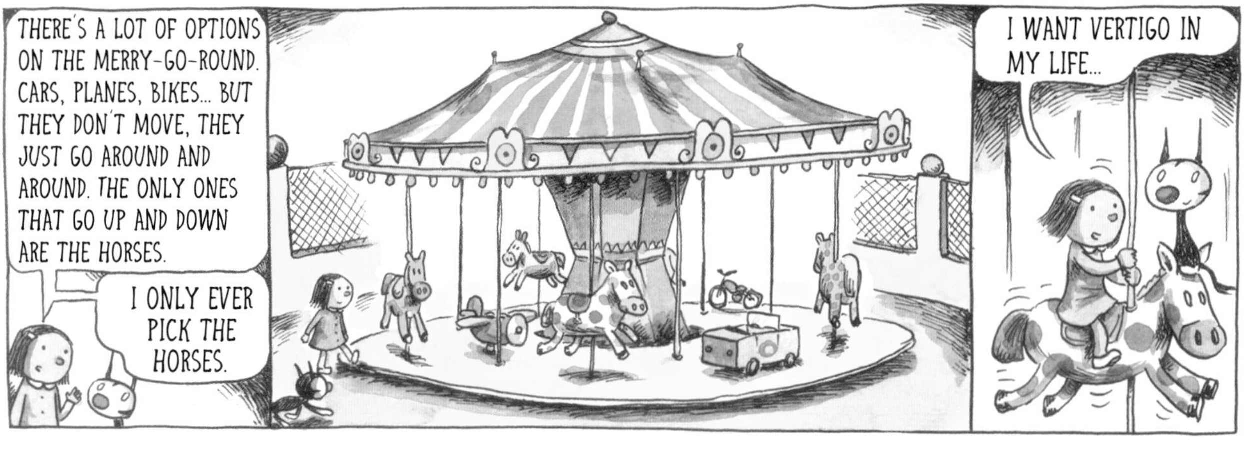
THERE'S A LOT OF OPTIONS ON THE MERRY-GO-ROUND. CARS, PLANES, BIKES... BUT THEY DON'T MOVE, THEY JUST GO AROUND AND AROUND. THE ONLY ONES THAT GO UP AND DOWN ARE THE HORSES.
I ONLY EVER PICK THE HORSES.
I WANT VERTIGO IN MY LIFE...

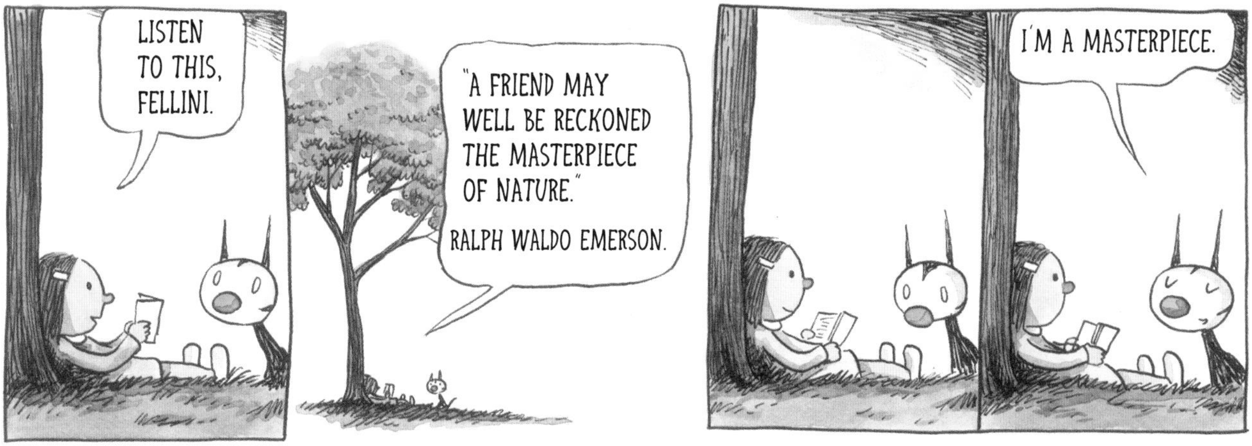
LISTEN TO THIS, FELLINI.
"A FRIEND MAY WELL BE RECKONED THE MASTERPIECE OF NATURE."
RALPH WALDO EMERSON.
I'M A MASTERPIECE.

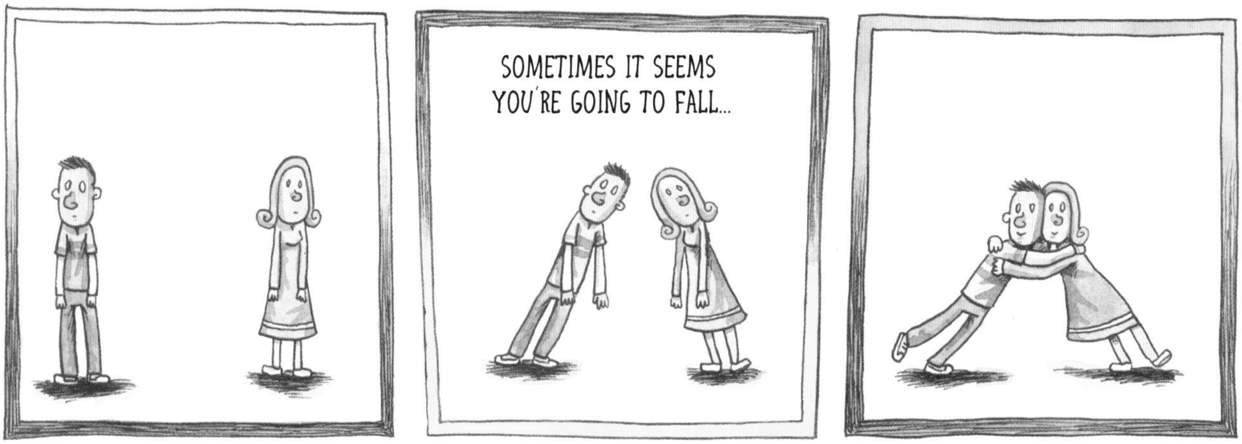
SOMETIMES IT SEEMS YOU'RE GOING TO FALL...

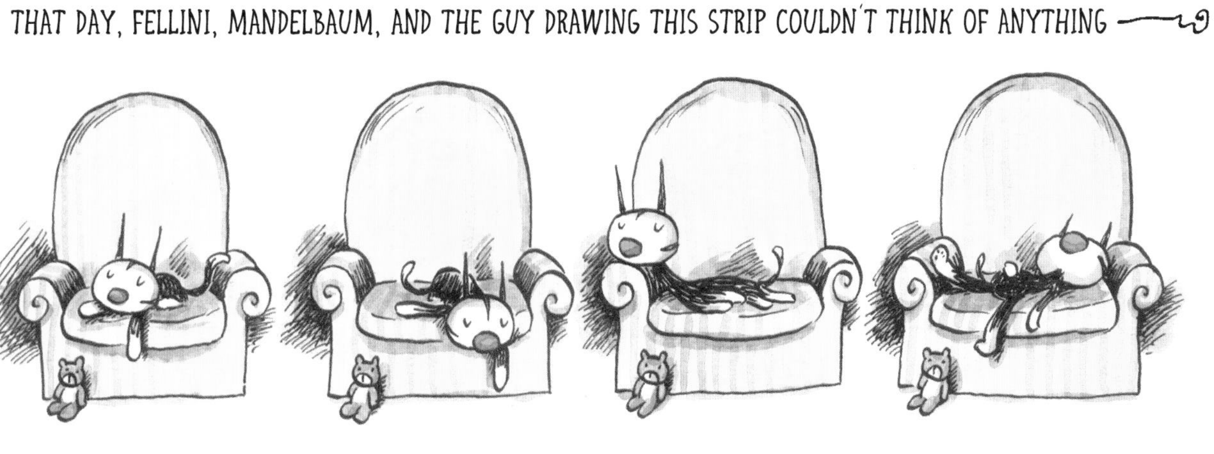
THAT DAY, FELLINI, MANDELBAUM, AND THE GUY DRAWING THIS STRIP COULDN'T THINK OF ANYTHING

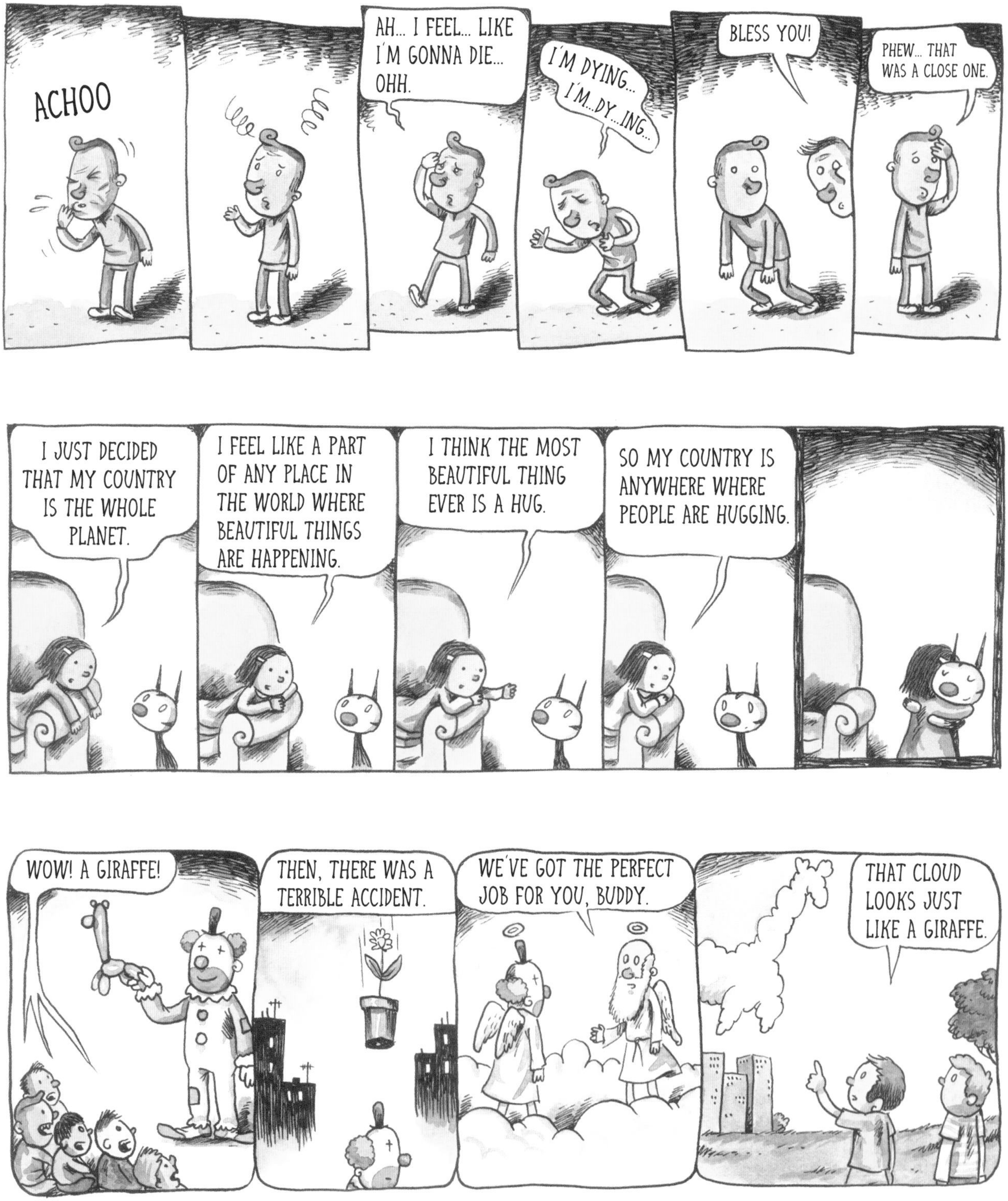
ACHOO
AH... I FEEL... LIKE I'M GONNA DIE... OHH.
I'M DYING... I'M...DY...ING...
BLESS YOU!
PHEW... THAT WAS A CLOSE ONE.
I JUST DECIDED THAT MY COUNTRY IS THE WHOLE PLANET.
I FEEL LIKE A PART OF ANY PLACE IN THE WORLD WHERE BEAUTIFUL THINGS ARE HAPPENING.
I THINK THE MOST BEAUTIFUL THING EVER IS A HUG.
SO MY COUNTRY IS ANYWHERE WHERE PEOPLE ARE HUGGING.
WOW! A GIRAFFE!
THEN, THERE WAS A TERRIBLE ACCIDENT.
WE'VE GOT THE PERFECT JOB FOR YOU, BUDDY.
THAT CLOUD LOOKS JUST LIKE A GIRAFFE.

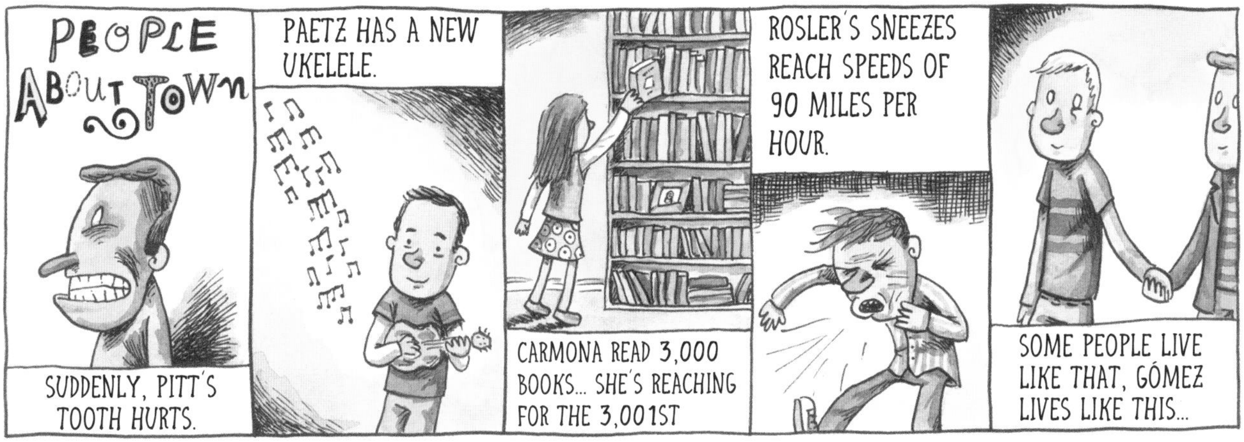
PEOPLE ABOUT TOWN
SUDDENLY, PITT'S TOOTH HURTS.
PAETZ HAS A NEW UKELELE.
CARMONA READ 3,000 BOOKS... SHE'S REACHING FOR THE 3,001ST
ROSLER'S SNEEZES REACH SPEEDS OF 90 MILES PER HOUR.
SOME PEOPLE LIVE LIKE THAT, GÓMEZ LIVES LIKE THIS...

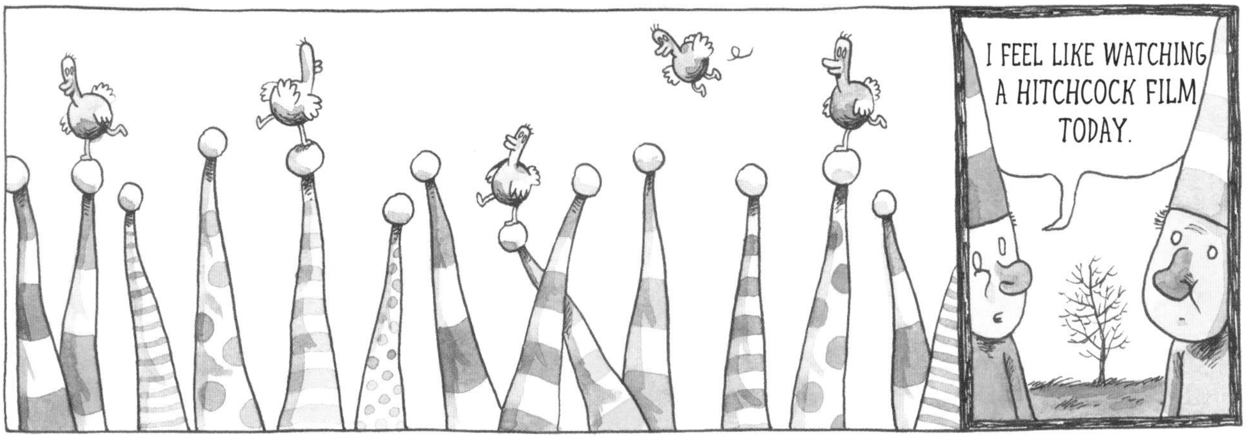
I FEEL LIKE WATCHING A HITCHCOCK FILM TODAY.

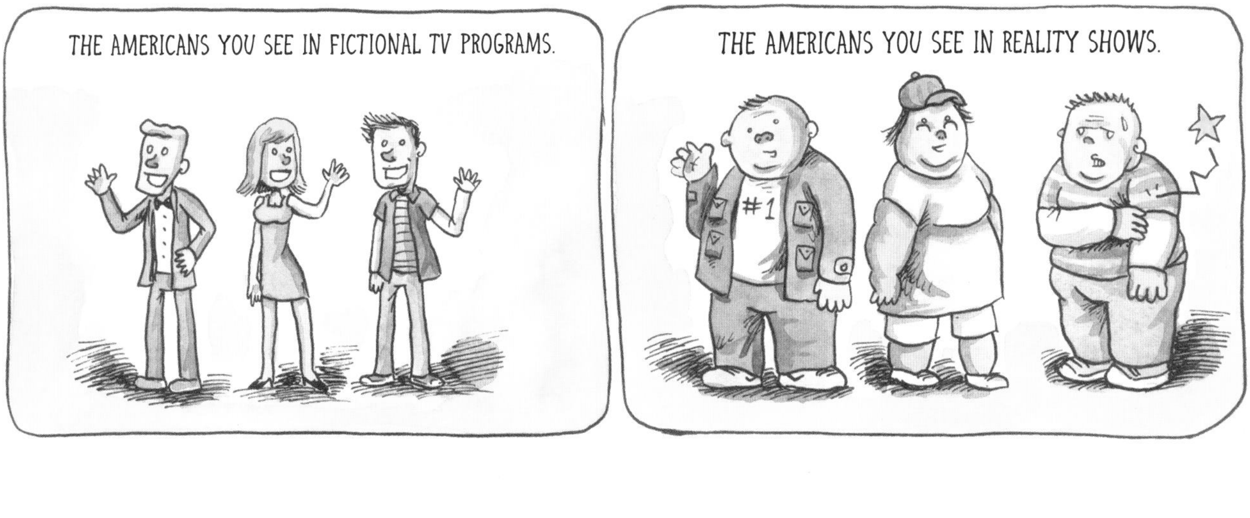
THE AMERICANS YOU SEE IN FICTIONAL TV PROGRAMS.
THE AMERICANS YOU SEE IN REALITY SHOWS.
#1

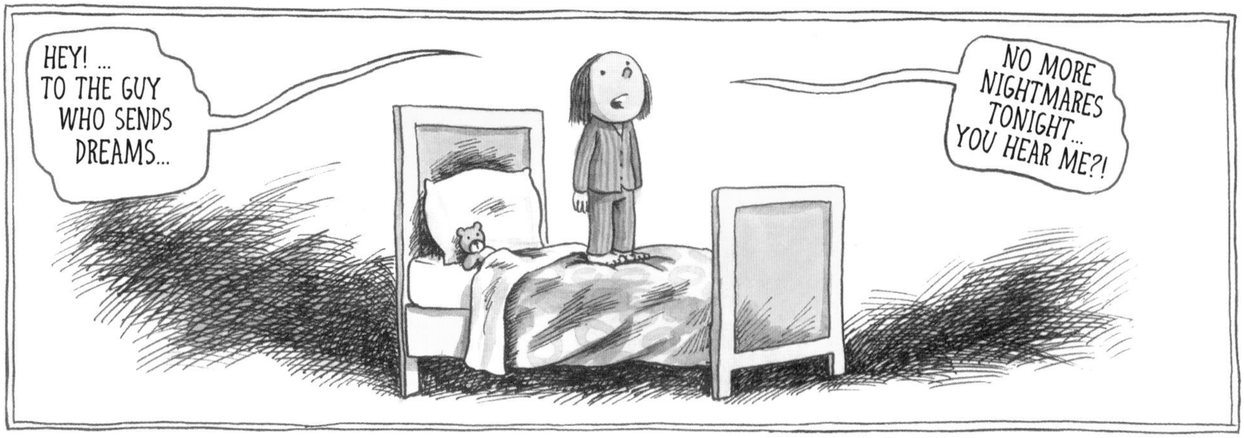
HEY! ...
TO THE GUY
WHO SENDS
DREAMS...
NO MORE
NIGHTMARES
TONIGHT...
YOU HEAR ME?!

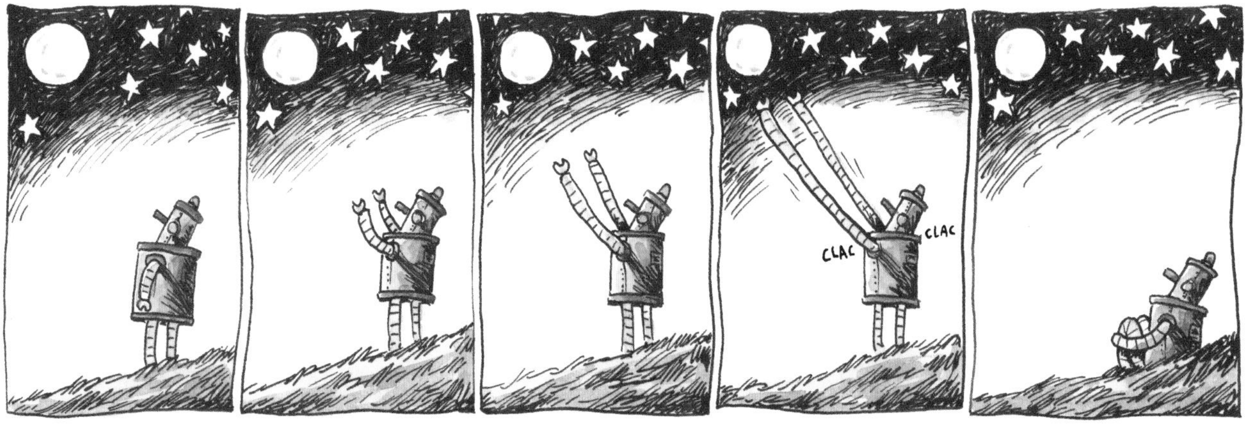
CLAC
CLAC

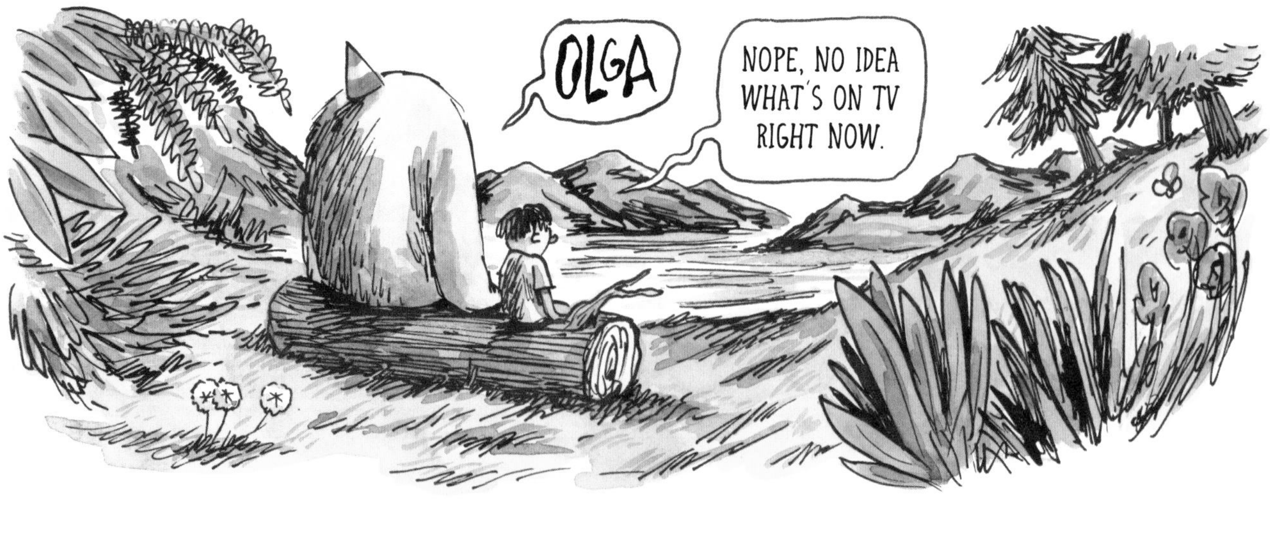
OLGA
NOPE, NO IDEA
WHAT'S ON TV
RIGHT NOW.

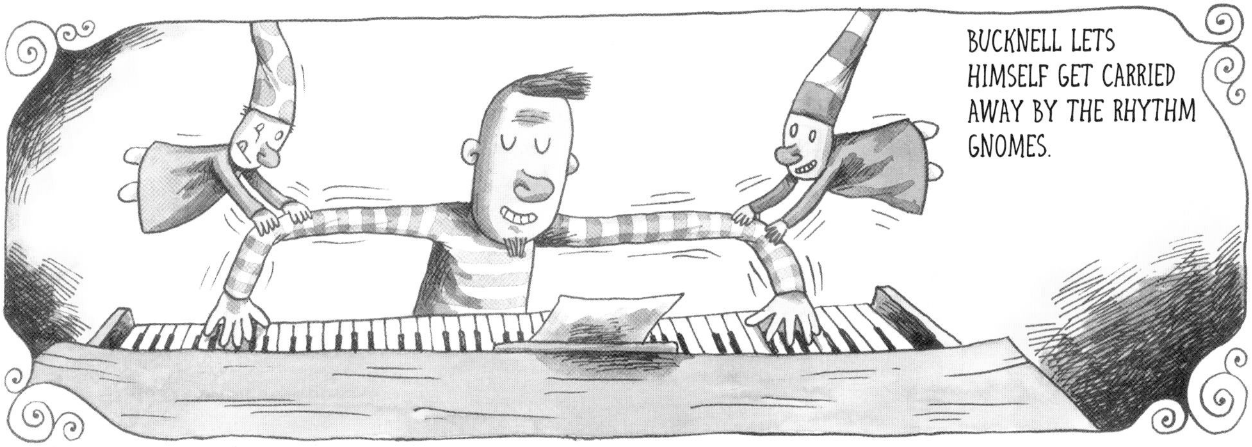
BUCKNELL LETS HIMSELF GET CARRIED AWAY BY THE RHYTHM GNOMES.

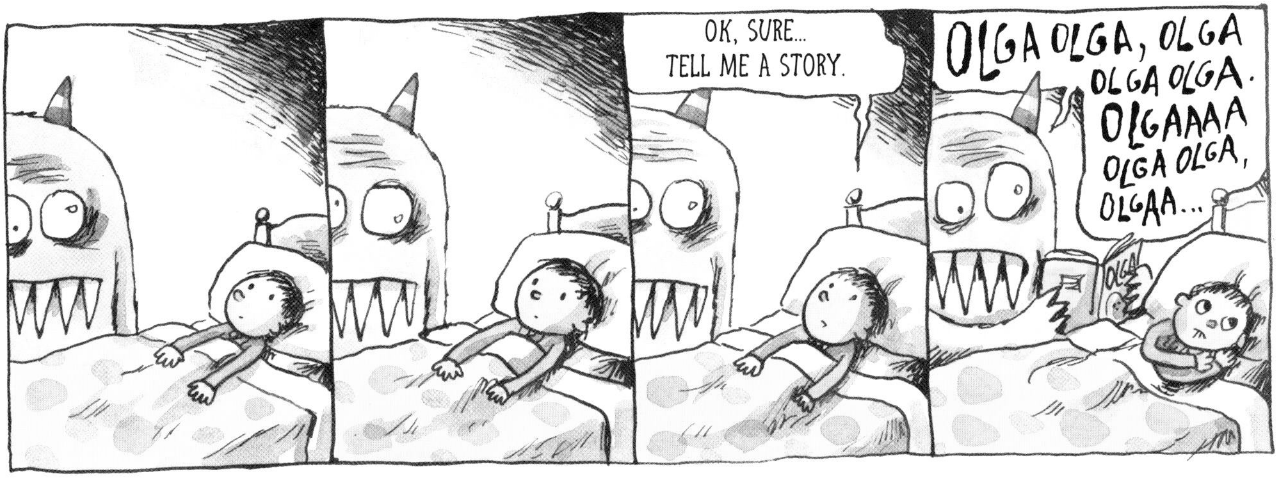
OK, SURE... TELL ME A STORY.
OLGA OLGA, OLGA OLGA OLGA. OLGAAAA OLGA OLGA, OLGAA...
OLGA

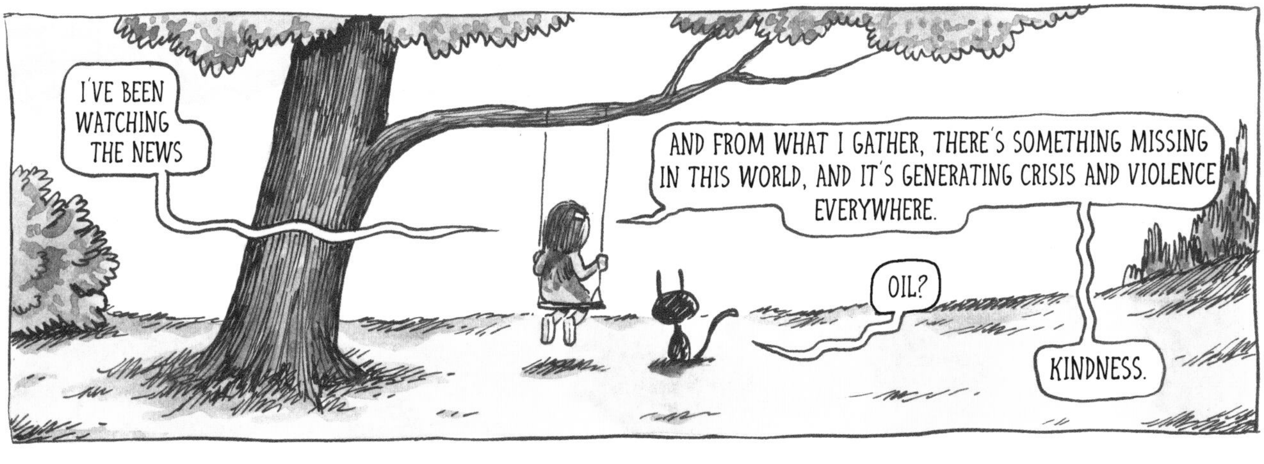
I'VE BEEN WATCHING THE NEWS
AND FROM WHAT I GATHER, THERE'S SOMETHING MISSING IN THIS WORLD, AND IT'S GENERATING CRISIS AND VIOLENCE EVERYWHERE.
OIL?
KINDNESS.

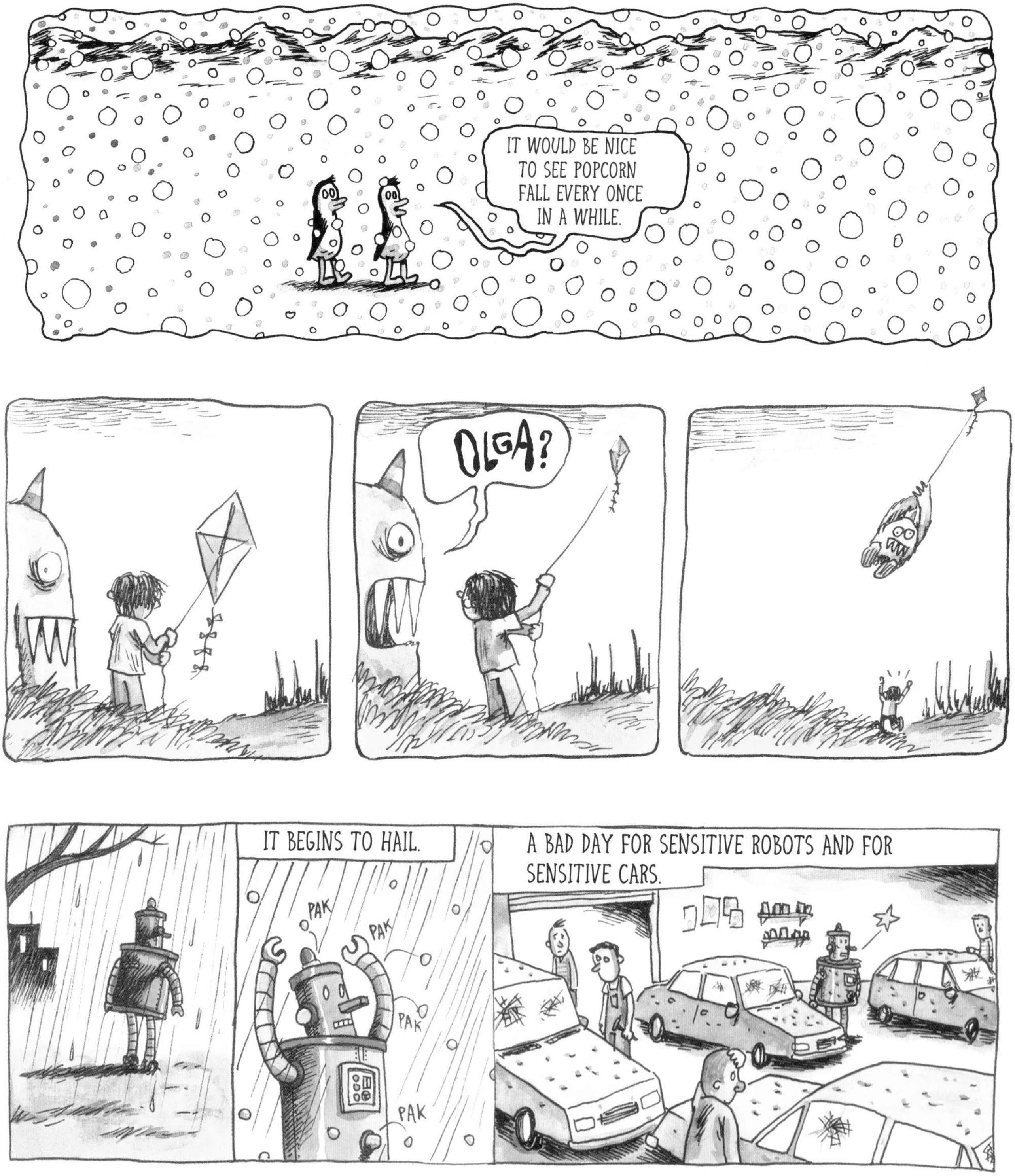
IT WOULD BE NICE TO SEE POPCORN FALL EVERY ONCE IN A WHILE.
OLGA?
IT BEGINS TO HAIL.
PAK
PAK
PAK
PAK
A BAD DAY FOR SENSITIVE ROBOTS AND FOR SENSITIVE CARS.

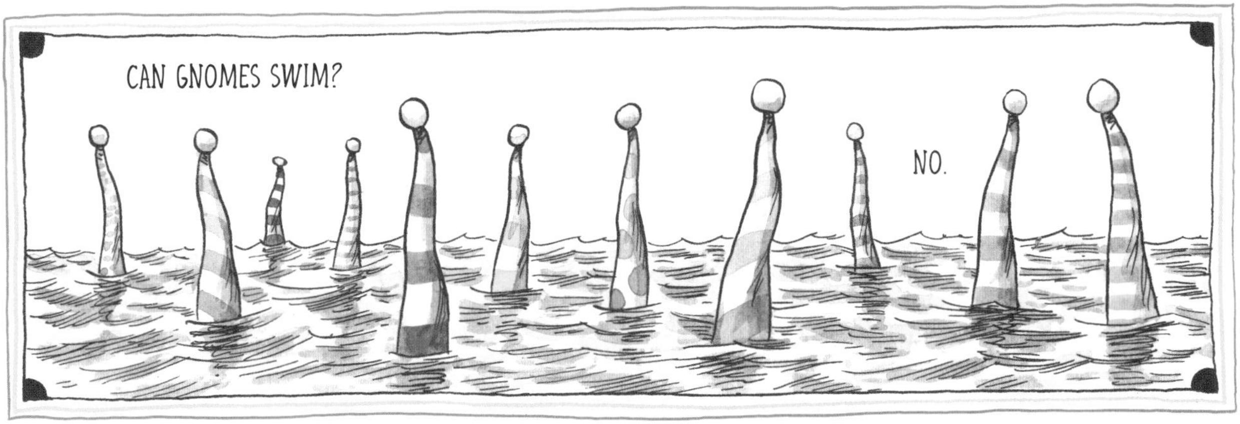
CAN GNOMES SWIM?
NO.

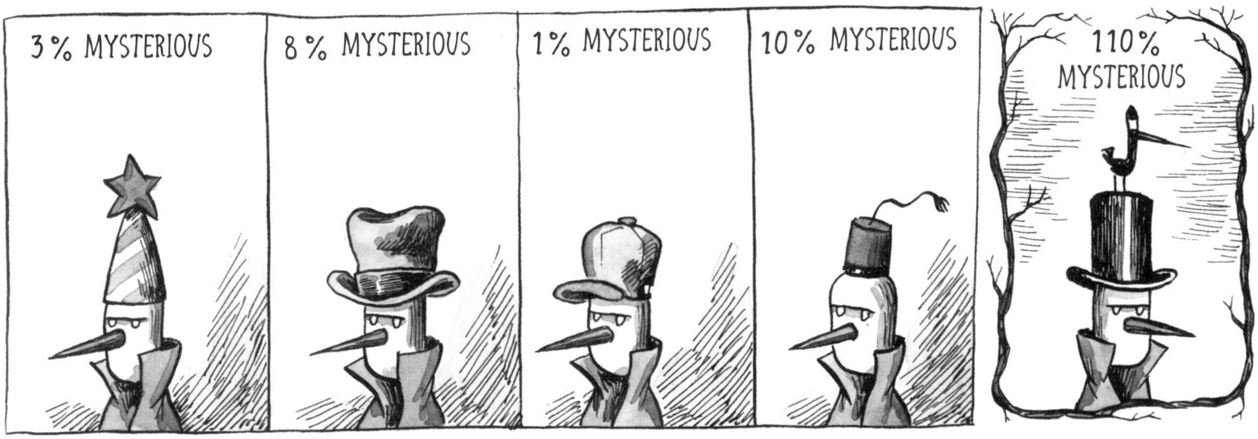
3% MYSTERIOUS
8% MYSTERIOUS
1% MYSTERIOUS
10% MYSTERIOUS
110% MYSTERIOUS

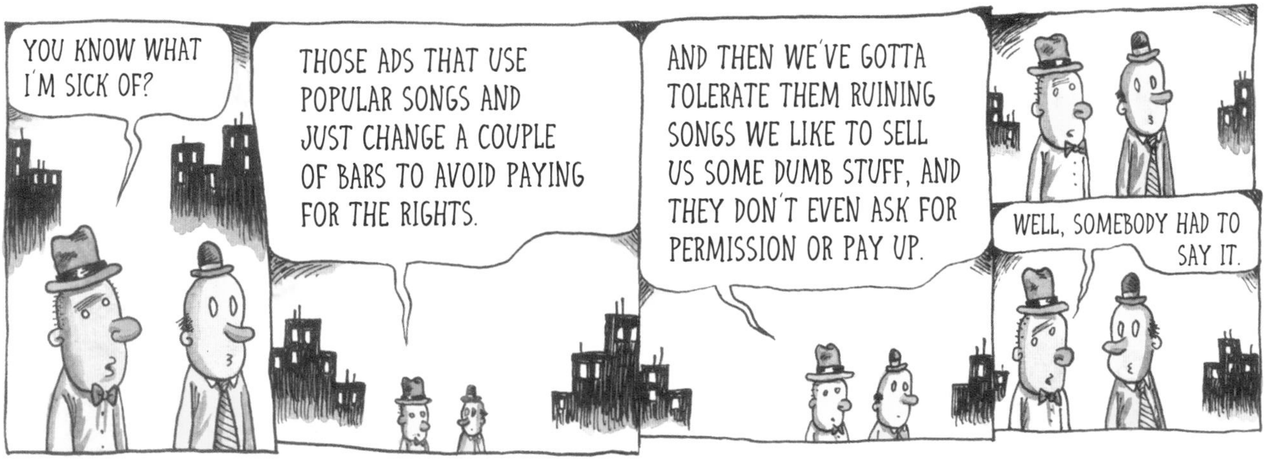
YOU KNOW WHAT I'M SICK OF?
THOSE ADS THAT USE POPULAR SONGS AND JUST CHANGE A COUPLE OF BARS TO AVOID PAYING FOR THE RIGHTS.
AND THEN WE'VE GOTTA TOLERATE THEM RUINING SONGS WE LIKE TO SELL US SOME DUMB STUFF, AND THEY DON'T EVEN ASK FOR PERMISSION OR PAY UP.
WELL, SOMEBODY HAD TO SAY IT.

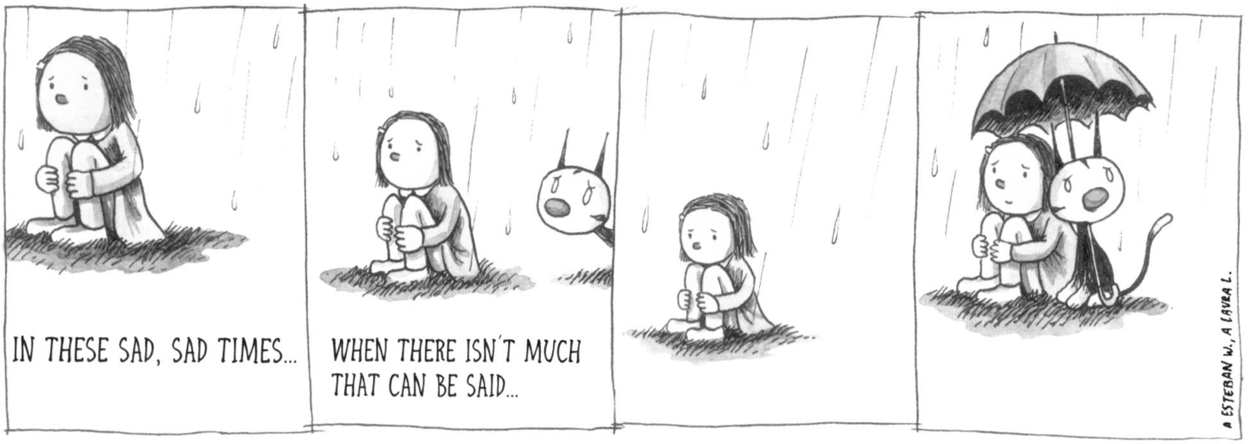
IN THESE SAD, SAD TIMES...
WHEN THERE ISN'T MUCH THAT CAN BE SAID...
A ESTEBAN W., A LAURA L.

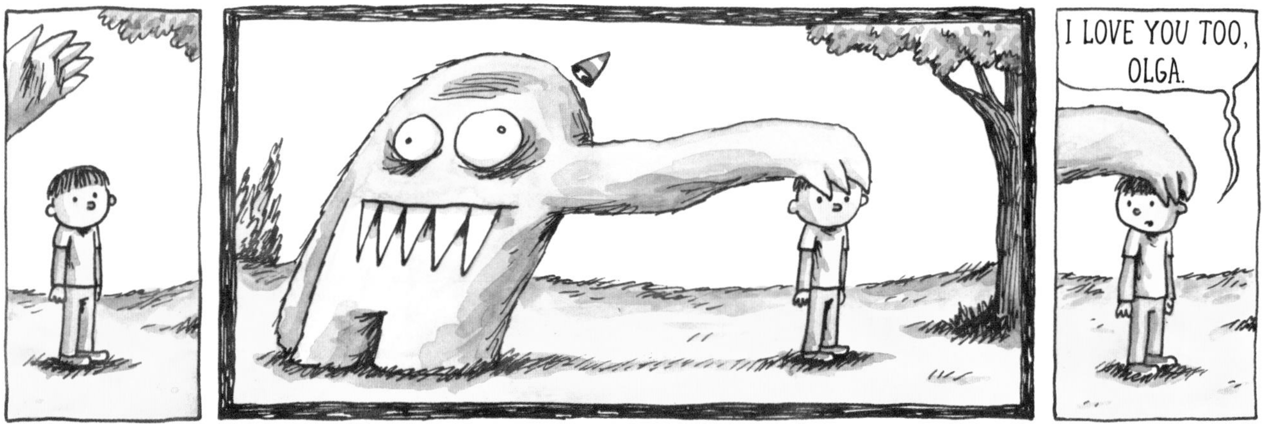
I LOVE YOU TOO, OLGA.

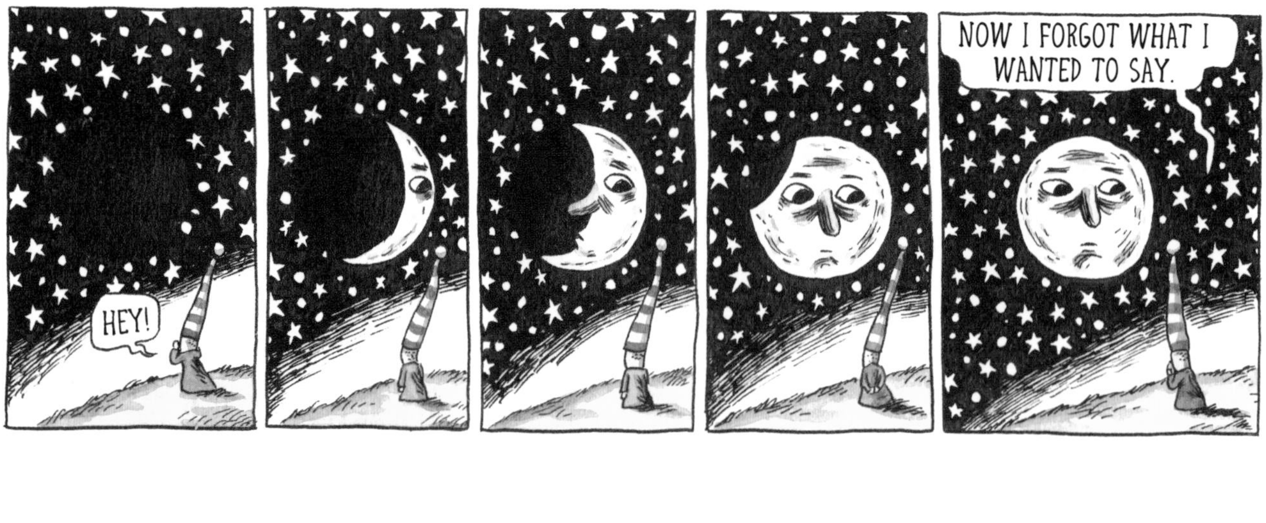
HEY!
NOW I FORGOT WHAT I WANTED TO SAY.

A big thanks to all the artists under ten years old who filled this book with Olgas: Abril, Agostina, Alan, Alejandra, Alex, Alexander, Ambar, Amir, Ana, Paula, Andoni, Andru, Antonia, Antonio, Ariala, Armando, Bauti, Bautista, Benjamín, Brian, Brisa, Bruno, Camilo, Candela, Carolina, Caroline, Casandra, Cata, Catalina, Chiara, Circe, Clarice, Clarita, Consuelo, Cristian, Damaris, Daniela, Darwin, Deiner, Delfina, Eli, Ema, Emilio, Emma, Evangelina, Ezequiel, Felipe, Fico, Fidel, Florencia, Francesca, Francisco, Franco, Franquita, Gabriel, Gianna, Gonzalo, Grethel, Griselda, Guada, Hans, Hossana, Ignacio, Iñigo, Isidro, Jazmín, Joaco, Joaquín, Joel, José Gabriel, Josefina, Juampi, Juan, Juan Isidro, Juan Jesús, Juan Martín, Juana, Juanita, Julián, Kamil, Kamila, Karú, Kim, Lady, Lara, Lautaro, León, Leonardo, Leydi, Lidia, Loli, Lorenzo, Lucía, Luciano, Ludovica, Luis, Luján, Lule, Lulu, Maggie, Malena, Maltiti, Manu, Manuel, Marco Antonio, Marcos, María, Mariel, Martín, Martina, Martuchi, Mateo, Mati, Matías, Matilda, Máximo, Mayck, Mechi, Melina, Merli, Mía, Miguel, Milena, Mili, Miranda, Mora, Naty, Nazareno, Nico, Nicolás, Olivia, Paloma, Paula, Pedro, Priscila, Quinto, Rafa, Ramiro, Rocco, Rocío, Sabrina, Samir, Sanai, Santi, Santiago, Sara, Simón, Sisela, Sofía, Sole, Tabata, Tadeo, Tatiana, Tiara, Tino, Titi, Tom, Tomás, Ulises, Uriel, Valentín, Valentina, Valentino, Vera, Vero, Verónica, Vicente, Victoria, Violeta, Vito, Yamileth, Yanina, Yasmín, Yoel, Yumi. My thanks go as well to Mara Faye Lethem, without whom the English-language *Macanudo* wouldn't exist.

Quiero entrar en la historieta,
cambiar mi piel por la piel
hecha de tinta y papel
que se usa en ese planeta.
Y flotar con Enriqueta
en dos pompas de jabón,
silbando a pleno pulmón
lo mejor de un estribillo.
(¡Olga y sus 5 colmillos
temblando de la emoción!)

Jorge Drexler

Dedicated to Federico
Erhart, with affection.

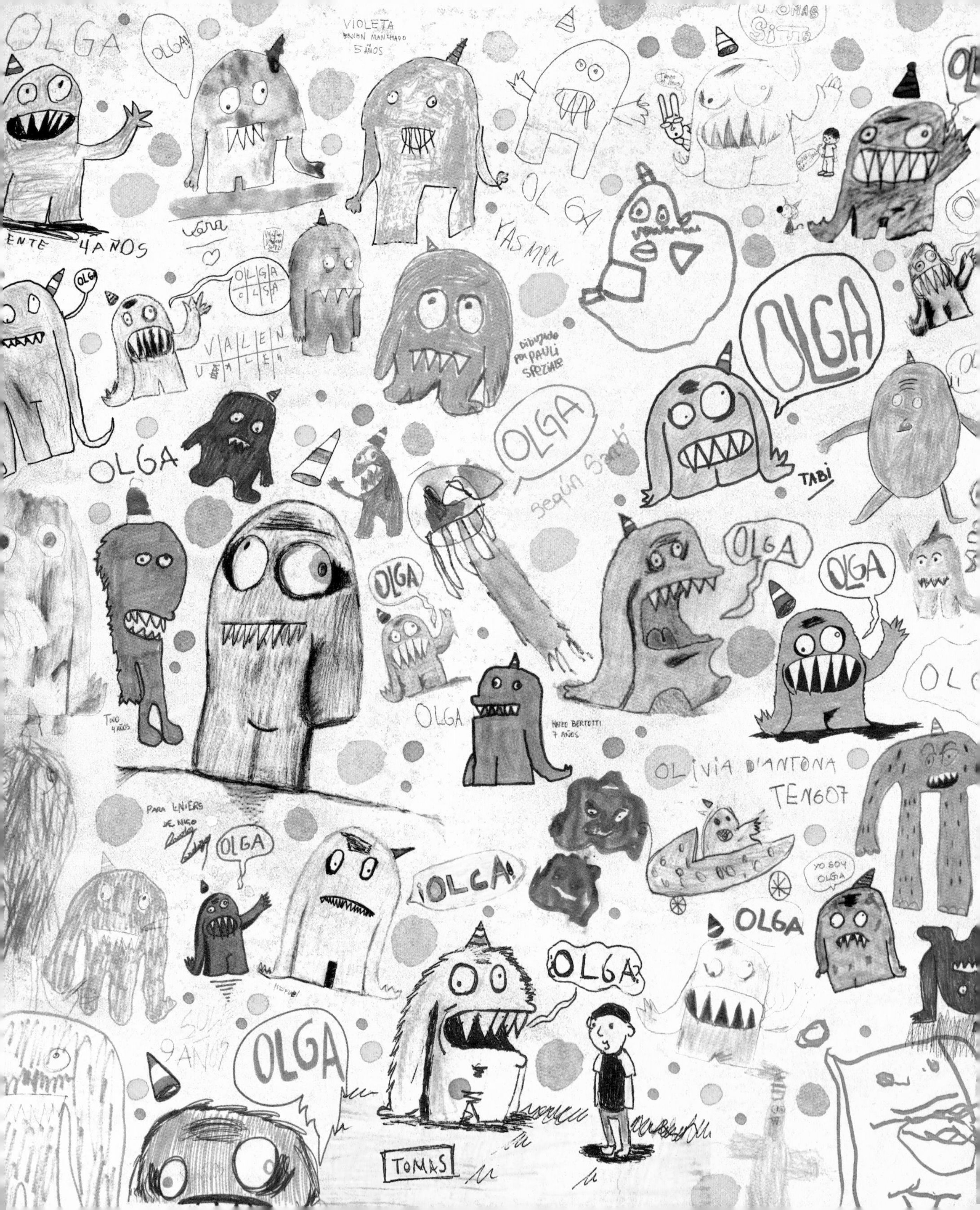
OLGA
OLGA
VIOLETA
5 AÑOS
4 AÑOS
YASMIN
OLGA
OLGA
VALEN
OLGA
Dibujado por PAULI SPEZIALE
OLGA
OLGA
OLGA
TABI
OLGA
OLGA
OLGA
TINO 4 AÑOS
OLGA
MATEO BERTOTTI 7 AÑOS
OLIVIA D'ANTONA
TENGO 7
OLGA
¡OLGA!
YO SOY OLGA
OLGA
OLGA?
OLGA
9 AÑOS
TOMAS